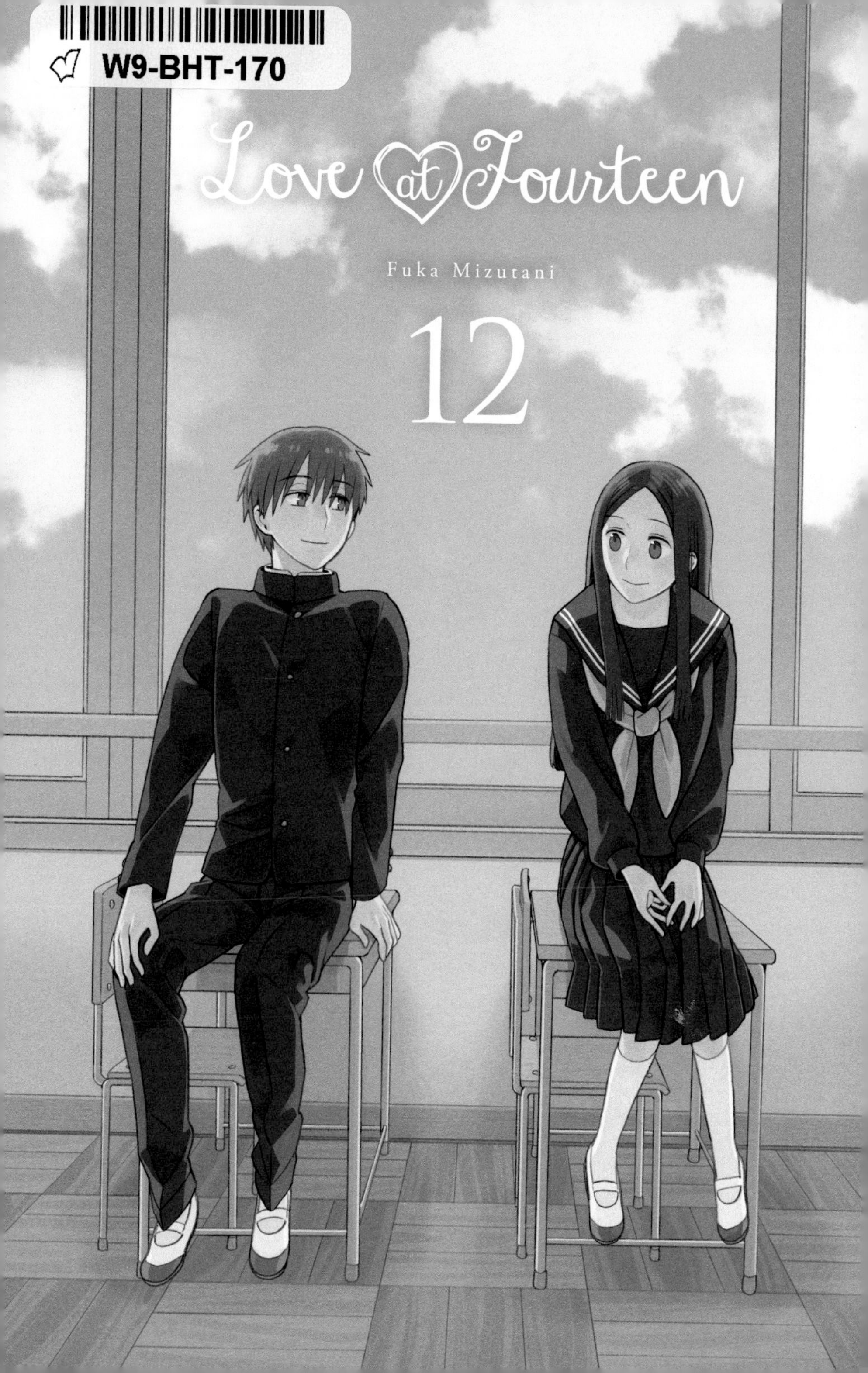
Love at Fourteen
Fuka Mizutani
12

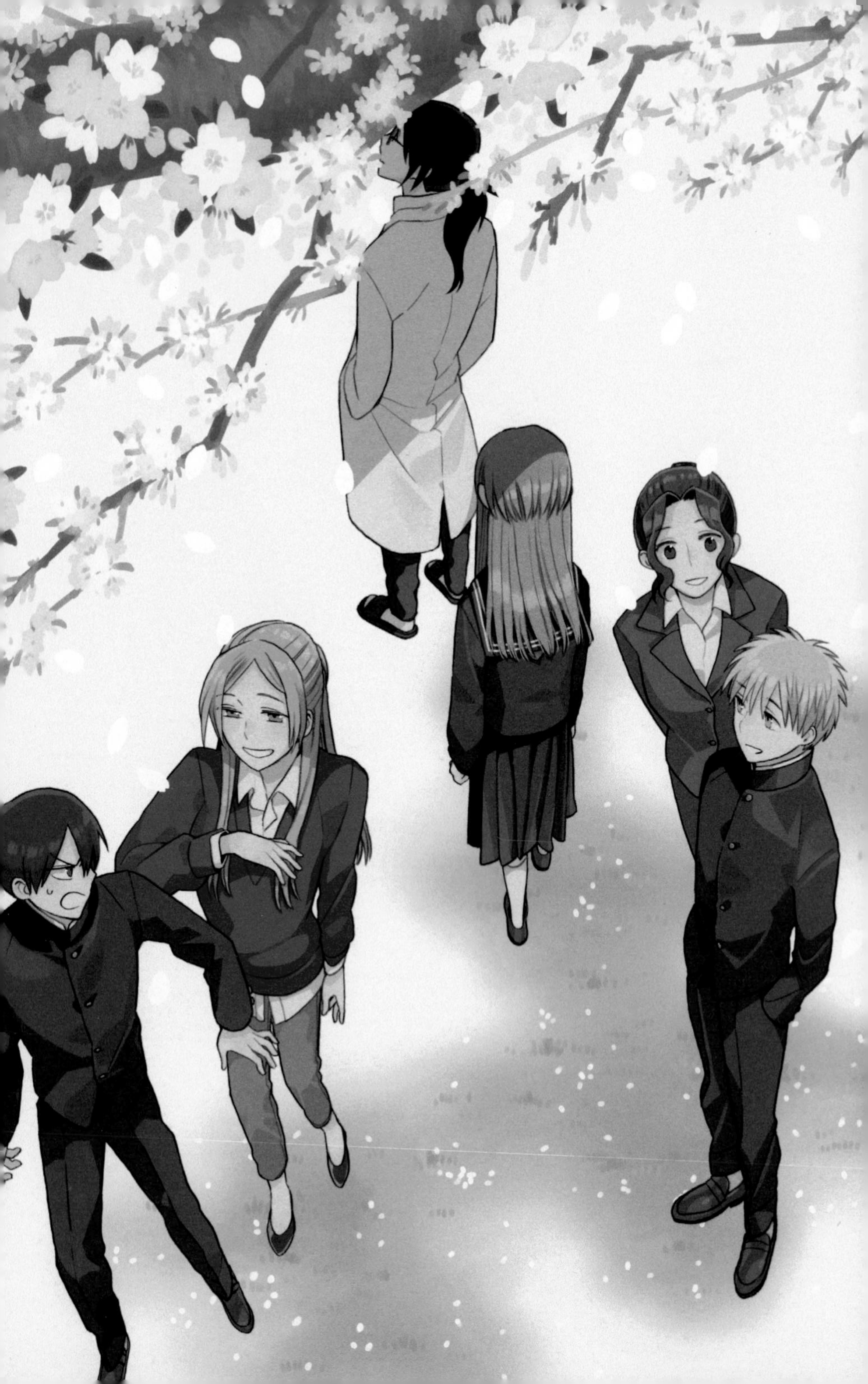

Contents

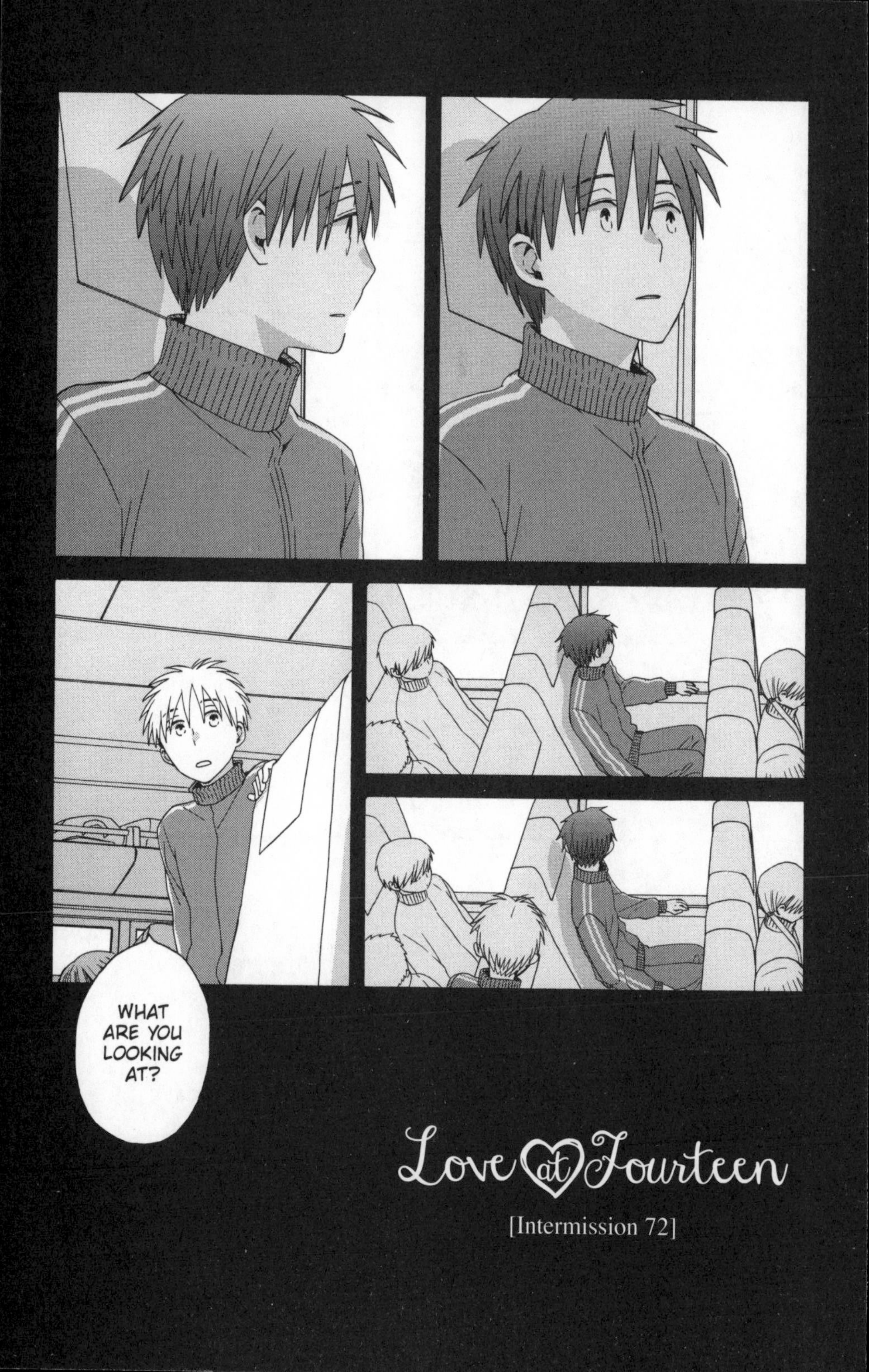
WHAT ARE YOU LOOKING AT?

Love at Fourteen

[Intermission 72]

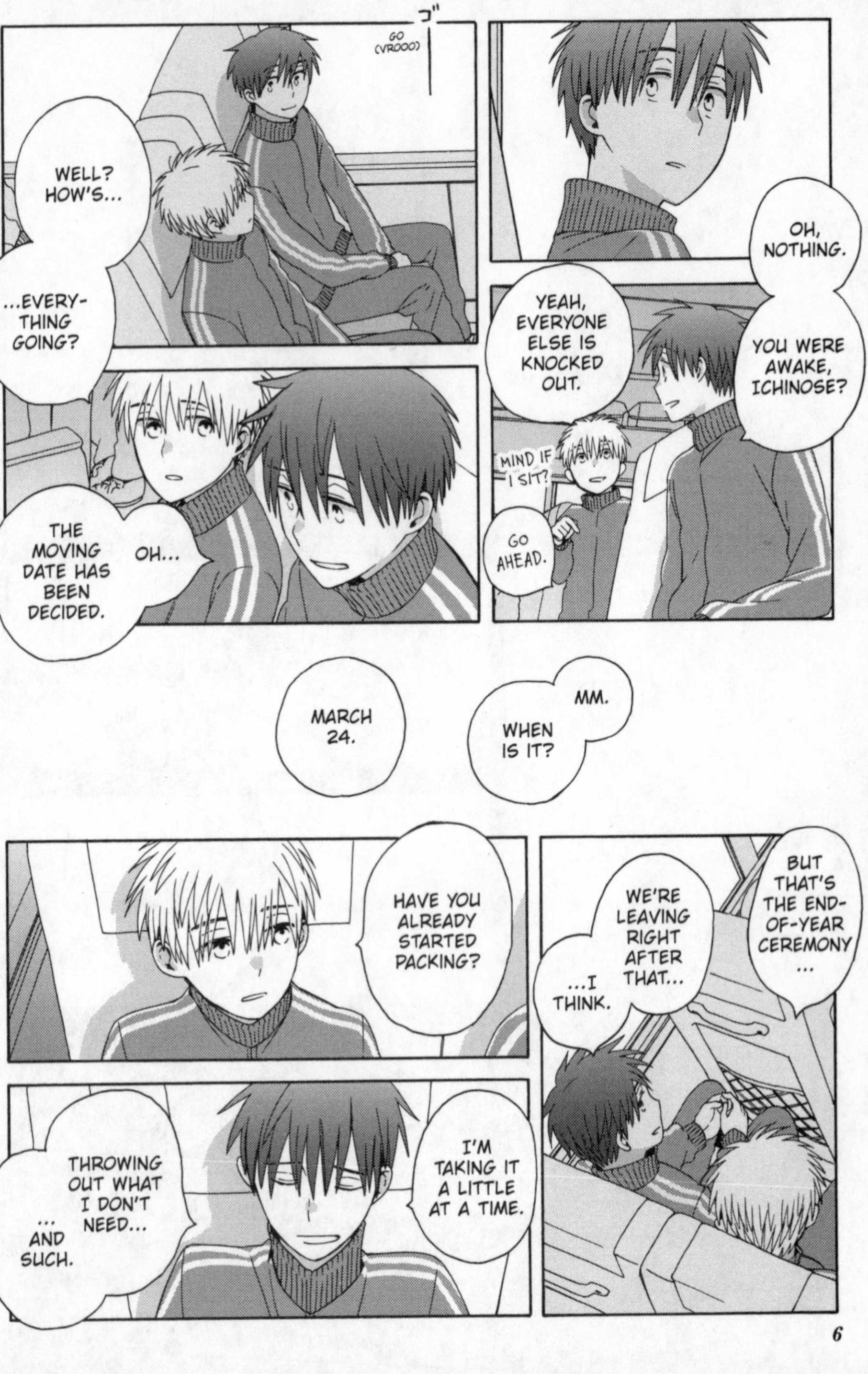
OH, NOTHING.
YOU WERE AWAKE, ICHINOSE?
YEAH, EVERYONE ELSE IS KNOCKED OUT.
MIND IF I SIT?
GO AHEAD.
ゴ
GO (VROOO)
WELL? HOW'S...
...EVERY-THING GOING?
OH...
THE MOVING DATE HAS BEEN DECIDED.
MM.
WHEN IS IT?
MARCH 24.
BUT THAT'S THE END-OF-YEAR CEREMONY...
WE'RE LEAVING RIGHT AFTER THAT...
...I THINK.
HAVE YOU ALREADY STARTED PACKING?
I'M TAKING IT A LITTLE AT A TIME.
THROWING OUT WHAT I DON'T NEED...
...AND SUCH.

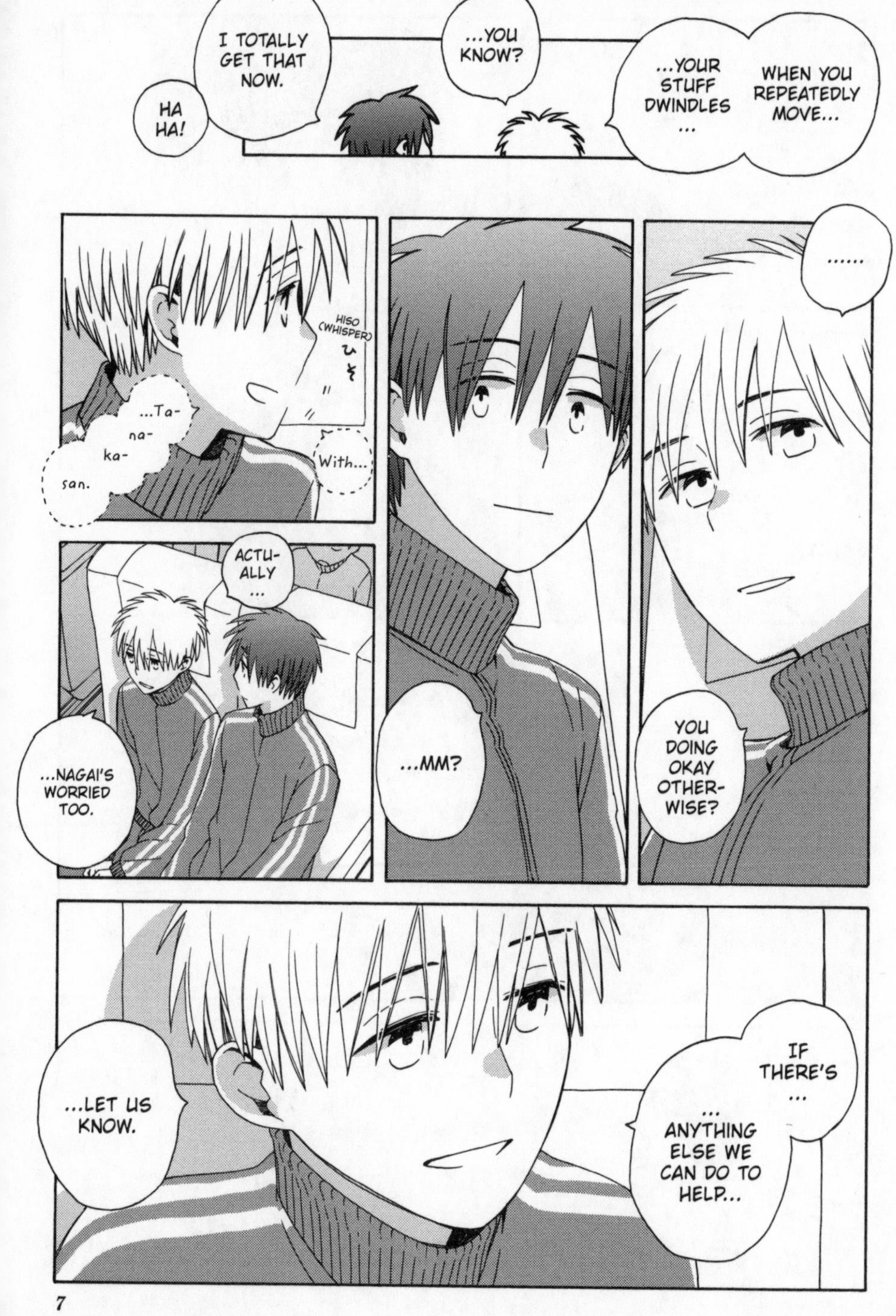
WHEN YOU REPEATEDLY MOVE...
...YOUR STUFF DWINDLES...
...YOU KNOW?
I TOTALLY GET THAT NOW.
HA HA!
......
YOU DOING OKAY OTHERWISE?
...MM?
HISO (WHISPER)
ひそ
With...
...Ta-na-ka-san.
ACTU-ALLY...
...NAGAI'S WORRIED TOO.
IF THERE'S... ...ANYTHING ELSE WE CAN DO TO HELP...
...LET US KNOW.

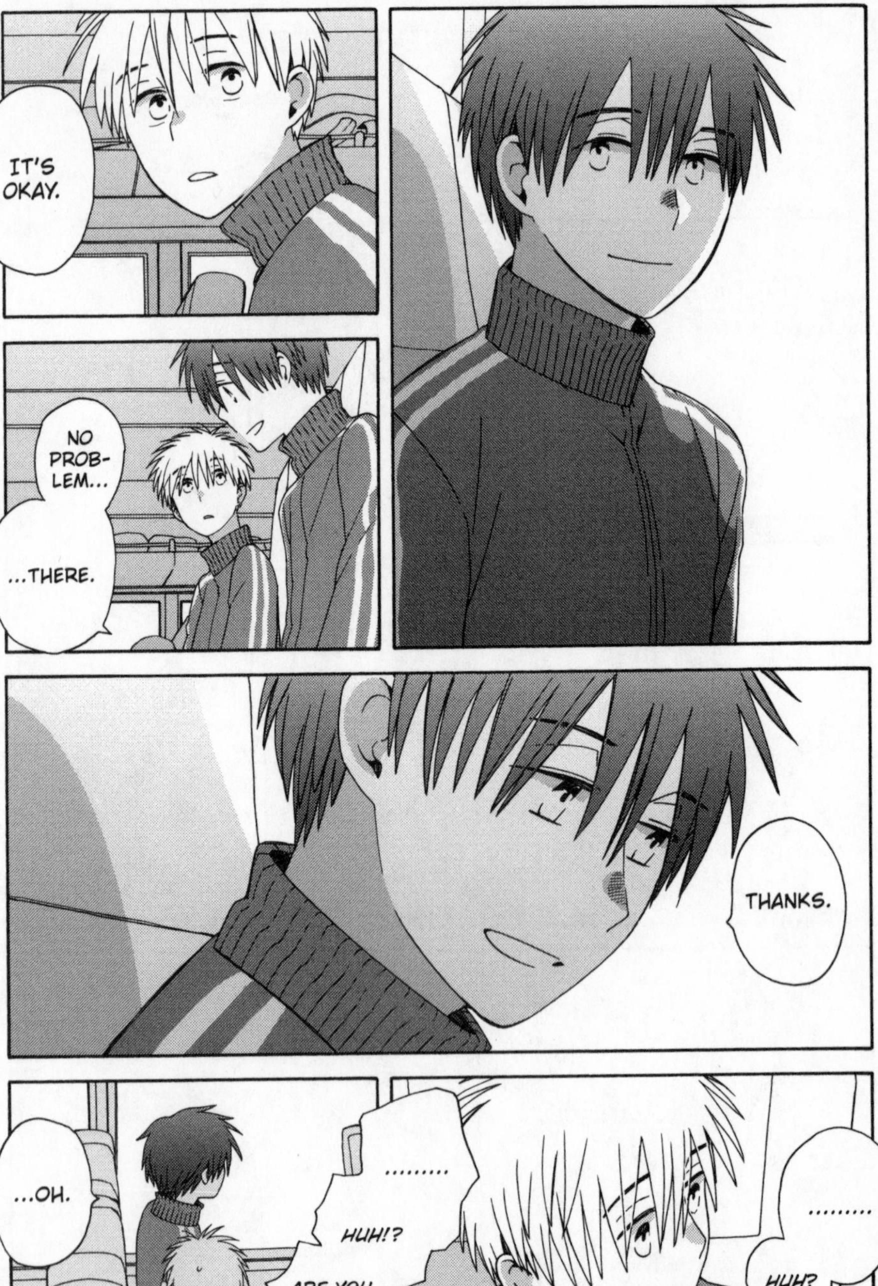
IT'S OKAY.
NO PROB-LEM...
...THERE.
THANKS.
....
HUH?
....
HUH!?
ARE YOU SERIOUS !?
...OH.

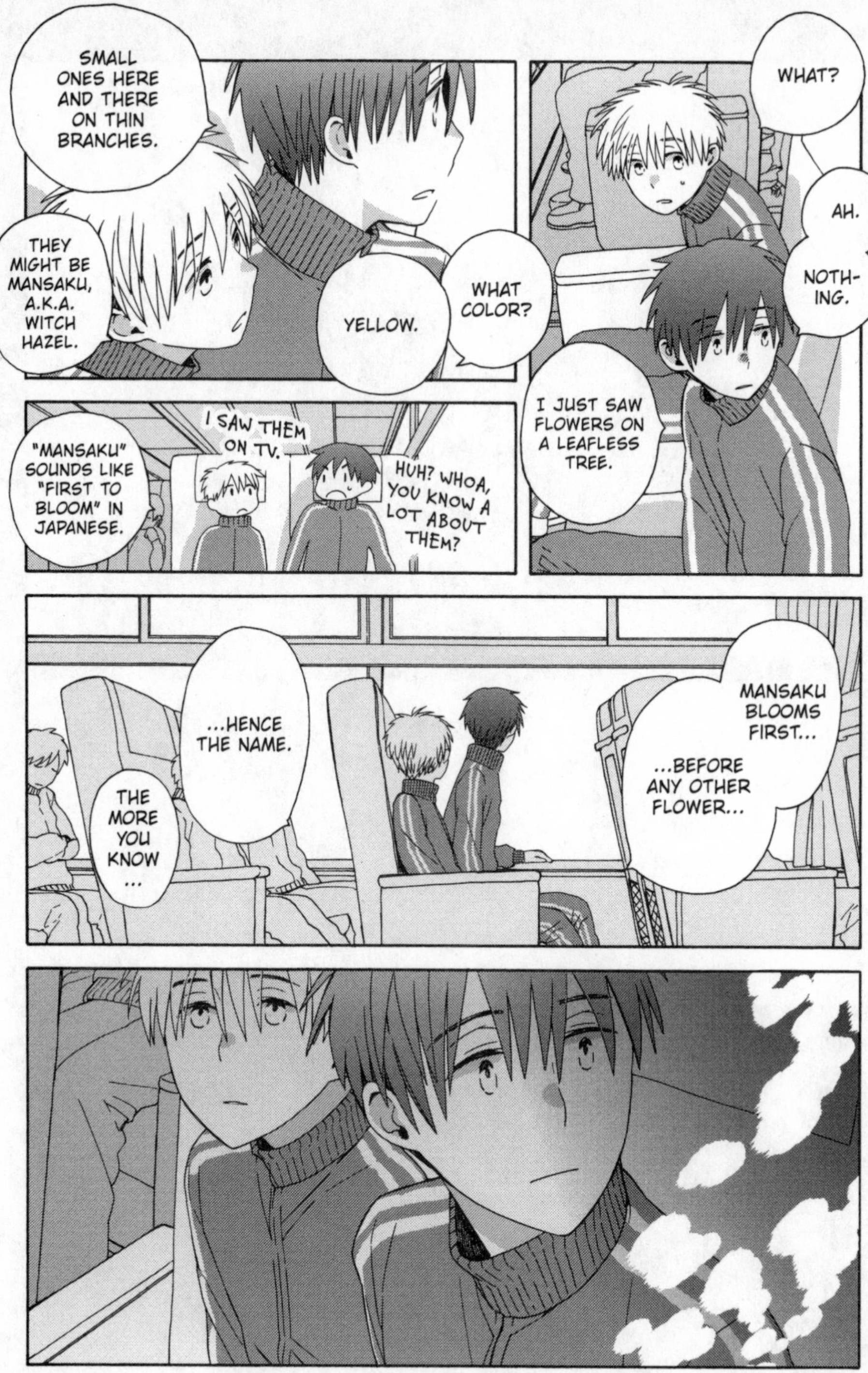

WHAT?
AH.
NOTH-ING.
I JUST SAW FLOWERS ON A LEAFLESS TREE.
WHAT COLOR?
YELLOW.
SMALL ONES HERE AND THERE ON THIN BRANCHES.
THEY MIGHT BE MANSAKU, A.K.A. WITCH HAZEL.
HUH? WHOA, YOU KNOW A LOT ABOUT THEM?
I SAW THEM ON TV.
"MANSAKU" SOUNDS LIKE "FIRST TO BLOOM" IN JAPANESE.
MANSAKU BLOOMS FIRST...
...BEFORE ANY OTHER FLOWER...
...HENCE THE NAME.
THE MORE YOU KNOW ...

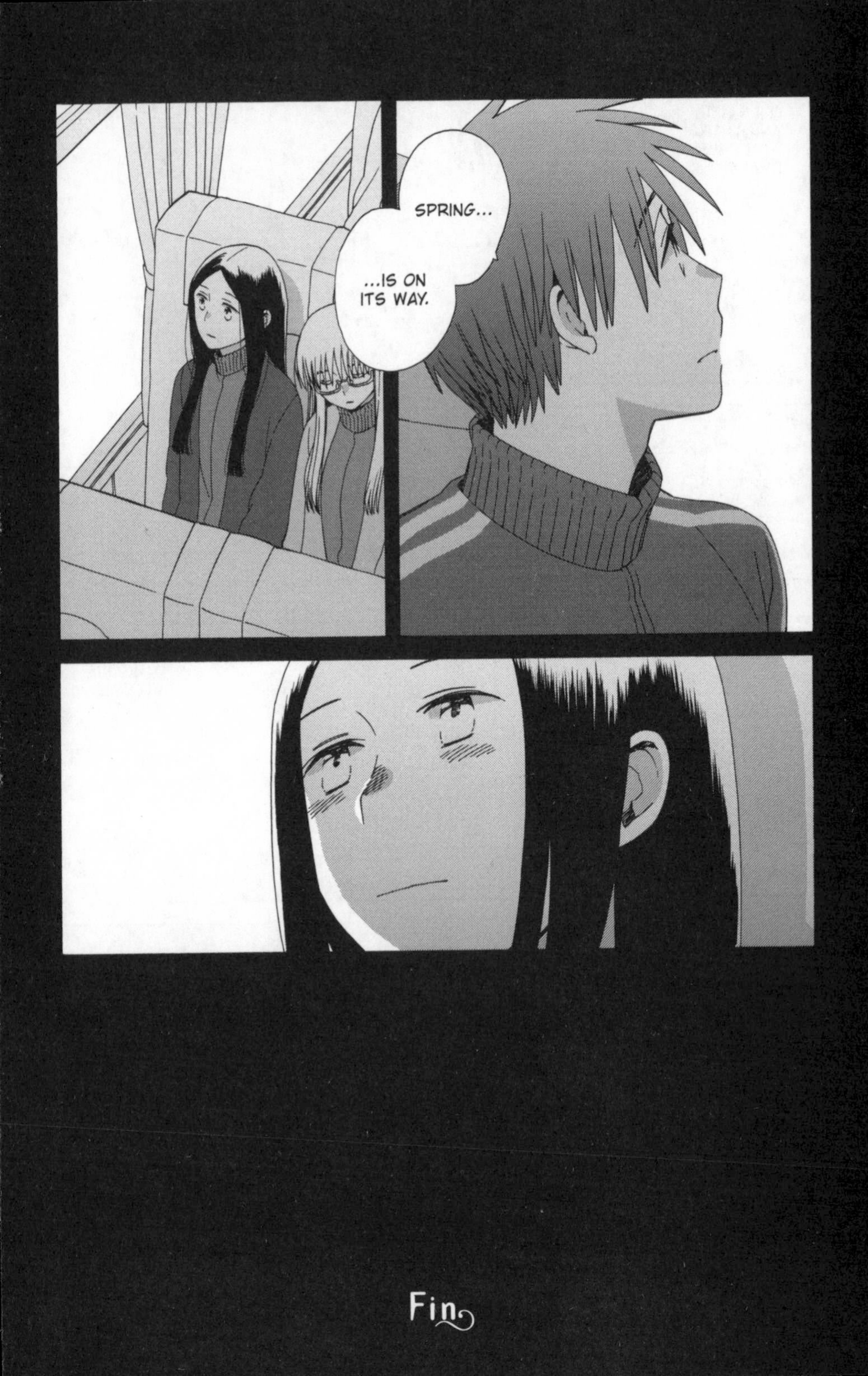
SPRING...
...IS ON ITS WAY.

Fin

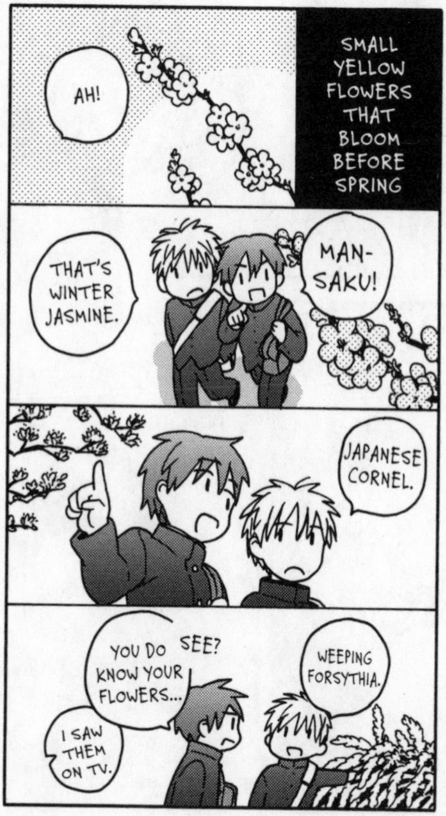
SMALL YELLOW FLOWERS THAT BLOOM BEFORE SPRING
AH!
MAN-SAKU!
THAT'S WINTER JASMINE.
JAPANESE CORNEL.
WEEPING FORSYTHIA.
SEE?
YOU DO KNOW YOUR FLOWERS...
I SAW THEM ON TV.

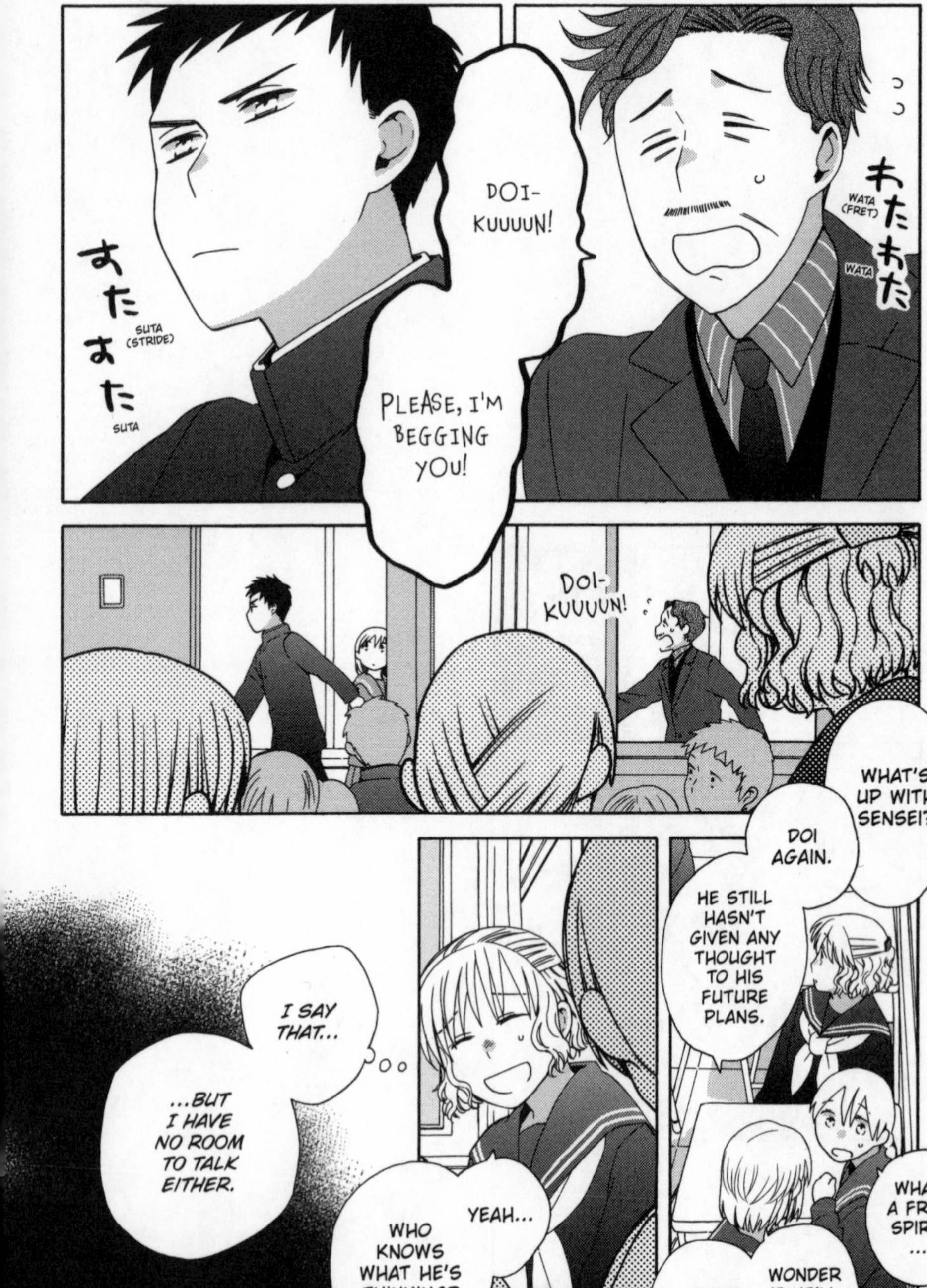
おたおた
WATA (FRET)
WATA
DOI-KUUUUN!
PLEASE, I'M BEGGING YOU!
すたすた
SUTA (STRIDE)
SUTA
DOI-KUUUUN!
WHAT'S UP WITH SENSEI?
DOI AGAIN.
HE STILL HASN'T GIVEN ANY THOUGHT TO HIS FUTURE PLANS.
WHAT A FREE SPIRIT ...
WONDER IF HE'LL BE OKAY ...
...RIGHT, SHAGGY?
YEAH...
WHO KNOWS WHAT HE'S THINKING?
I SAY THAT...
...BUT I HAVE NO ROOM TO TALK EITHER.

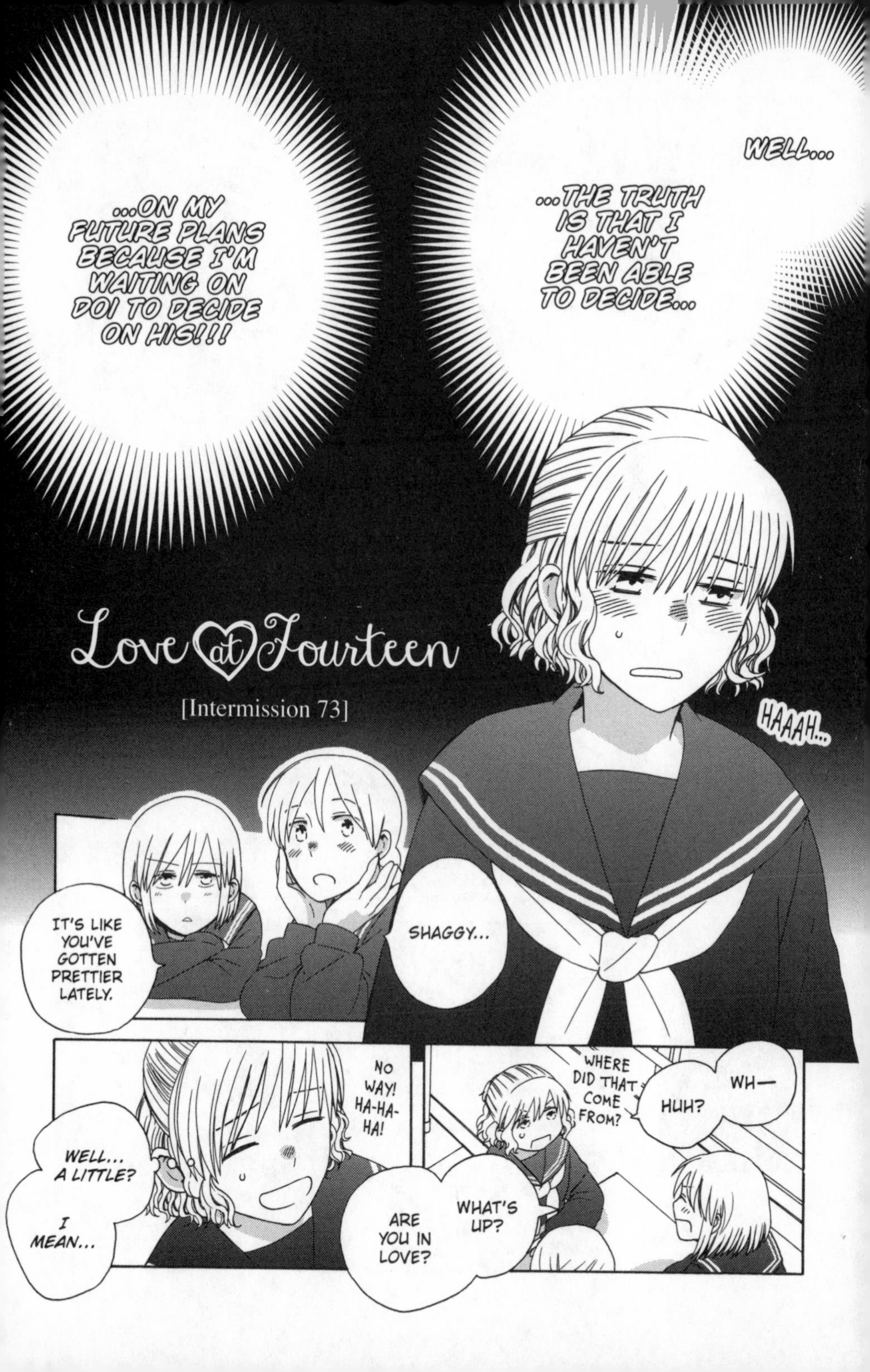
WELL...
...THE TRUTH IS THAT I HAVEN'T BEEN ABLE TO DECIDE...
...ON MY FUTURE PLANS BECAUSE I'M WAITING ON DOI TO DECIDE ON HIS!!!
Love at Fourteen
[Intermission 73]
HAAAH...
SHAGGY...
IT'S LIKE YOU'VE GOTTEN PRETTIER LATELY.
WH—
HUH?
WHERE DID THAT COME FROM?
WHAT'S UP?
ARE YOU IN LOVE?
NO WAY! HA-HA-HA!
WELL... A LITTLE?
I MEAN...

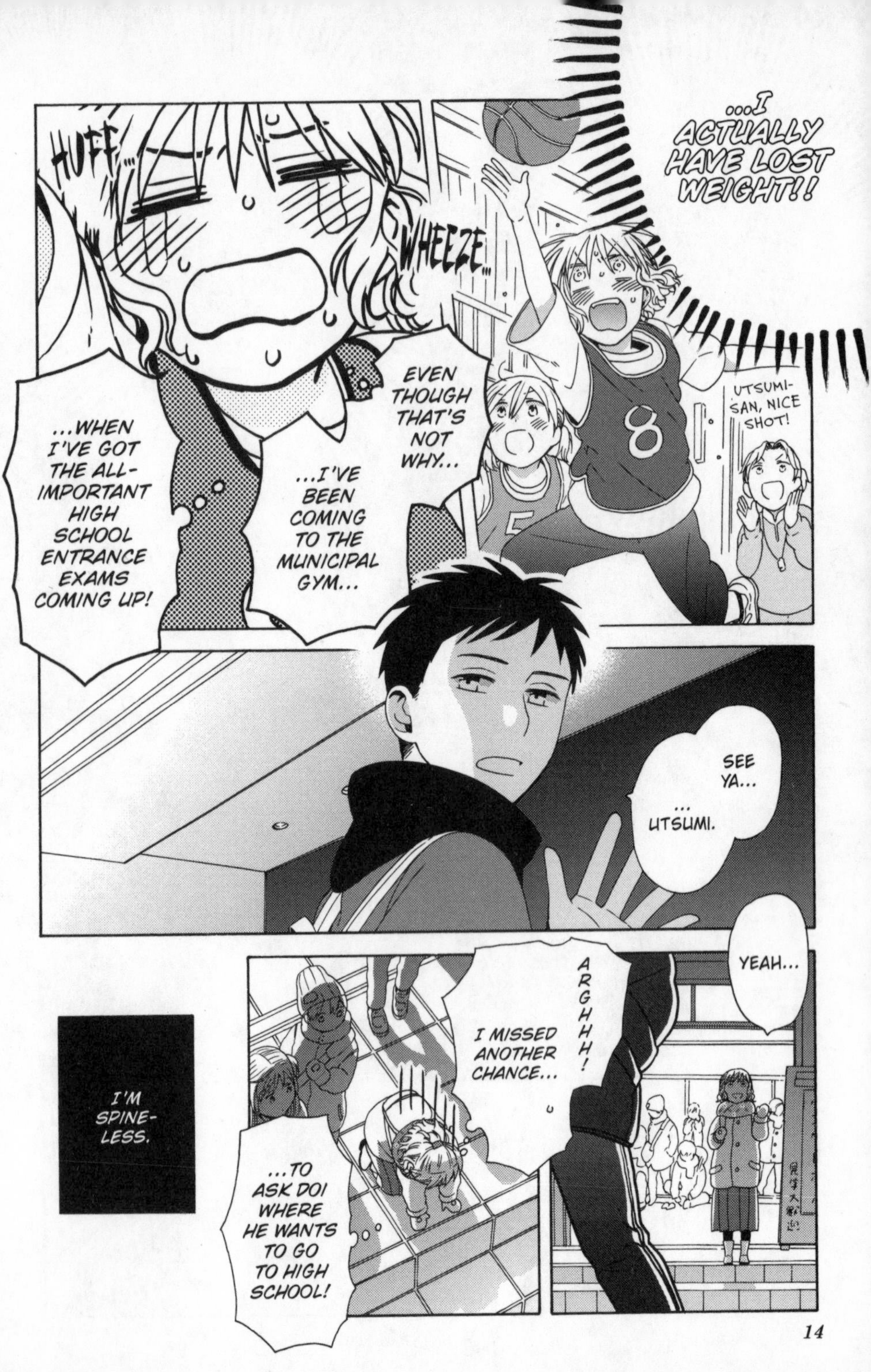
...I ACTUALLY HAVE LOST WEIGHT!!
UTSUMI-SAN, NICE SHOT!
EVEN THOUGH THAT'S NOT WHY...
...I'VE BEEN COMING TO THE MUNICIPAL GYM...
HUFF...
WHEEZE...
...WHEN I'VE GOT THE ALL-IMPORTANT HIGH SCHOOL ENTRANCE EXAMS COMING UP!
SEE YA...
...UTSUMI.
YEAH...
ARGHHH!
I MISSED ANOTHER CHANCE...
...TO ASK DOI WHERE HE WANTS TO GO TO HIGH SCHOOL!
I'M SPINELESS.

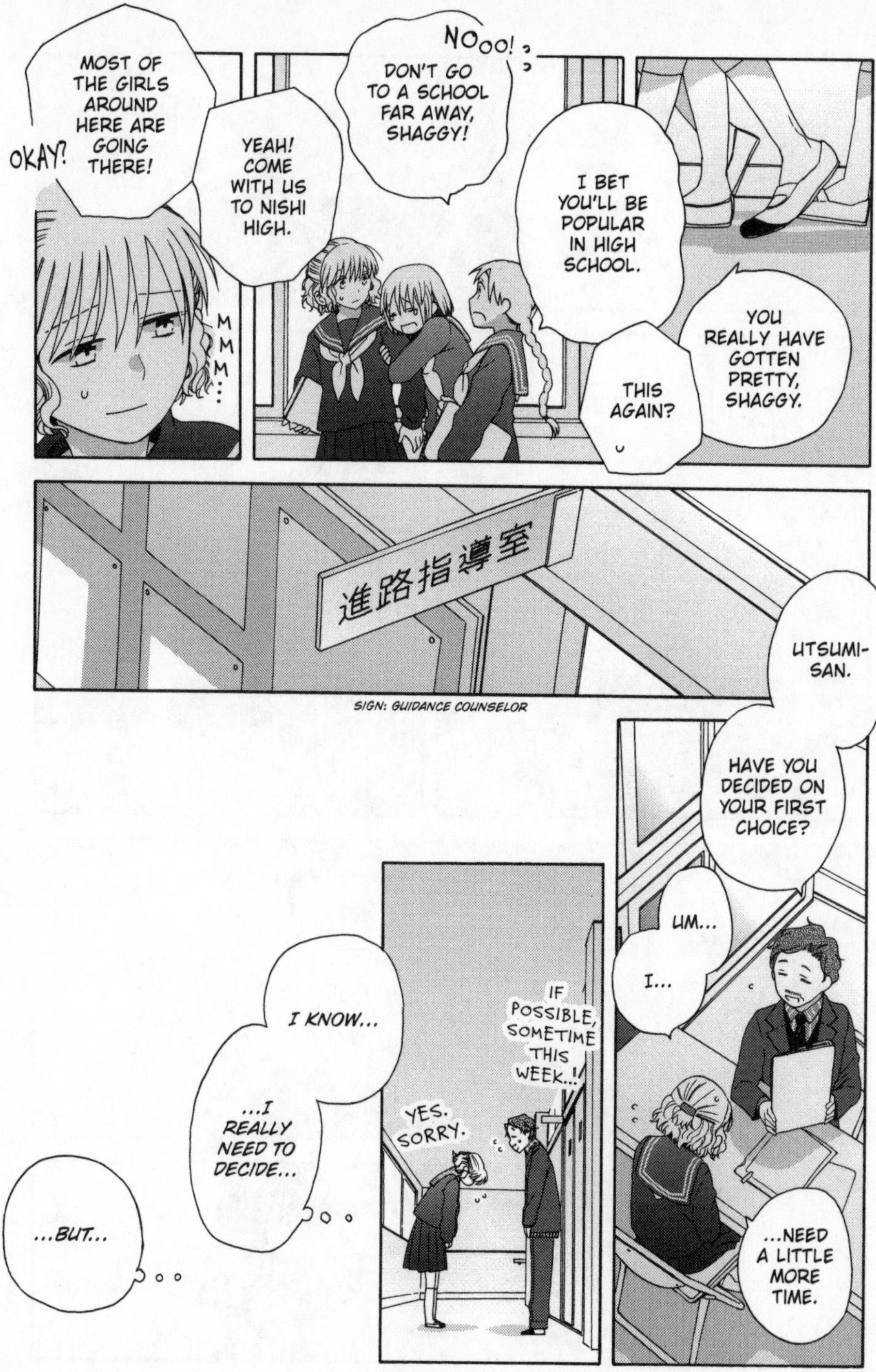
YOU REALLY HAVE GOTTEN PRETTY, SHAGGY.
I BET YOU'LL BE POPULAR IN HIGH SCHOOL.
THIS AGAIN?
NOooo!
DON'T GO TO A SCHOOL FAR AWAY, SHAGGY!
YEAH! COME WITH US TO NISHI HIGH.
MOST OF THE GIRLS AROUND HERE ARE GOING THERE!
OKAY?
MMM...
進路指導室
UTSUMI-SAN.
HAVE YOU DECIDED ON YOUR FIRST CHOICE?
UM...
I...
...NEED A LITTLE MORE TIME.
IF POSSIBLE, SOMETIME THIS WEEK...!
YES. SORRY.
I KNOW...
...I REALLY NEED TO DECIDE...
...BUT...
SIGN: GUIDANCE COUNSELOR

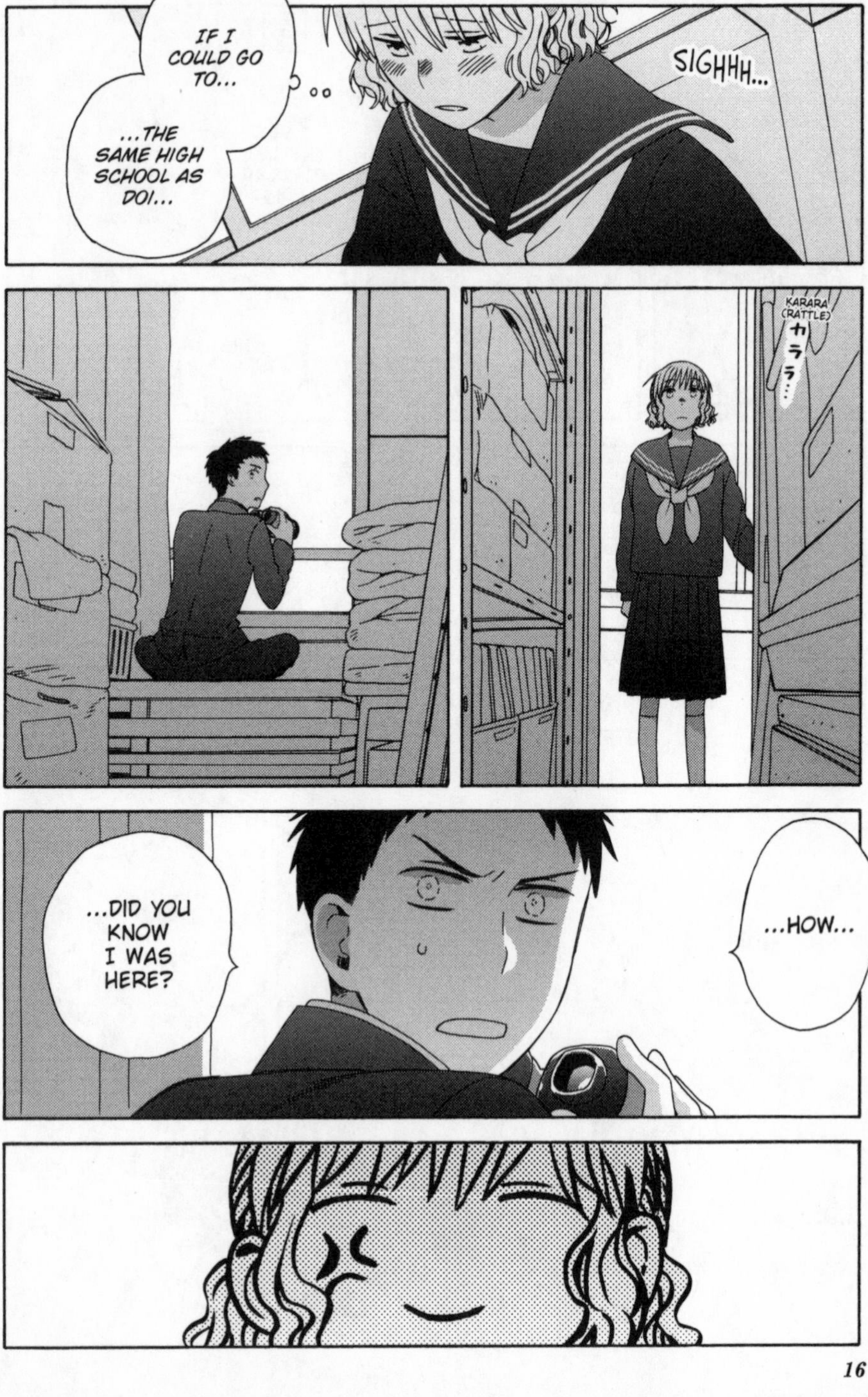
IF I COULD GO TO...
...THE SAME HIGH SCHOOL AS DOI...
SIGHHH...
KARARA (RATTLE)
カララ…
...HOW...
...DID YOU KNOW I WAS HERE?

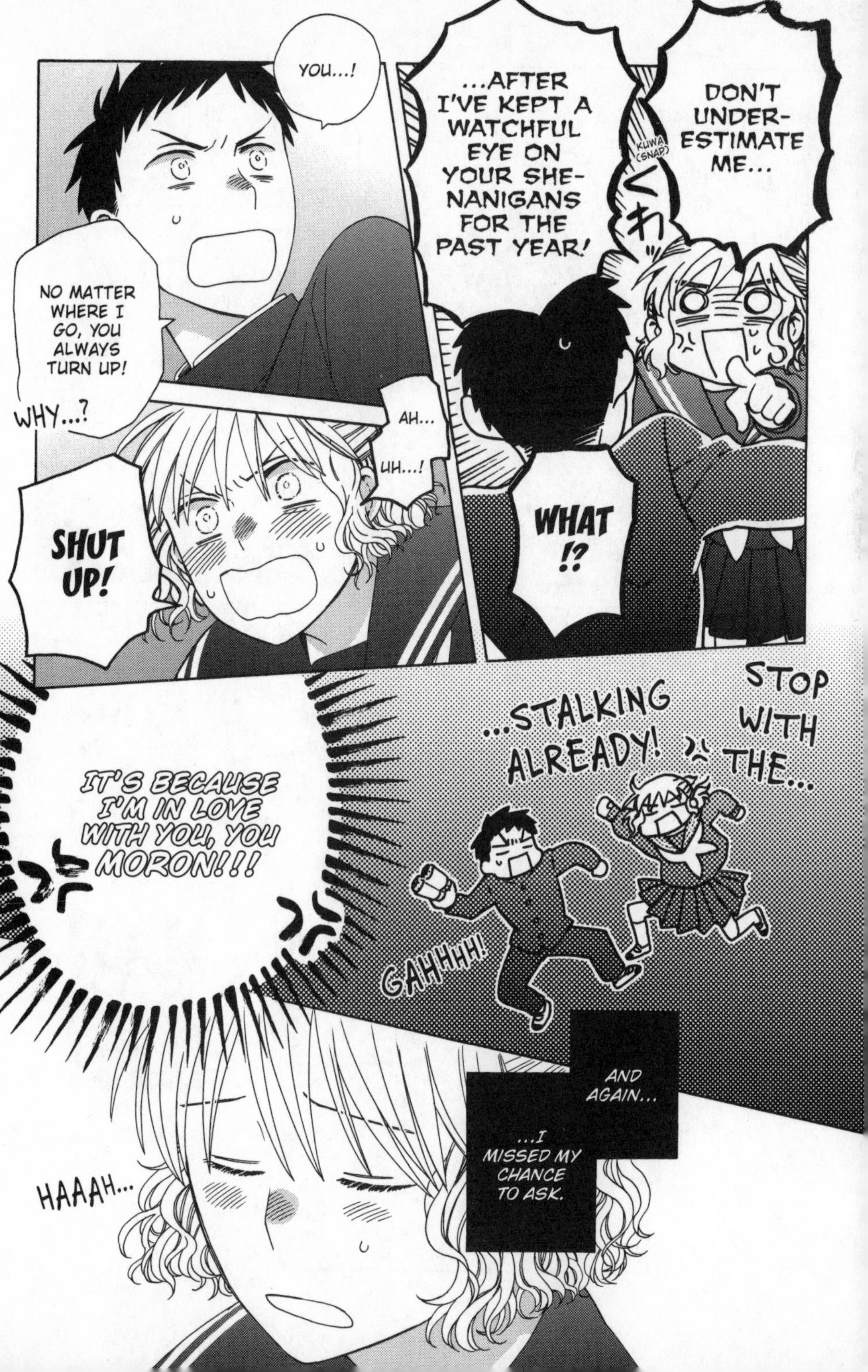
DON'T UNDER-ESTIMATE ME...
くわッ
KUWA (SNAP)
...AFTER I'VE KEPT A WATCHFUL EYE ON YOUR SHE-NANIGANS FOR THE PAST YEAR!
WHAT!?
YOU...!
NO MATTER WHERE I GO, YOU ALWAYS TURN UP!
WHY...?
AH...
UH...!
SHUT UP!
STOP WITH THE...
...STALKING ALREADY!
GAHHHH!
IT'S BECAUSE I'M IN LOVE WITH YOU, YOU MORON!!!
AND AGAIN...
...I MISSED MY CHANCE TO ASK.
HAAAH...

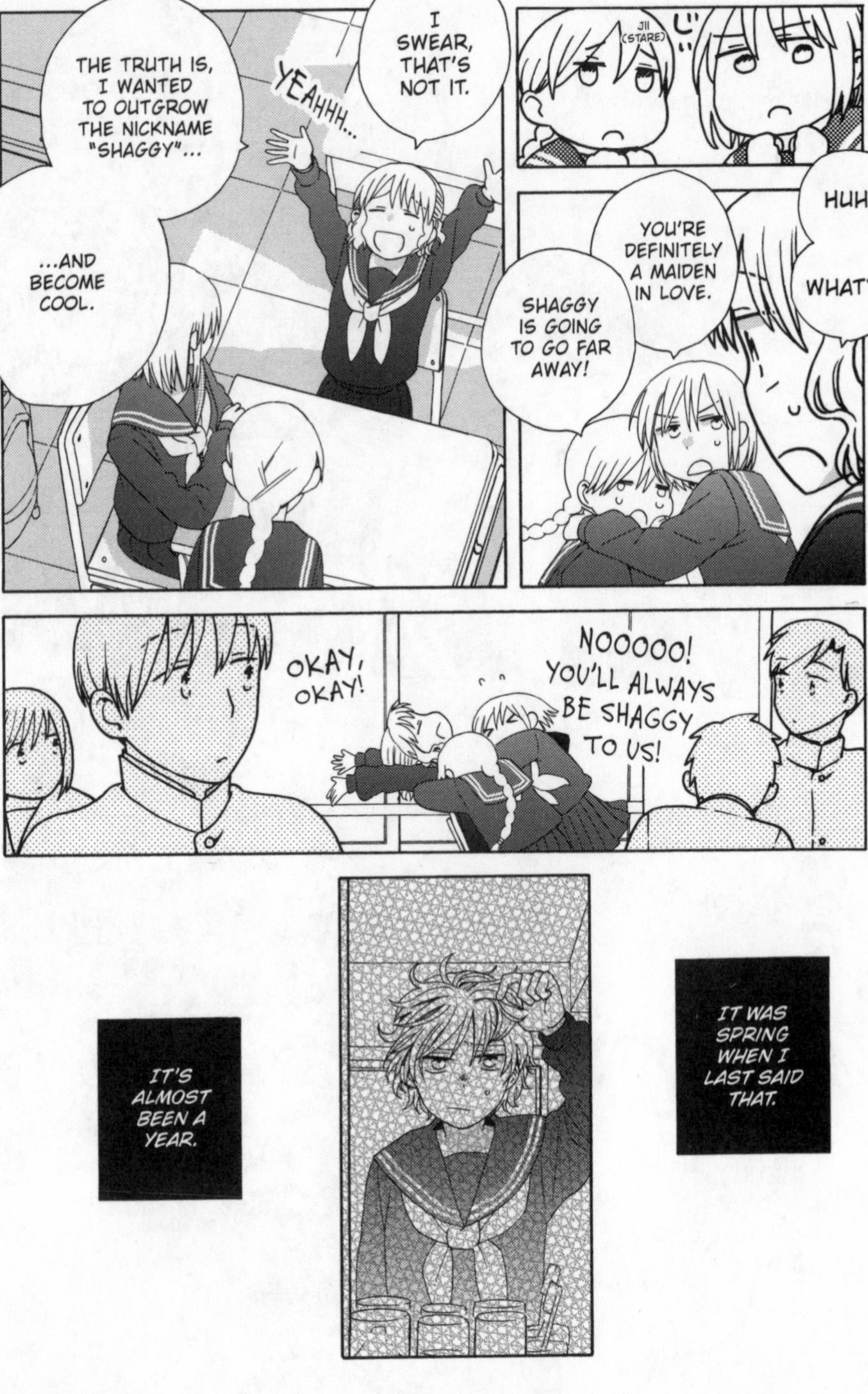
JII (STARE)
じ
HUH?
WHAT?
YOU'RE DEFINITELY A MAIDEN IN LOVE.
SHAGGY IS GOING TO GO FAR AWAY!
I SWEAR, THAT'S NOT IT.
YEAHHH...
THE TRUTH IS, I WANTED TO OUTGROW THE NICKNAME "SHAGGY"...
...AND BECOME COOL.
NOOOOO! YOU'LL ALWAYS BE SHAGGY TO US!
OKAY, OKAY!
IT WAS SPRING WHEN I LAST SAID THAT.
IT'S ALMOST BEEN A YEAR.

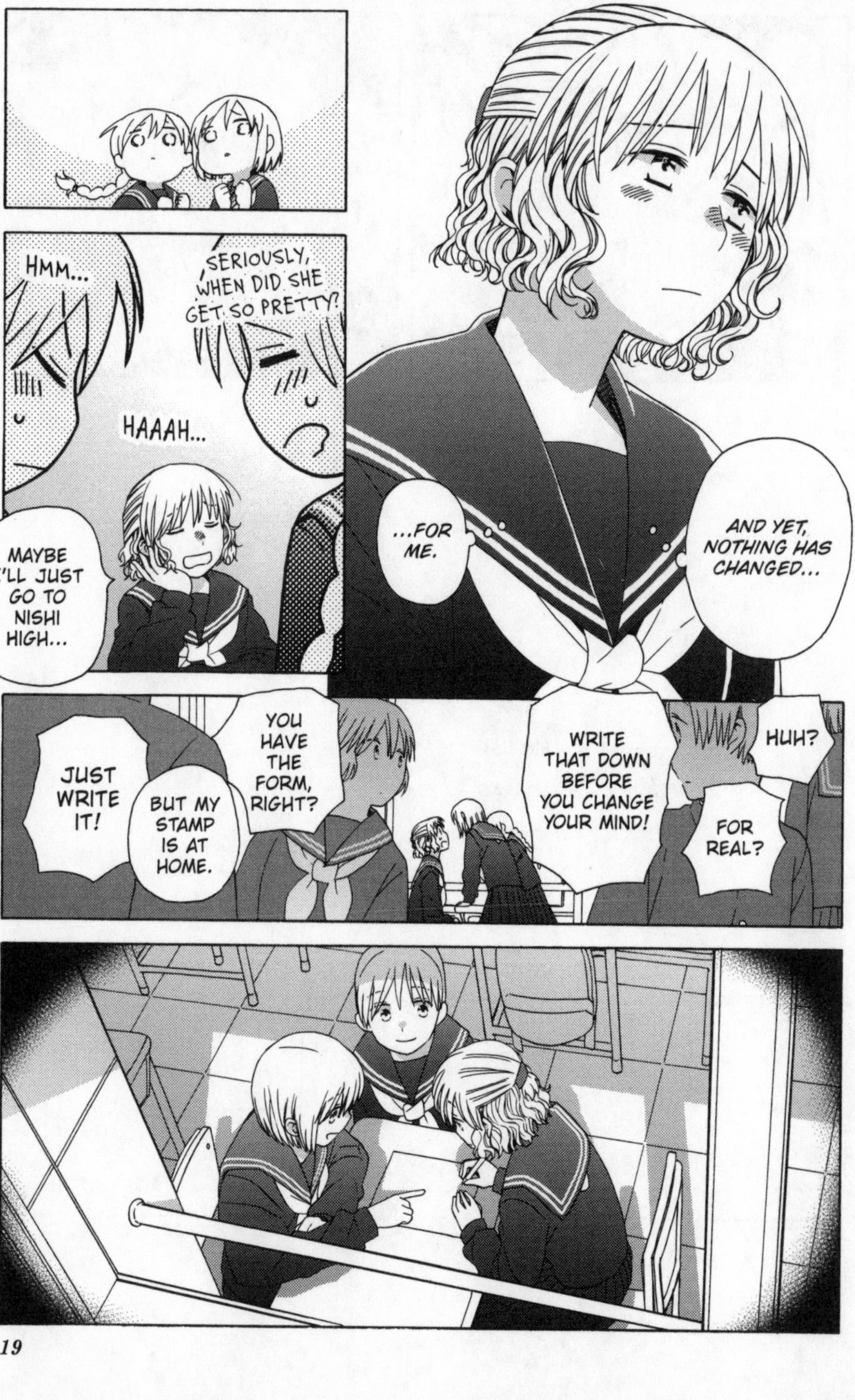
AND YET, NOTHING HAS CHANGED...
...FOR ME.
SERIOUSLY, WHEN DID SHE GET SO PRETTY?
HMM...
HAAAH...
MAYBE I'LL JUST GO TO NISHI HIGH...
HUH?
FOR REAL?
WRITE THAT DOWN BEFORE YOU CHANGE YOUR MIND!
YOU HAVE THE FORM, RIGHT?
BUT MY STAMP IS AT HOME.
JUST WRITE IT!

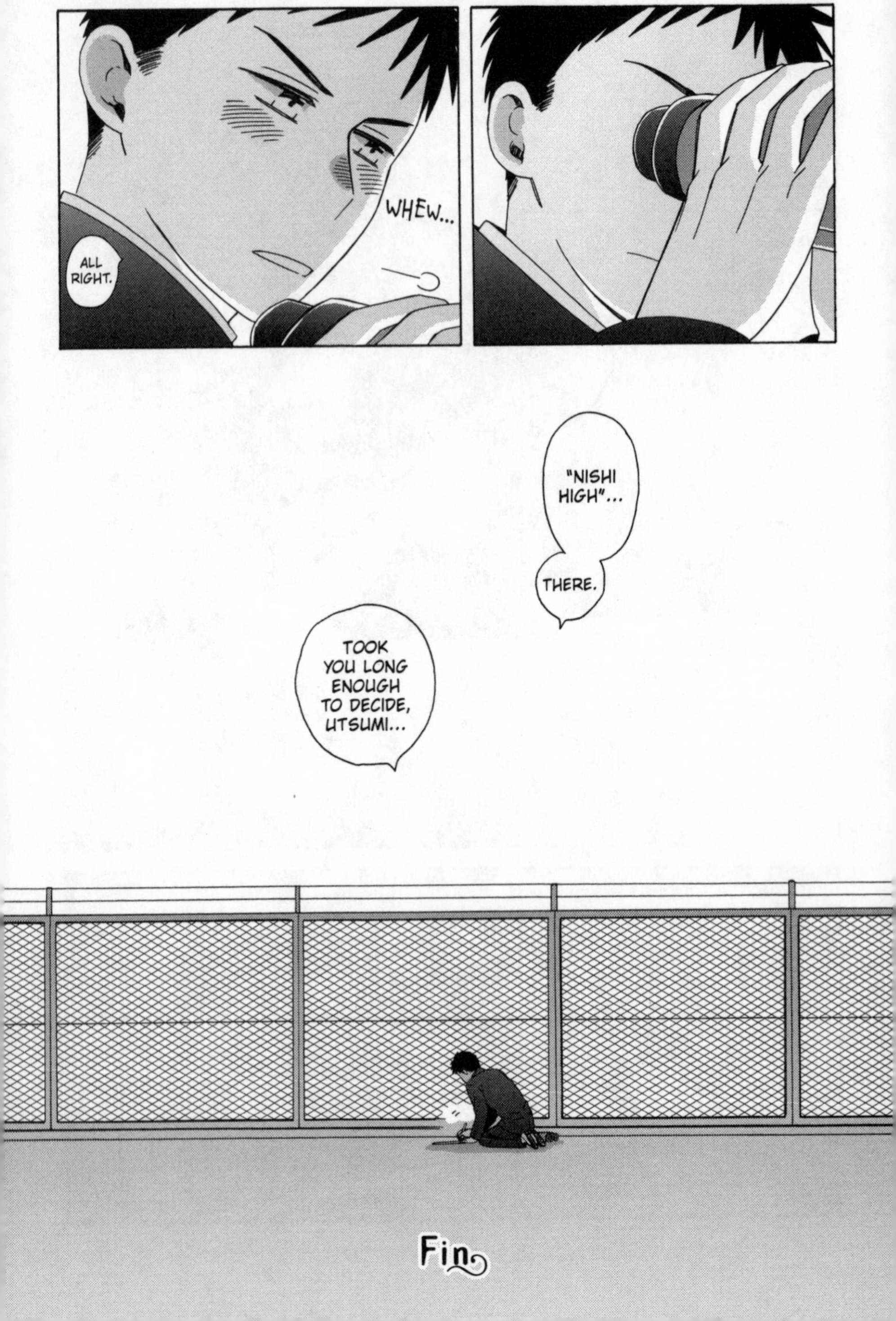
WHEW...
ALL RIGHT.
"NISHI HIGH"...
THERE.
TOOK YOU LONG ENOUGH TO DECIDE, UTSUMI...
Fin

Love at Fourteen

[Intermission 74]

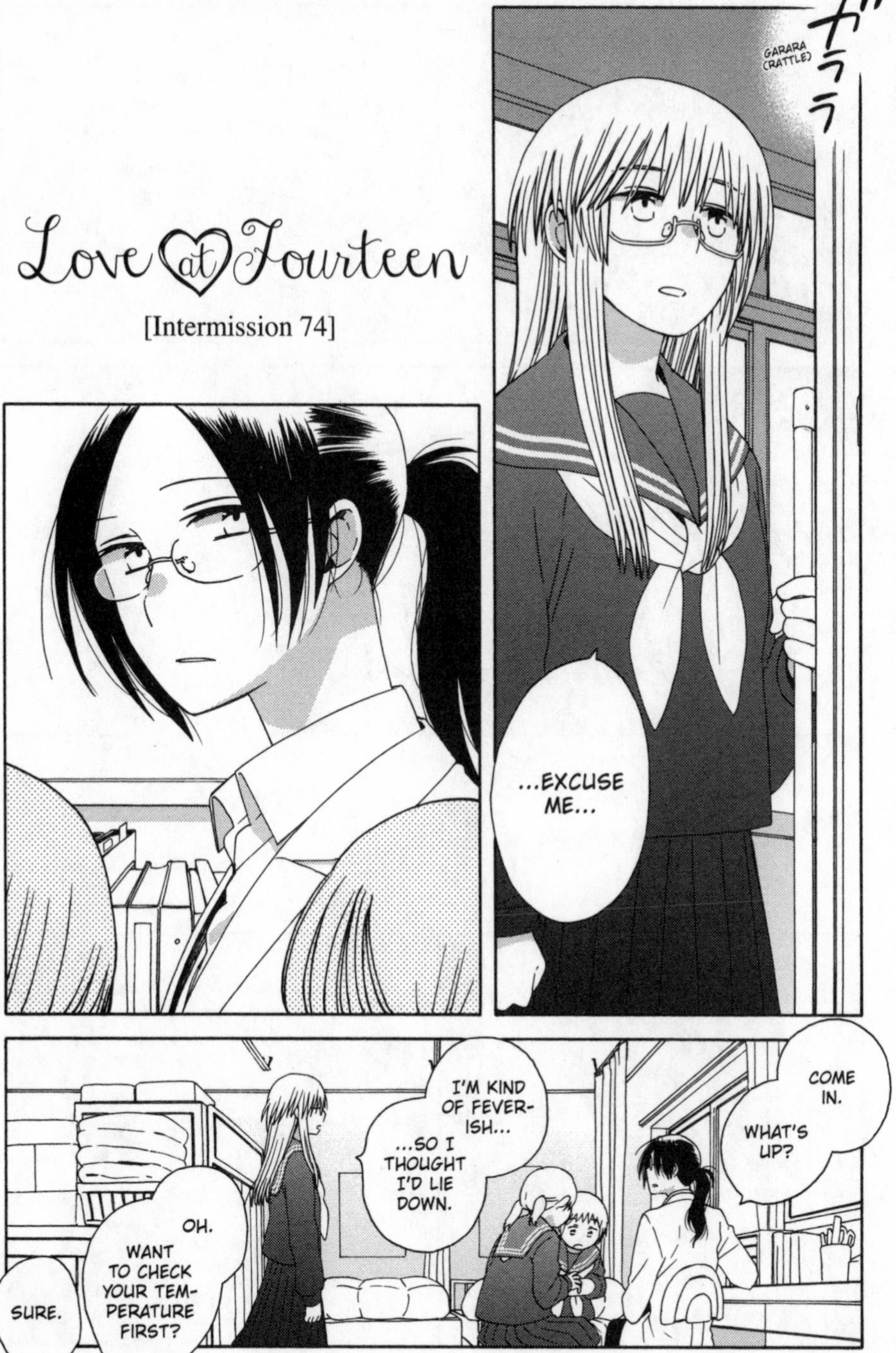
ガララ
GARARA (RATTLE)
...EXCUSE ME...
COME IN.
WHAT'S UP?
I'M KIND OF FEVER-ISH...
...SO I THOUGHT I'D LIE DOWN.
OH.
WANT TO CHECK YOUR TEM-PERATURE FIRST?
SURE.

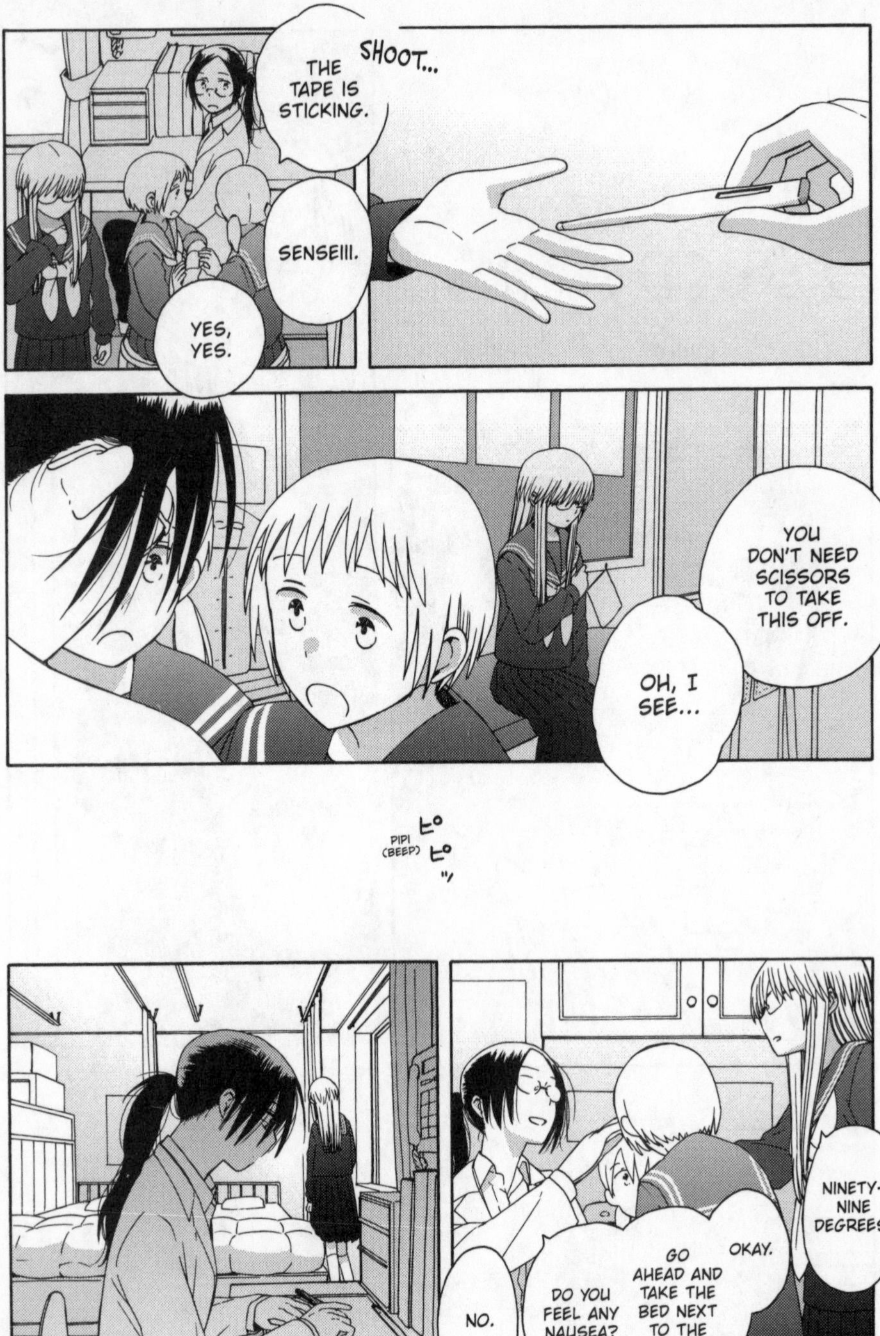
SHOOT...
THE TAPE IS STICKING.
SENSEIII.
YES, YES.
YOU DON'T NEED SCISSORS TO TAKE THIS OFF.
OH, I SEE...
ピピッ
PIPI (BEEP)
NINETY-NINE DEGREES.
OKAY.
GO AHEAD AND TAKE THE BED NEXT TO THE WINDOW.
DO YOU FEEL ANY NAUSEA?
NO.

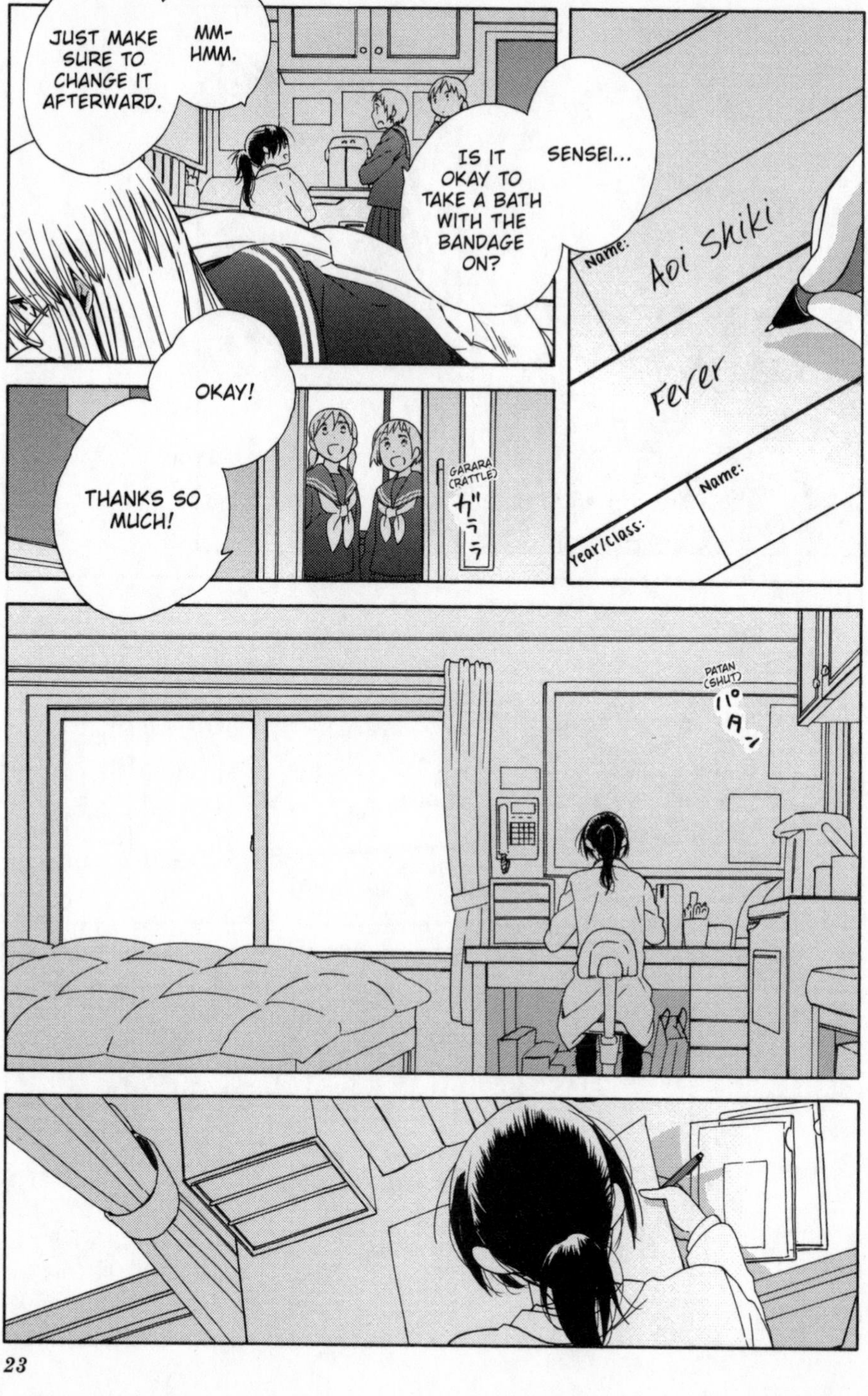
Name:
Aoi Shiki
Fever
Year/Class:
Name:
SENSEI...
IS IT OKAY TO TAKE A BATH WITH THE BANDAGE ON?
MM-HMM.
JUST MAKE SURE TO CHANGE IT AFTERWARD.
OKAY!
THANKS SO MUCH!
GARARA (RATTLE)
ガララ
PATAN (SHUT)
パタン

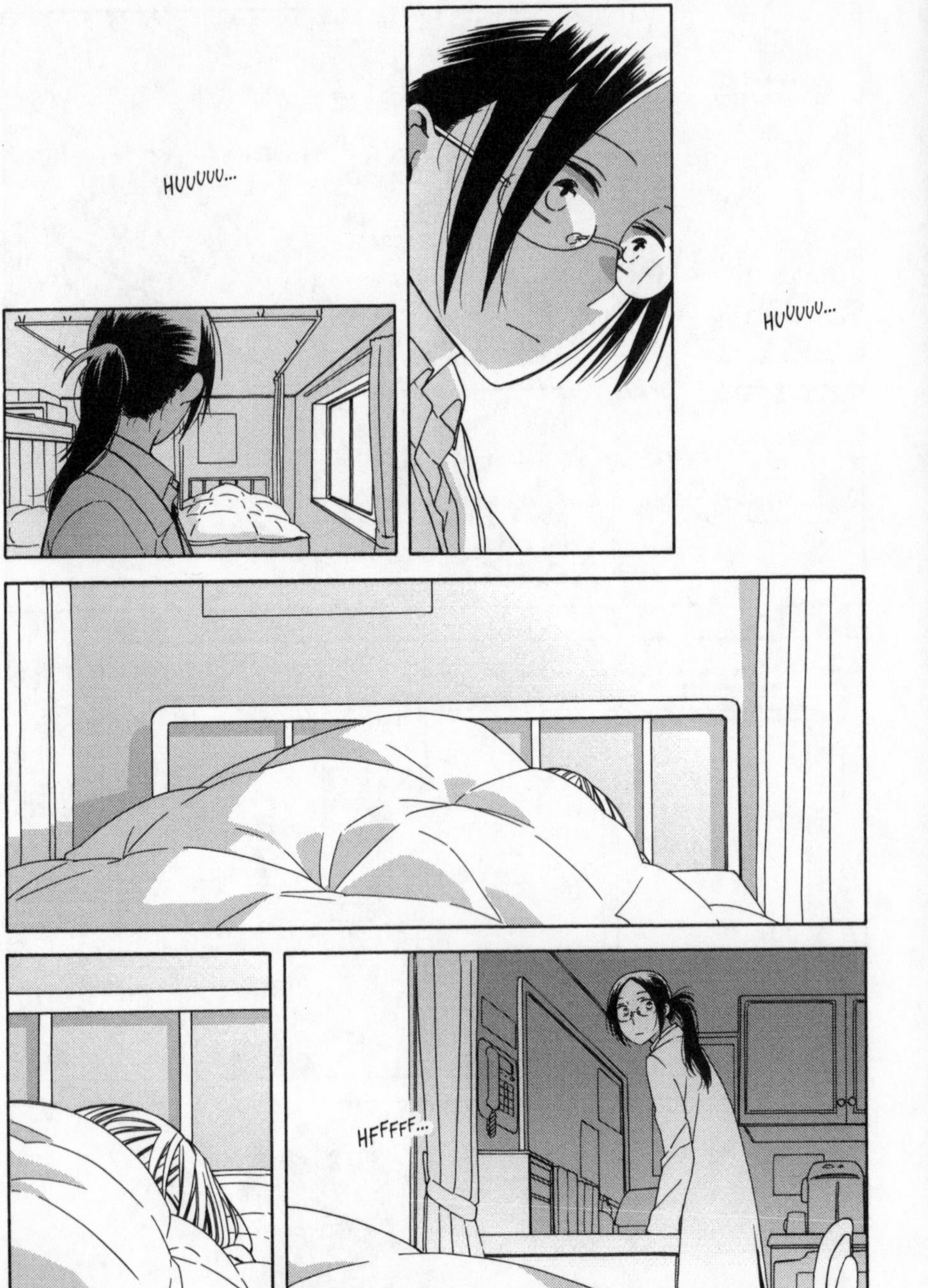
HUUUUU...
HUUUUU...
HFFFFF...

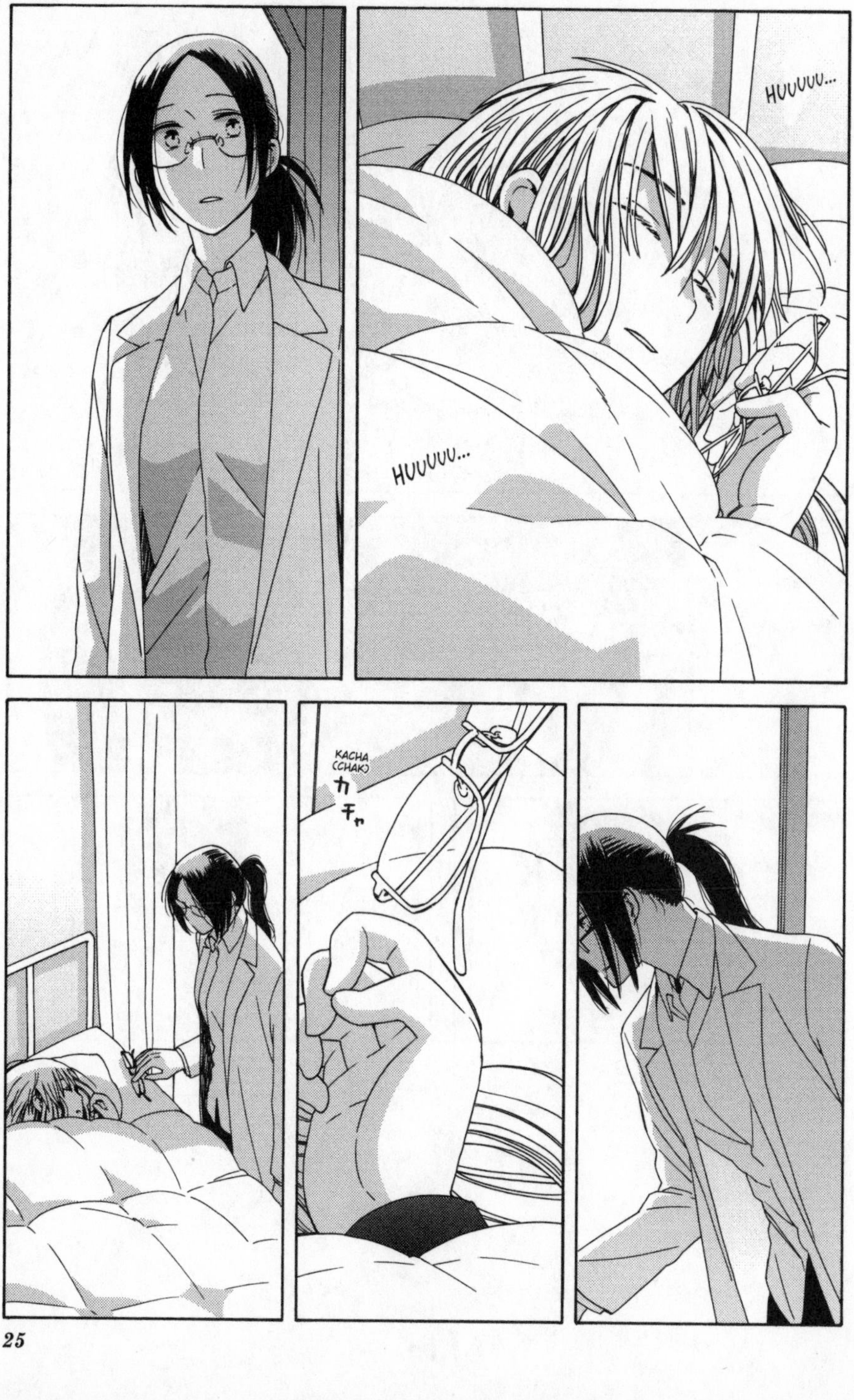
HUUUUU...
HUUUUU...
KACHA (CHAK)
カチャ

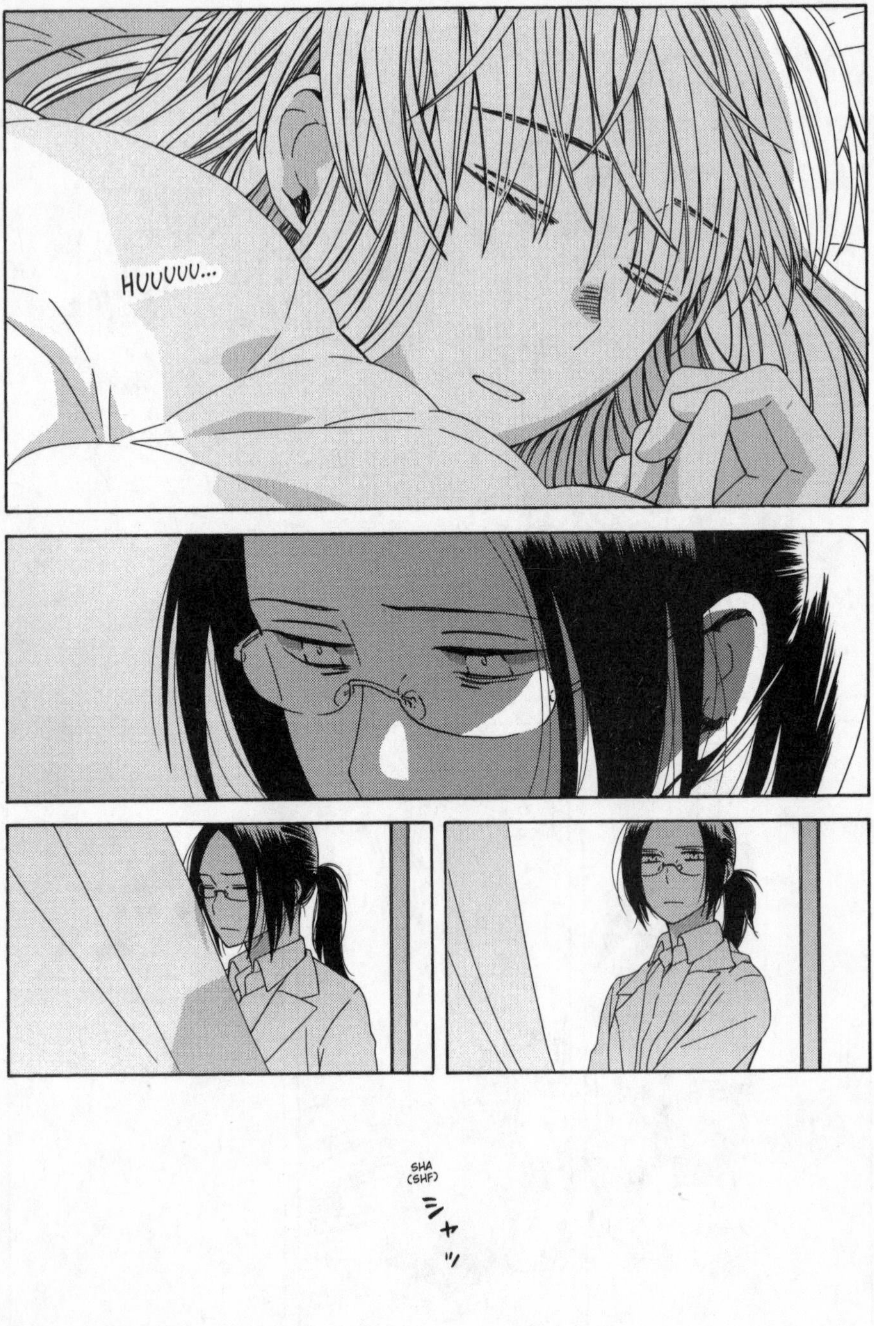
HUUUUU...
SHA (SHF)
シャッ

Fin

Love at Fourteen

[Chapter 48]

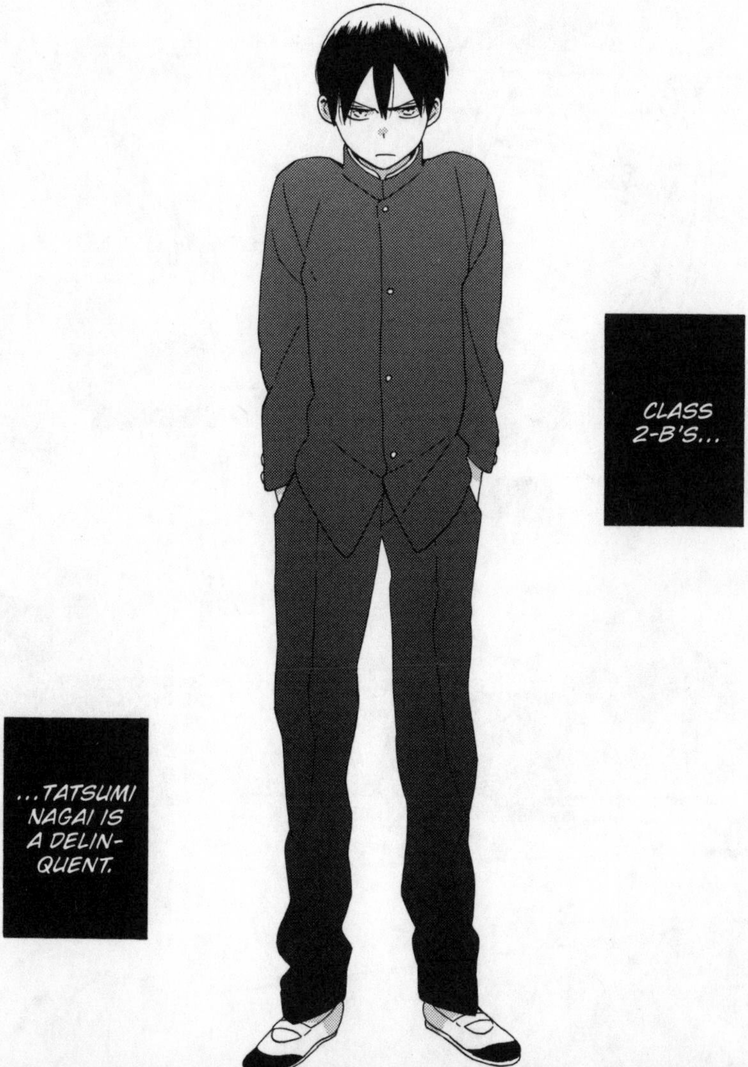
CLASS 2-B'S...
...TATSUMI NAGAI IS A DELIN-QUENT.

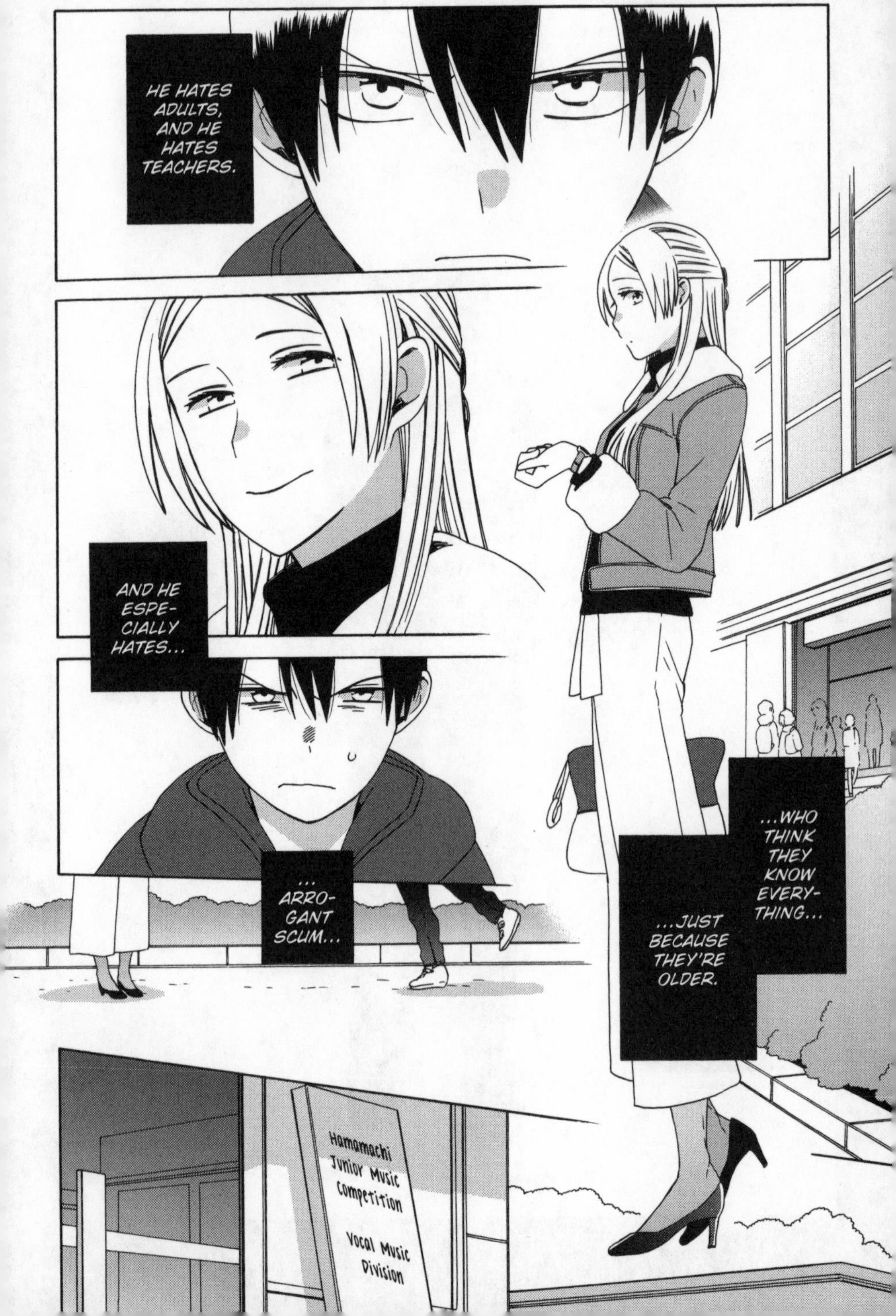
HE HATES ADULTS, AND HE HATES TEACHERS.
AND HE ESPE-CIALLY HATES...
... ARRO-GANT SCUM...
...WHO THINK THEY KNOW EVERY-THING...
...JUST BECAUSE THEY'RE OLDER.
Hamamachi Junior Music Competition
Vocal Music Division

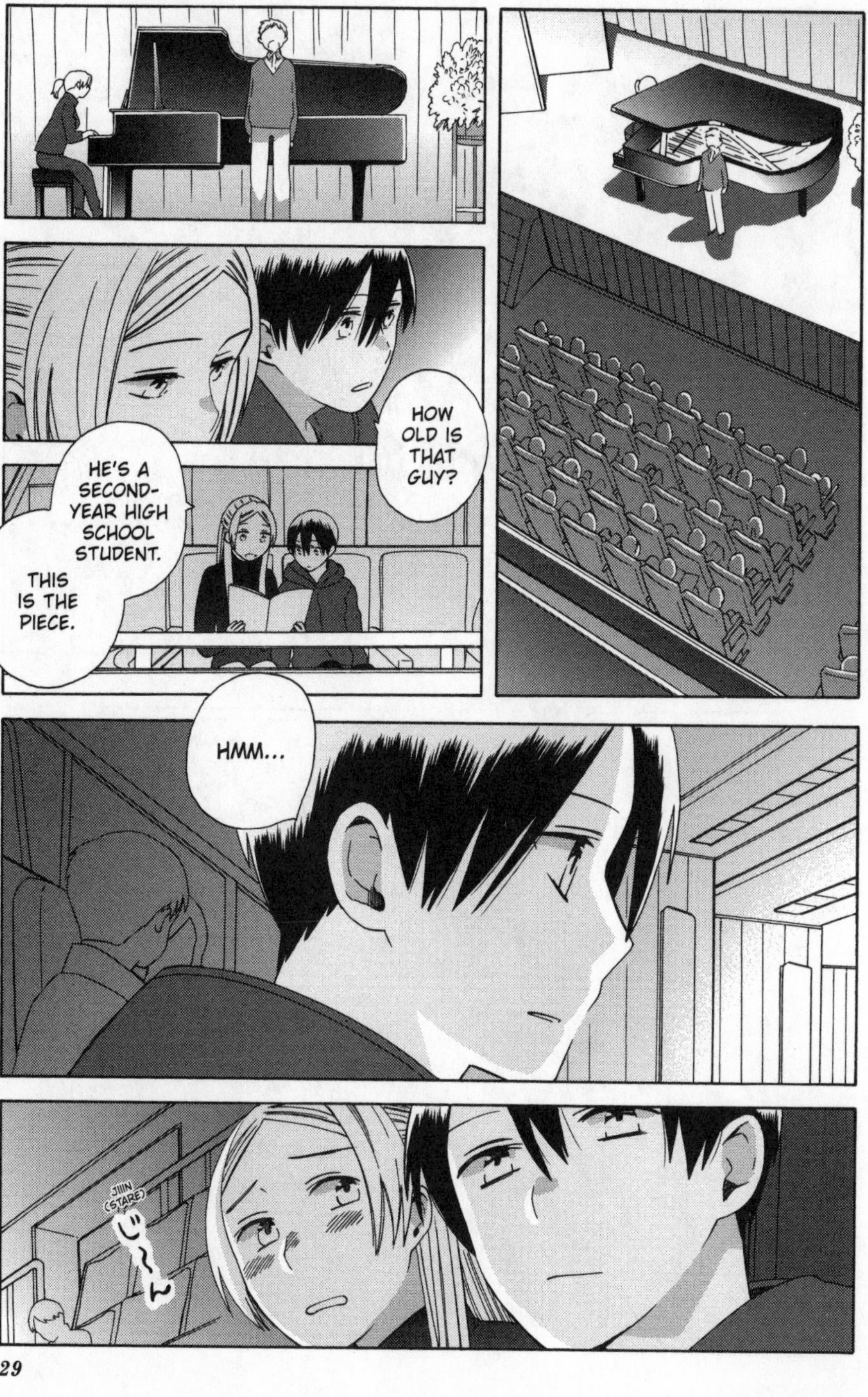
HOW OLD IS THAT GUY?
HE'S A SECOND-YEAR HIGH SCHOOL STUDENT.
THIS IS THE PIECE.
HMM...
JIIN (STARE)
じ〜ん

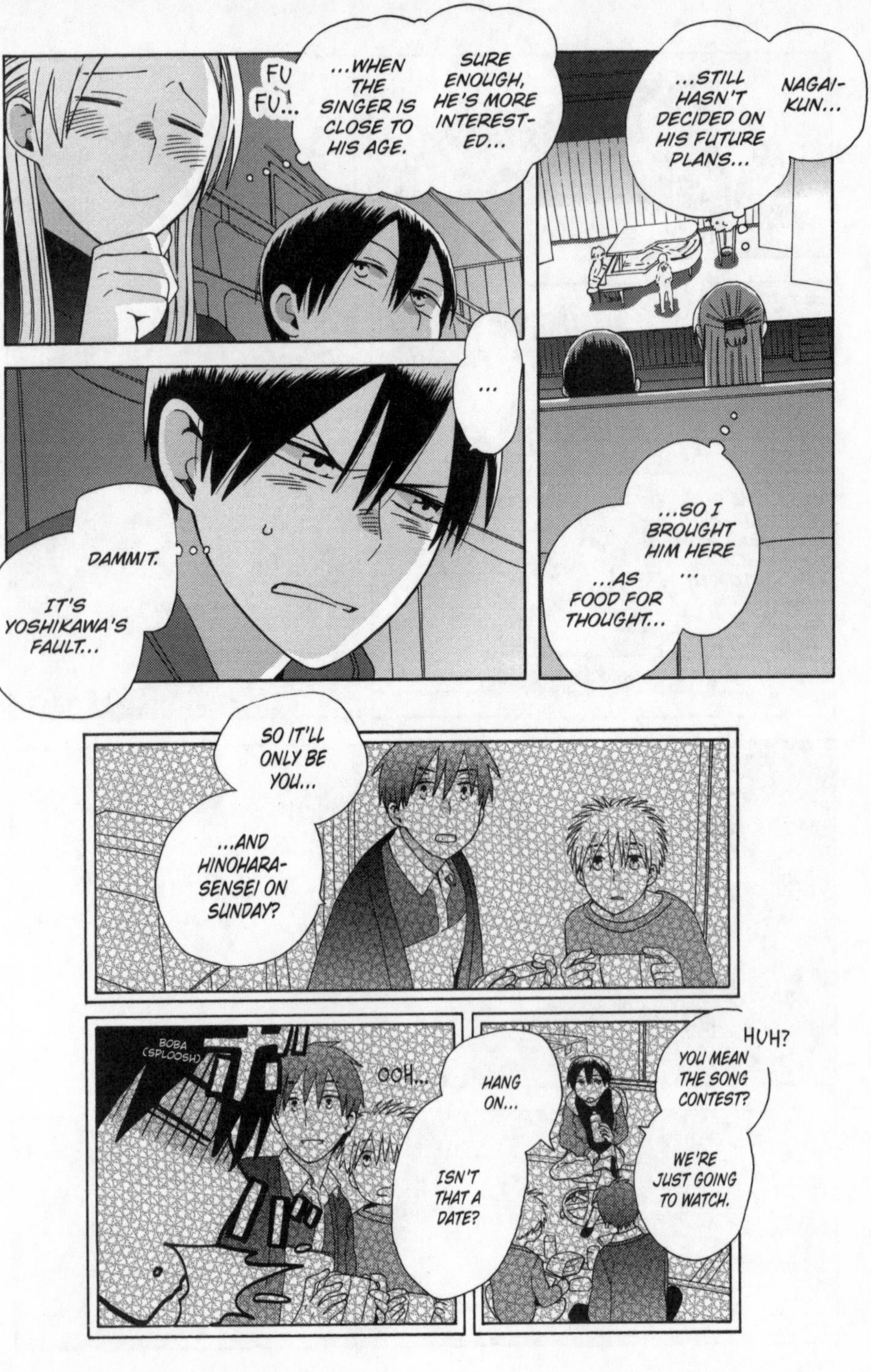
NAGAI-KUN...
...STILL HASN'T DECIDED ON HIS FUTURE PLANS...
SURE ENOUGH, HE'S MORE INTERESTED...
...WHEN THE SINGER IS CLOSE TO HIS AGE.
FU FU...
...SO I BROUGHT HIM HERE ...
...AS FOOD FOR THOUGHT...
...
DAMMIT.
IT'S YOSHIKAWA'S FAULT...
SO IT'LL ONLY BE YOU...
...AND HINOHARA-SENSEI ON SUNDAY?
HUH?
YOU MEAN THE SONG CONTEST?
WE'RE JUST GOING TO WATCH.
HANG ON...
ISN'T THAT A DATE?
OOH...
BOBA (SPLOOSH)

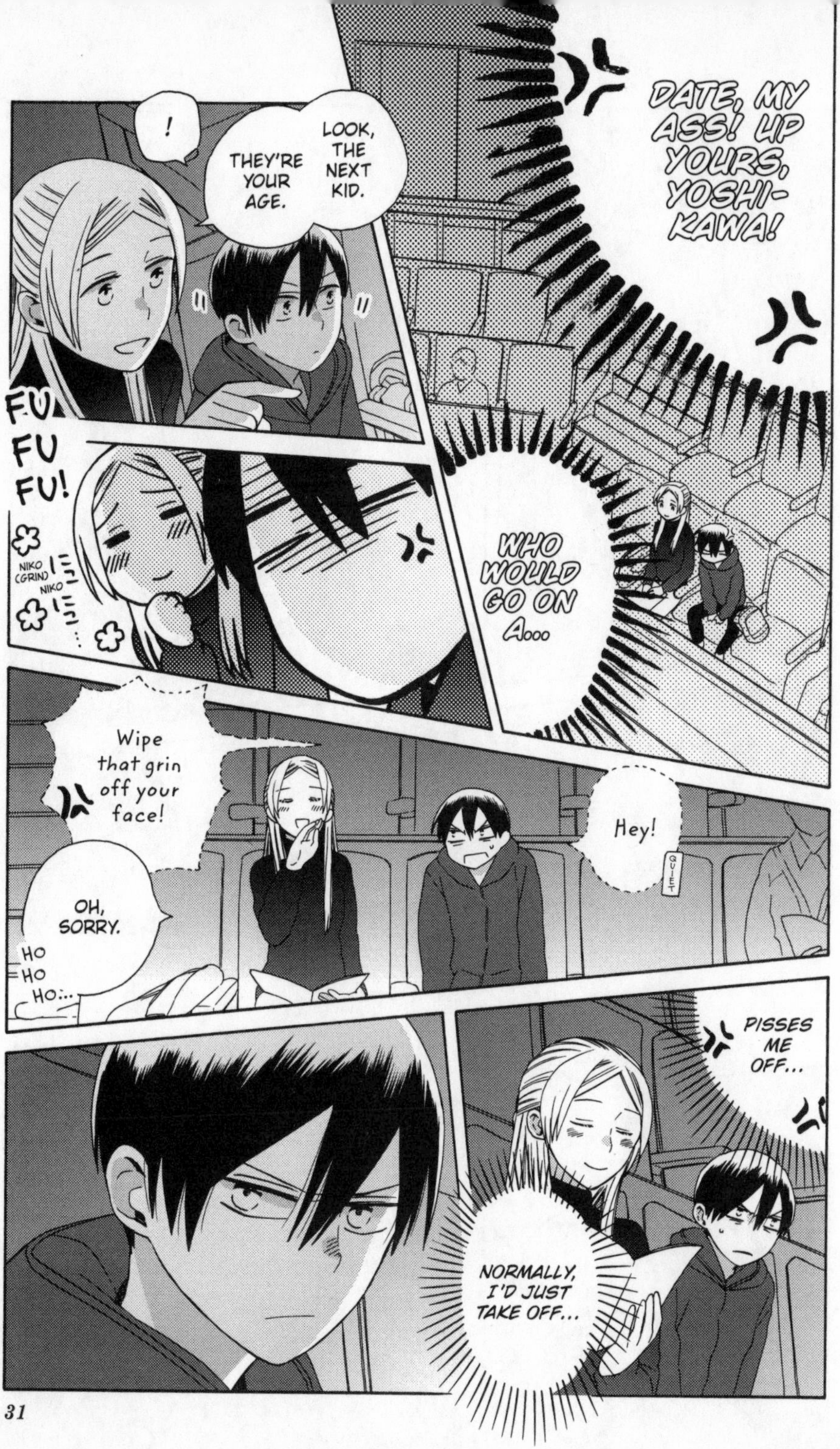
DATE, MY ASS! UP YOURS, YOSHI-KAWA!
WHO WOULD GO ON A...
LOOK, THE NEXT KID.
THEY'RE YOUR AGE.
!
FU FU FU!
NIKO (GRIN) NIKO
Hey!
QUIET
Wipe that grin off your face!
OH, SORRY.
HO HO HO...
PISSES ME OFF...
NORMALLY, I'D JUST TAKE OFF...

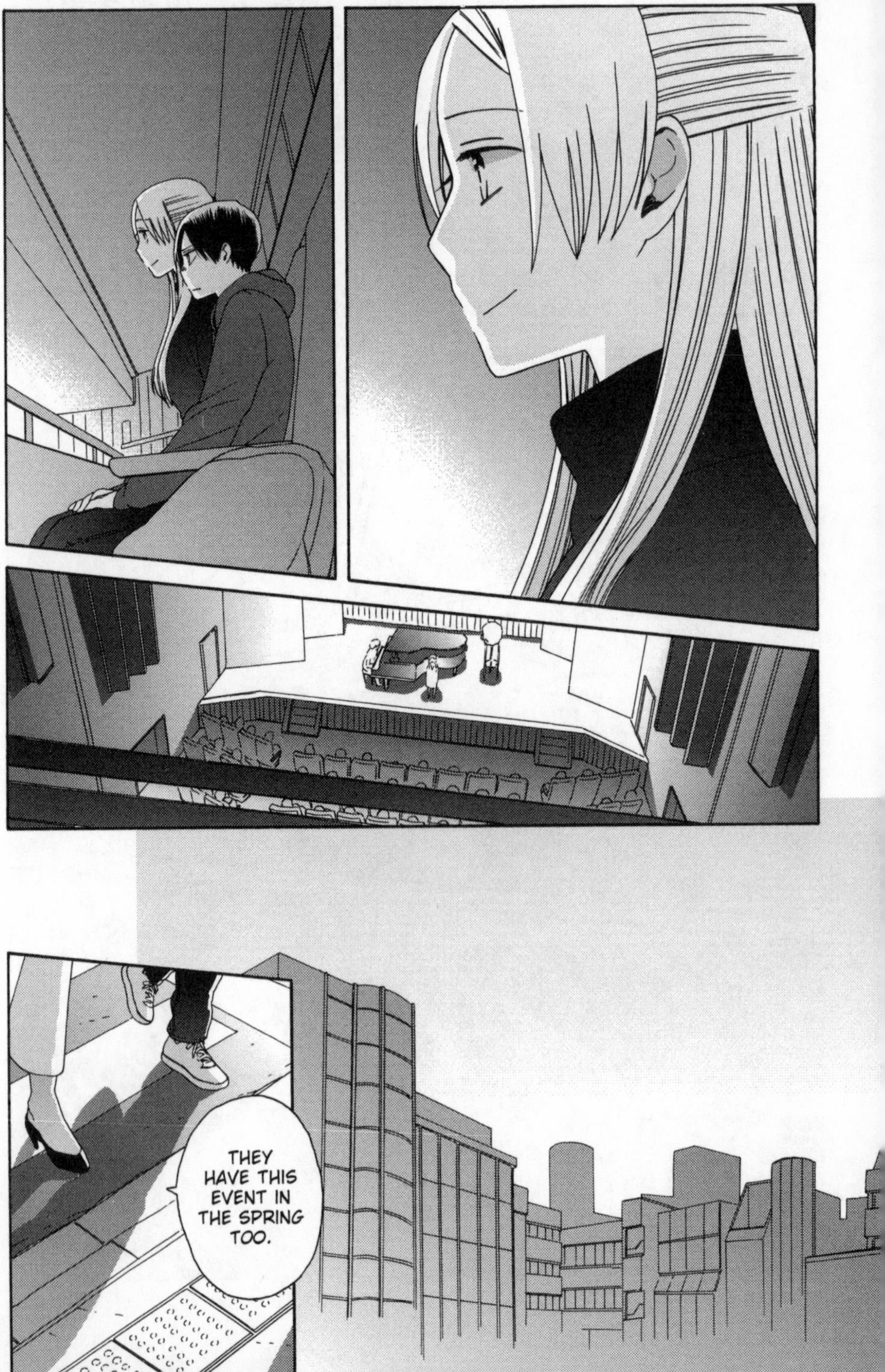
THEY HAVE THIS EVENT IN THE SPRING TOO.

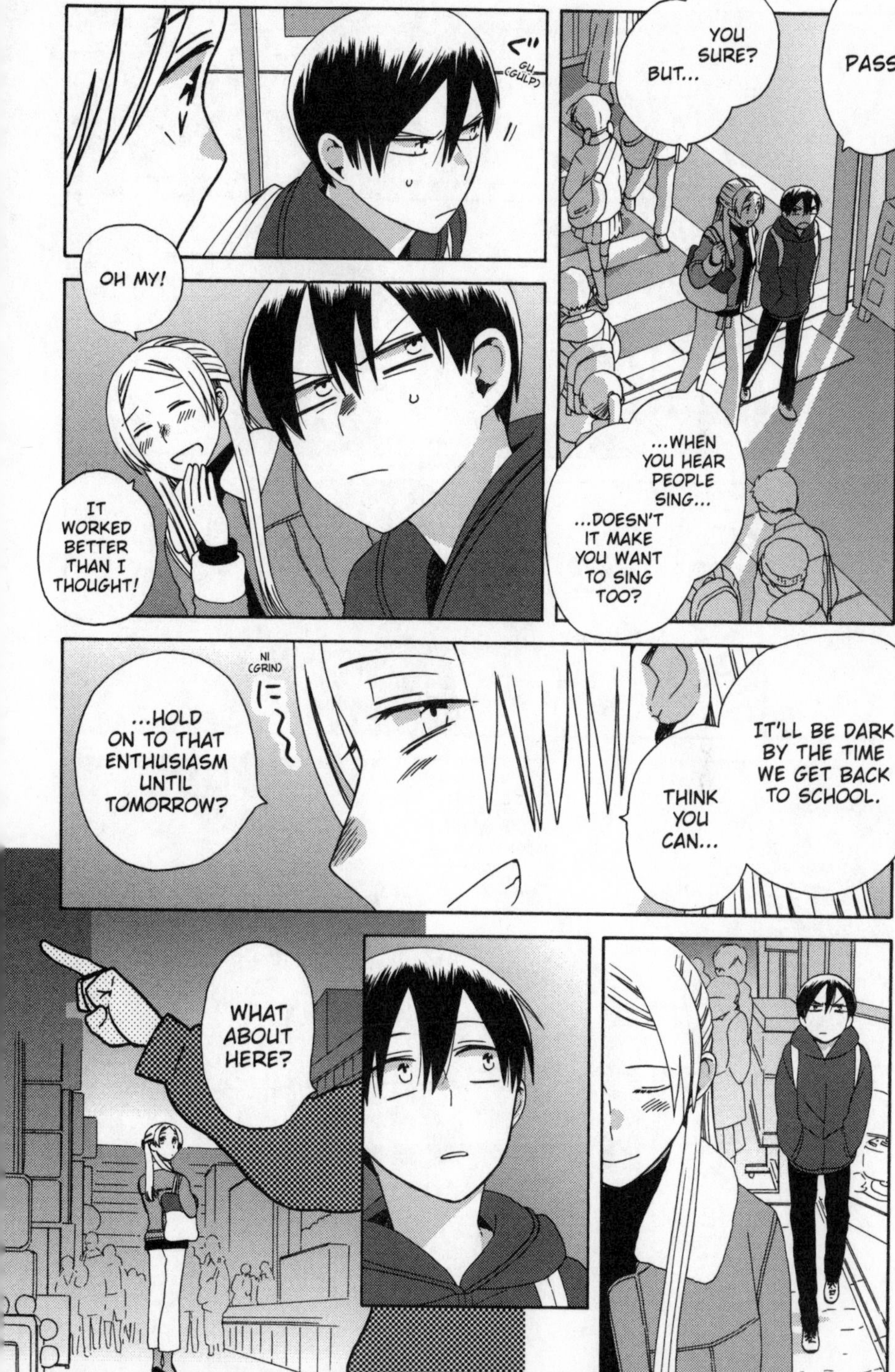
PASS.
BUT... YOU SURE?
...WHEN YOU HEAR PEOPLE SING...
...DOESN'T IT MAKE YOU WANT TO SING TOO?
ぐ"
GU (GULP)
OH MY!
IT WORKED BETTER THAN I THOUGHT!
IT'LL BE DARK BY THE TIME WE GET BACK TO SCHOOL.
THINK YOU CAN...
に~
NI (GRIN)
...HOLD ON TO THAT ENTHUSIASM UNTIL TOMORROW?
WHAT ABOUT HERE?

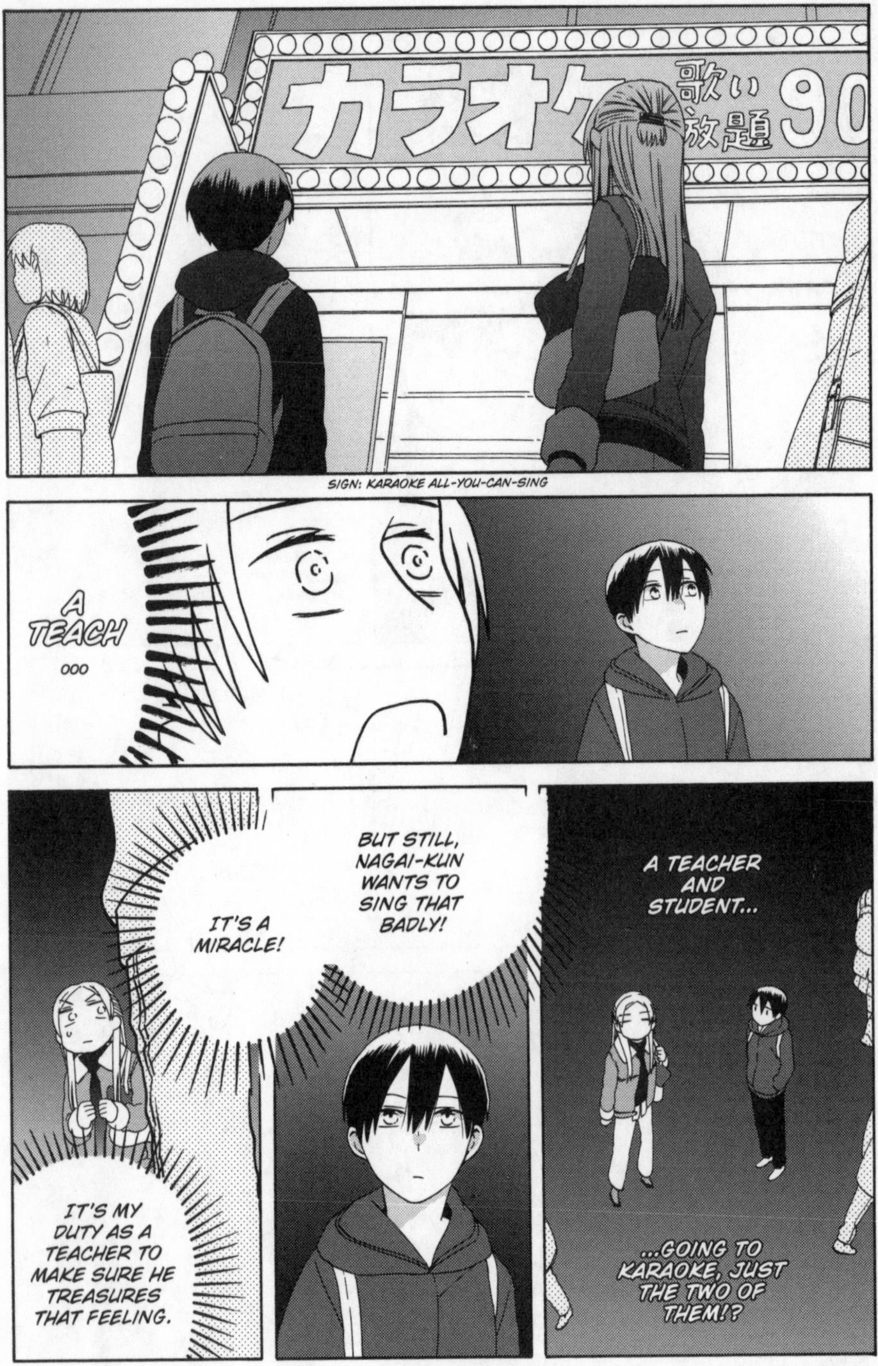
カラオ
歌い放題
90
SIGN: KARAOKE ALL-YOU-CAN-SING
A TEACH ooo
A TEACHER AND STUDENT...
...GOING TO KARAOKE, JUST THE TWO OF THEM!?
BUT STILL, NAGAI-KUN WANTS TO SING THAT BADLY!
IT'S A MIRACLE!
IT'S MY DUTY AS A TEACHER TO MAKE SURE HE TREASURES THAT FEELING.

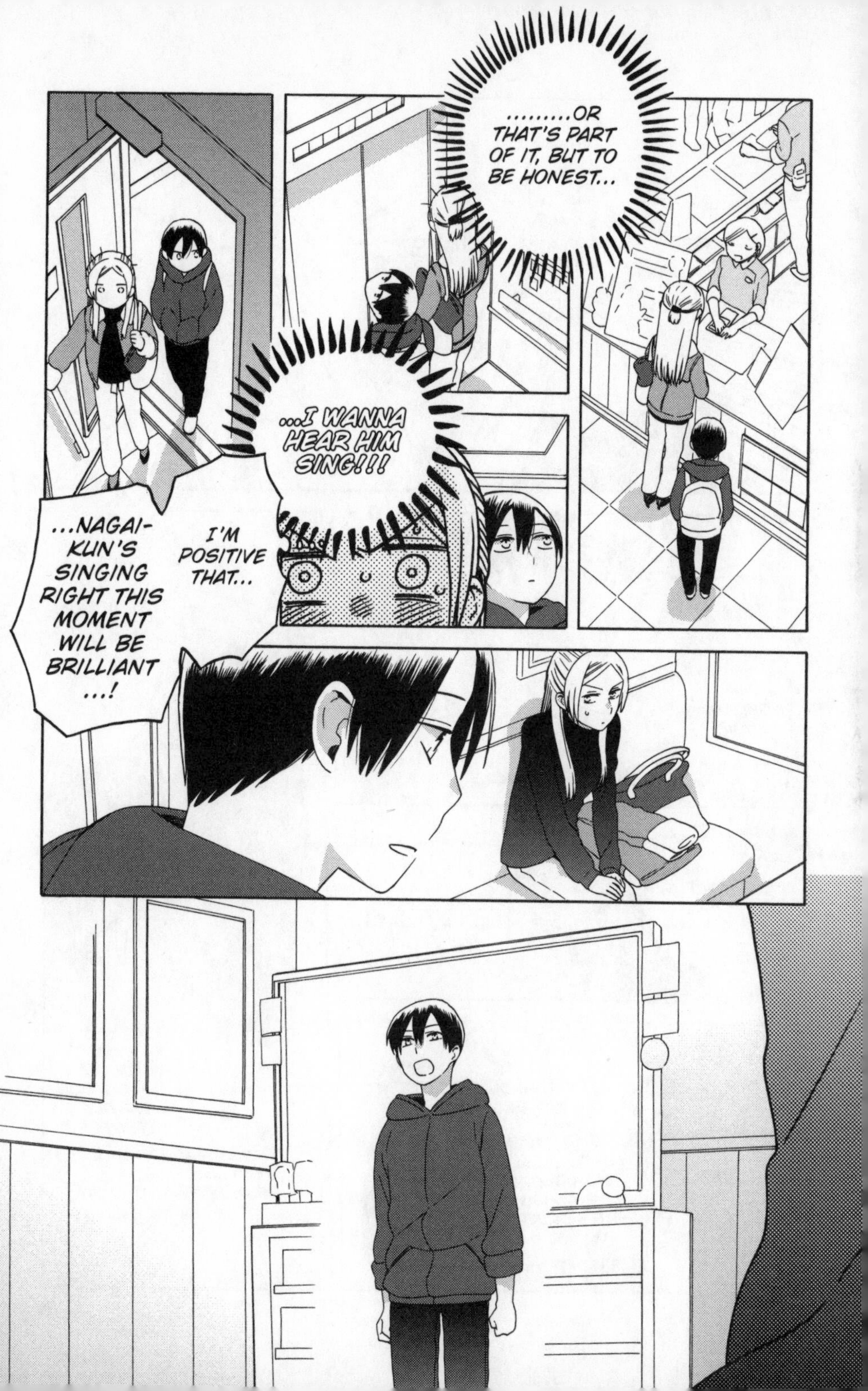
.........OR THAT'S PART OF IT, BUT TO BE HONEST...
...I WANNA HEAR HIM SING!!!
I'M POSITIVE THAT...
...NAGAI-KUN'S SINGING RIGHT THIS MOMENT WILL BE BRILLIANT ...!

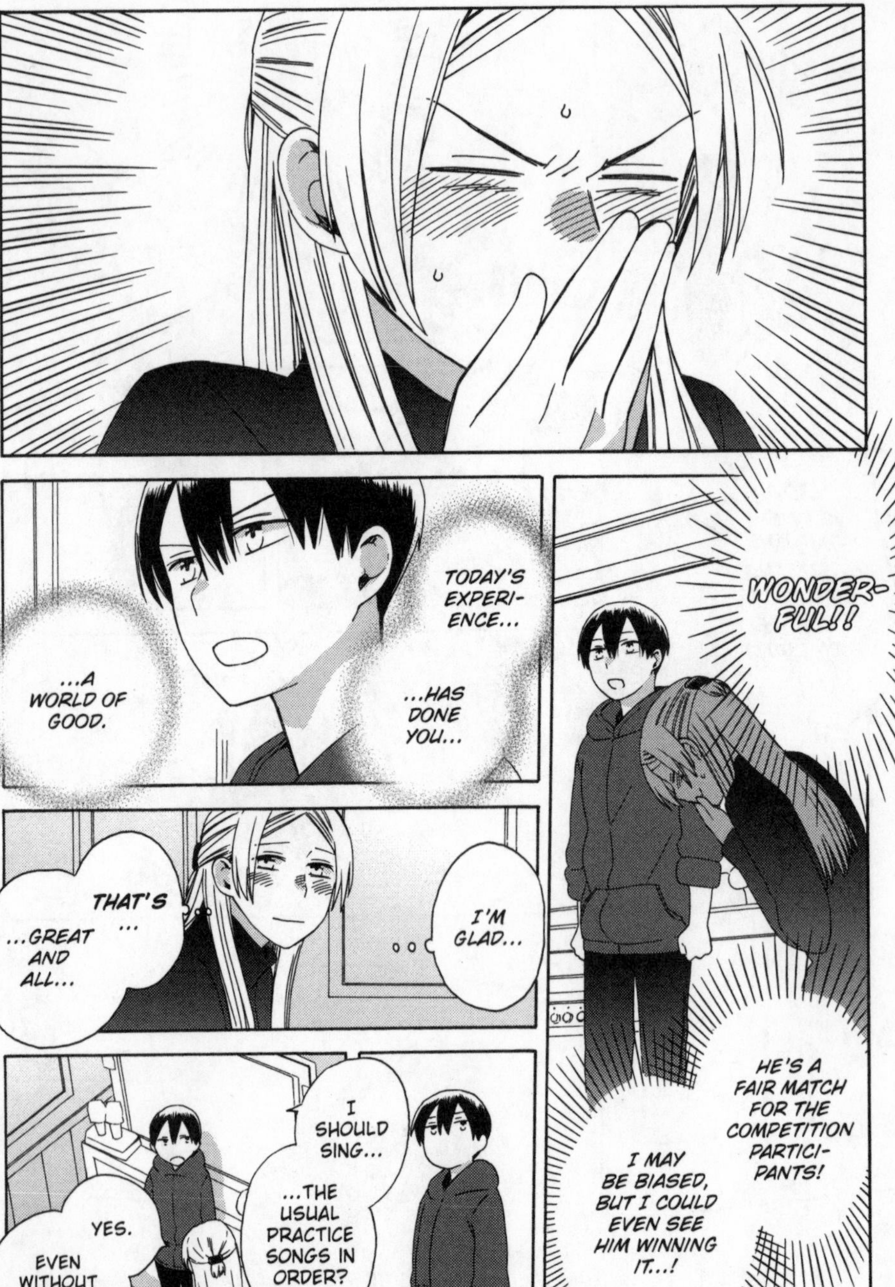
WONDER-FUL!!
HE'S A FAIR MATCH FOR THE COMPETITION PARTICI-PANTS!
I MAY BE BIASED, BUT I COULD EVEN SEE HIM WINNING IT...!
TODAY'S EXPERI-ENCE...
...HAS DONE YOU...
...A WORLD OF GOOD.
I'M GLAD...
THAT'S...
...GREAT AND ALL...
I SHOULD SING...
...THE USUAL PRACTICE SONGS IN ORDER?
YES.
EVEN WITHOUT ACCOMPANI-MENT, MIND THE TEMPO, OKAY?

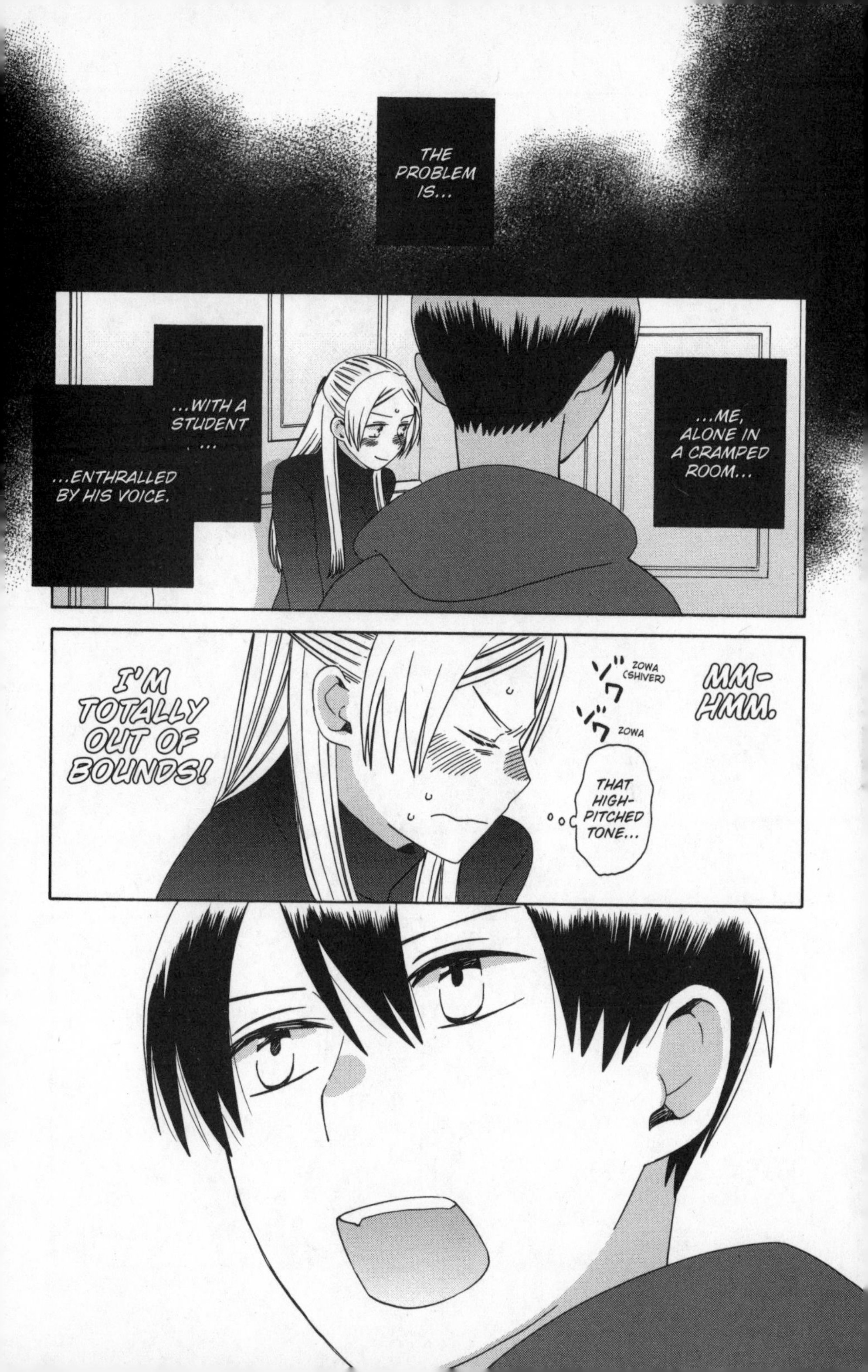
THE PROBLEM IS...
...ME, ALONE IN A CRAMPED ROOM...
...WITH A STUDENT ...
...ENTHRALLED BY HIS VOICE.
MM-HMM.
ゾワ ZOWA (SHIVER)
ゾワ ZOWA
THAT HIGH-PITCHED TONE...
I'M TOTALLY OUT OF BOUNDS!

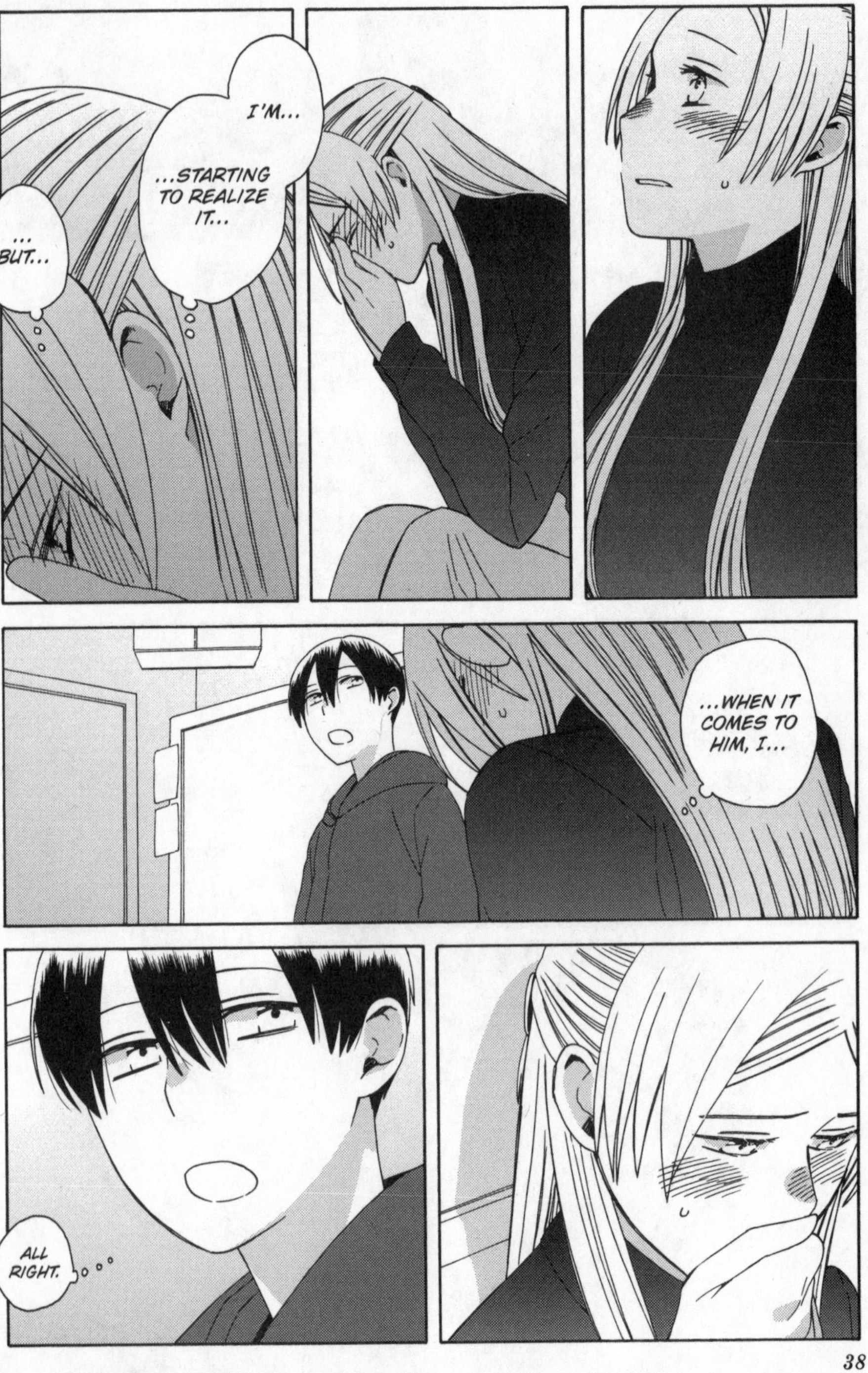
I'M...
...STARTING TO REALIZE IT...
... BUT...
...WHEN IT COMES TO HIM, I...
ALL RIGHT.

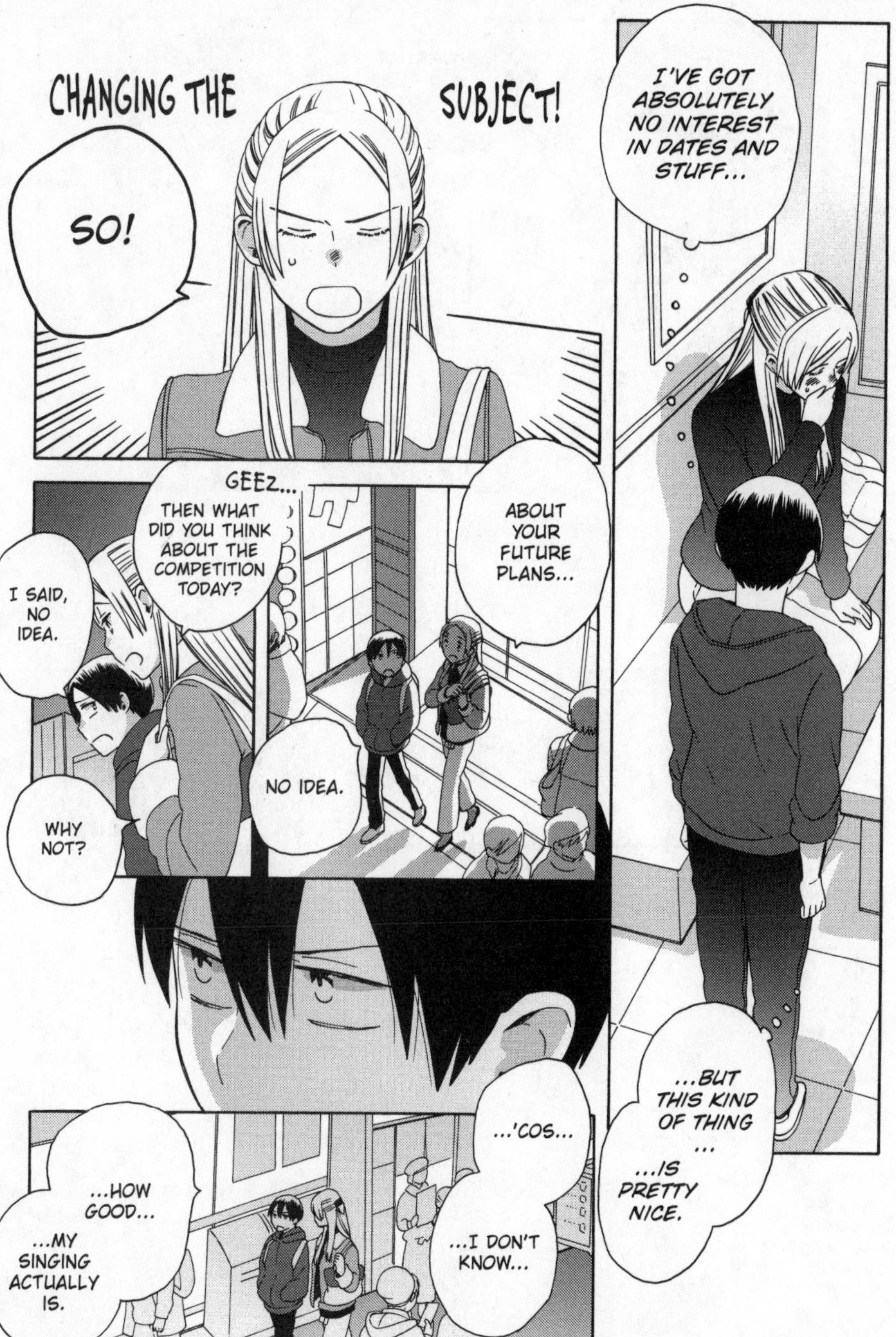

I'VE GOT ABSOLUTELY NO INTEREST IN DATES AND STUFF...
...BUT THIS KIND OF THING ...
...IS PRETTY NICE.
CHANGING THE SUBJECT!
SO!
ABOUT YOUR FUTURE PLANS...
GEEZ...
THEN WHAT DID YOU THINK ABOUT THE COMPETITION TODAY?
NO IDEA.
I SAID, NO IDEA.
WHY NOT?
...'COS...
...I DON'T KNOW...
...HOW GOOD...
...MY SINGING ACTUALLY IS.

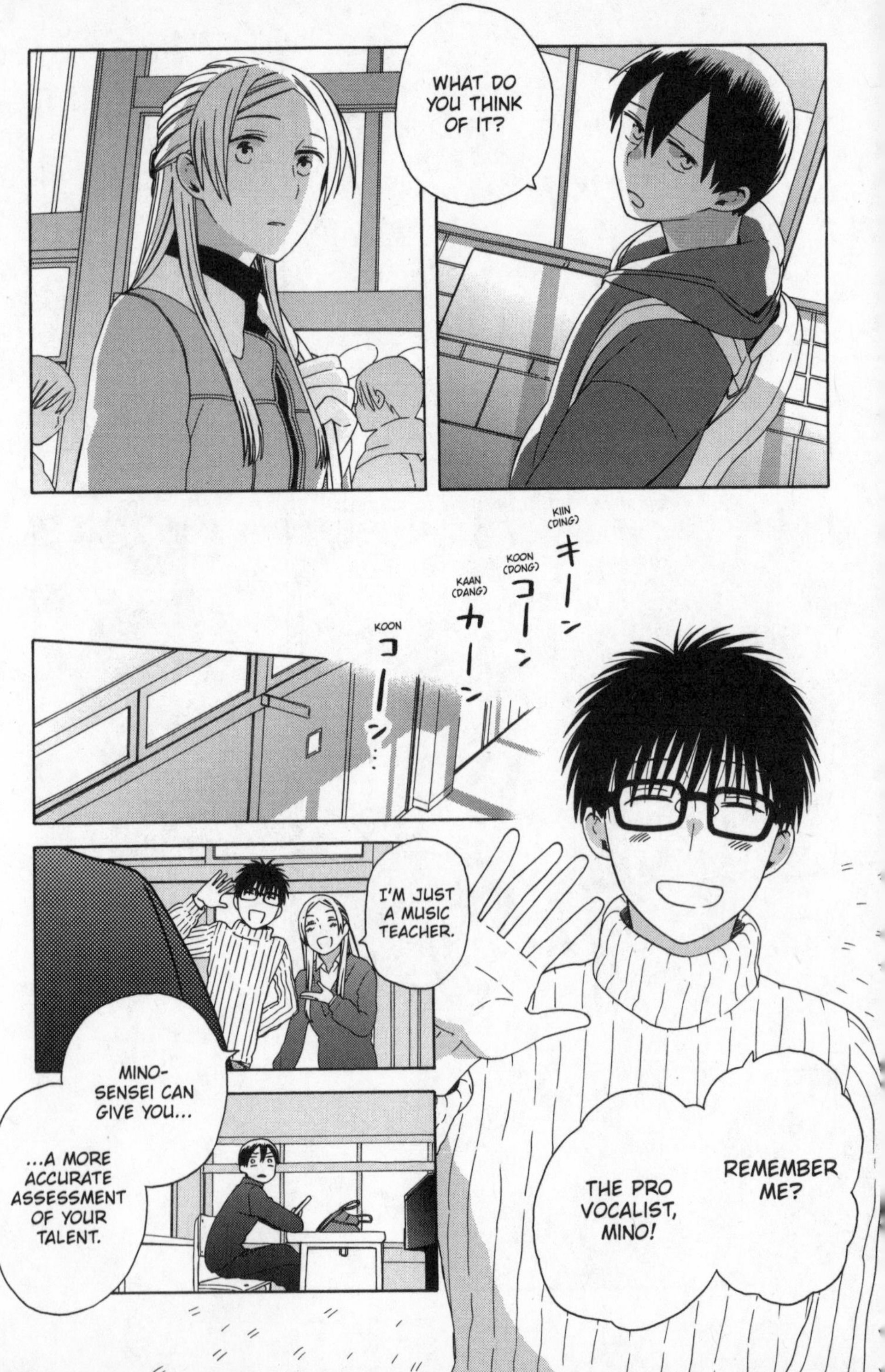
WHAT DO YOU THINK OF IT?
KIIN (DING)
キーン
KOON (DONG)
コーン
KAAN (DANG)
カーン
KOON
コーン…
REMEMBER ME?
THE PRO VOCALIST, MINO!
I'M JUST A MUSIC TEACHER.
MINO-SENSEI CAN GIVE YOU...
...A MORE ACCURATE ASSESSMENT OF YOUR TALENT.

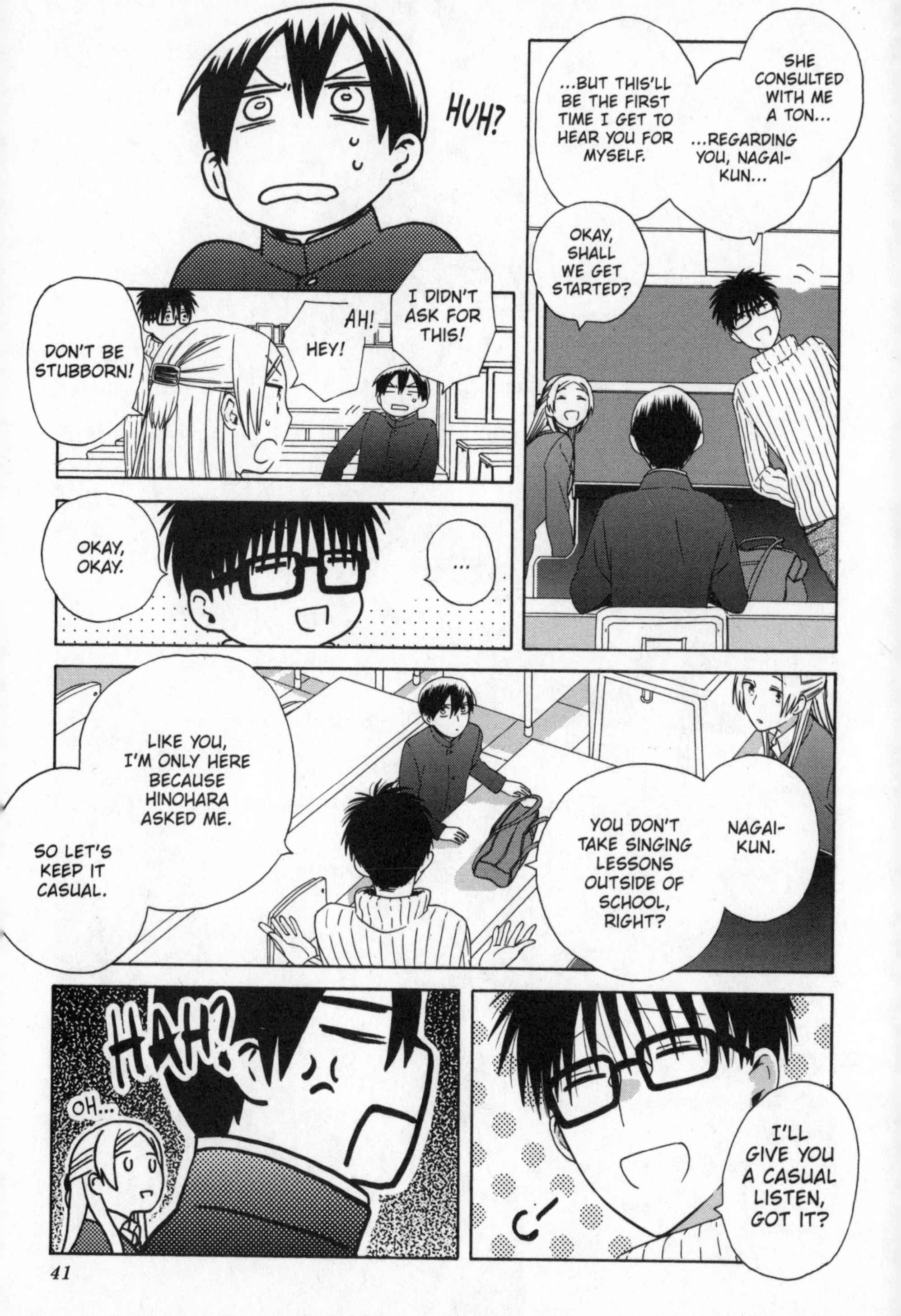
SHE CONSULTED WITH ME A TON...
...REGARDING YOU, NAGAI-KUN...
...BUT THIS'LL BE THE FIRST TIME I GET TO HEAR YOU FOR MYSELF.
OKAY, SHALL WE GET STARTED?
HUH?
I DIDN'T ASK FOR THIS!
AH!
HEY!
DON'T BE STUBBORN!
...
OKAY, OKAY.
NAGAI-KUN.
YOU DON'T TAKE SINGING LESSONS OUTSIDE OF SCHOOL, RIGHT?
LIKE YOU, I'M ONLY HERE BECAUSE HINOHARA ASKED ME.
SO LET'S KEEP IT CASUAL.
I'LL GIVE YOU A CASUAL LISTEN, GOT IT?
HAH!?
OH...

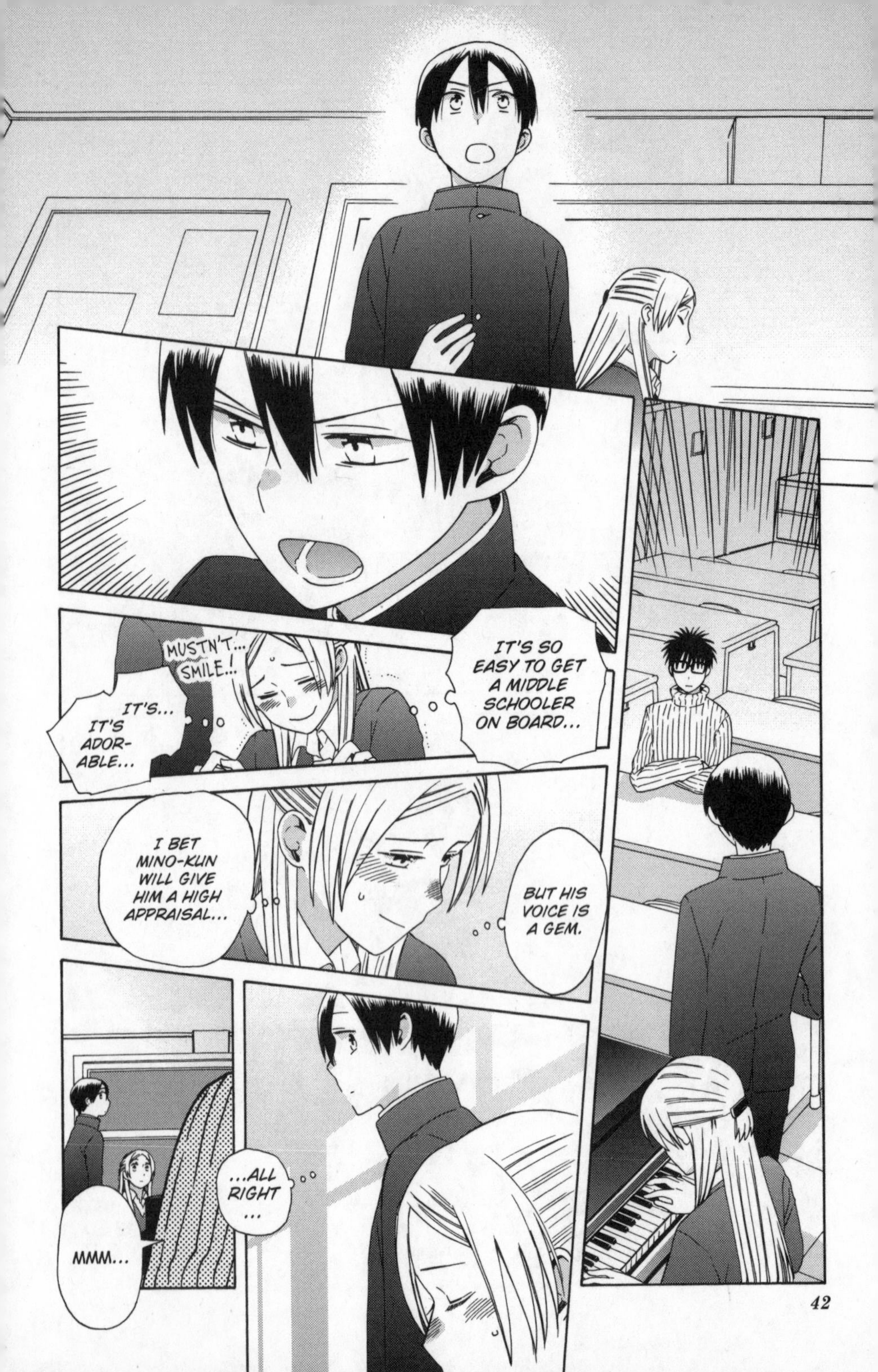
IT'S SO EASY TO GET A MIDDLE SCHOOLER ON BOARD...
MUSTN'T... SMILE...!
IT'S... IT'S ADORABLE...
BUT HIS VOICE IS A GEM.
I BET MINO-KUN WILL GIVE HIM A HIGH APPRAISAL...
...ALL RIGHT...
MMM...

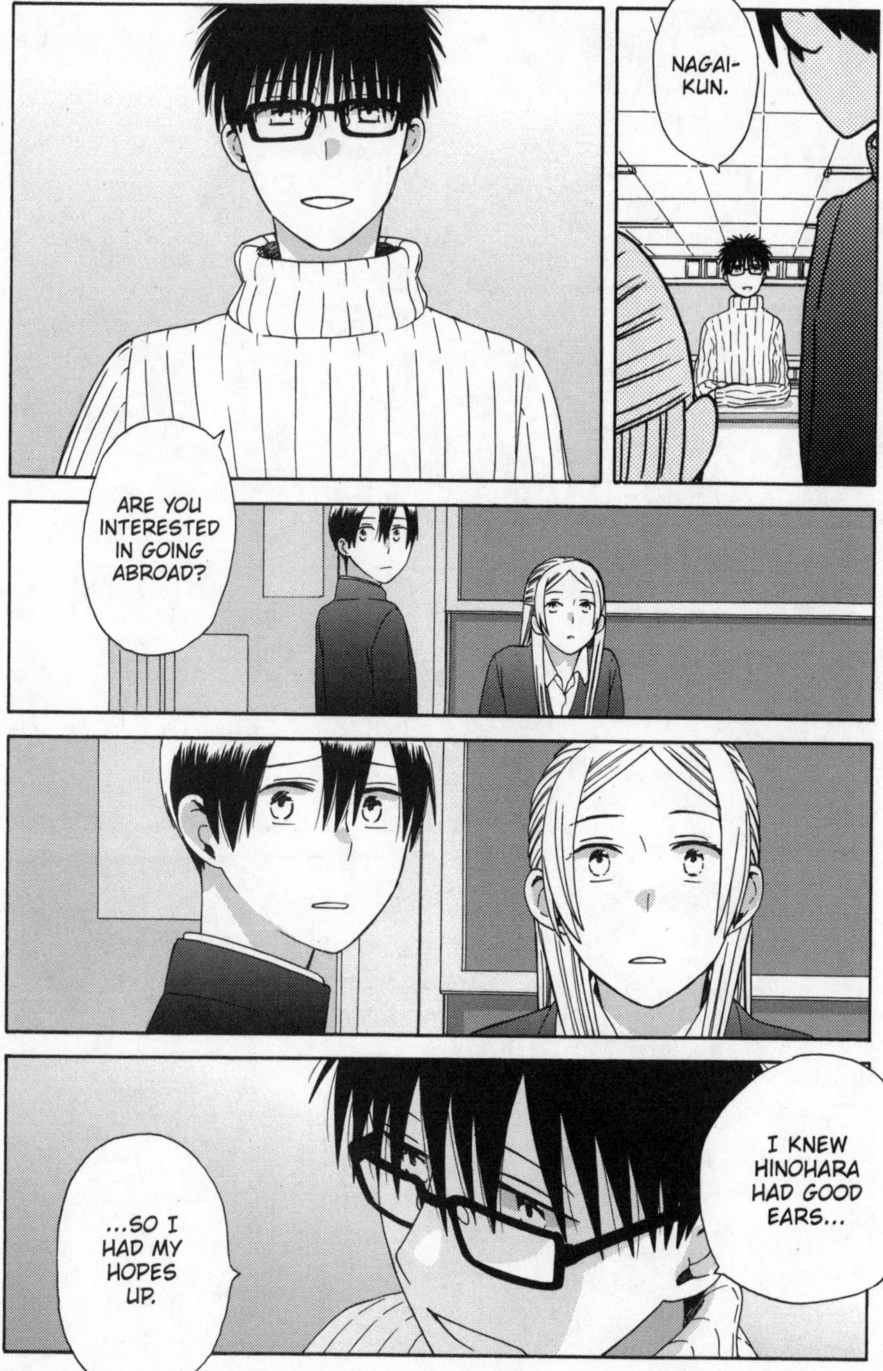
NAGAI-KUN.
ARE YOU INTERESTED IN GOING ABROAD?
I KNEW HINOHARA HAD GOOD EARS...
...SO I HAD MY HOPES UP.

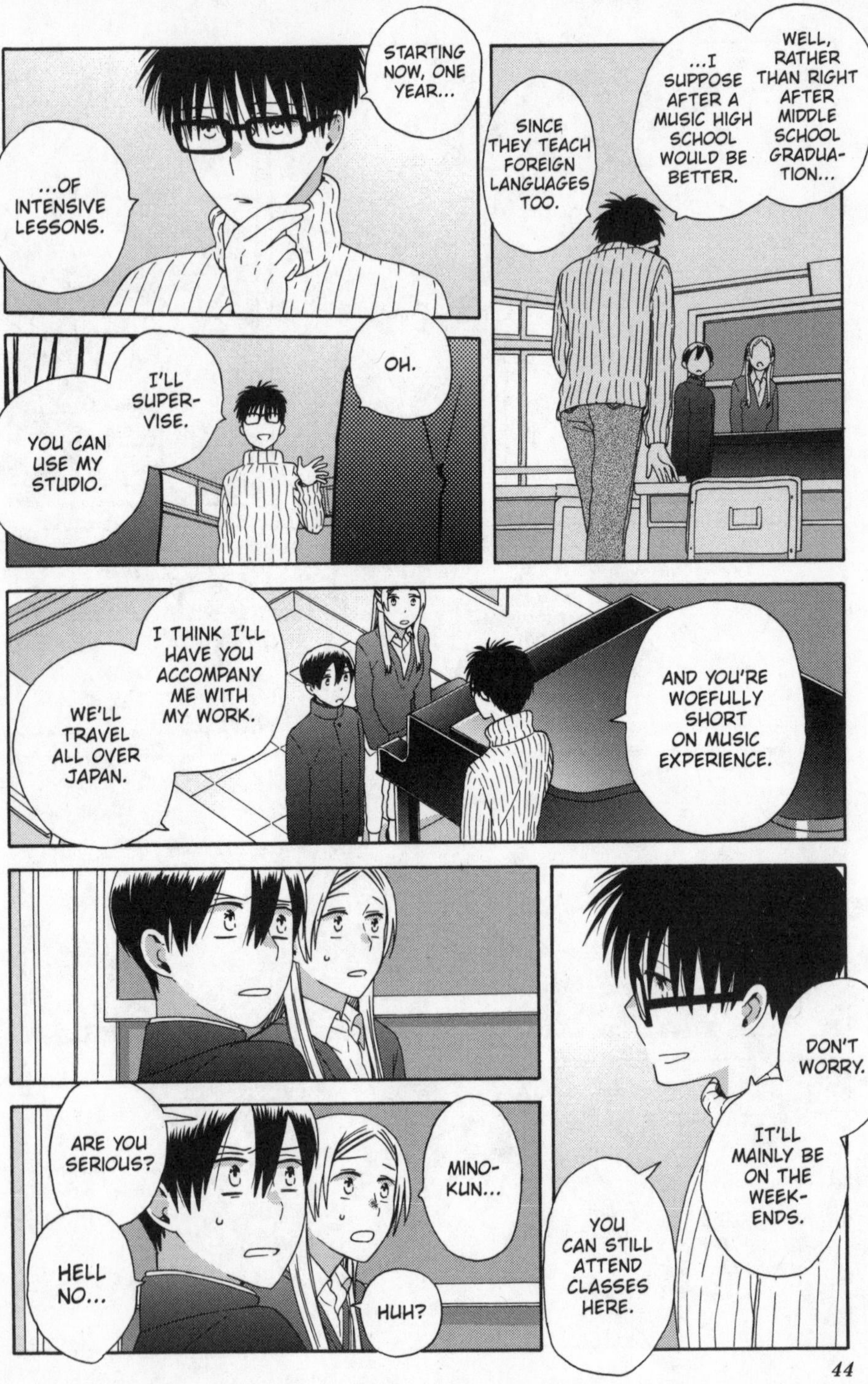
WELL, RATHER THAN RIGHT AFTER MIDDLE SCHOOL GRADUATION...
...I SUPPOSE AFTER A MUSIC HIGH SCHOOL WOULD BE BETTER.
SINCE THEY TEACH FOREIGN LANGUAGES TOO.
STARTING NOW, ONE YEAR...
...OF INTENSIVE LESSONS.
OH.
I'LL SUPERVISE.
YOU CAN USE MY STUDIO.
AND YOU'RE WOEFULLY SHORT ON MUSIC EXPERIENCE.
I THINK I'LL HAVE YOU ACCOMPANY ME WITH MY WORK.
WE'LL TRAVEL ALL OVER JAPAN.
DON'T WORRY.
IT'LL MAINLY BE ON THE WEEKENDS.
YOU CAN STILL ATTEND CLASSES HERE.
MINO-KUN...
ARE YOU SERIOUS?
HUH?
HELL NO...

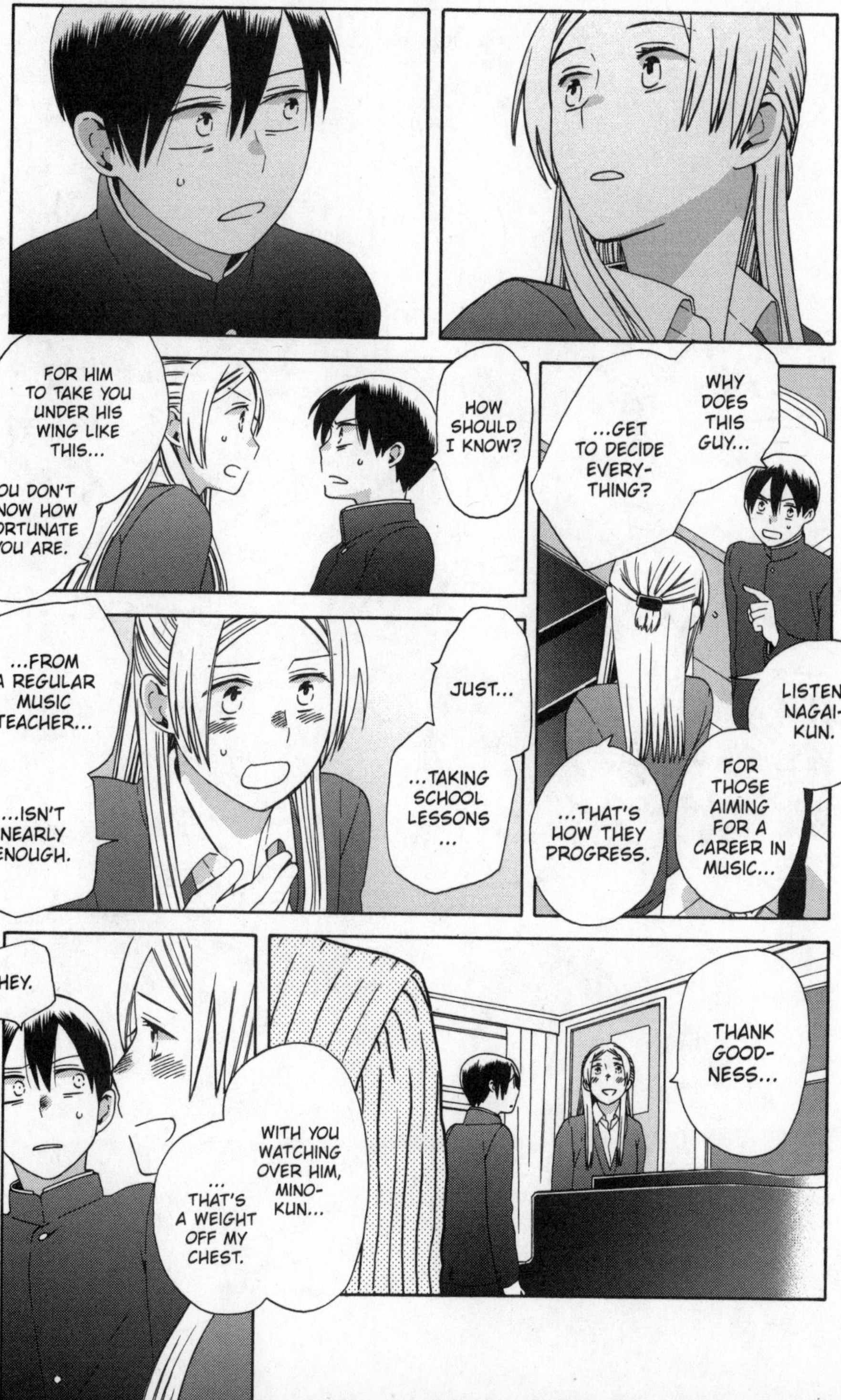
WHY DOES THIS GUY...
...GET TO DECIDE EVERYTHING?
LISTEN, NAGAI-KUN.
FOR THOSE AIMING FOR A CAREER IN MUSIC...
...THAT'S HOW THEY PROGRESS.
HOW SHOULD I KNOW?
FOR HIM TO TAKE YOU UNDER HIS WING LIKE THIS...
YOU DON'T KNOW HOW FORTUNATE YOU ARE.
JUST...
...TAKING SCHOOL LESSONS...
...FROM A REGULAR MUSIC TEACHER...
...ISN'T NEARLY ENOUGH.
THANK GOODNESS...
WITH YOU WATCHING OVER HIM, MINO-KUN...
...THAT'S A WEIGHT OFF MY CHEST.
HEY.

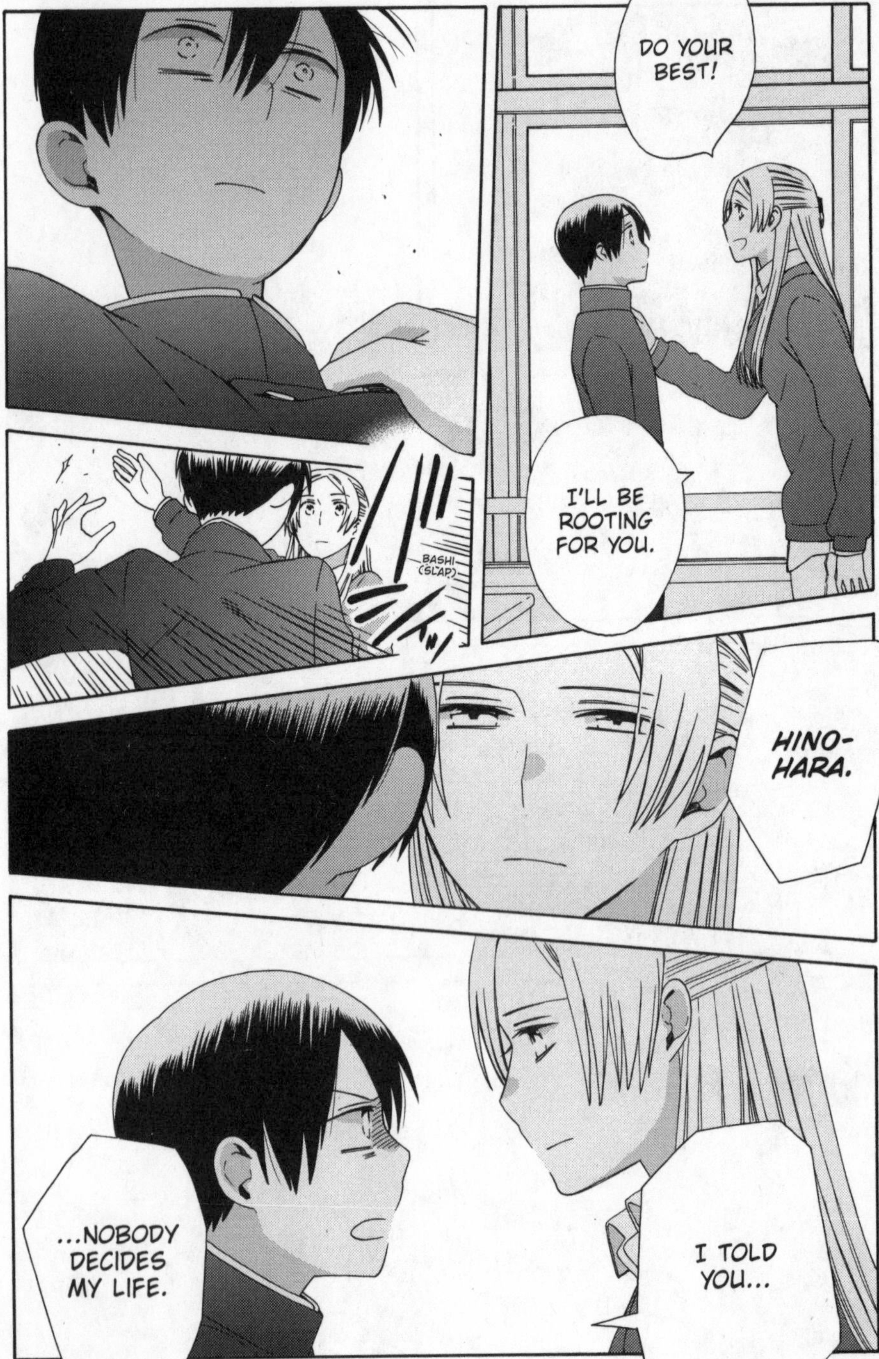
DO YOUR BEST!
I'LL BE ROOTING FOR YOU.
BASHI (SLAP)
HINO-HARA.
I TOLD YOU...
...NOBODY DECIDES MY LIFE.

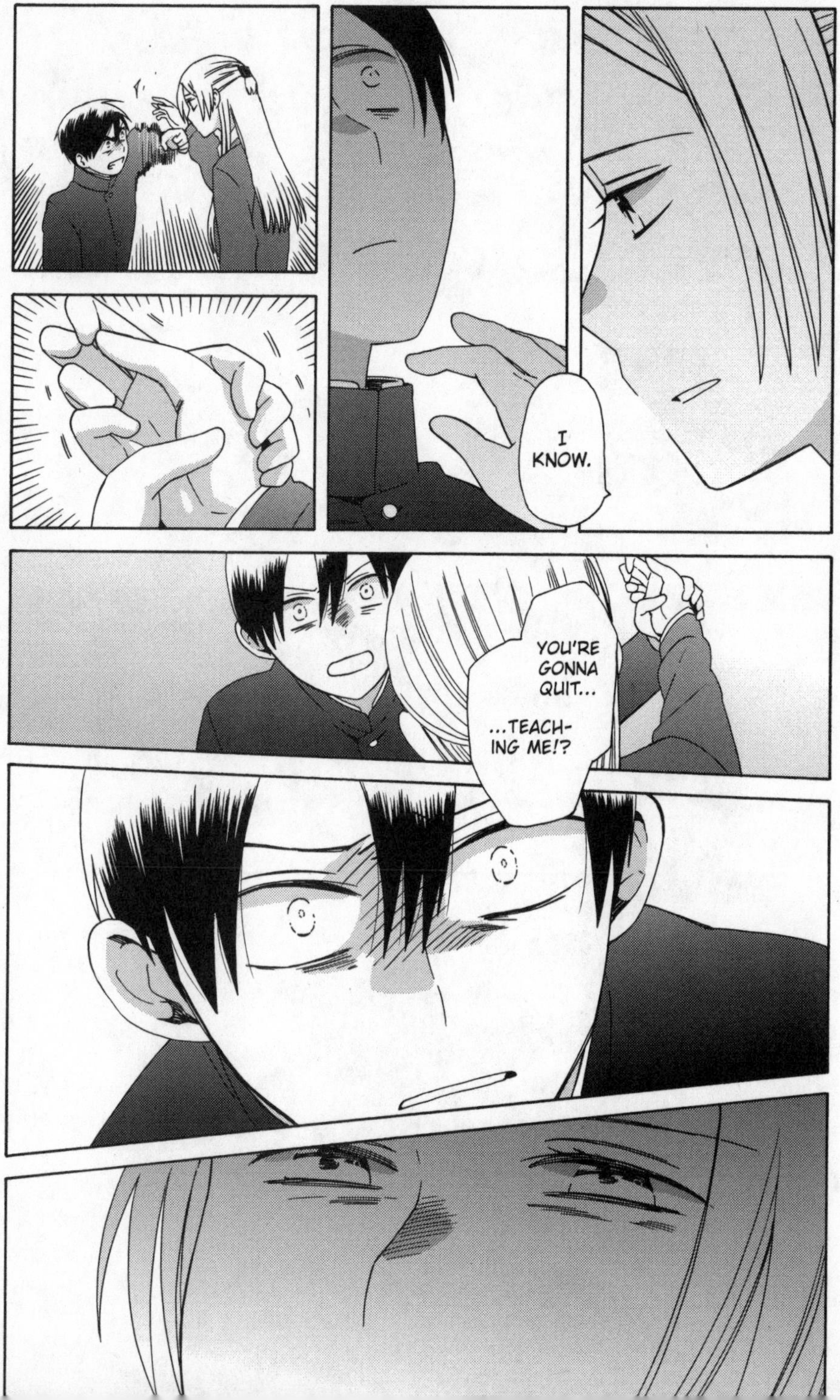
I KNOW.
YOU'RE GONNA QUIT... ...TEACHING ME!?

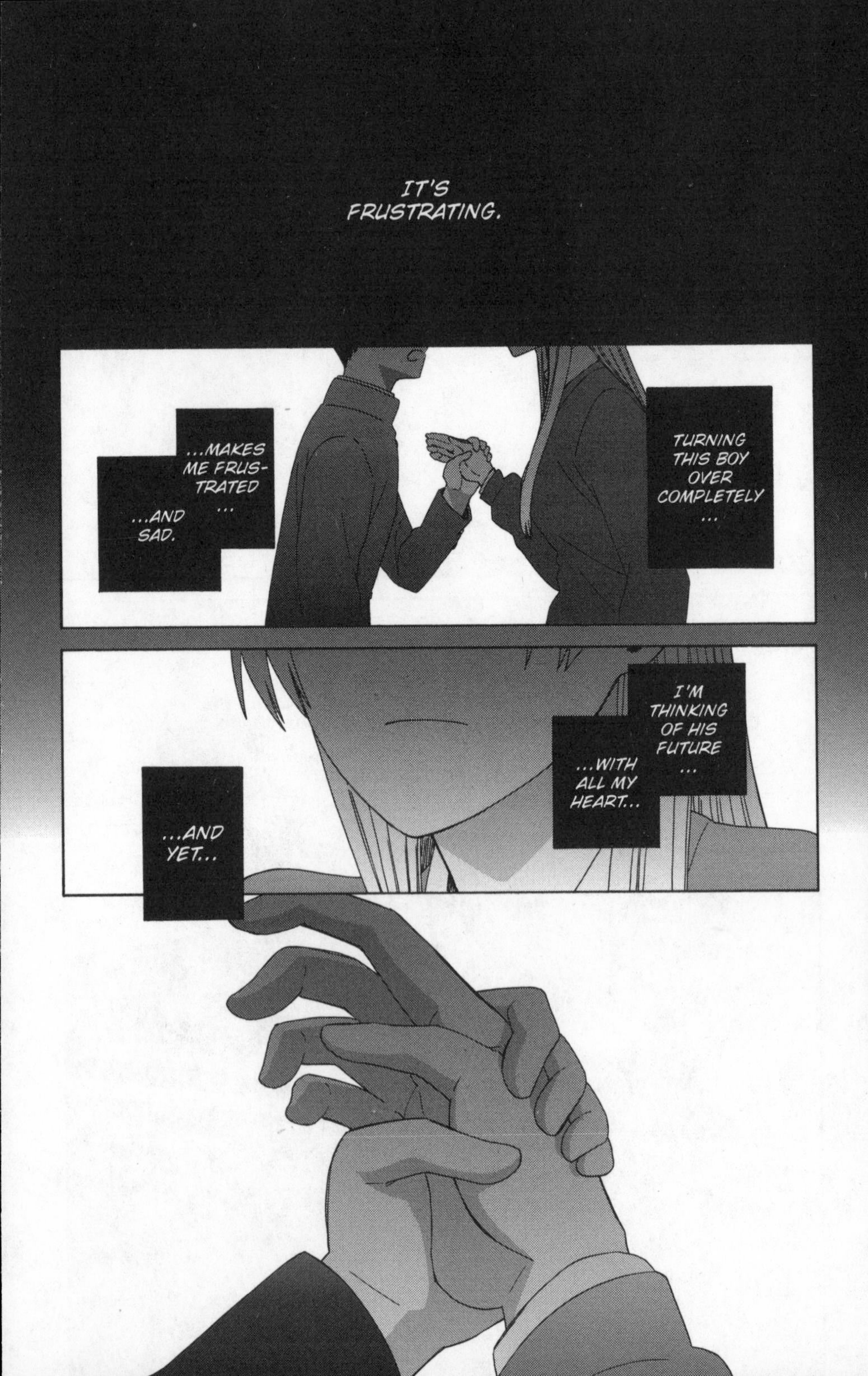
IT'S FRUSTRATING.
TURNING THIS BOY OVER COMPLETELY...
...MAKES ME FRUS-TRATED...
...AND SAD.
I'M THINKING OF HIS FUTURE...
...WITH ALL MY HEART...
...AND YET...

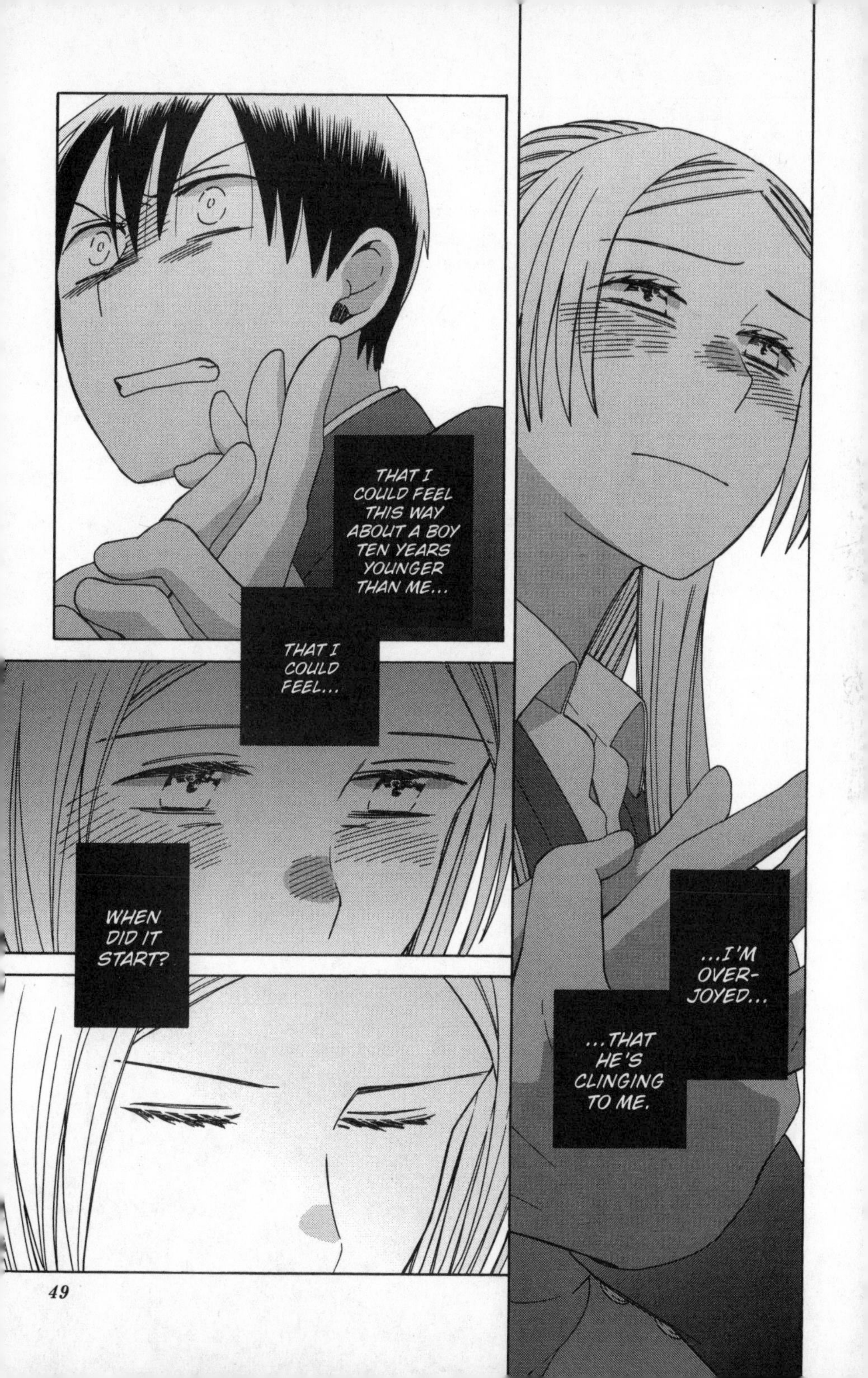
...I'M OVER-JOYED...
...THAT HE'S CLINGING TO ME.
THAT I COULD FEEL THIS WAY ABOUT A BOY TEN YEARS YOUNGER THAN ME...
THAT I COULD FEEL...
WHEN DID IT START?

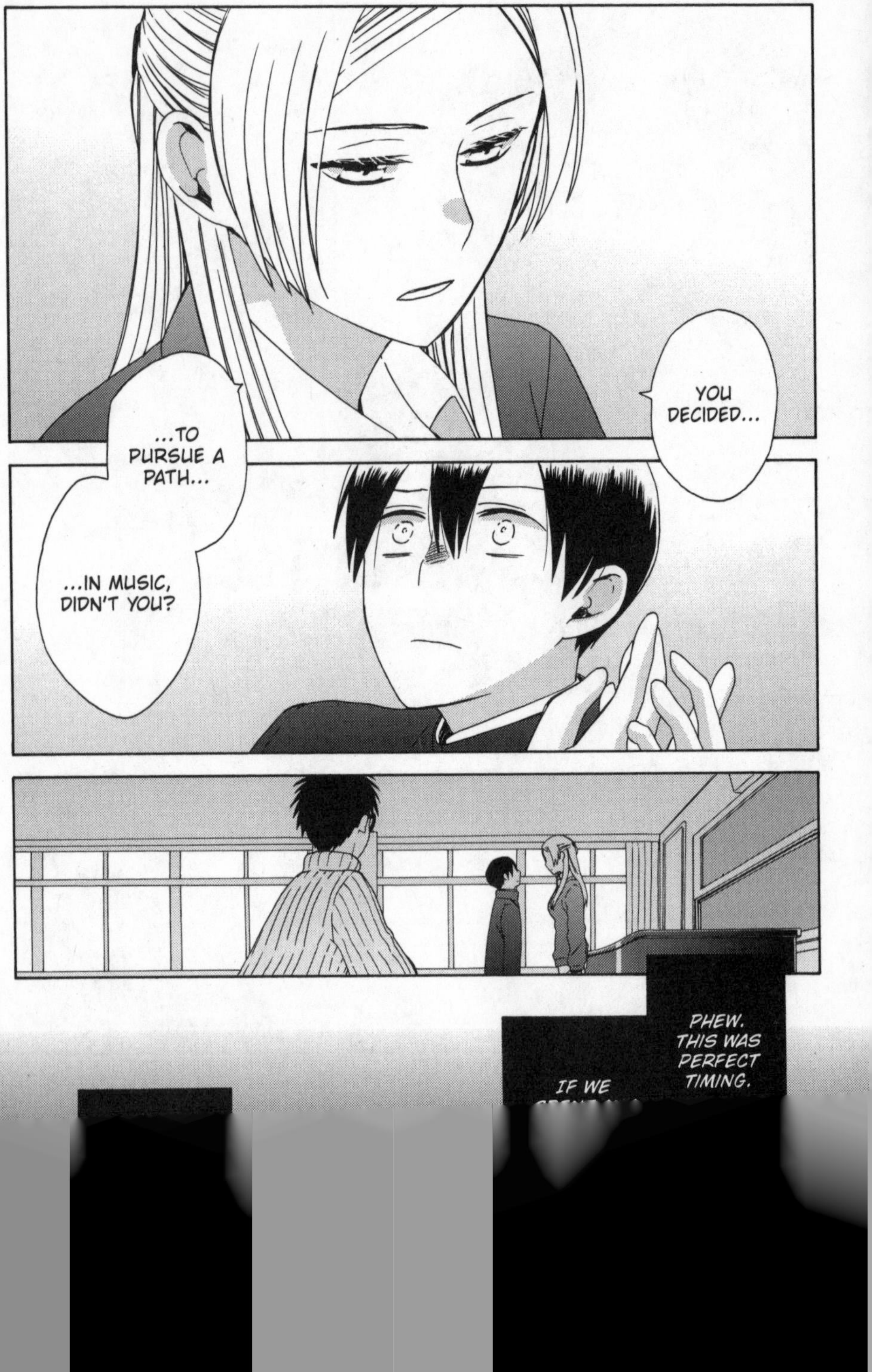
YOU DECIDED...
...TO PURSUE A PATH...
...IN MUSIC, DIDN'T YOU?
PHEW. THIS WAS PERFECT TIMING.
IF WE

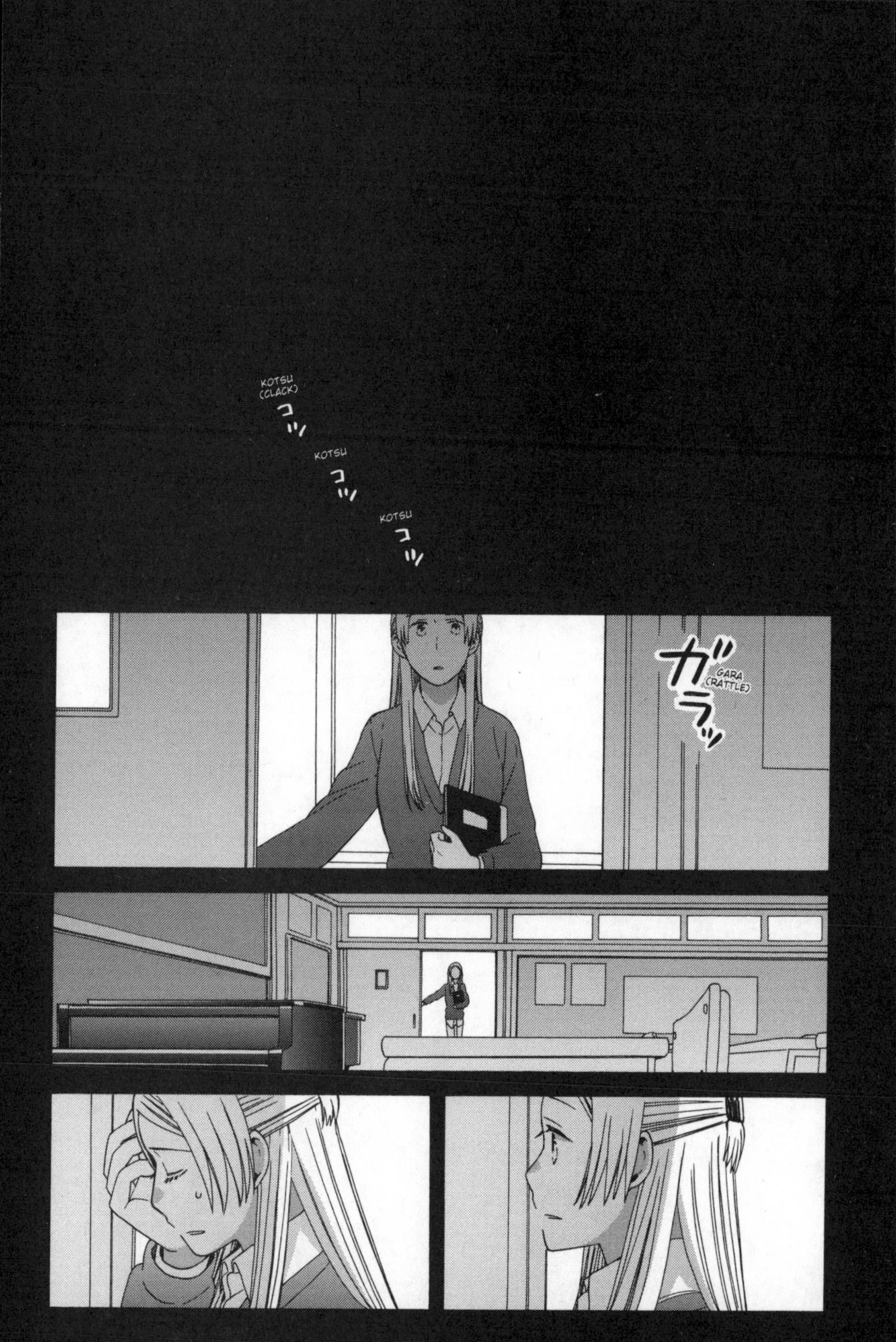
KOTSU (CLACK)
コツ
KOTSU
コツ
KOTSU
コツ
ガラッ
GARA (RATTLE)

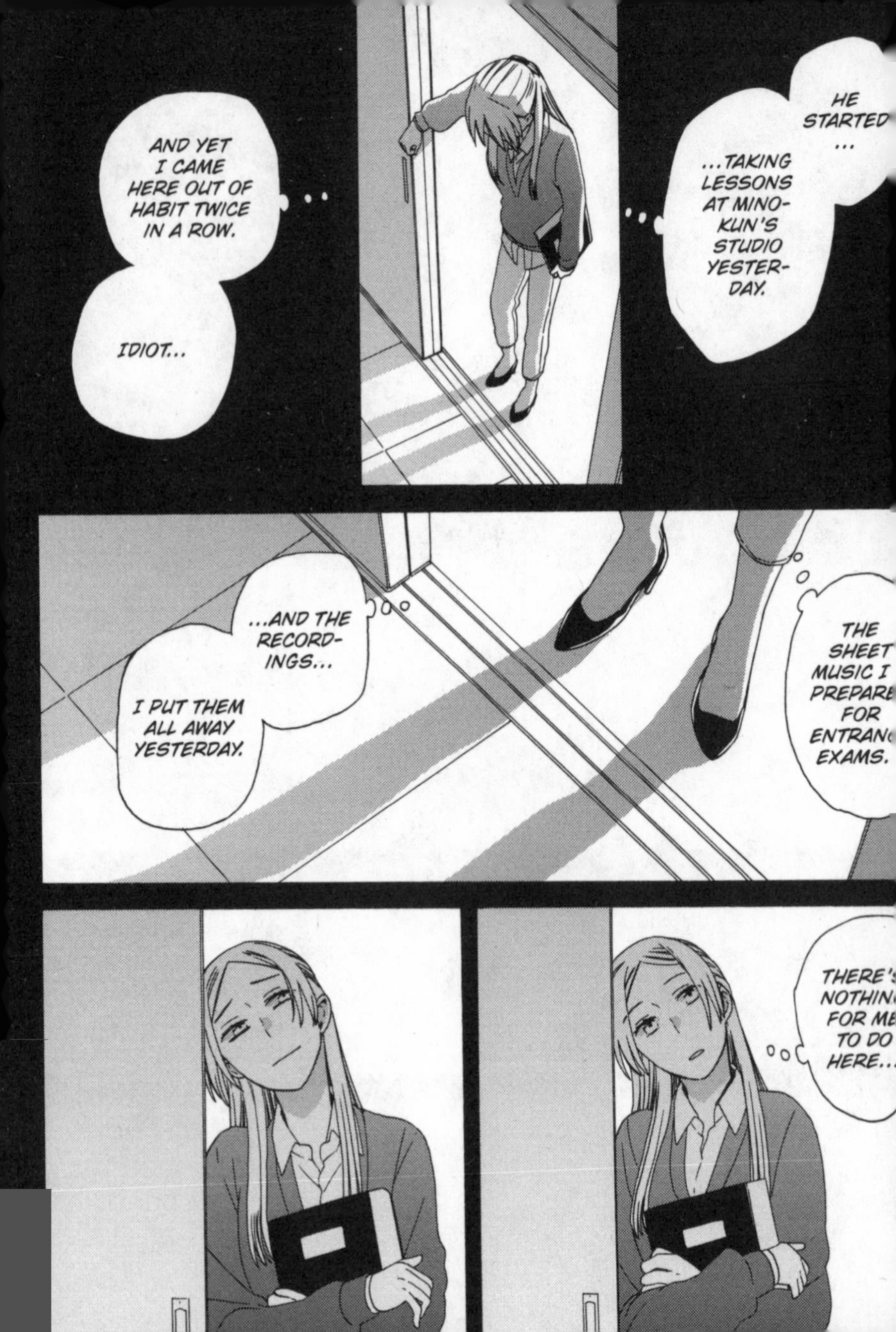
HE STARTED ...
...TAKING LESSONS AT MINO-KUN'S STUDIO YESTER-DAY.
AND YET I CAME HERE OUT OF HABIT TWICE IN A ROW.
IDIOT...
THE SHEET MUSIC I PREPARE FOR ENTRANC EXAMS.
...AND THE RECORD-INGS...
I PUT THEM ALL AWAY YESTERDAY.
THERE'S NOTHIN FOR ME TO DO HERE...

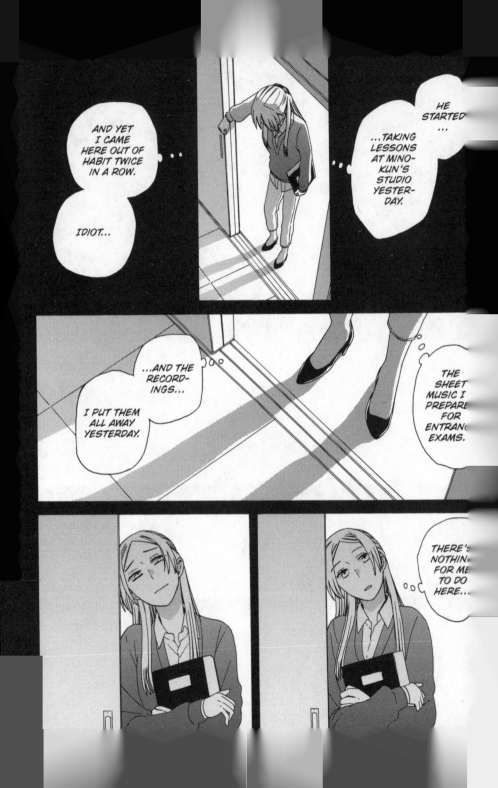

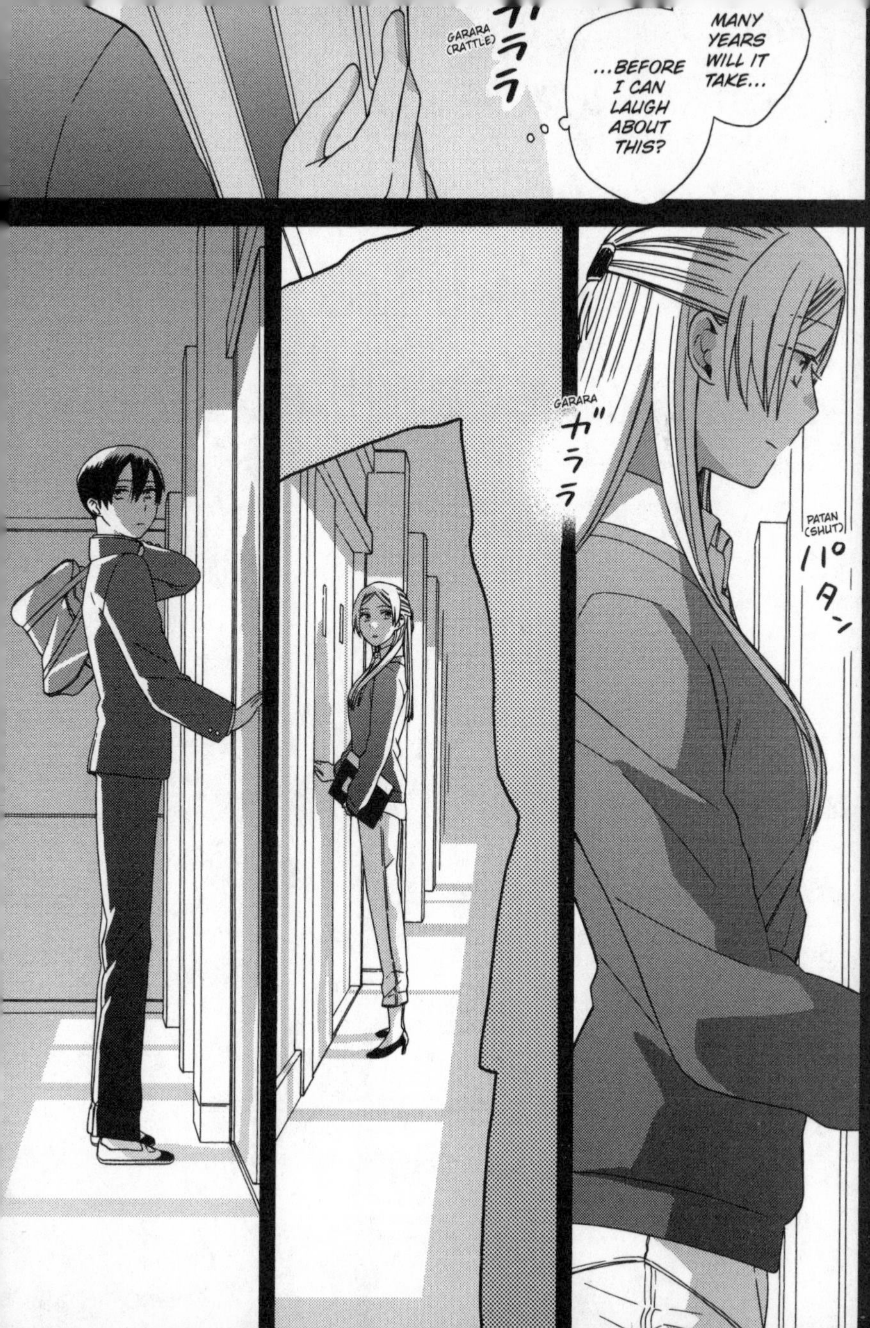
MANY YEARS WILL IT TAKE...
...BEFORE I CAN LAUGH ABOUT THIS?
GARARA (RATTLE)
ガララ
GARARA
ガララ
PATAN (SHUT)
パタン

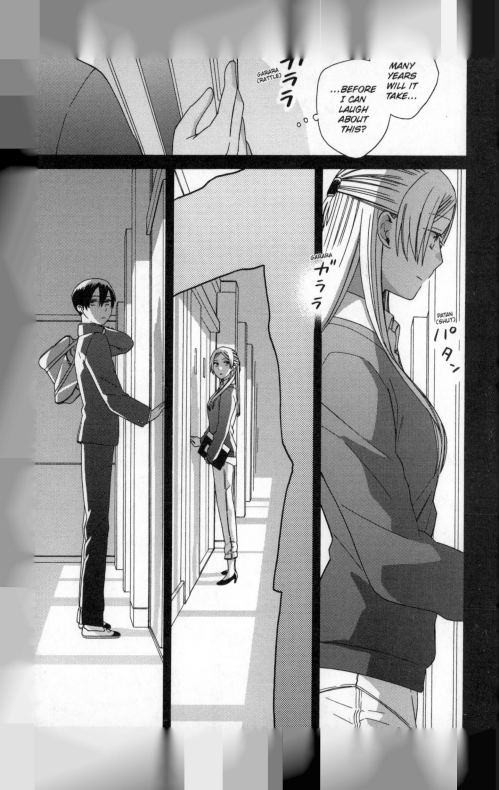

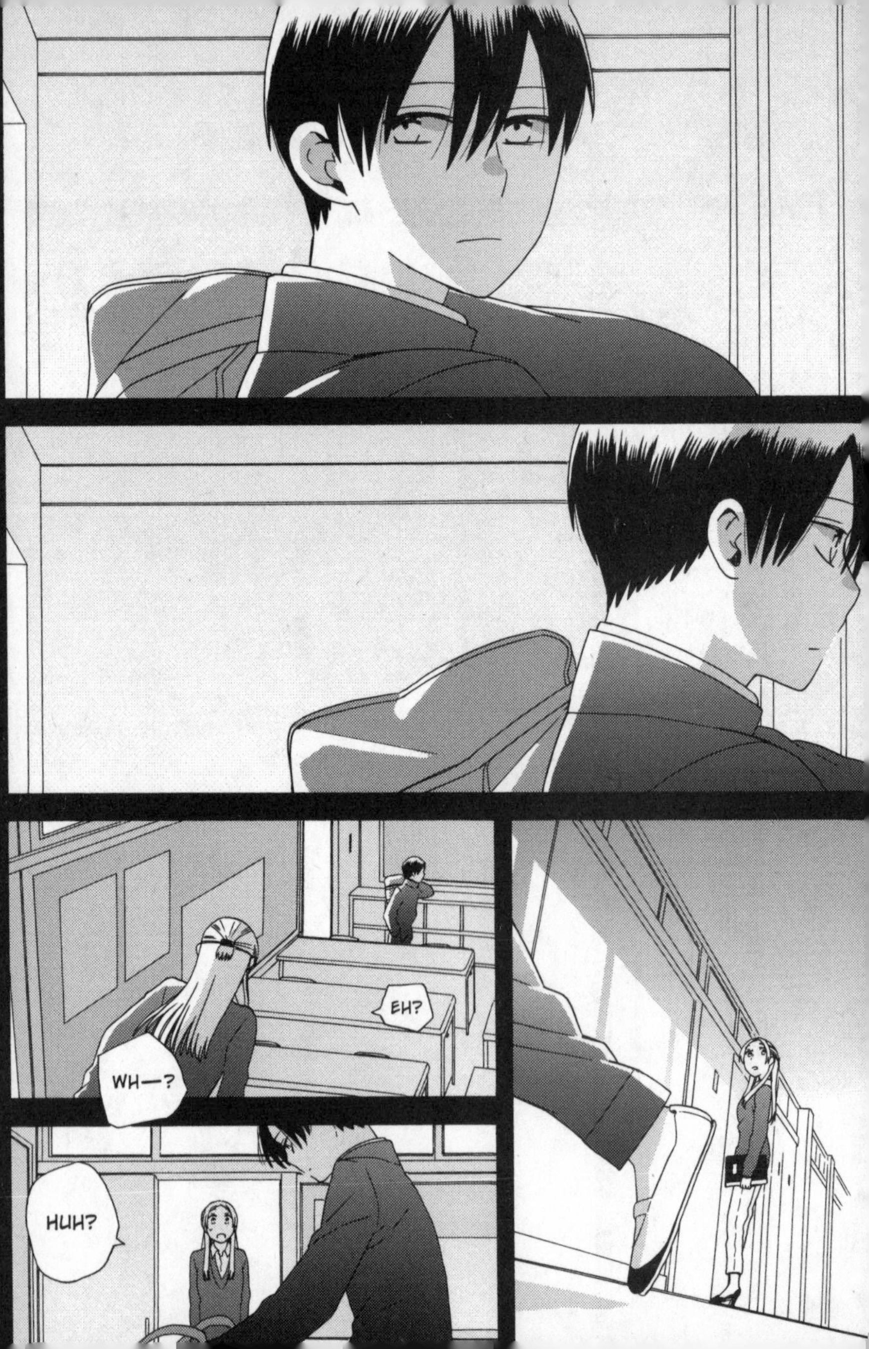
EH?
WH—?
HUH?

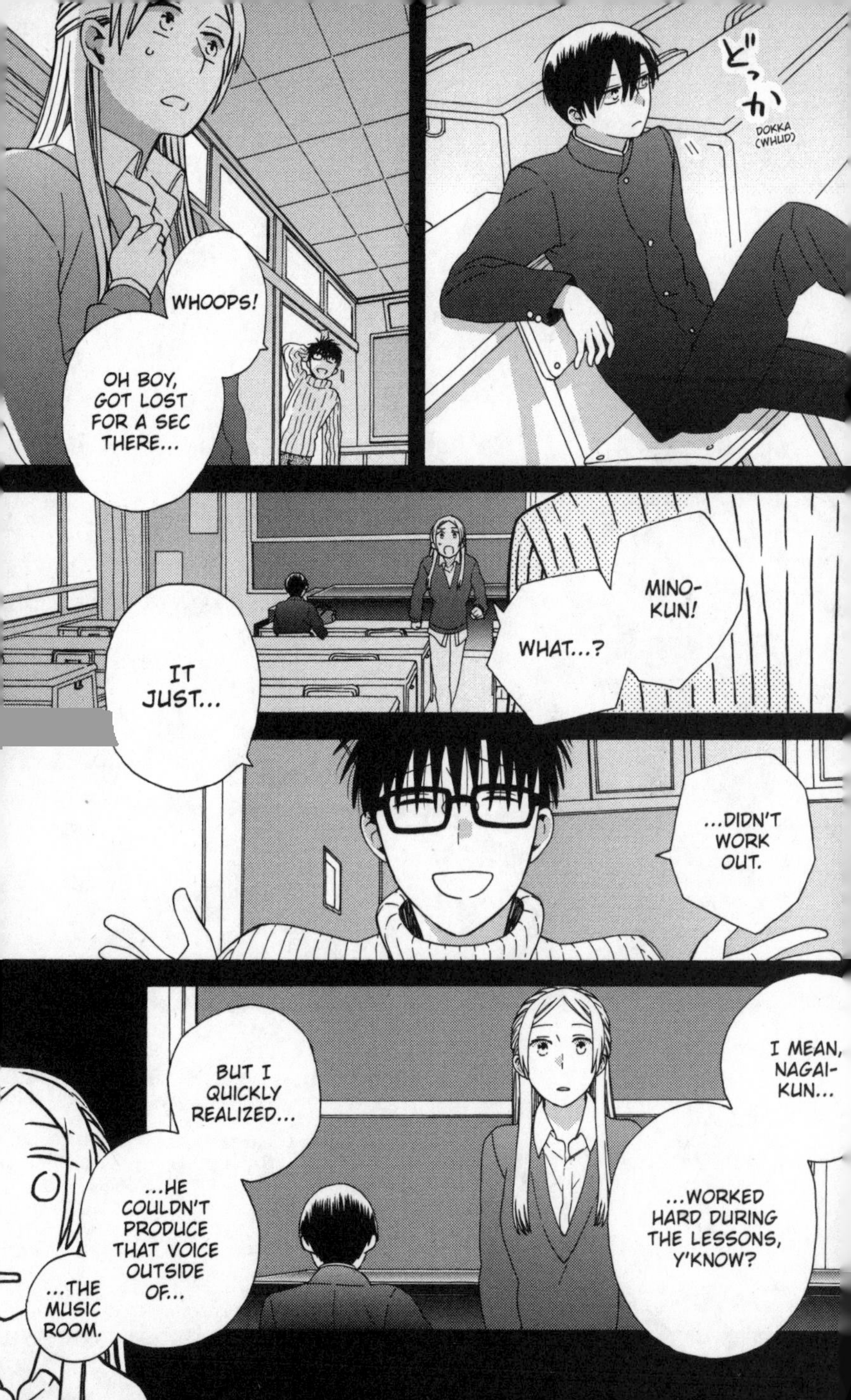

どっか
DOKKA (WHUD)
WHOOPS!
OH BOY, GOT LOST FOR A SEC THERE...
MINO-KUN!
WHAT...?
IT JUST...
...DIDN'T WORK OUT.
I MEAN, NAGAI-KUN...
...WORKED HARD DURING THE LESSONS, Y'KNOW?
BUT I QUICKLY REALIZED...
...HE COULDN'T PRODUCE THAT VOICE OUTSIDE OF...
...THE MUSIC ROOM.

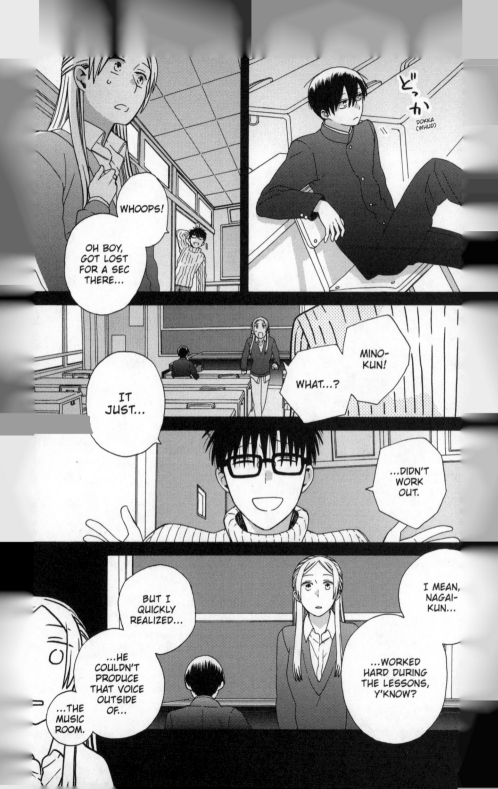

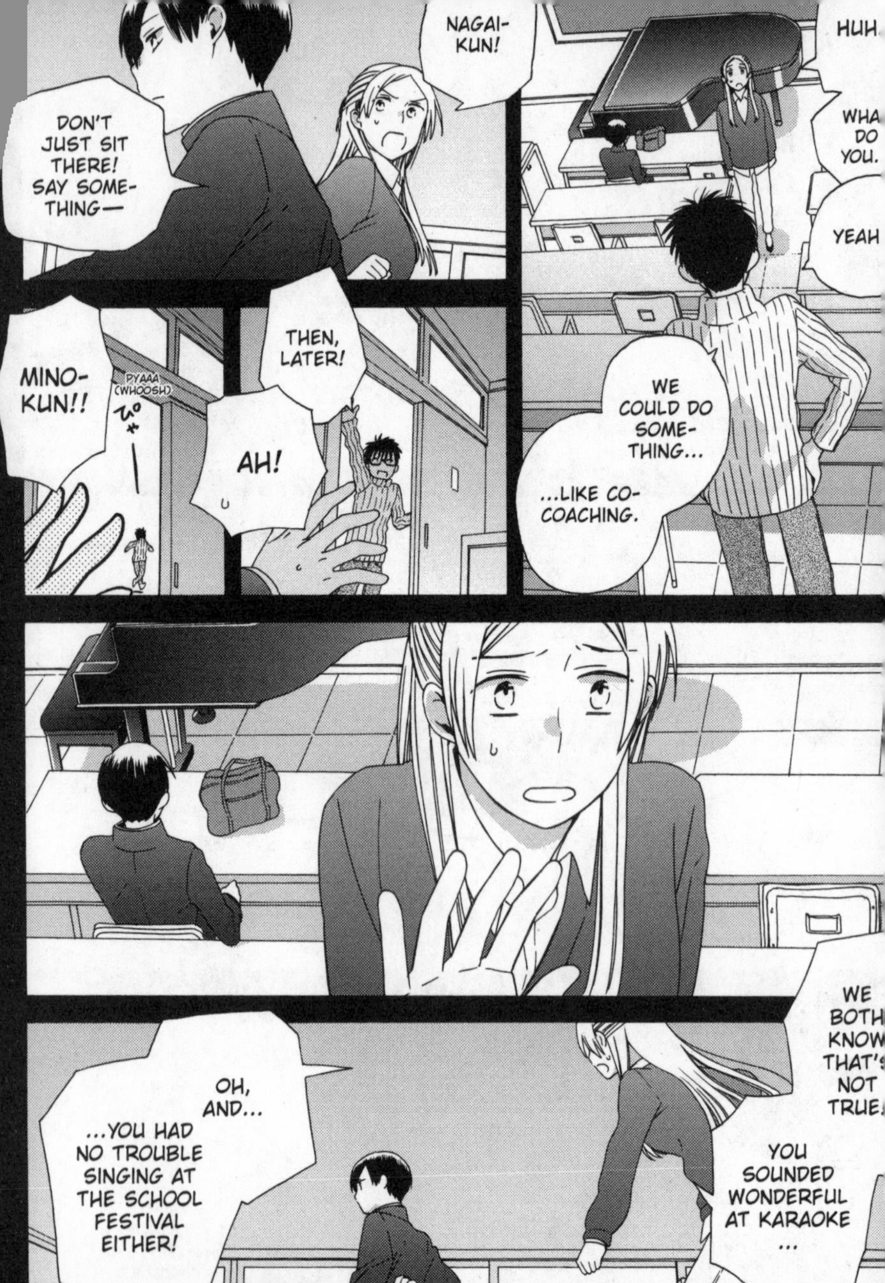
HUH
WHA DO YOU.
YEAH
WE COULD DO SOMETHING...
...LIKE CO-COACHING.
NAGAI-KUN!
DON'T JUST SIT THERE! SAY SOMETHING—
THEN, LATER!
AH!
MINO-KUN!!
PYAAA (WHOOSH)
WE BOTH KNOW THAT'S NOT TRUE.
YOU SOUNDED WONDERFUL AT KARAOKE ...
OH, AND...
...YOU HAD NO TROUBLE SINGING AT THE SCHOOL FESTIVAL EITHER!

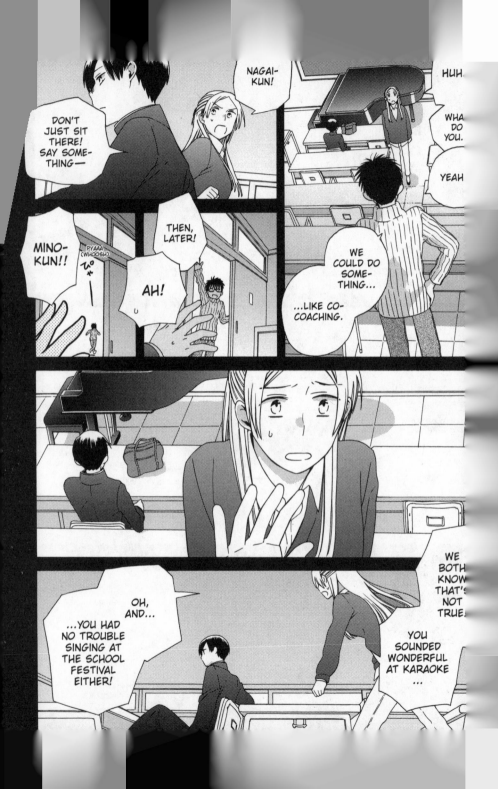

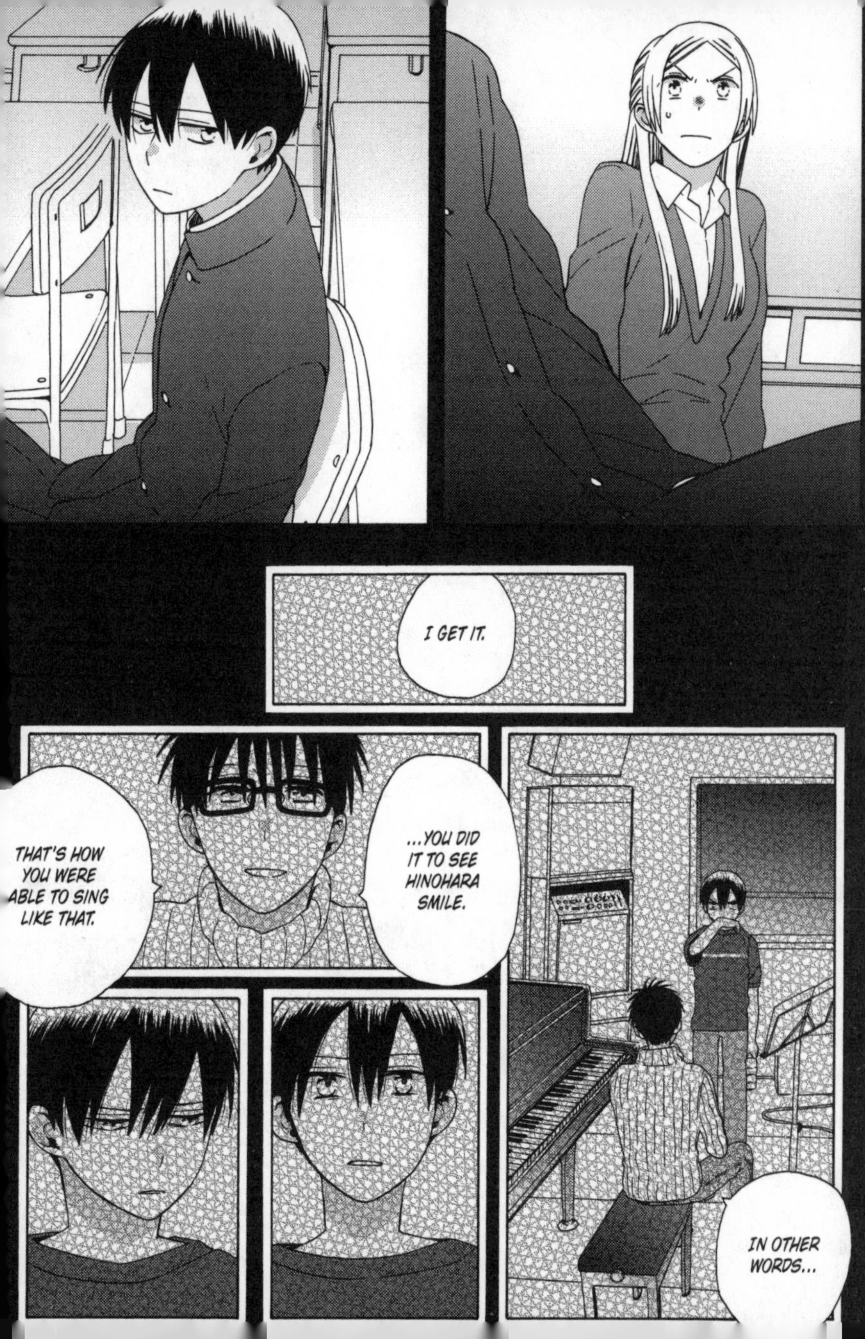
I GET IT.
IN OTHER WORDS...
...YOU DID IT TO SEE HINOHARA SMILE.
THAT'S HOW YOU WERE ABLE TO SING LIKE THAT.

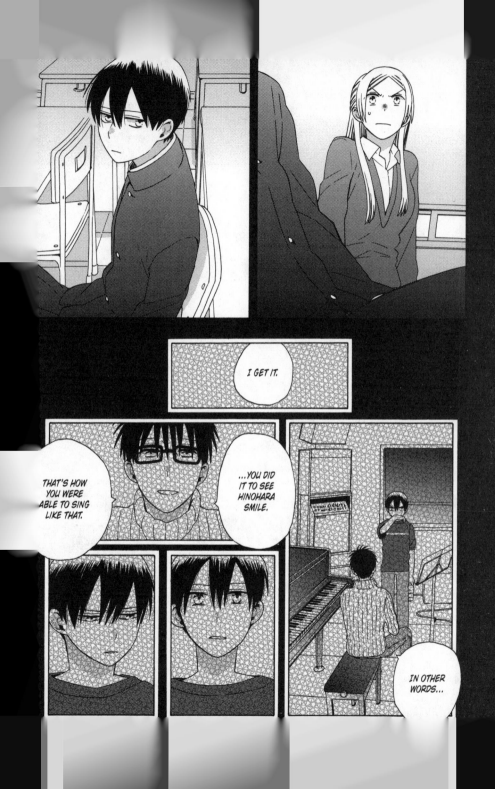

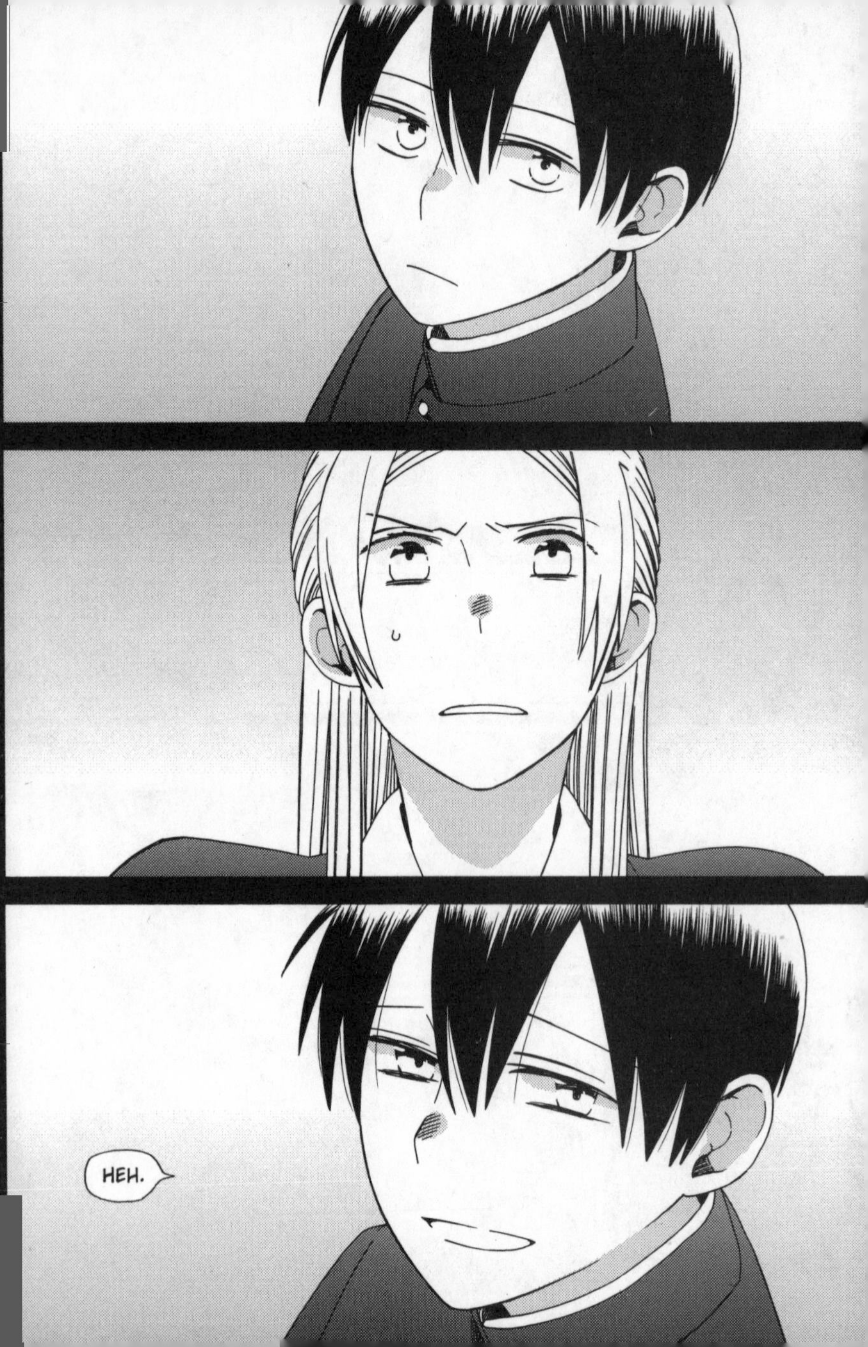
HEH.

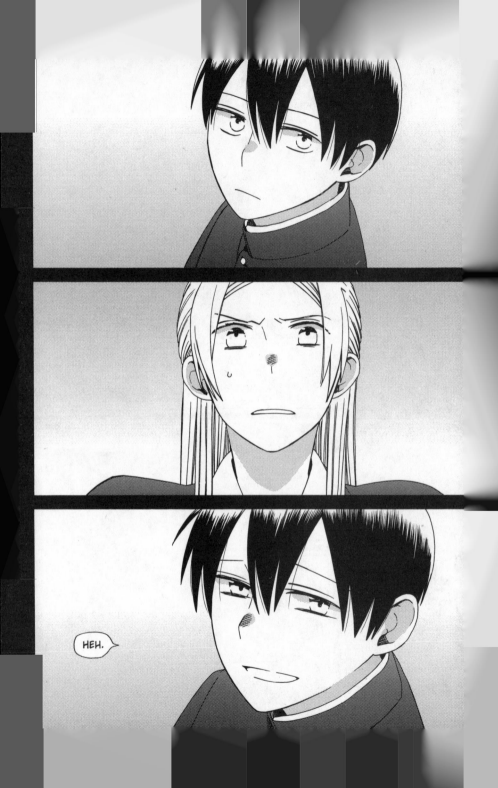

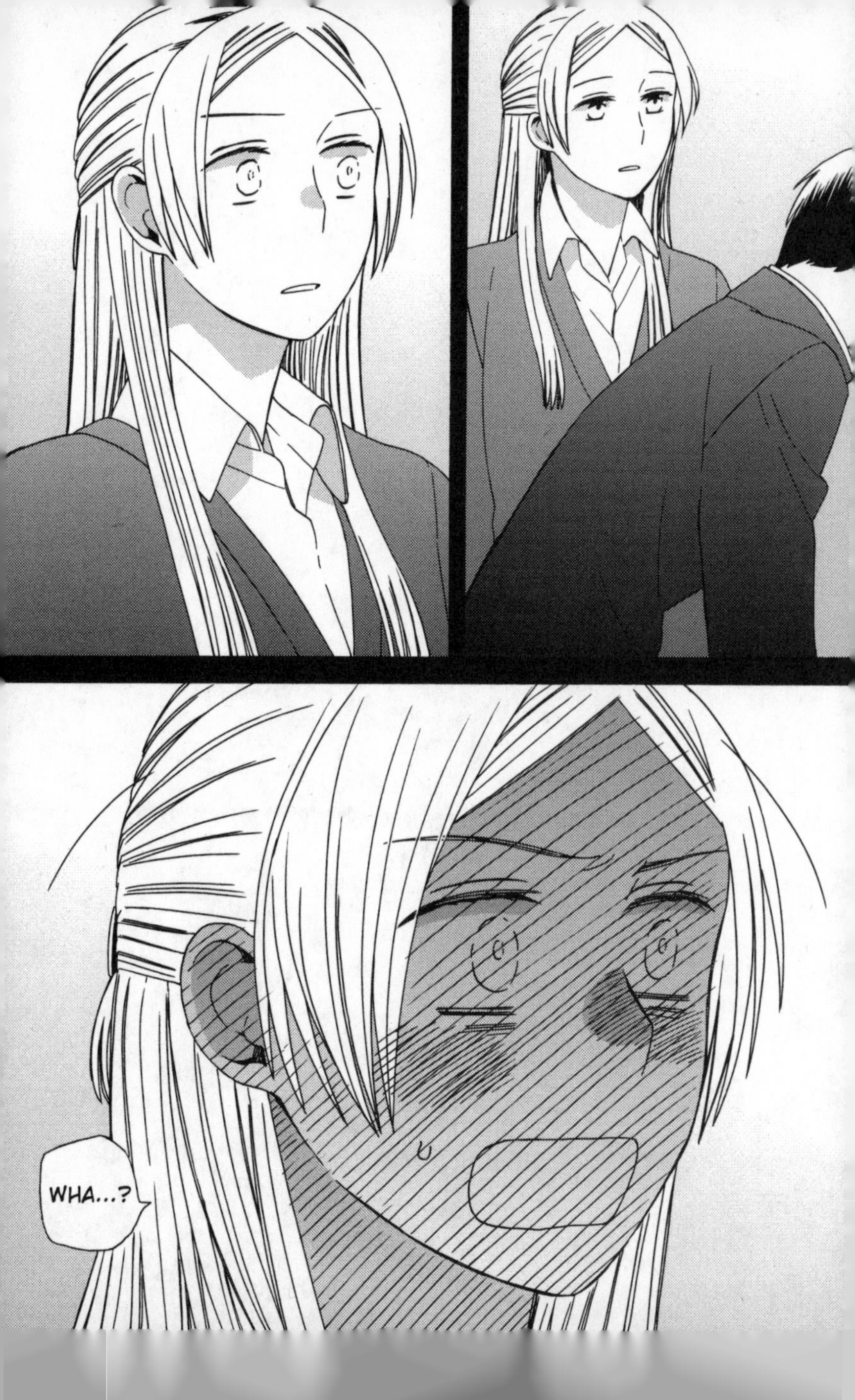
WHA...?

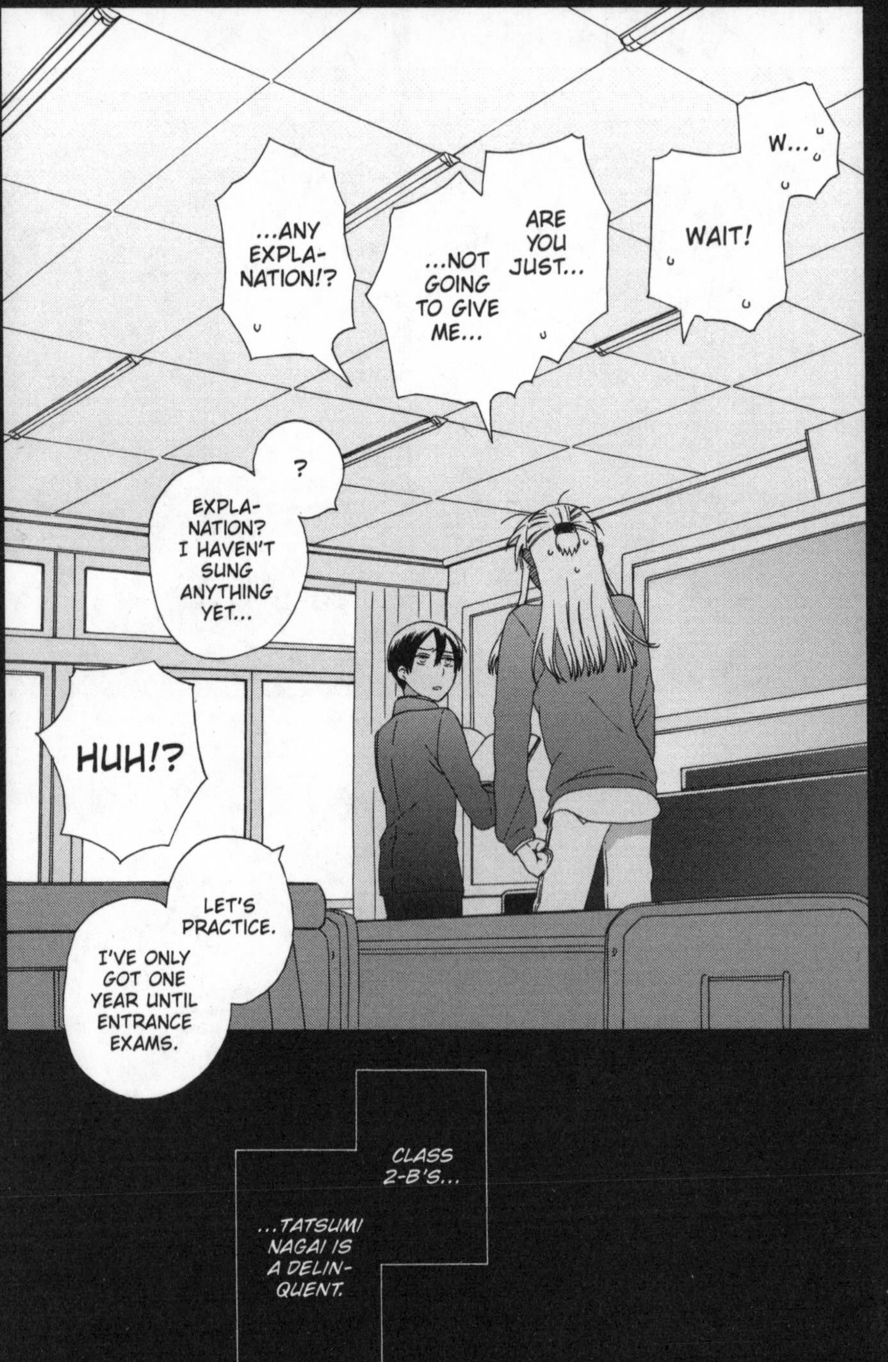
W... WAIT!
ARE YOU JUST... ...NOT GOING TO GIVE ME...
...ANY EXPLANATION!?
?
EXPLANATION? I HAVEN'T SUNG ANYTHING YET...
HUH!?
LET'S PRACTICE.
I'VE ONLY GOT ONE YEAR UNTIL ENTRANCE EXAMS.
CLASS 2-B'S...
...TATSUMI NAGAI IS A DELINQUENT.

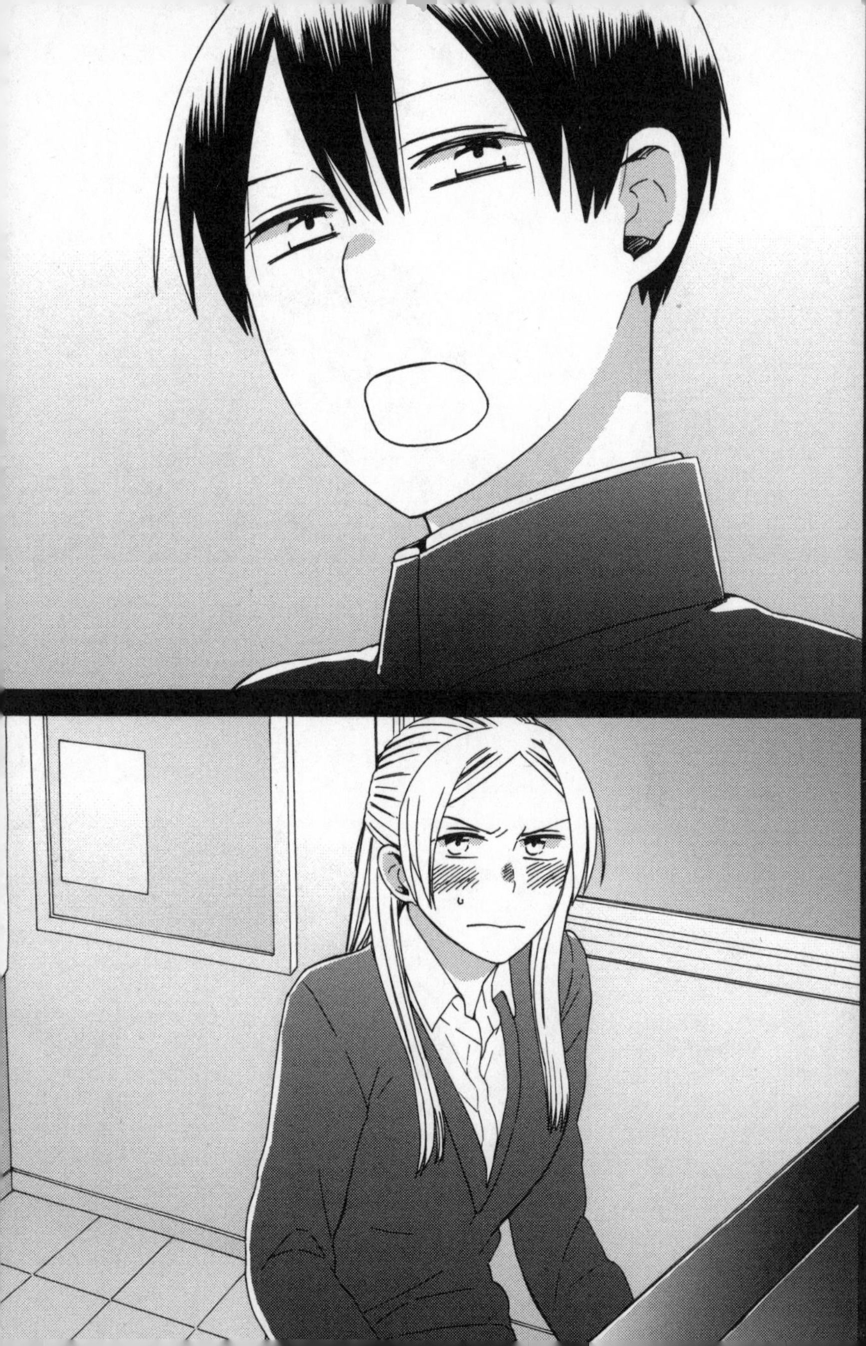

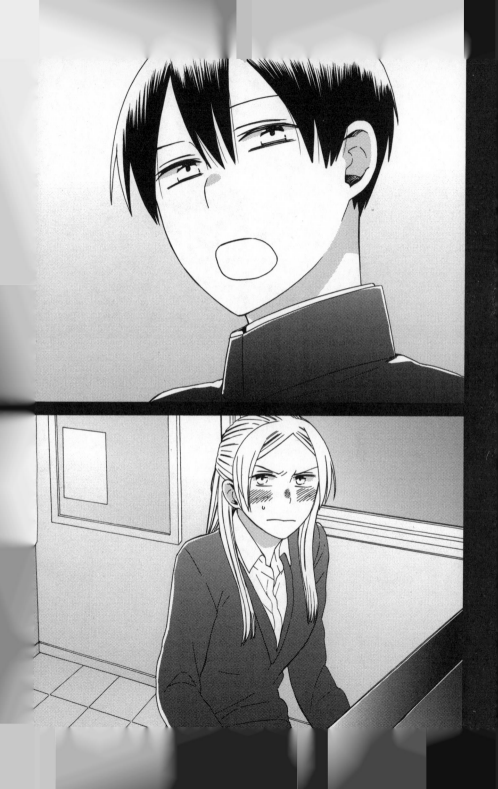

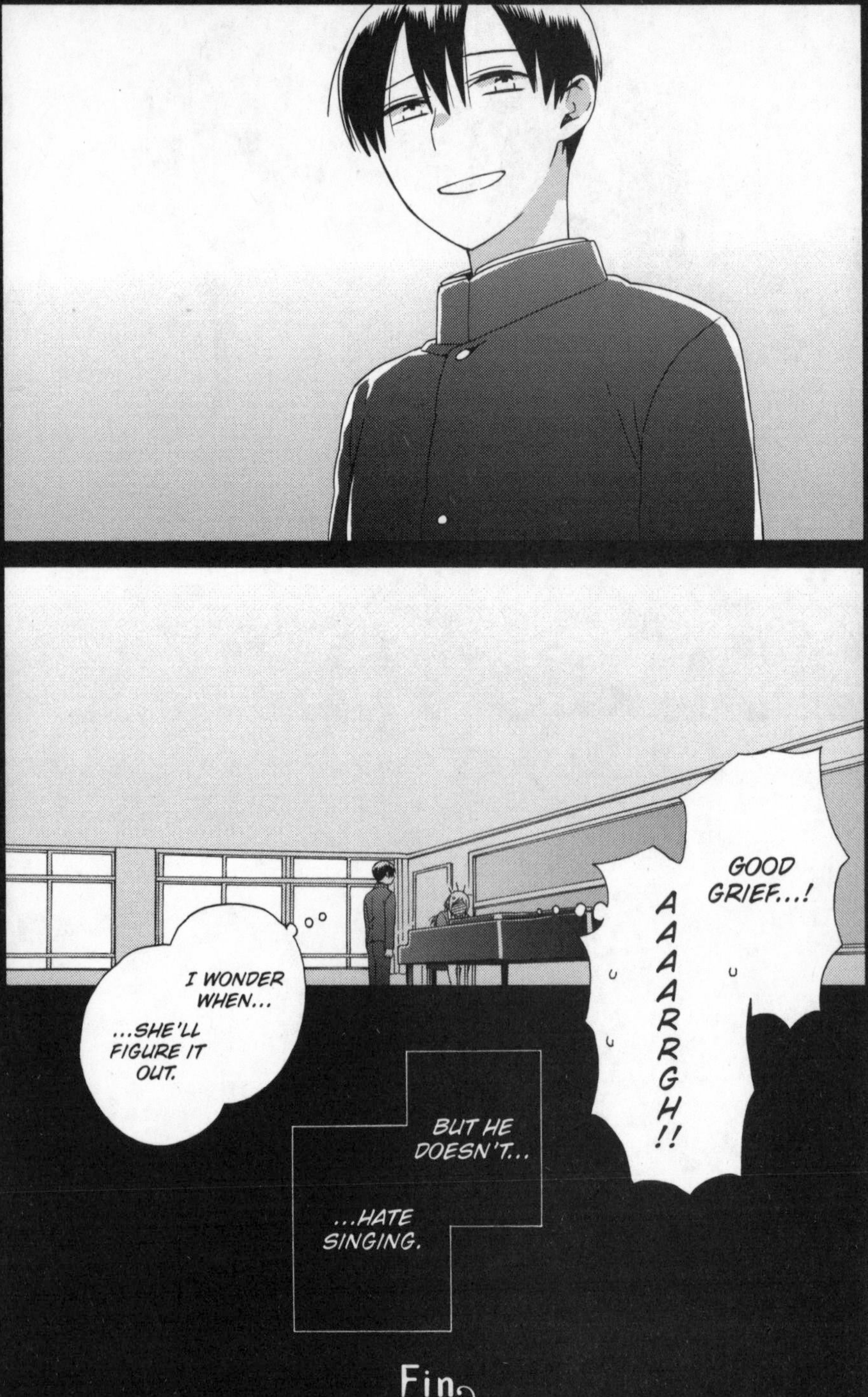
GOOD GRIEF...!
AAAAARRGH!!
I WONDER WHEN...
...SHE'LL FIGURE IT OUT.
BUT HE DOESN'T...
...HATE SINGING.
Fin

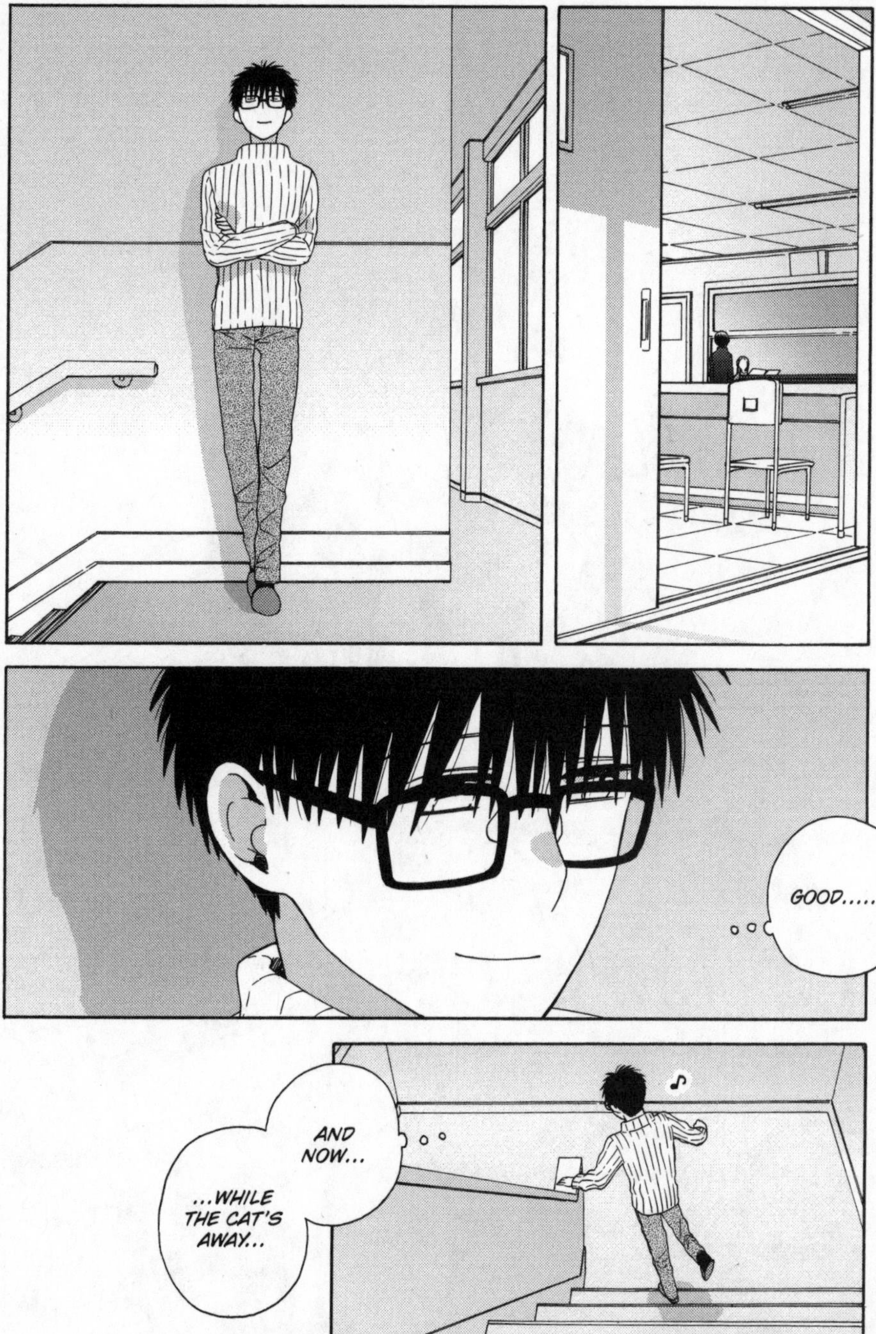
GOOD......
AND NOW...
...WHILE THE CAT'S AWAY...

Love at Fourteen

[Intermission 75]

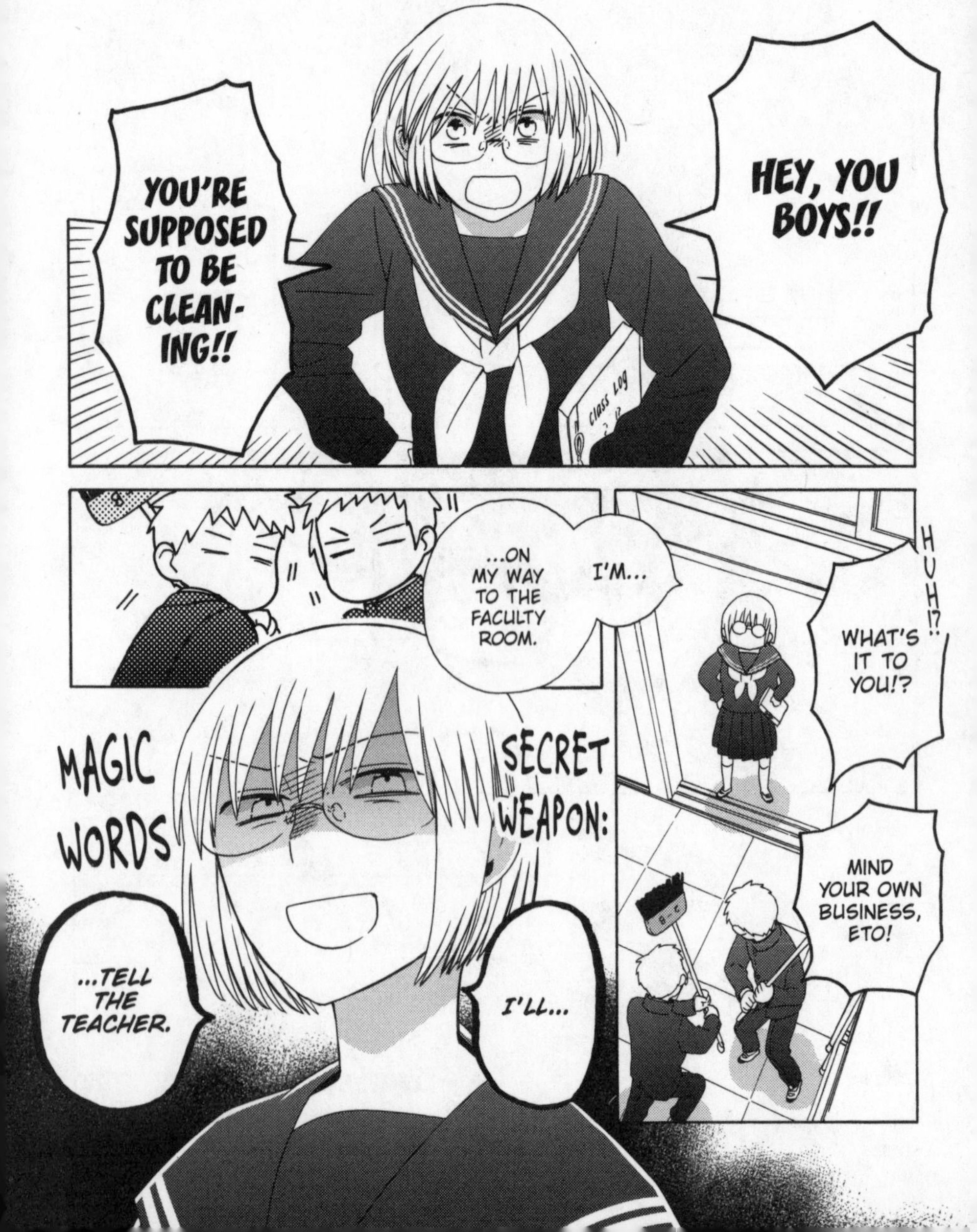
HEY, YOU BOYS!!
YOU'RE SUPPOSED TO BE CLEAN-ING!!
CLASS LOG
HUH!?
WHAT'S IT TO YOU!?
MIND YOUR OWN BUSINESS, ETO!
I'M...
...ON MY WAY TO THE FACULTY ROOM.
SECRET WEAPON:
MAGIC WORDS
I'LL...
...TELL THE TEACHER.

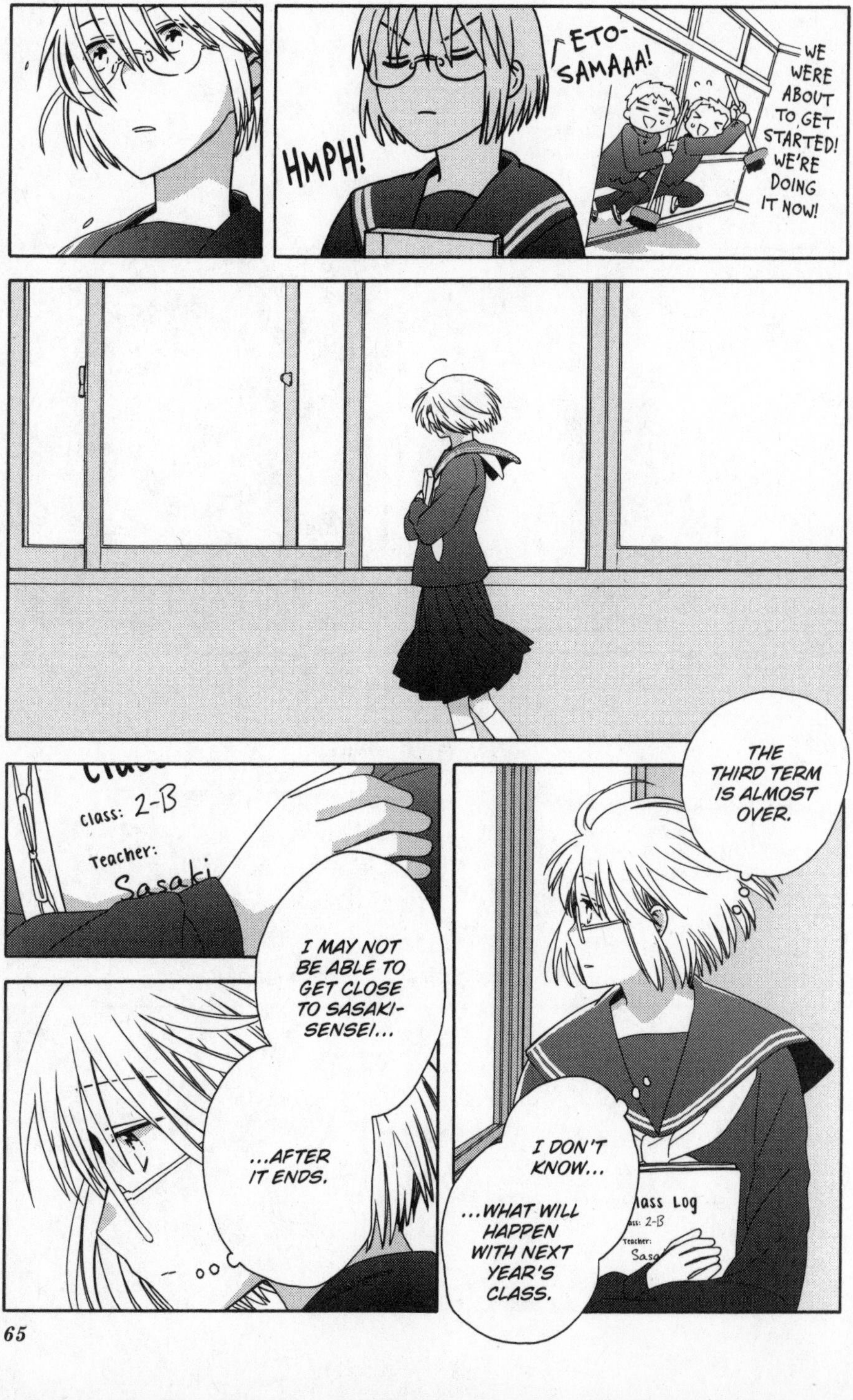
ETO-SAMAAA!
WE WERE ABOUT TO GET STARTED! WE'RE DOING IT NOW!
HMPH!
THE THIRD TERM IS ALMOST OVER.
I DON'T KNOW...
...WHAT WILL HAPPEN WITH NEXT YEAR'S CLASS.
Class: 2-B
Teacher: Sasaki
I MAY NOT BE ABLE TO GET CLOSE TO SASAKI-SENSEI...
...AFTER IT ENDS.

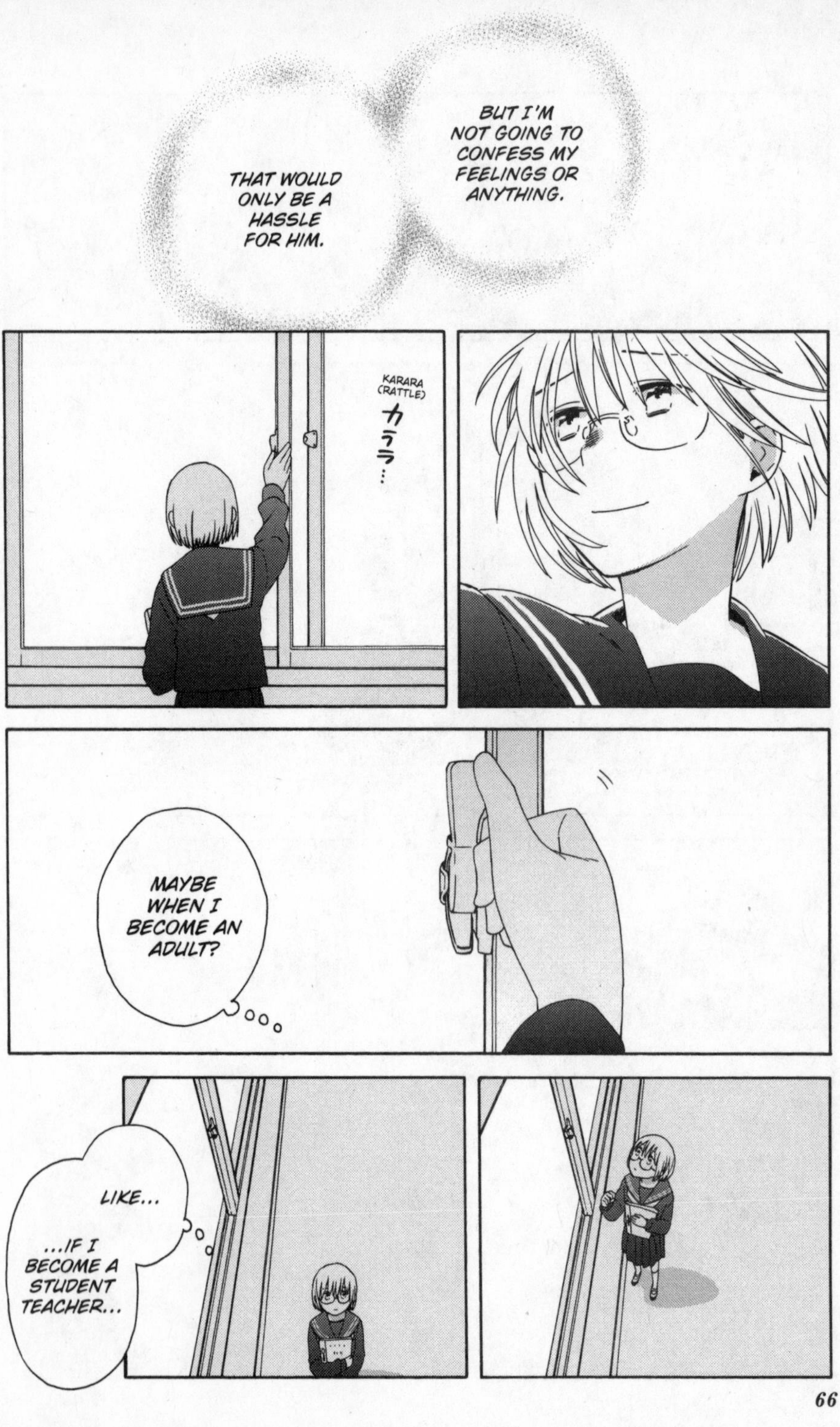
BUT I'M NOT GOING TO CONFESS MY FEELINGS OR ANYTHING.
THAT WOULD ONLY BE A HASSLE FOR HIM.
KARARA (RATTLE)
カララ…
MAYBE WHEN I BECOME AN ADULT?
LIKE...
...IF I BECOME A STUDENT TEACHER...

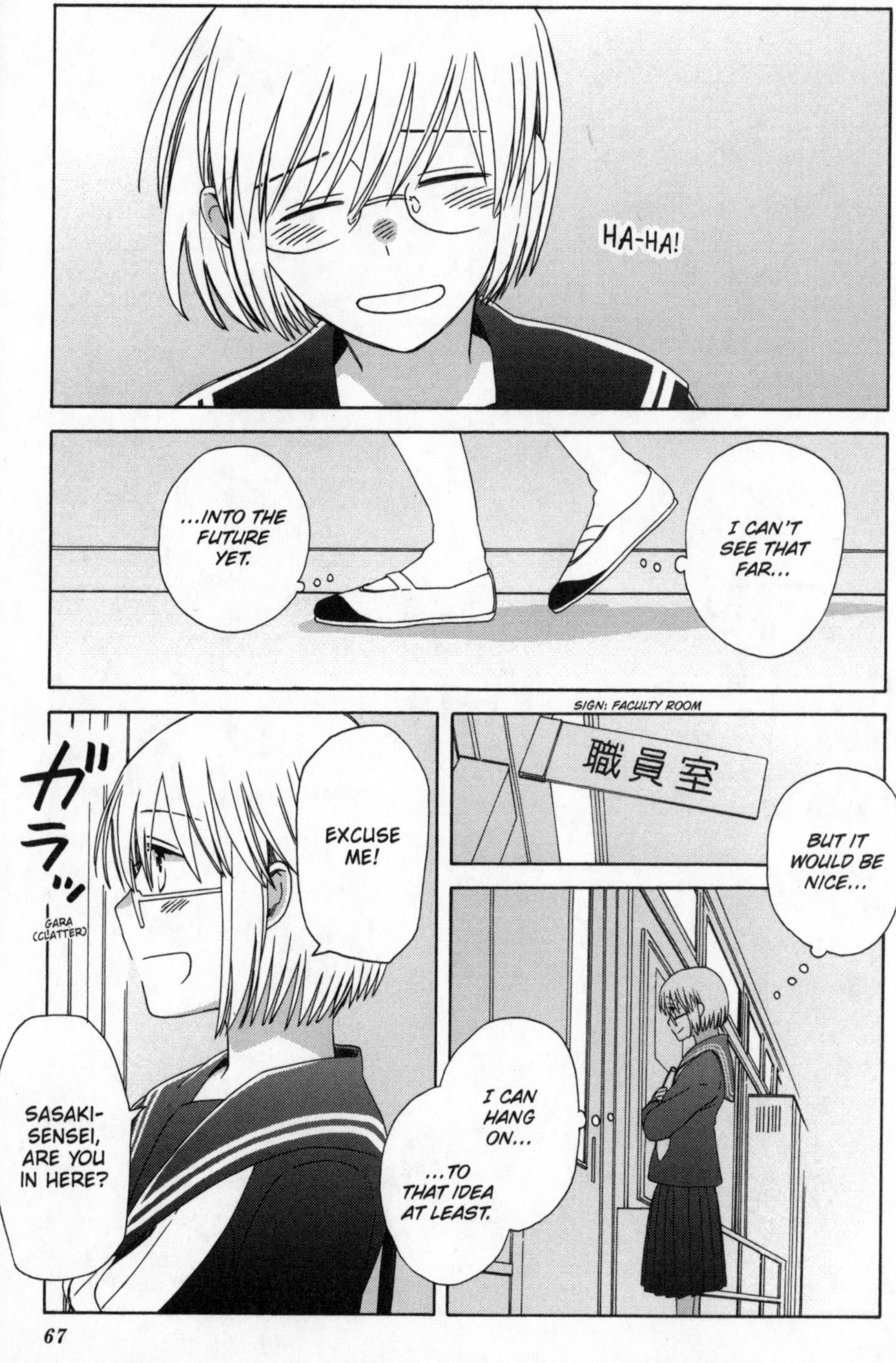
HA-HA!
I CAN'T SEE THAT FAR...
...INTO THE FUTURE YET.
SIGN: FACULTY ROOM
職員室
BUT IT WOULD BE NICE...
I CAN HANG ON...
...TO THAT IDEA AT LEAST.
ガラッ
GARA (CLATTER)
EXCUSE ME!
SASAKI-SENSEI, ARE YOU IN HERE?

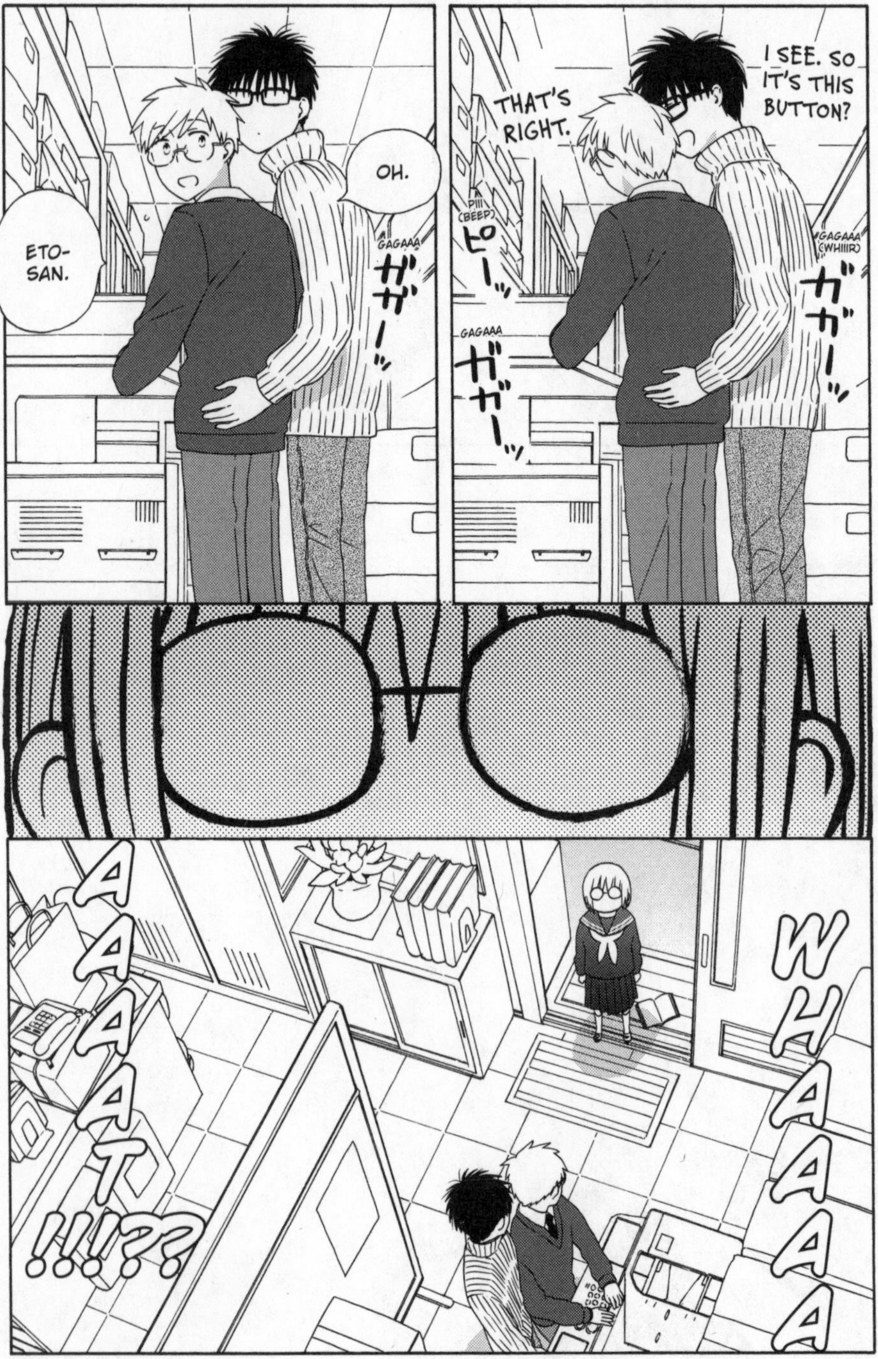
I SEE. SO IT'S THIS BUTTON?
THAT'S RIGHT.
GAGAAA (WHIIIR)
ガガーッ
PIII (BEEP)
ピーッ
GAGAAA
ガガーッ
OH.
GAGAAA
ガガーッ
ETO-SAN.
WHAAAAAA
AAAAT!!!??

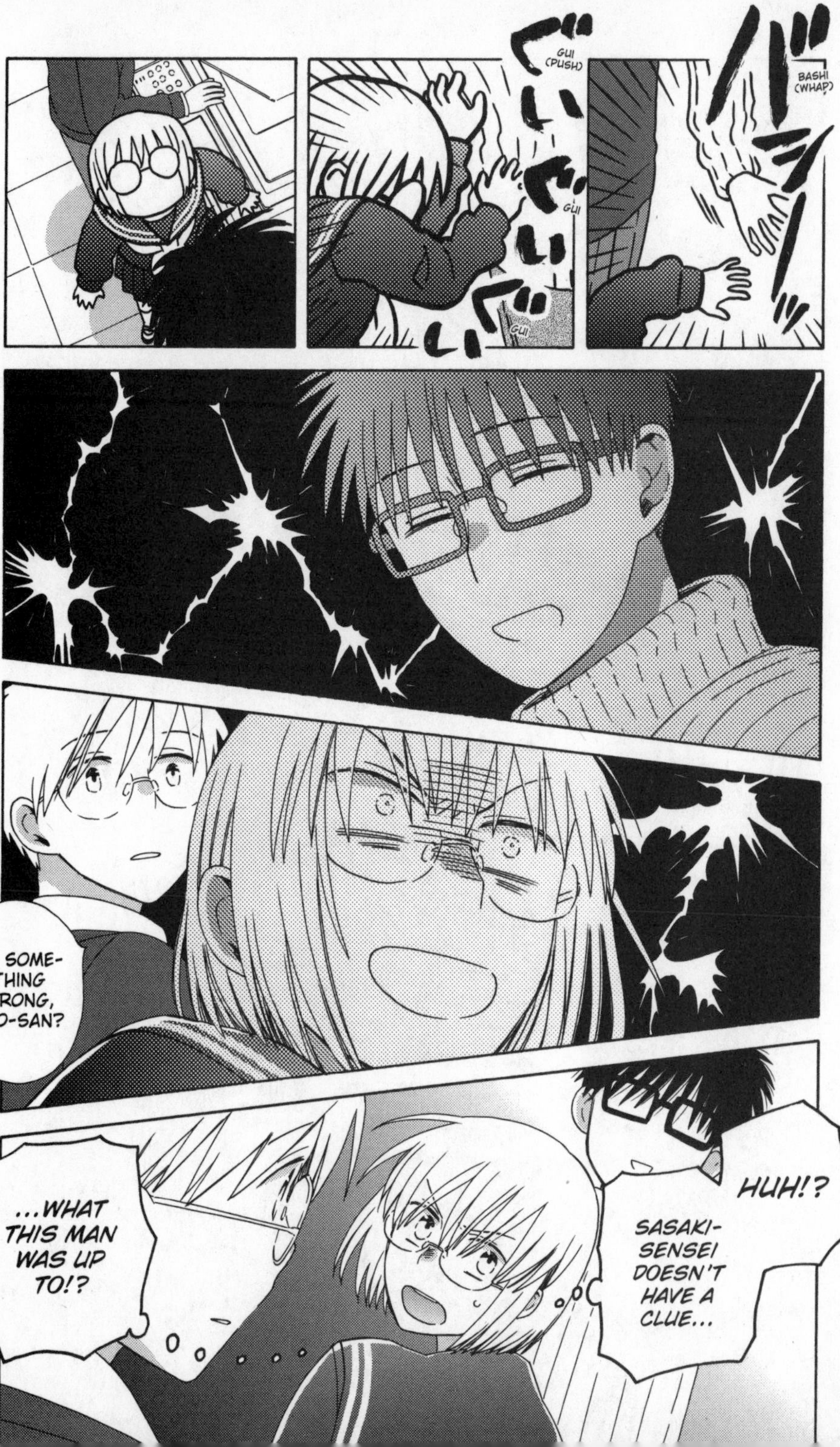
BASHI (WHAP)
GUI (PUSH)
GUI
GUI
IS SOME-THING WRONG, ETO-SAN?
HUH!?
SASAKI-SENSEI DOESN'T HAVE A CLUE...
...WHAT THIS MAN WAS UP TO!?

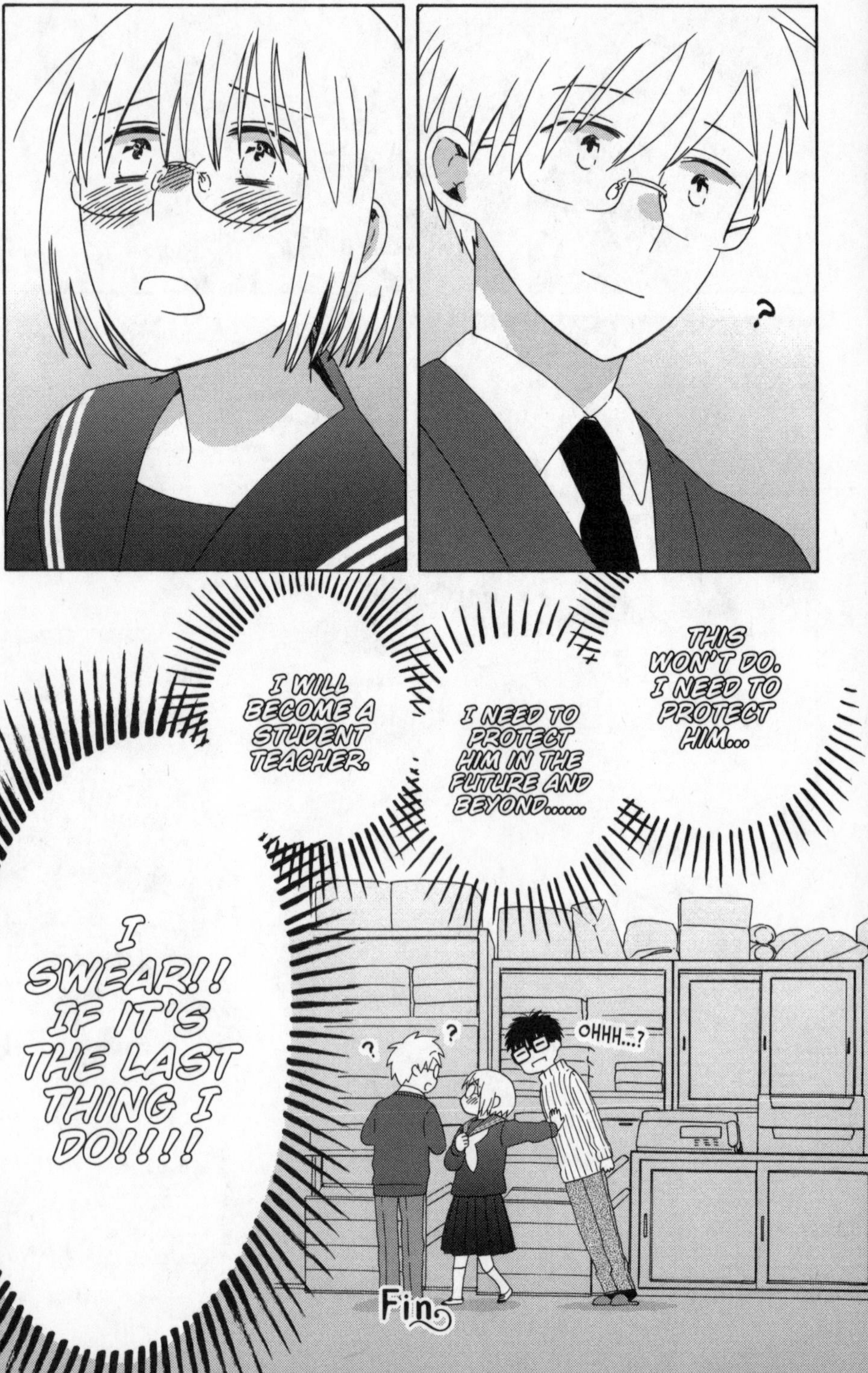
?
THIS WON'T DO. I NEED TO PROTECT HIM...
I NEED TO PROTECT HIM IN THE FUTURE AND BEYOND......
I WILL BECOME A STUDENT TEACHER.
OHHH...?
?
?
I SWEAR!! IF IT'S THE LAST THING I DO!!!!
Fin

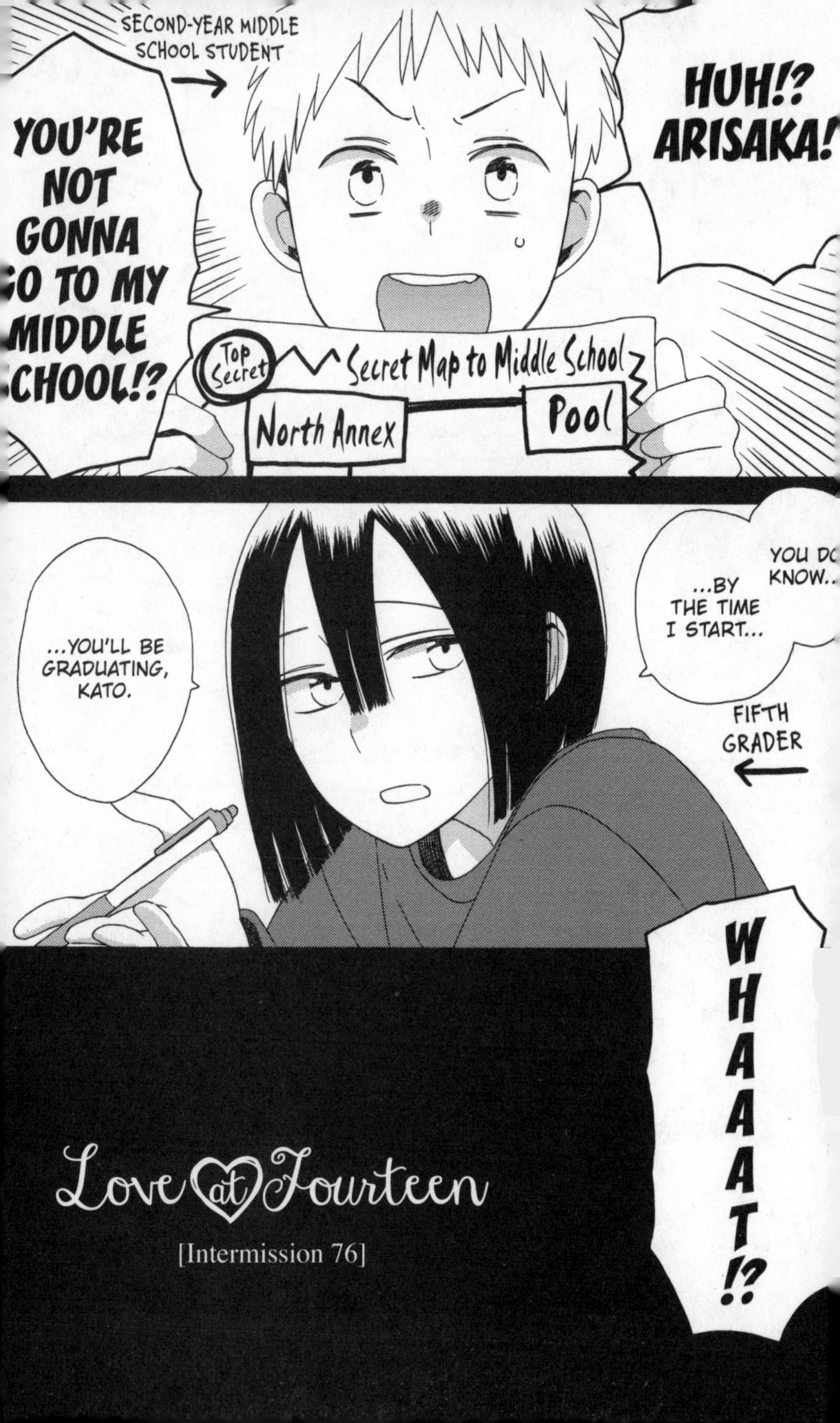
HUH!? ARISAKA!
SECOND-YEAR MIDDLE SCHOOL STUDENT
YOU'RE NOT GONNA GO TO MY MIDDLE SCHOOL!?
Top Secret
Secret Map to Middle School
Pool
North Annex
YOU DO KNOW...
...BY THE TIME I START...
FIFTH GRADER
...YOU'LL BE GRADUATING, KATO.
WHAAAAT!?
Love at Fourteen
[Intermission 76]

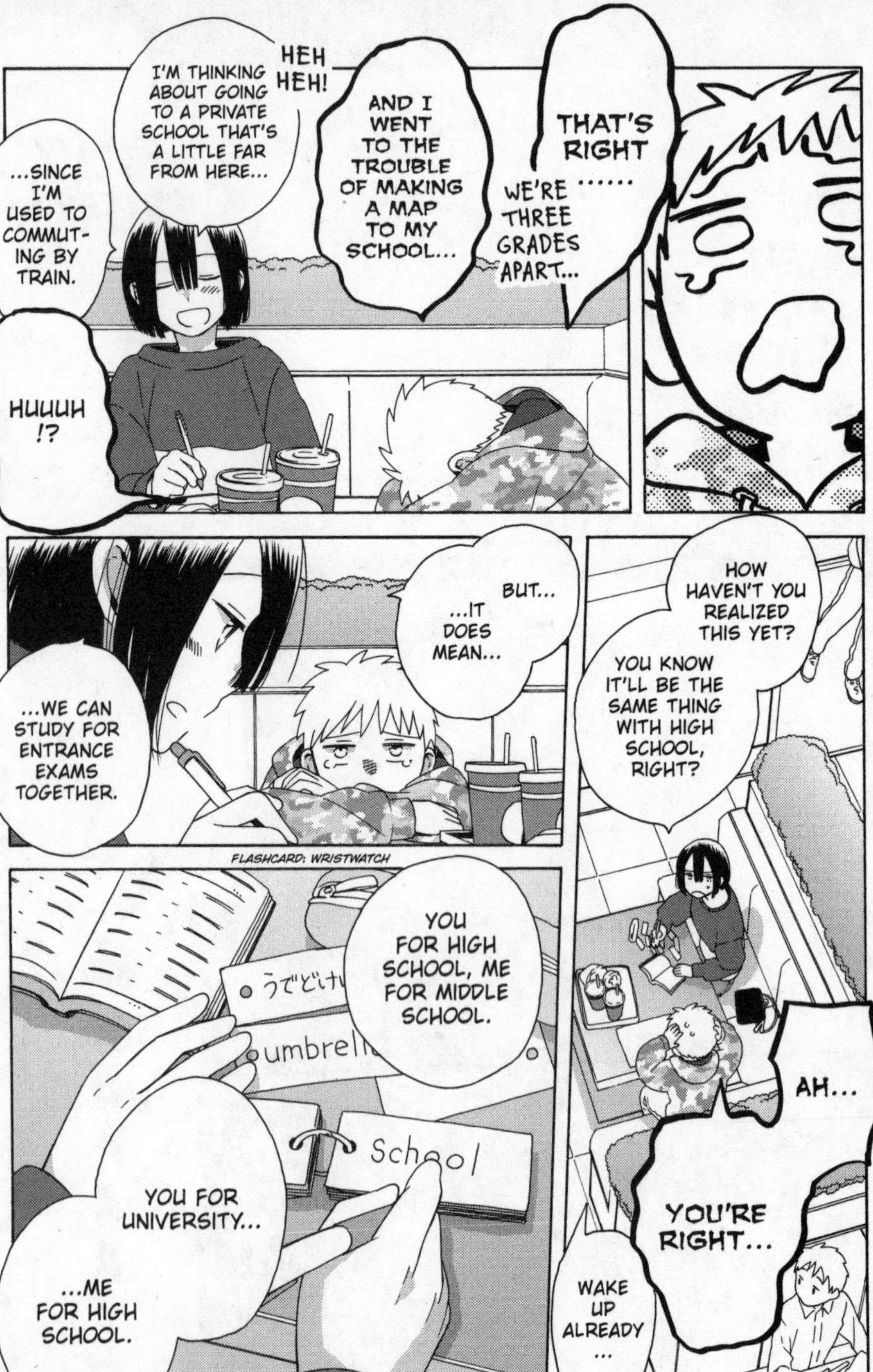
THAT'S RIGHT ......
WE'RE THREE GRADES APART...
AND I WENT TO THE TROUBLE OF MAKING A MAP TO MY SCHOOL...
HEH HEH!
I'M THINKING ABOUT GOING TO A PRIVATE SCHOOL THAT'S A LITTLE FAR FROM HERE...
...SINCE I'M USED TO COMMUTING BY TRAIN.
HUUUH !?
HOW HAVEN'T YOU REALIZED THIS YET?
YOU KNOW IT'LL BE THE SAME THING WITH HIGH SCHOOL, RIGHT?
AH...
YOU'RE RIGHT...
WAKE UP ALREADY ...
BUT...
...IT DOES MEAN...
...WE CAN STUDY FOR ENTRANCE EXAMS TOGETHER.
FLASHCARD: WRISTWATCH
うでどけい
YOU FOR HIGH SCHOOL, ME FOR MIDDLE SCHOOL.
School
YOU FOR UNIVERSITY...
...ME FOR HIGH SCHOOL.

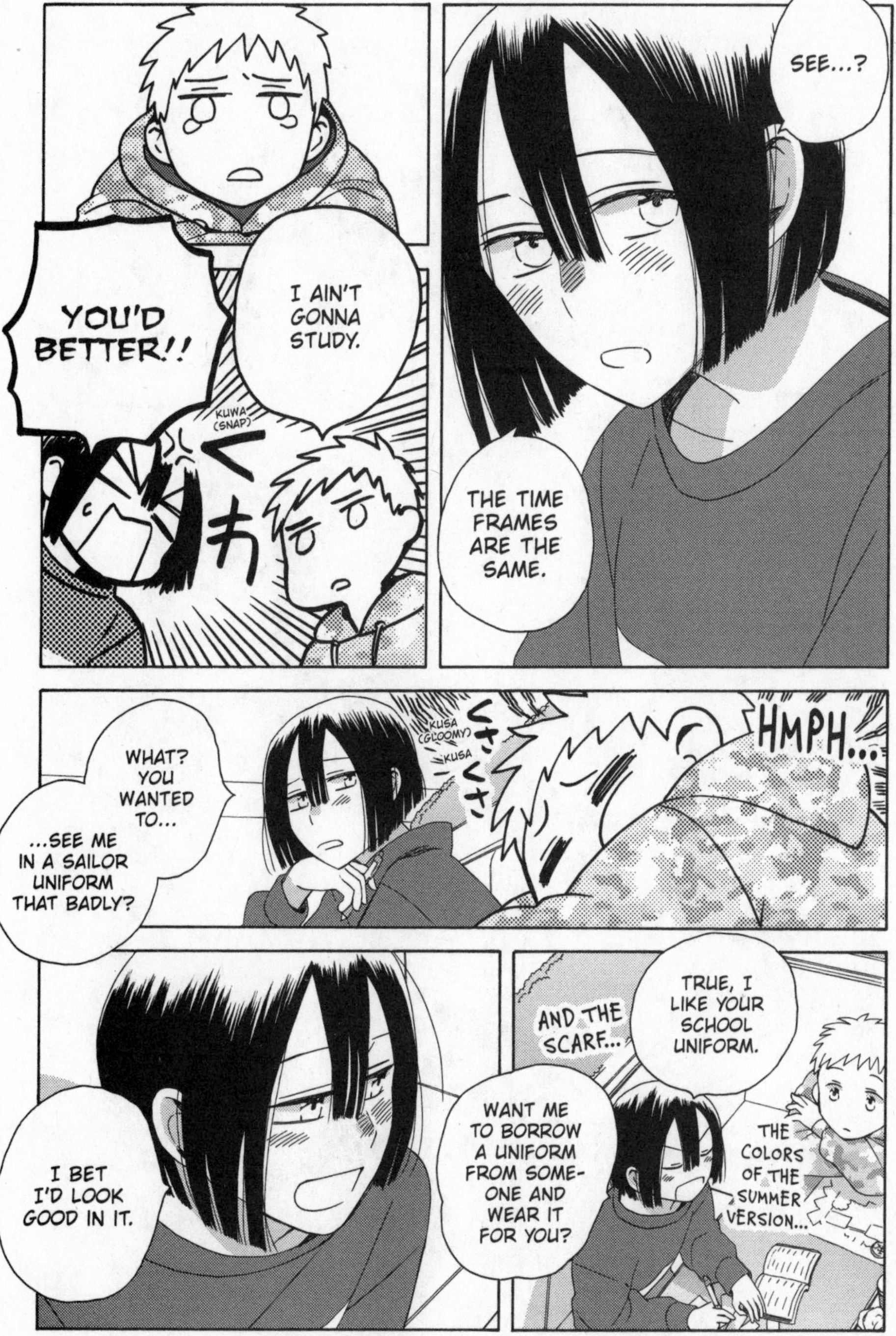
SEE...?
THE TIME FRAMES ARE THE SAME.
I AIN'T GONNA STUDY.
YOU'D BETTER!!
KUWA (SNAP)
HMPH...
KUSA (GLOOMY) KUSA
WHAT? YOU WANTED TO...
...SEE ME IN A SAILOR UNIFORM THAT BADLY?
TRUE, I LIKE YOUR SCHOOL UNIFORM.
AND THE SCARF...
THE COLORS OF THE SUMMER VERSION...
WANT ME TO BORROW A UNIFORM FROM SOME-ONE AND WEAR IT FOR YOU?
I BET I'D LOOK GOOD IN IT.

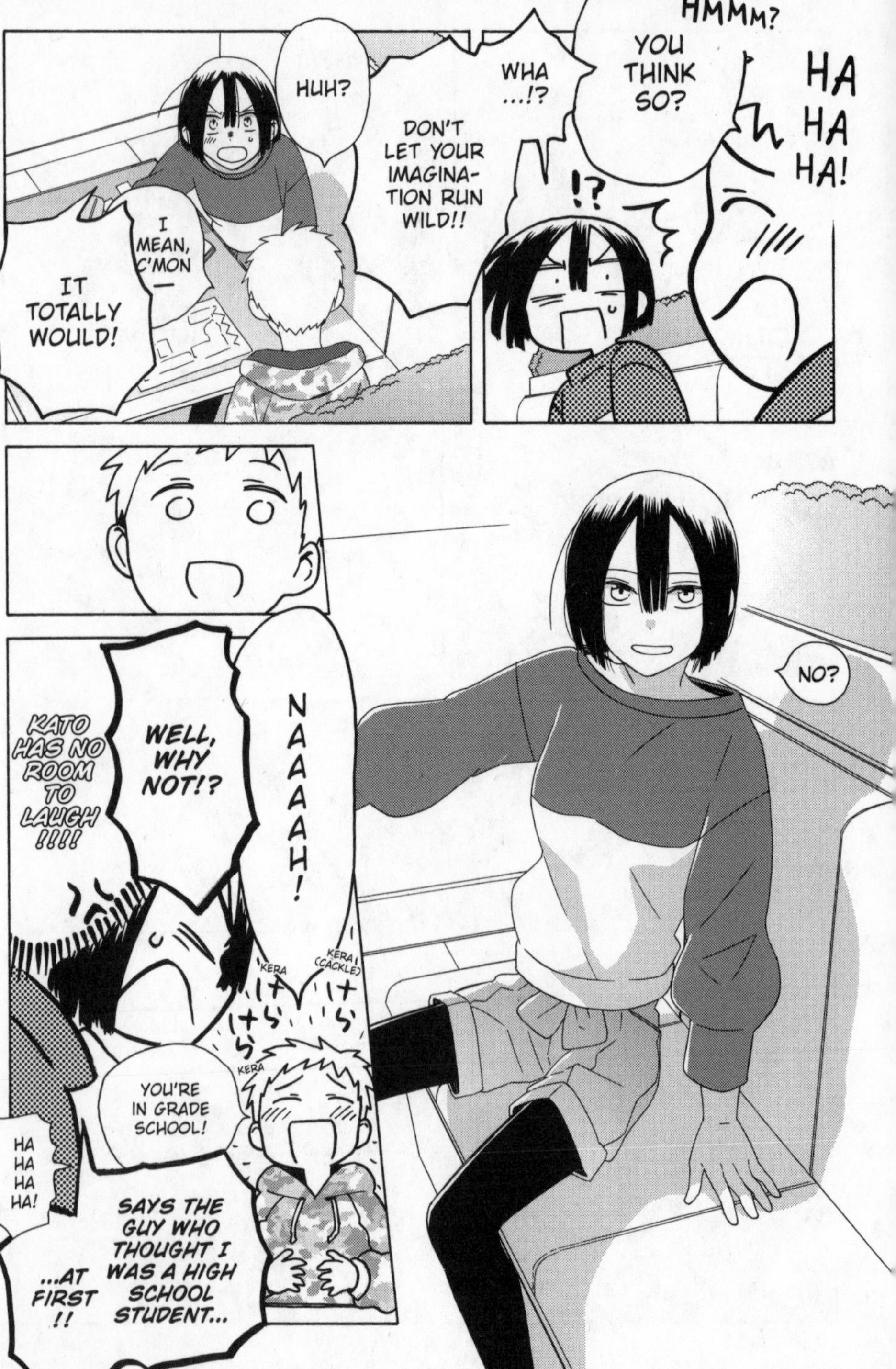
HA HA HA!
HMMM? YOU THINK SO?
WHA ...!?
!?
DON'T LET YOUR IMAGINATION RUN WILD!!
HUH?
I MEAN, C'MON—
IT TOTALLY WOULD!
NO?
NAAAAAH!
WELL, WHY NOT!?
KATO HAS NO ROOM TO LAUGH!!!!
KERA (CACKLE)
けら
KERA
けら
KERA
ら
YOU'RE IN GRADE SCHOOL!
HA HA HA HA!
SAYS THE GUY WHO THOUGHT I WAS A HIGH SCHOOL STUDENT...
...AT FIRST!!

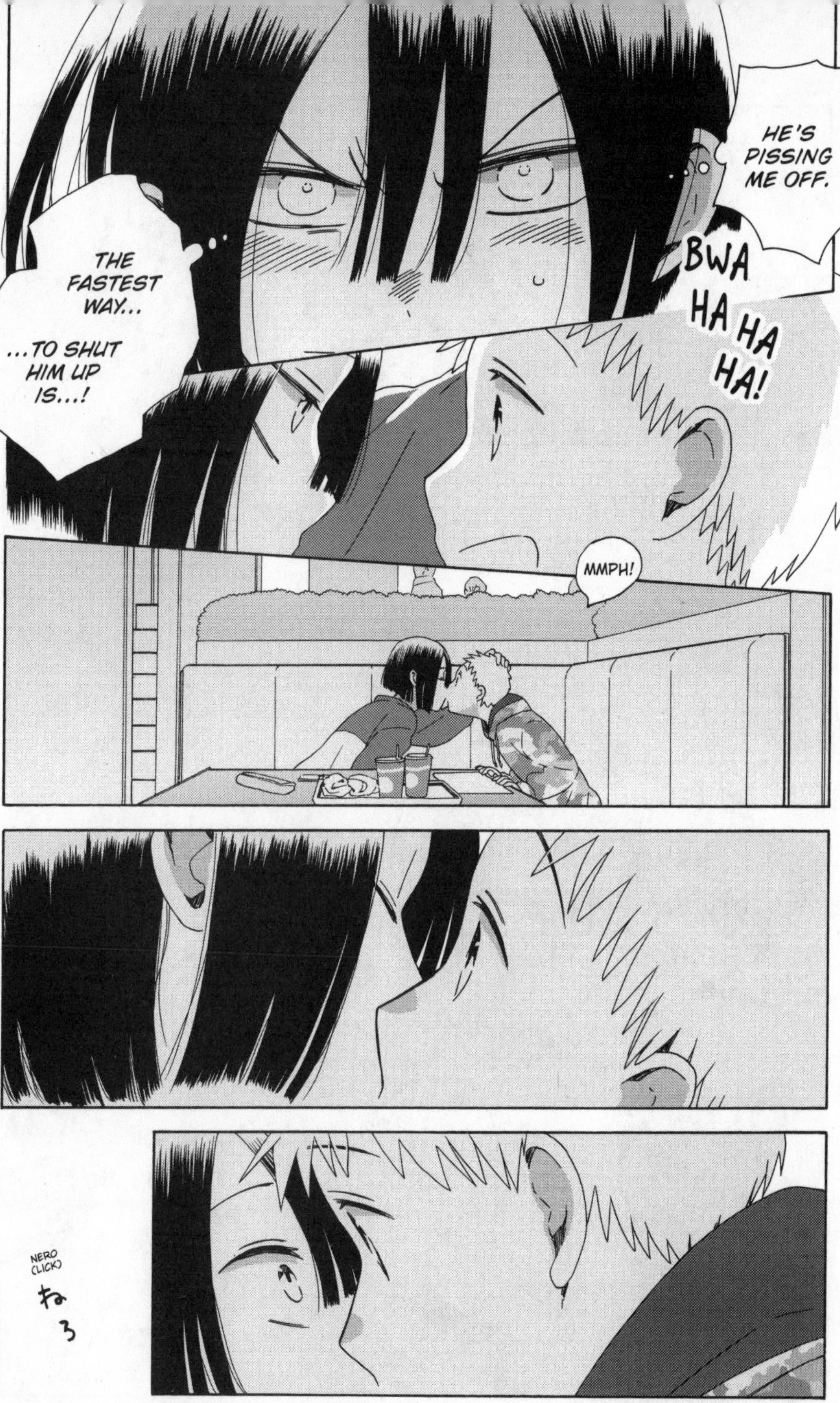
HE'S PISSING ME OFF.
BWA HA HA HA!
THE FASTEST WAY...
...TO SHUT HIM UP IS...!
MMPH!
NERO (LICK)
ねろ

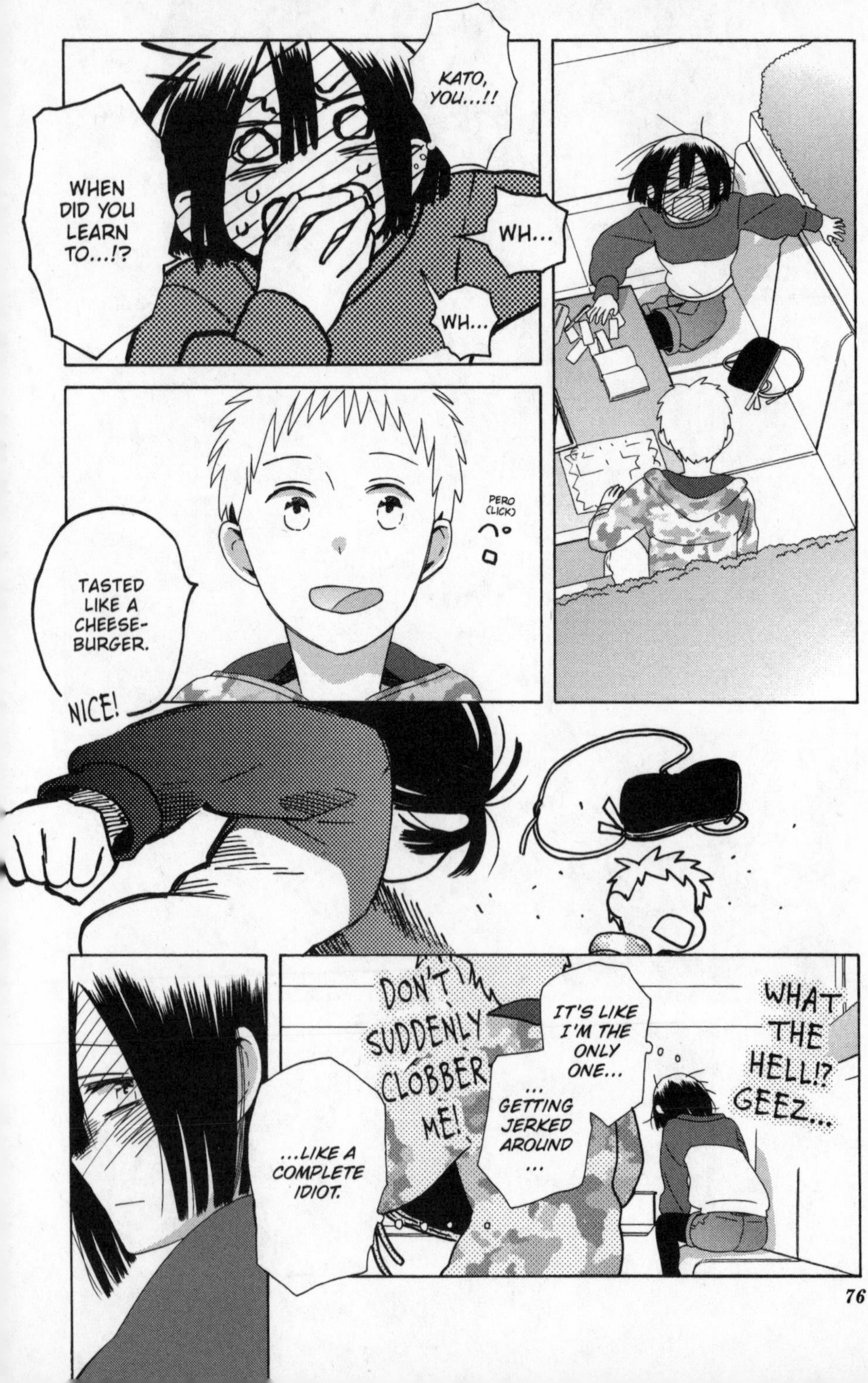
KATO, YOU...!!
WH...
WH...
WHEN DID YOU LEARN TO...!?
PERO (LICK)
TASTED LIKE A CHEESE-BURGER.
NICE!
WHAT THE HELL!? GEEZ...
DON'T SUDDENLY CLOBBER ME!
IT'S LIKE I'M THE ONLY ONE...
...GETTING JERKED AROUND...
...LIKE A COMPLETE IDIOT.

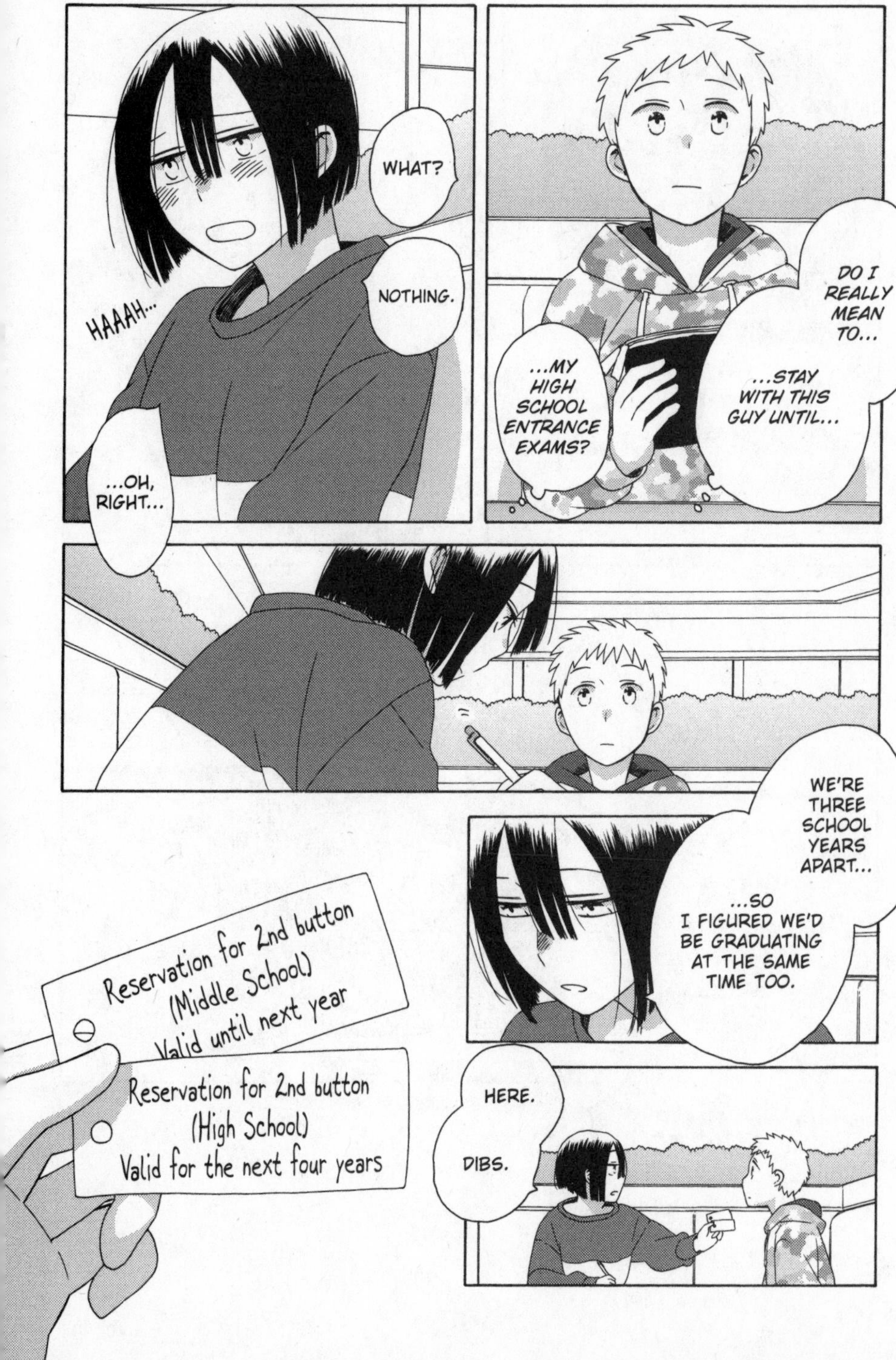
DO I REALLY MEAN TO...
...STAY WITH THIS GUY UNTIL...
...MY HIGH SCHOOL ENTRANCE EXAMS?
WHAT?
NOTHING.
HAAAH...
...OH, RIGHT...
WE'RE THREE SCHOOL YEARS APART...
...SO I FIGURED WE'D BE GRADUATING AT THE SAME TIME TOO.
HERE.
DIBS.
Reservation for 2nd button (Middle School) Valid until next year
Reservation for 2nd button (High School) Valid for the next four years

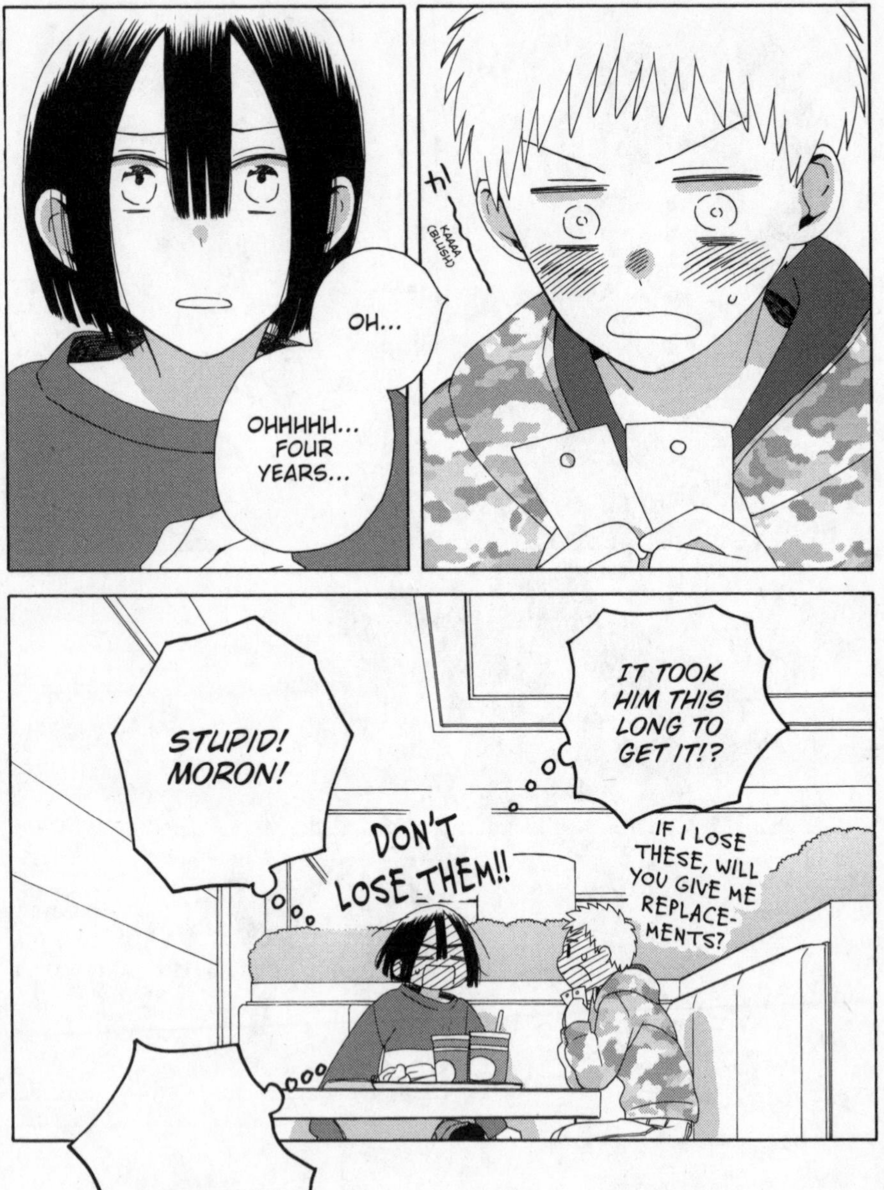
カー
KAAAA (BLUSH)
OH...
OHHHHH... FOUR YEARS...
IT TOOK HIM THIS LONG TO GET IT!?
IF I LOSE THESE, WILL YOU GIVE ME REPLACE-MENTS?
DON'T LOSE THEM!!
STUPID! MORON!
IDIOT!!!

Fin

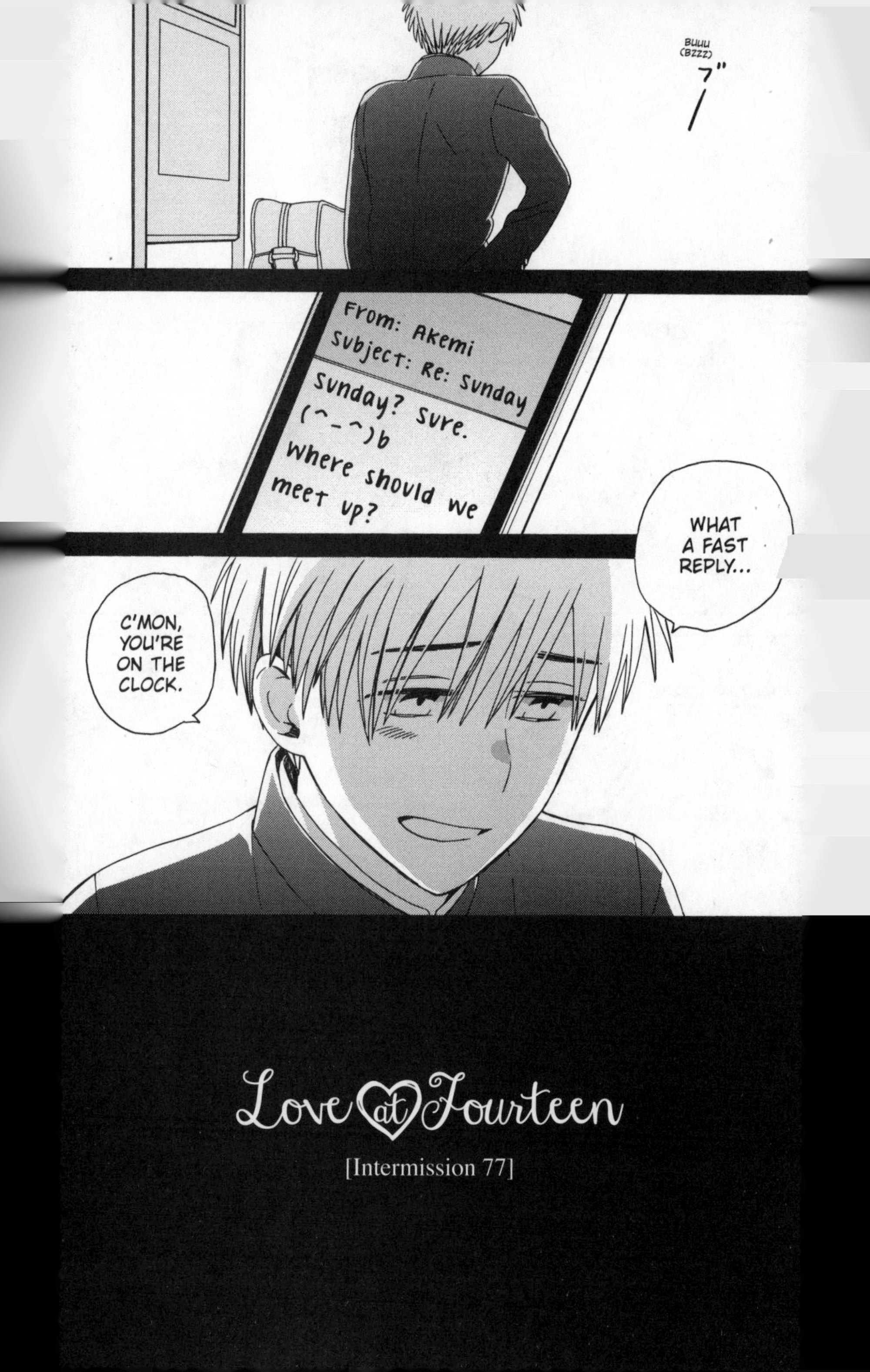
BUUU (BZZZ)
From: Akemi
Subject: Re: Sunday
Sunday? Sure. (^_^)b
Where should we meet up?
WHAT A FAST REPLY...
C'MON, YOU'RE ON THE CLOCK.

Love at Fourteen

[Intermission 77]

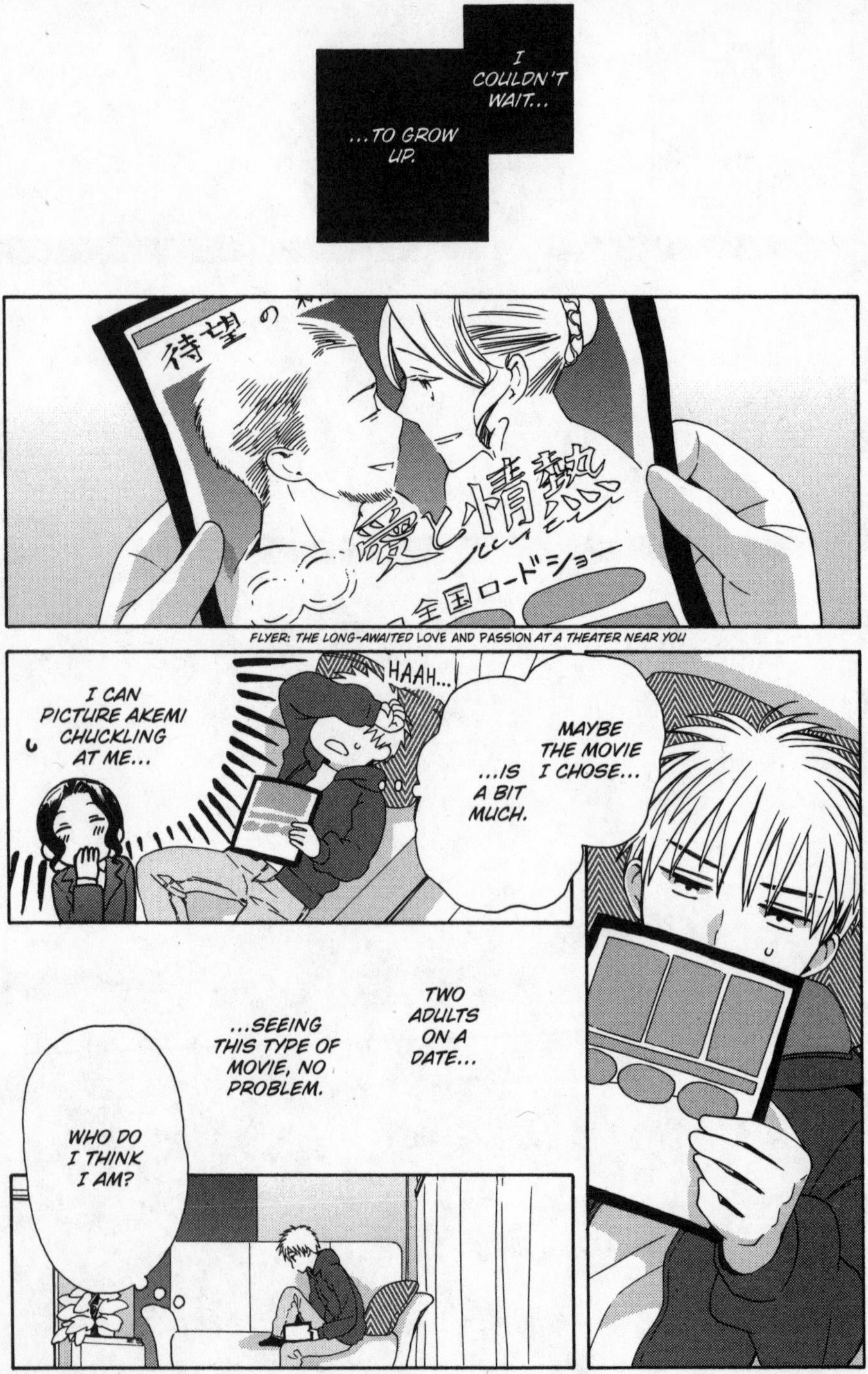
I COULDN'T WAIT...
...TO GROW UP.
待望の
愛と情熱
全国ロードショー
FLYER: THE LONG-AWAITED LOVE AND PASSION AT A THEATER NEAR YOU
MAYBE THE MOVIE I CHOSE...
...IS A BIT MUCH.
HAAH...
I CAN PICTURE AKEMI CHUCKLING AT ME...
TWO ADULTS ON A DATE...
...SEEING THIS TYPE OF MOVIE, NO PROBLEM.
WHO DO I THINK I AM?

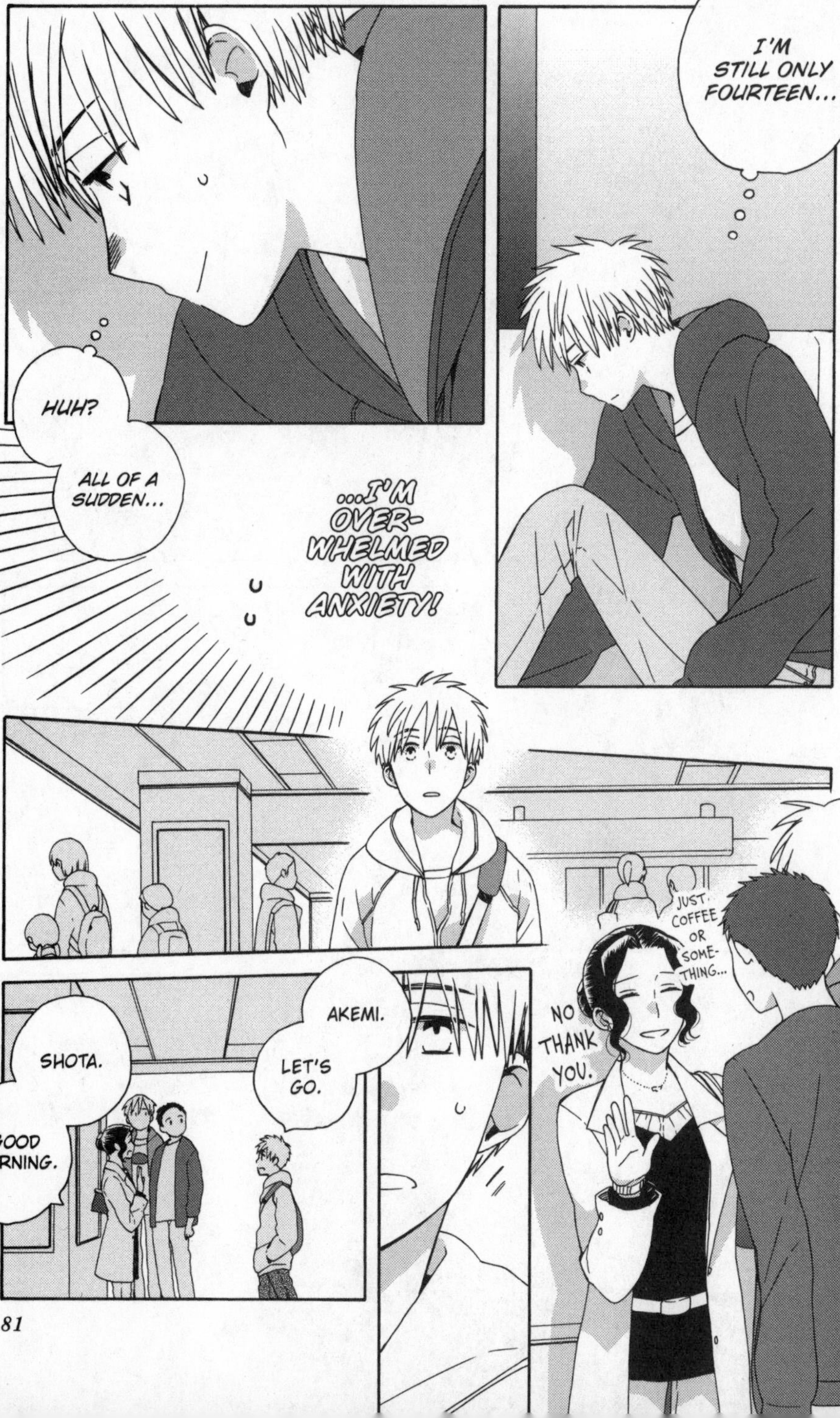
I'M STILL ONLY FOURTEEN...
HUH?
ALL OF A SUDDEN...
...I'M OVER-WHELMED WITH ANXIETY!
JUST COFFEE OR SOME-THING...
NO THANK YOU.
AKEMI.
LET'S GO.
SHOTA.
GOOD MORNING.

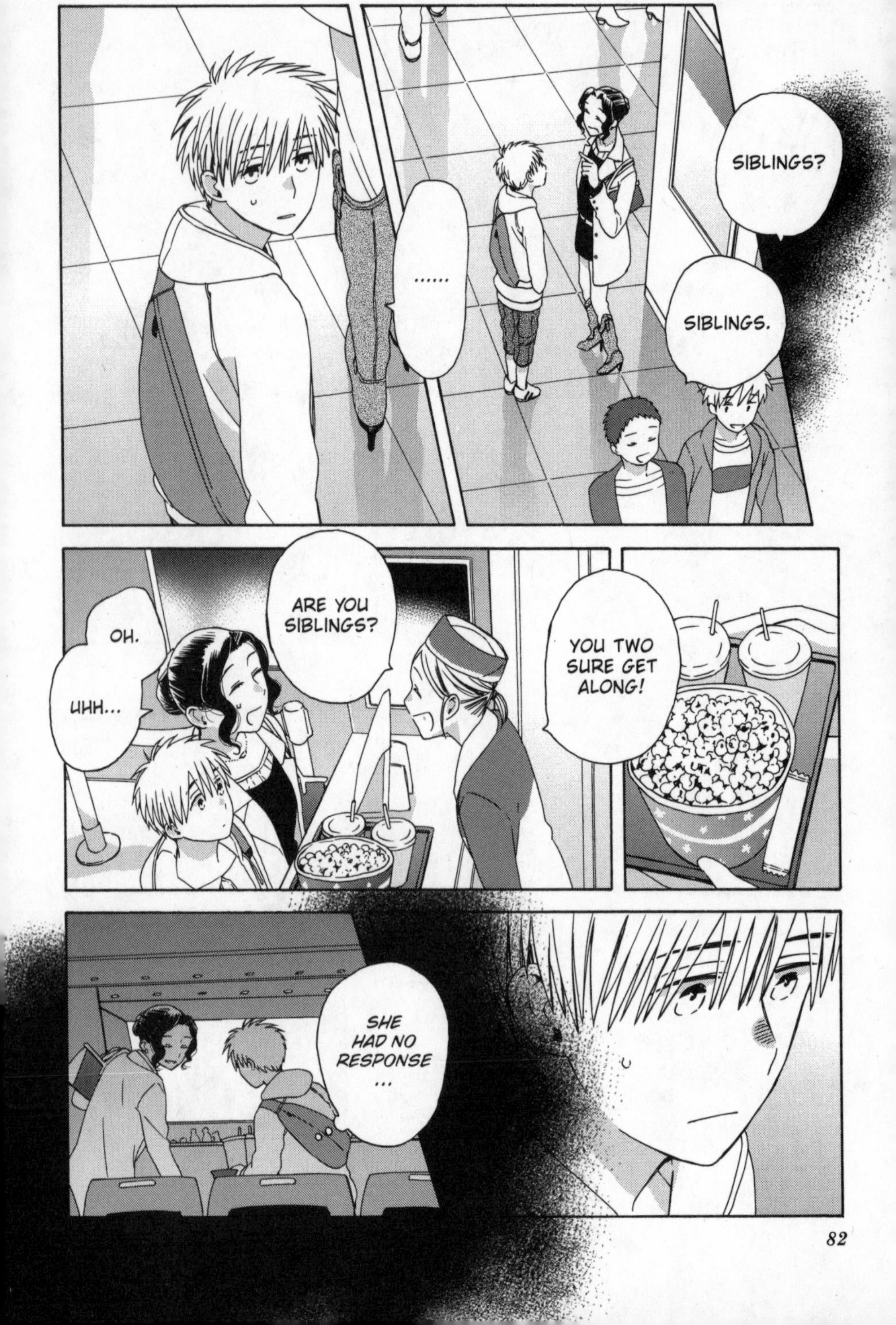
SIBLINGS?
SIBLINGS.
......
YOU TWO SURE GET ALONG!
ARE YOU SIBLINGS?
OH.
UHH...
SHE HAD NO RESPONSE ...

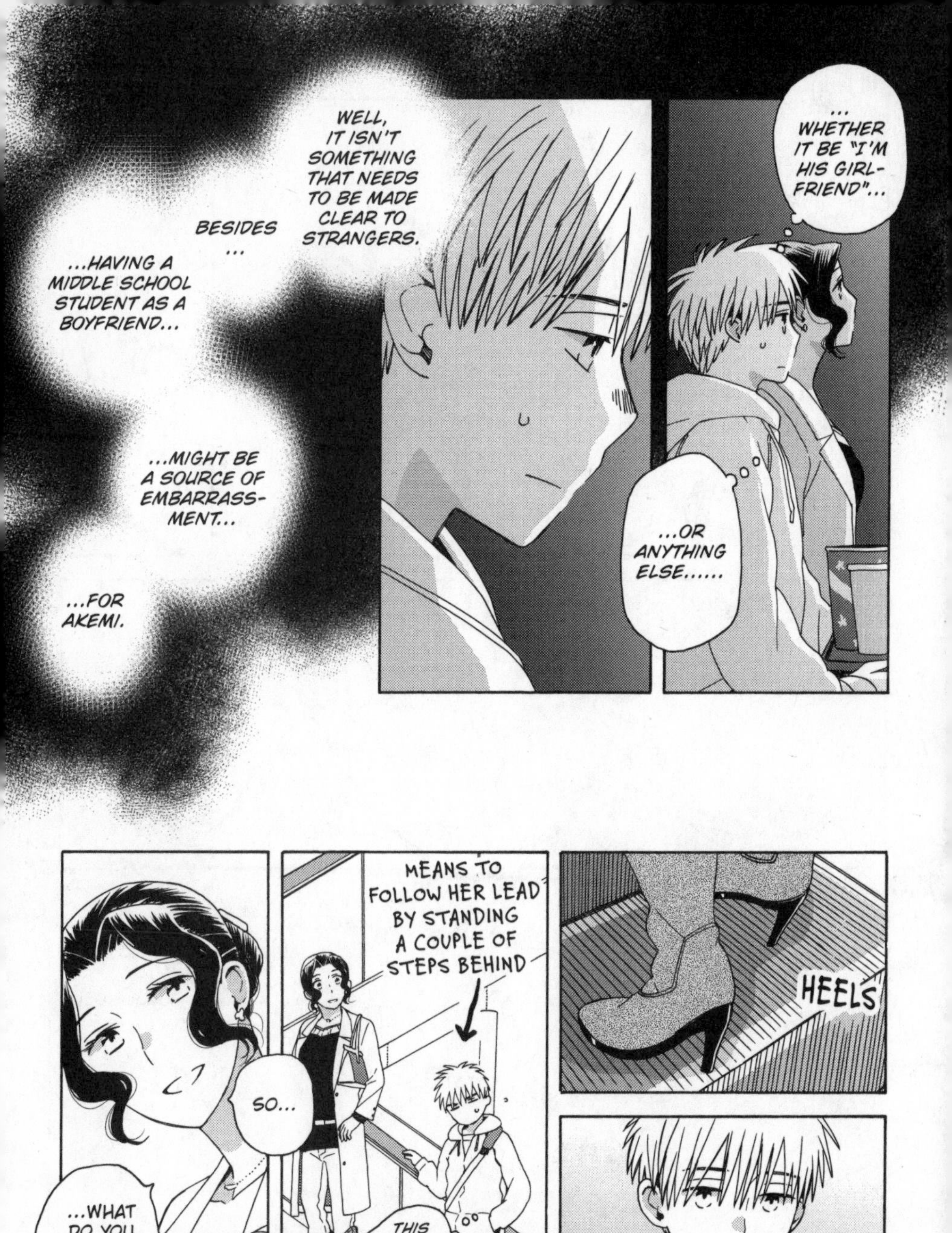
...WHETHER IT BE "I'M HIS GIRL-FRIEND"...
...OR ANYTHING ELSE......
WELL, IT ISN'T SOMETHING THAT NEEDS TO BE MADE CLEAR TO STRANGERS.
BESIDES ...
...HAVING A MIDDLE SCHOOL STUDENT AS A BOYFRIEND...
...MIGHT BE A SOURCE OF EMBARRASS-MENT...
...FOR AKEMI.
HEELS
MEANS TO FOLLOW HER LEAD BY STANDING A COUPLE OF STEPS BEHIND
THIS ISN'T THE PLACE TO ASSERT MYSELF AS HER BOYFRIEND EITHER ...
SO...
...WHAT DO YOU WANT TO DO FOR LUNCH?

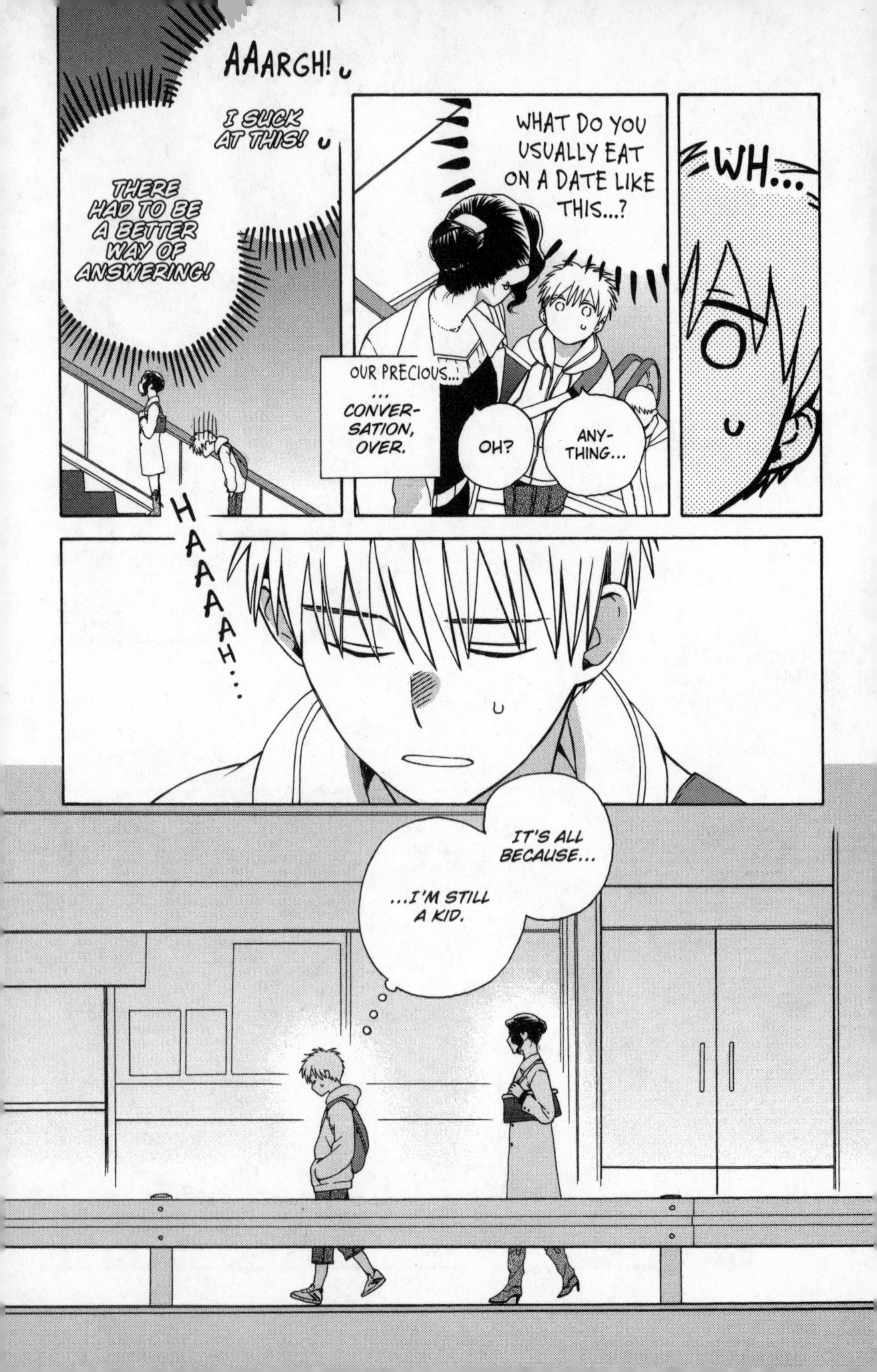
WH...
WHAT DO YOU USUALLY EAT ON A DATE LIKE THIS...?
ANY-THING...
OH?
OUR PRECIOUS... ...CONVER-SATION, OVER.
AAARGH!
I SUCK AT THIS!
THERE HAD TO BE A BETTER WAY OF ANSWERING!
HAAAAH...
IT'S ALL BECAUSE...
...I'M STILL A KID.

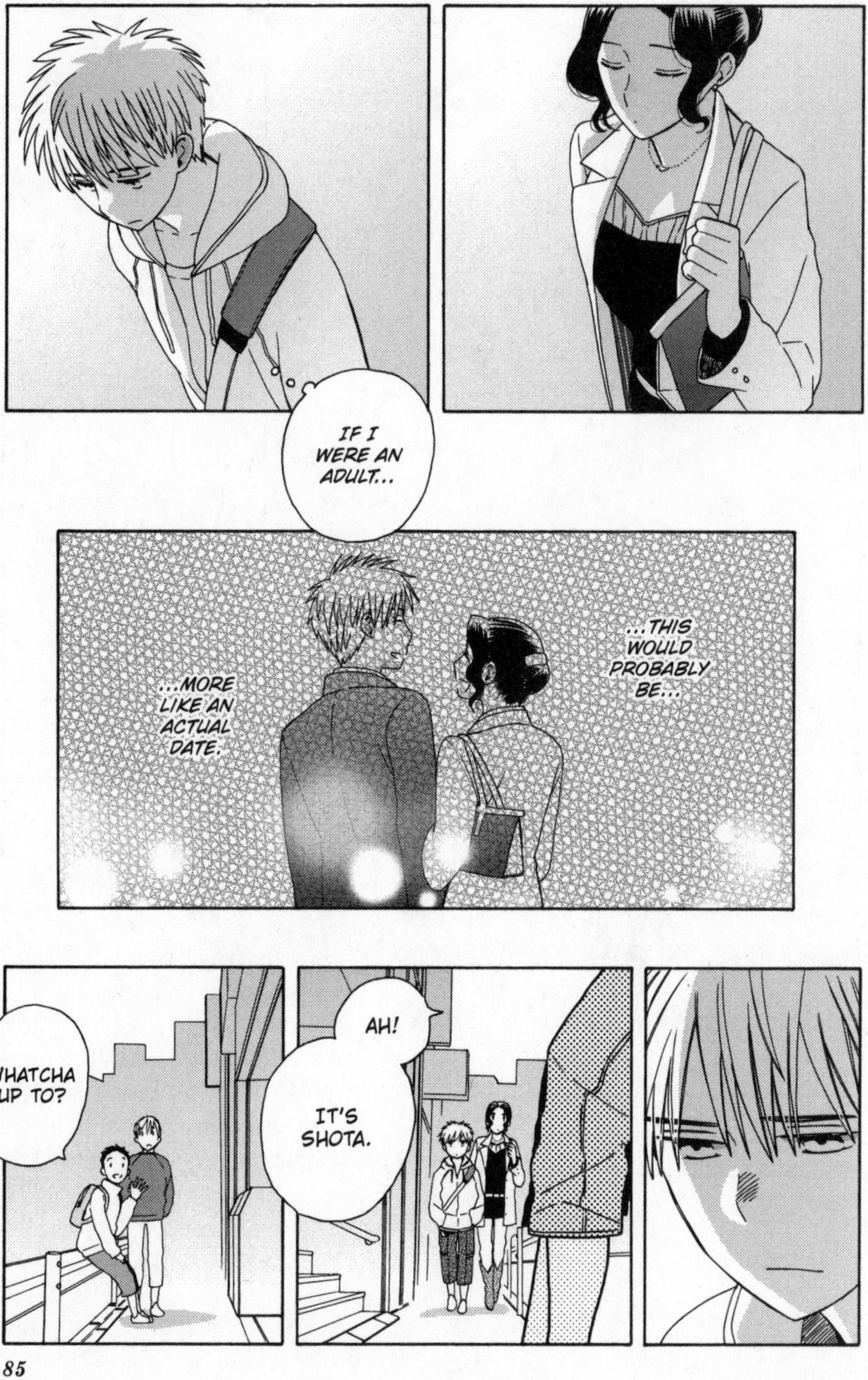
IF I WERE AN ADULT...
...THIS WOULD PROBABLY BE...
...MORE LIKE AN ACTUAL DATE.
AH!
IT'S SHOTA.
WHATCHA UP TO?

—BUT.

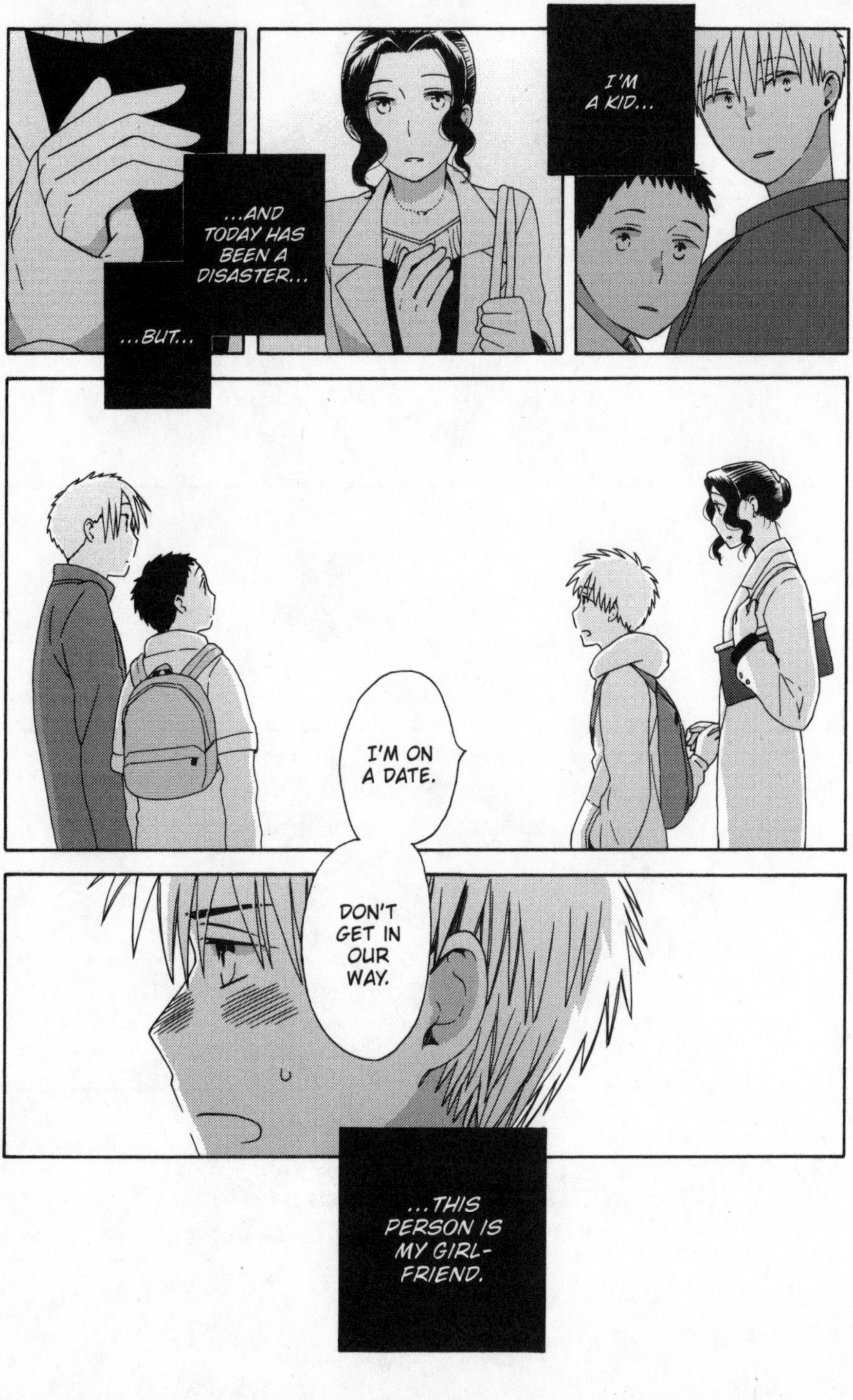
I'M A KID...
...AND TODAY HAS BEEN A DISASTER...
...BUT...
I'M ON A DATE.
DON'T GET IN OUR WAY.
...THIS PERSON IS MY GIRL-FRIEND.

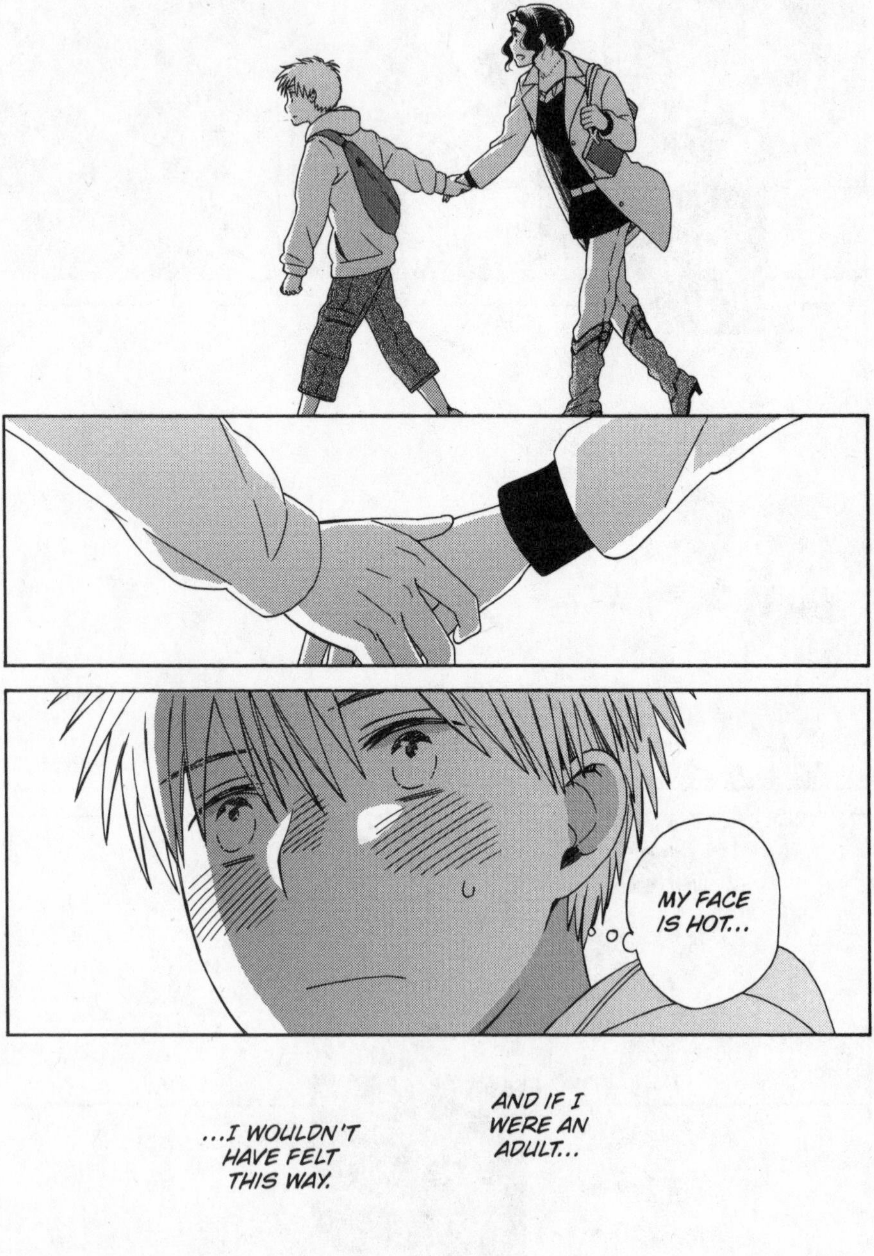
MY FACE IS HOT...
AND IF I WERE AN ADULT...
...I WOULDN'T HAVE FELT THIS WAY.

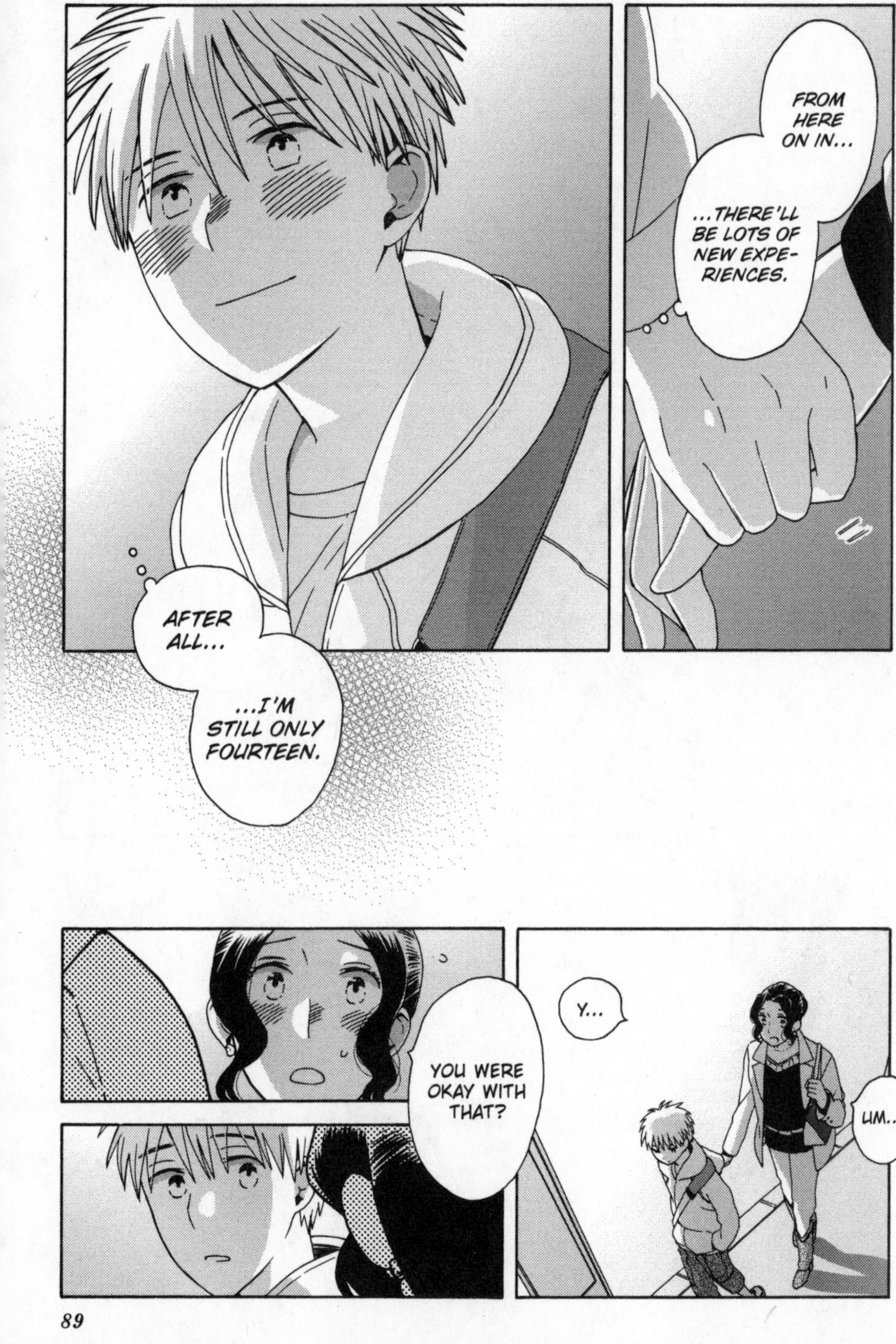
FROM HERE ON IN...
...THERE'LL BE LOTS OF NEW EXPE-RIENCES.
AFTER ALL...
...I'M STILL ONLY FOURTEEN.
Y...
UM...
YOU WERE OKAY WITH THAT?

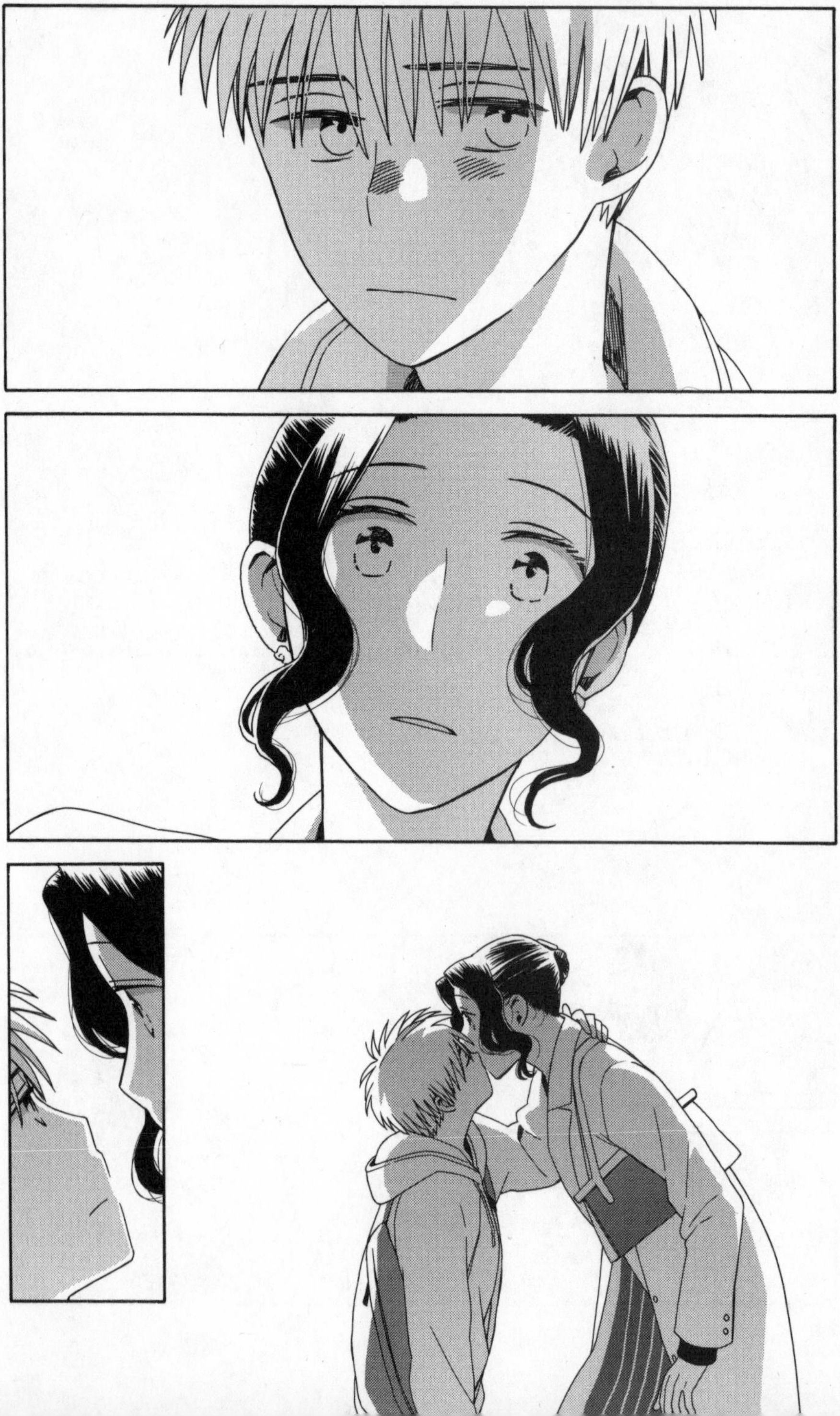

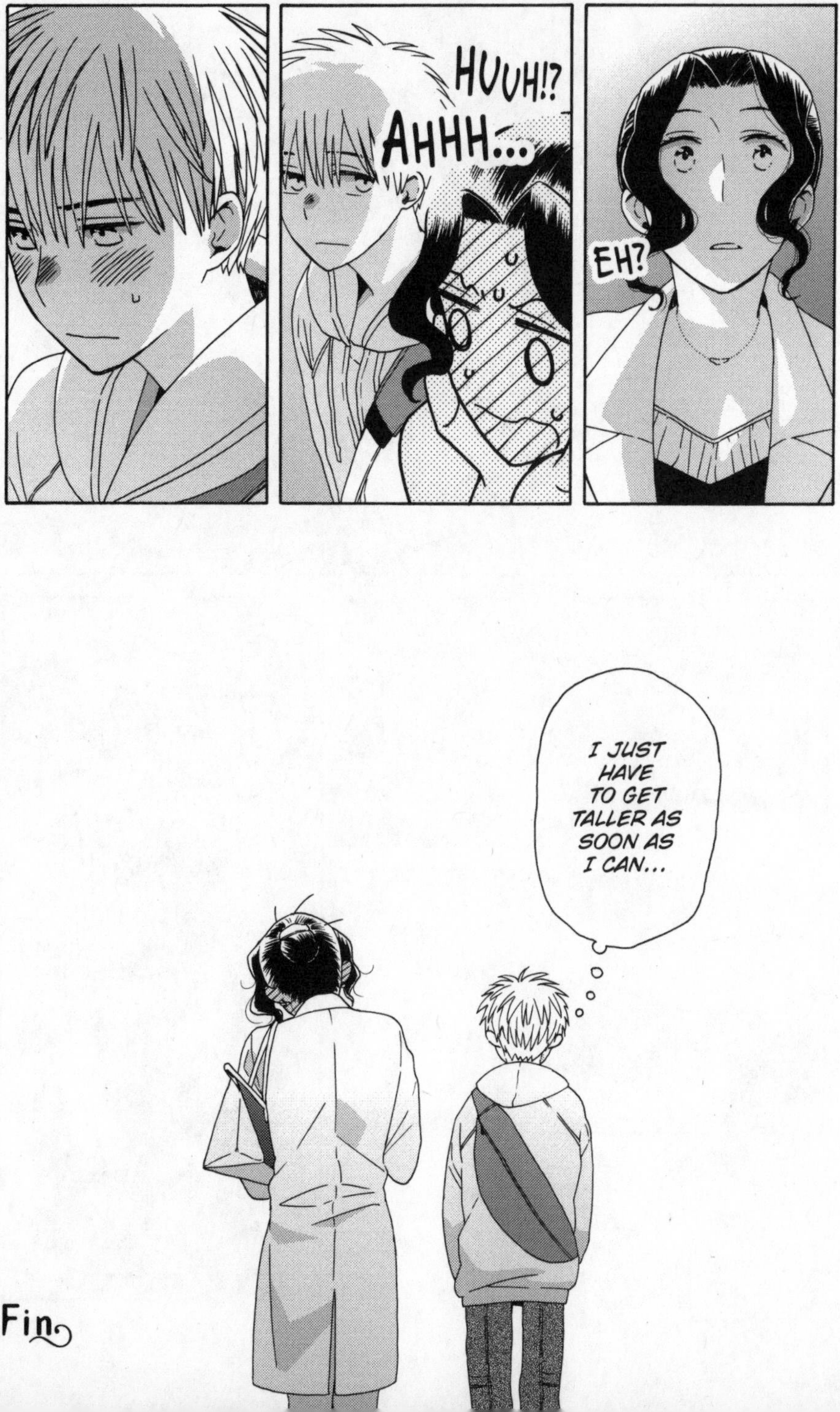
EH?
HUUH!?
AHHH...
I JUST HAVE TO GET TALLER AS SOON AS I CAN...
Fin

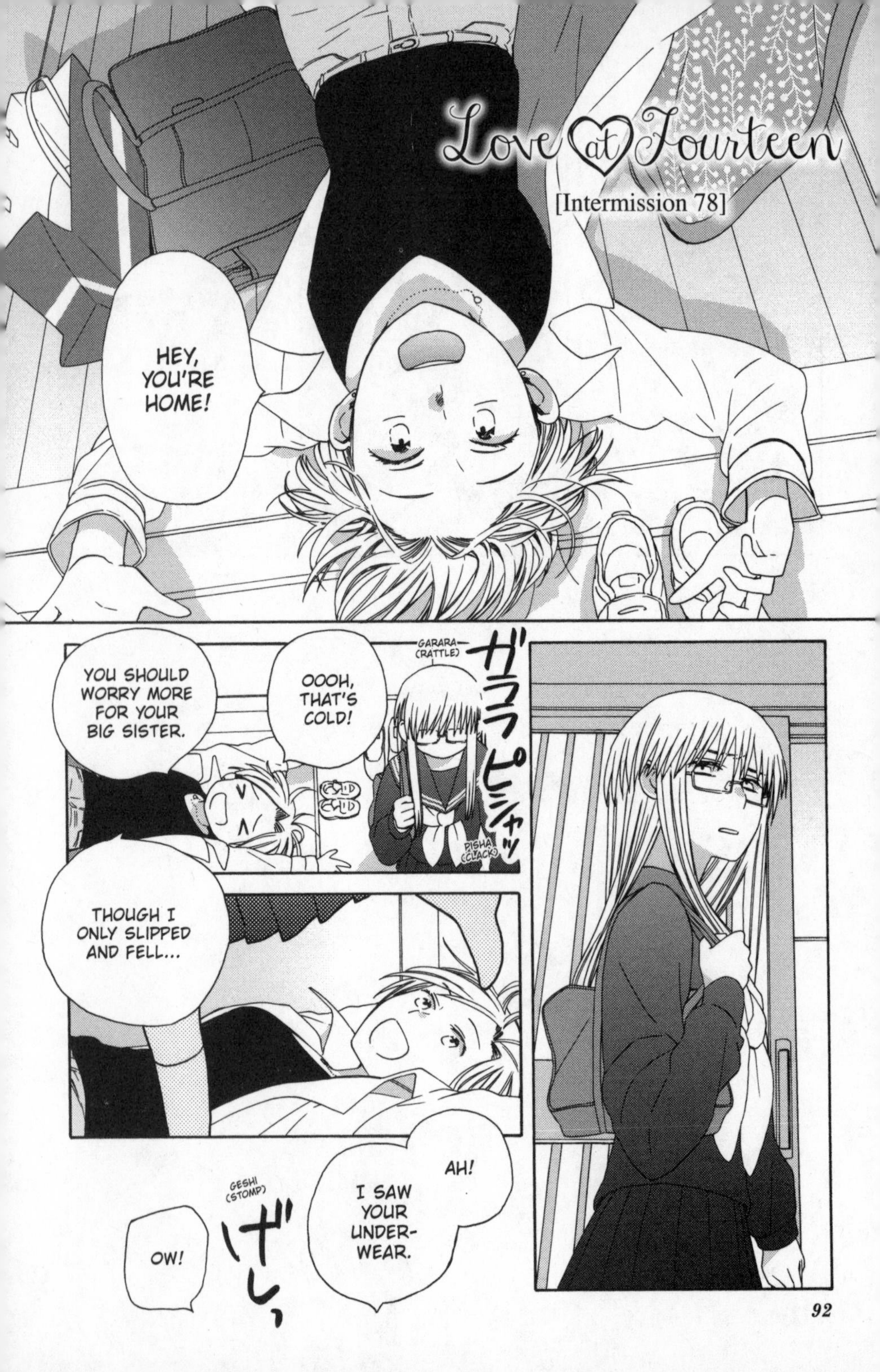
Love at Fourteen
[Intermission 78]
HEY, YOU'RE HOME!
GARARA (RATTLE)
ガララ
OOOH, THAT'S COLD!
YOU SHOULD WORRY MORE FOR YOUR BIG SISTER.
ピシャッ
PISHA (CLACK)
THOUGH I ONLY SLIPPED AND FELL...
AH!
I SAW YOUR UNDER-WEAR.
GESHI (STOMP)
げしっ
OW!

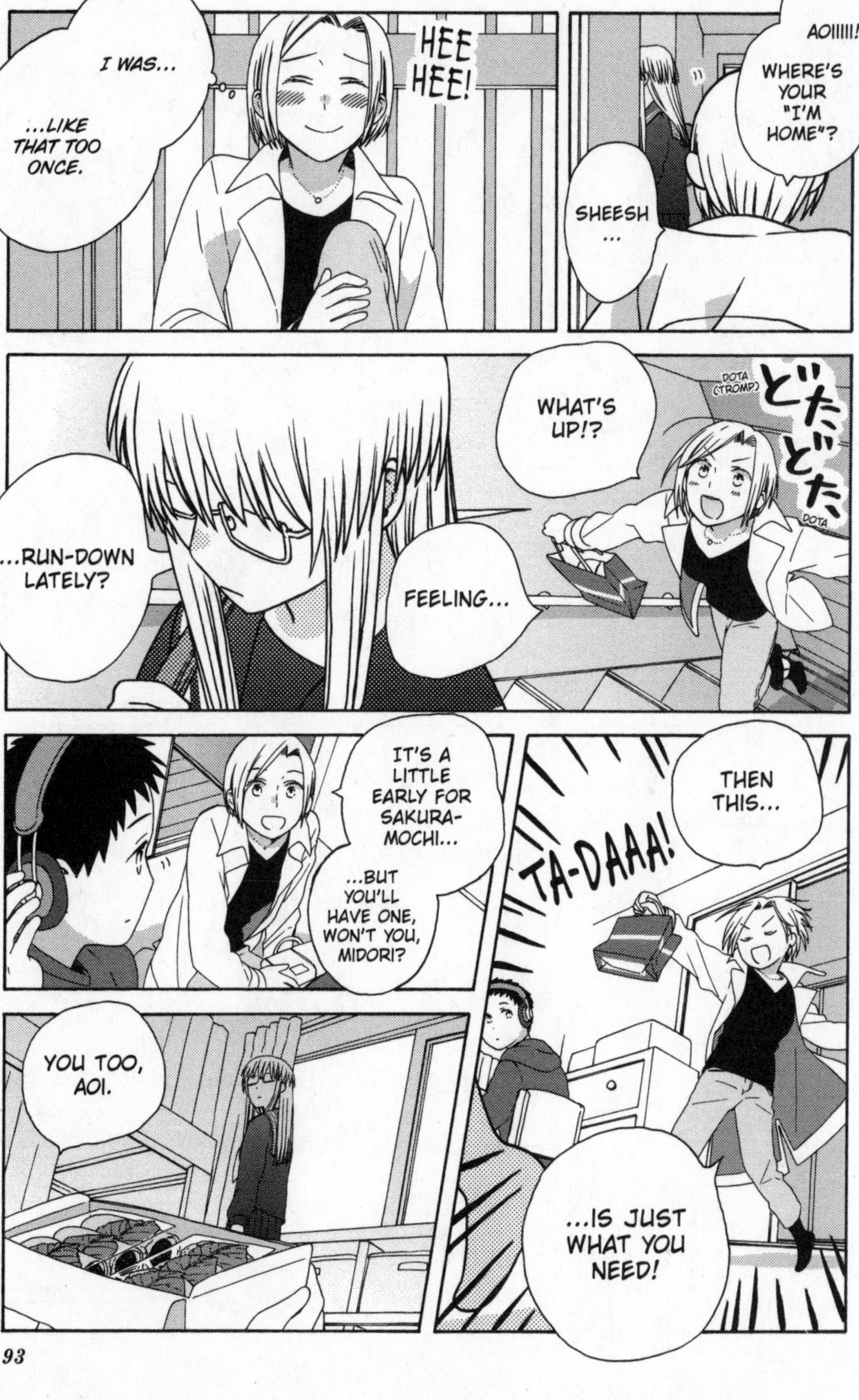
AOIIIII!
WHERE'S YOUR "I'M HOME"?
SHEESH ...
HEE HEE!
I WAS...
...LIKE THAT TOO ONCE.
DOTA (TROMP)
どたどた
DOTA
WHAT'S UP!?
FEELING...
...RUN-DOWN LATELY?
THEN THIS...
TA-DAAA!
...IS JUST WHAT YOU NEED!
IT'S A LITTLE EARLY FOR SAKURA-MOCHI...
...BUT YOU'LL HAVE ONE, WON'T YOU, MIDORI?
YOU TOO, AOI.

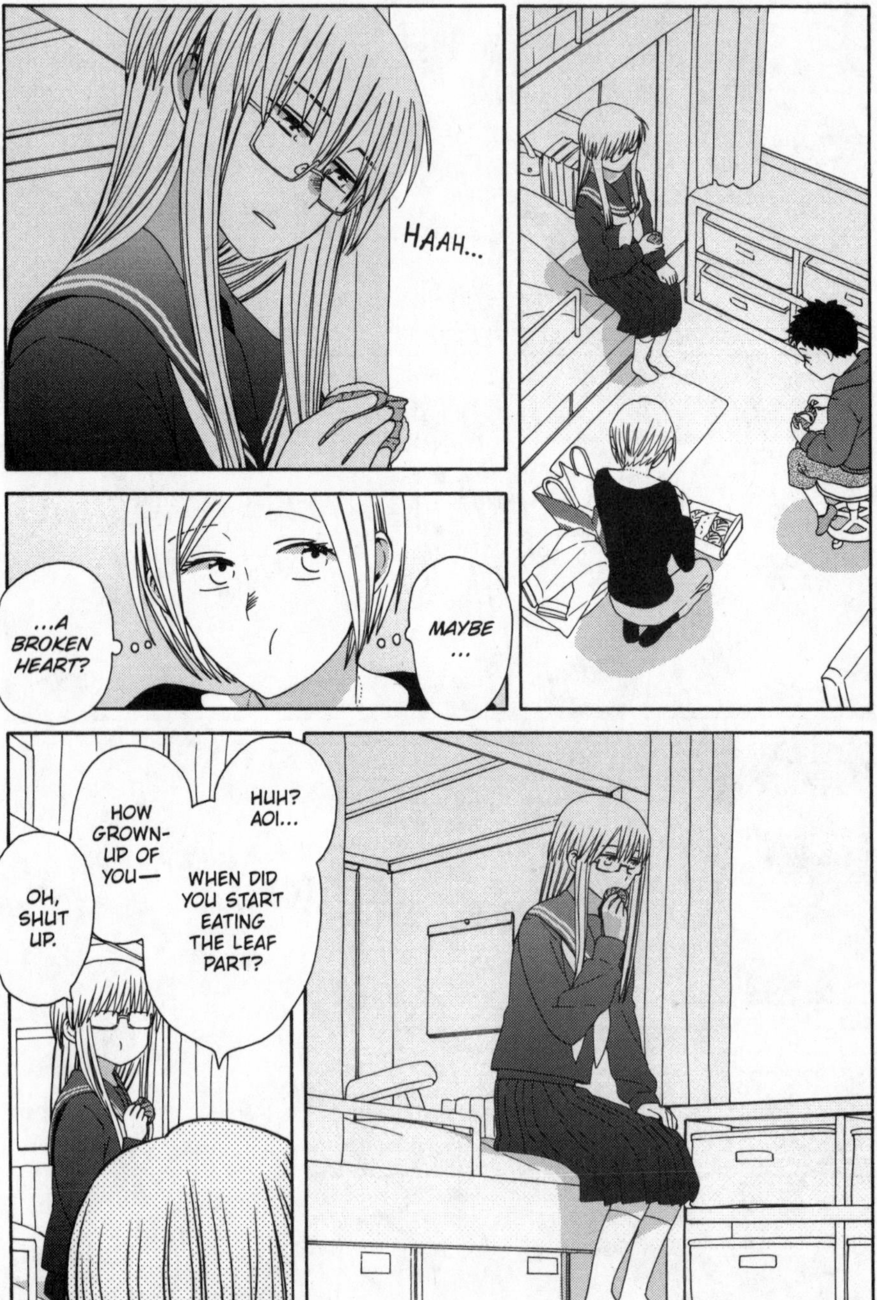
HAAH...
MAYBE ...
...A BROKEN HEART?
HUH? AOI...
WHEN DID YOU START EATING THE LEAF PART?
HOW GROWN-UP OF YOU—
OH, SHUT UP.

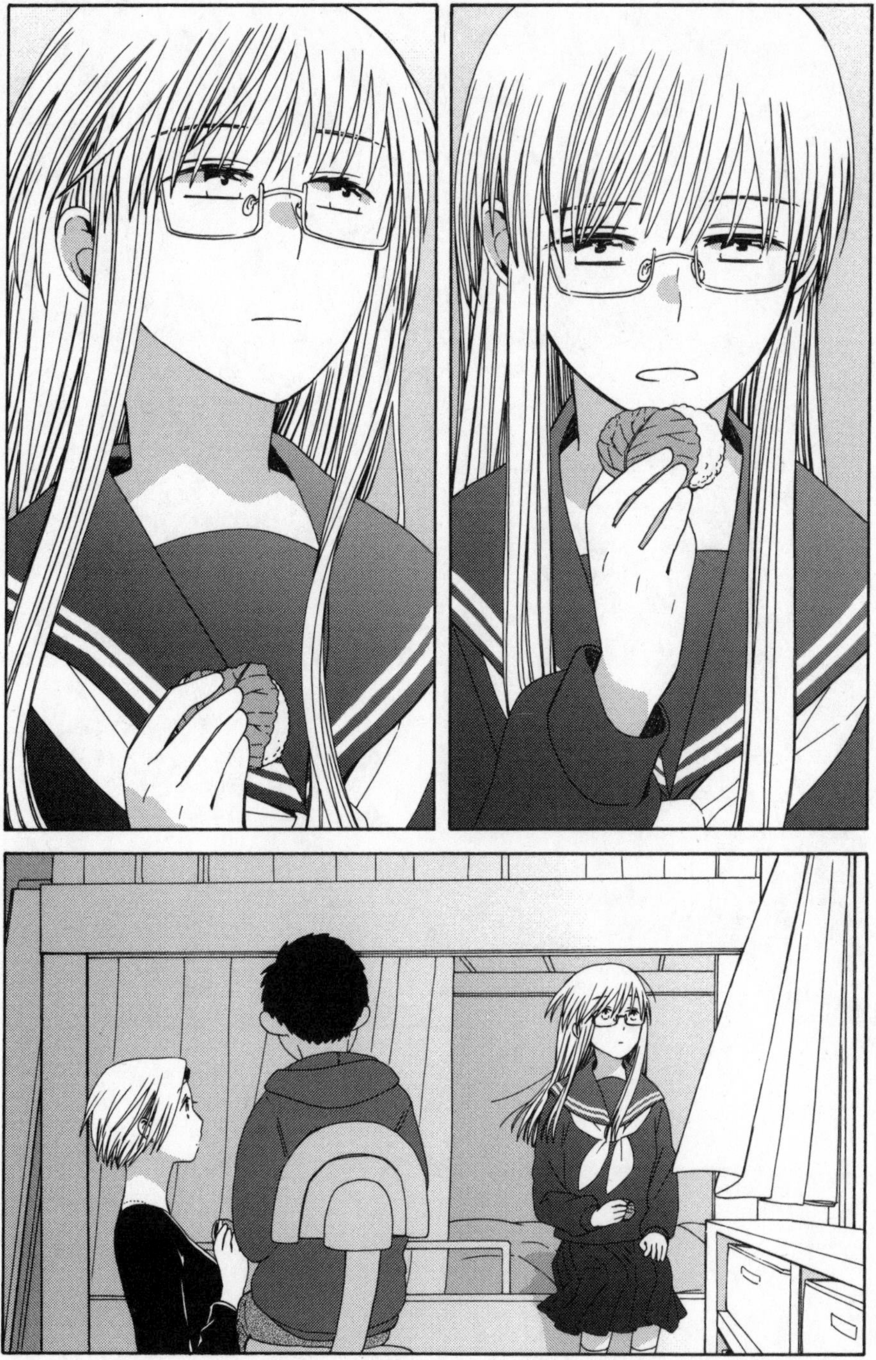

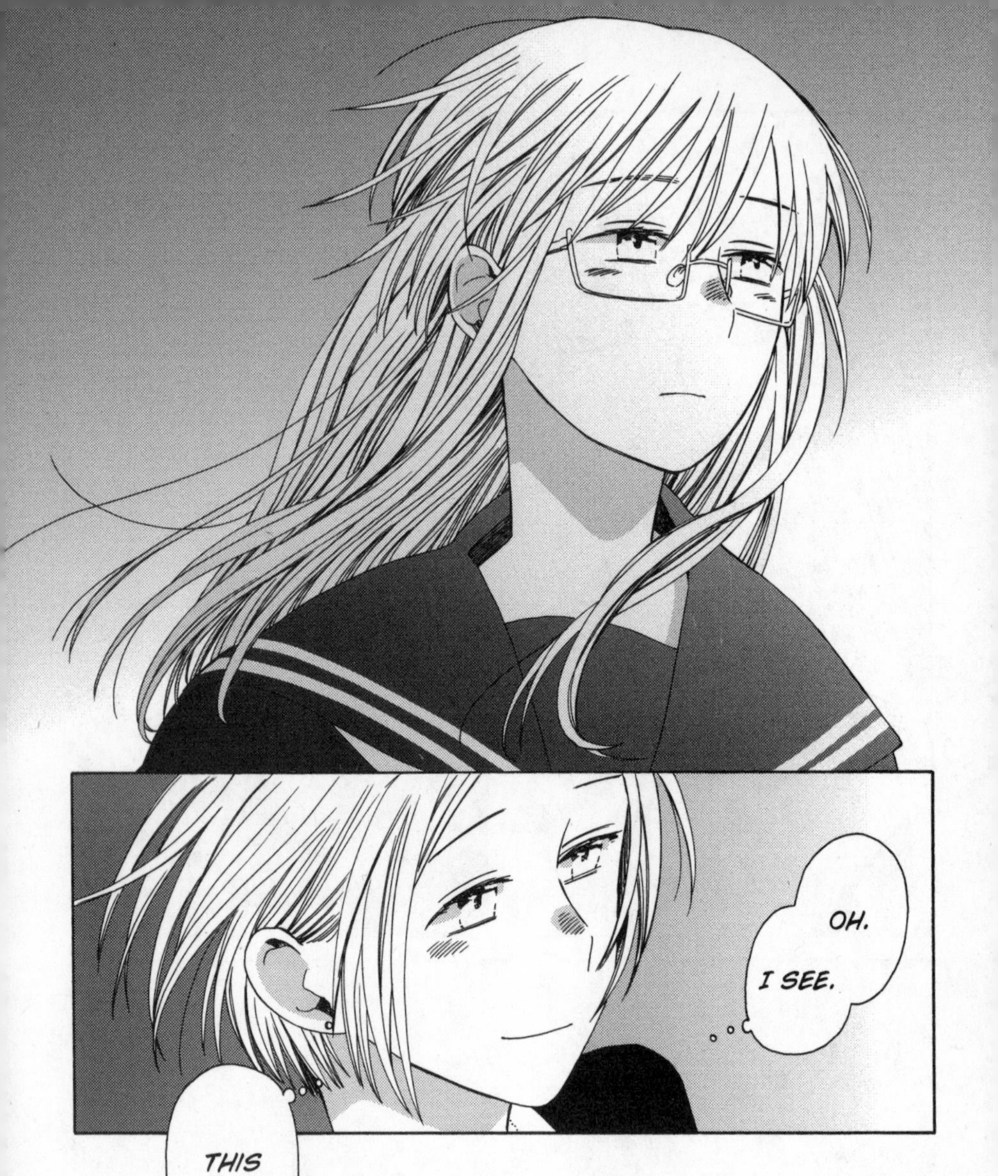
OH. I SEE.
THIS IS......

Fin

Love at Fourteen

[Chapter 49]

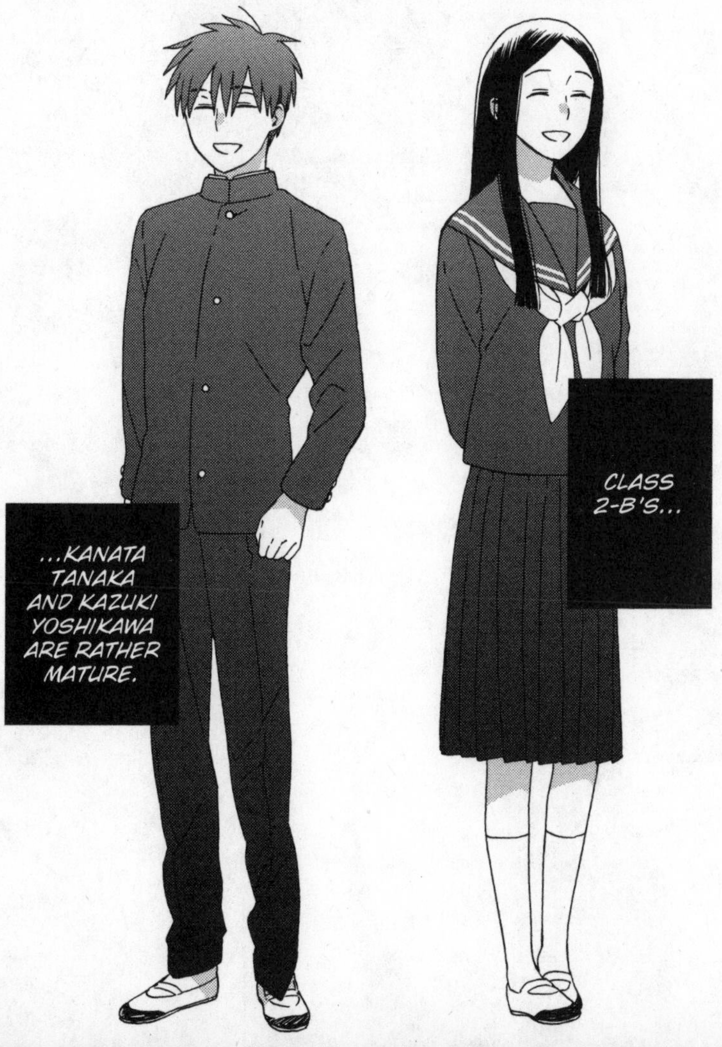
CLASS 2-B'S...
...KANATA TANAKA AND KAZUKI YOSHIKAWA ARE RATHER MATURE.

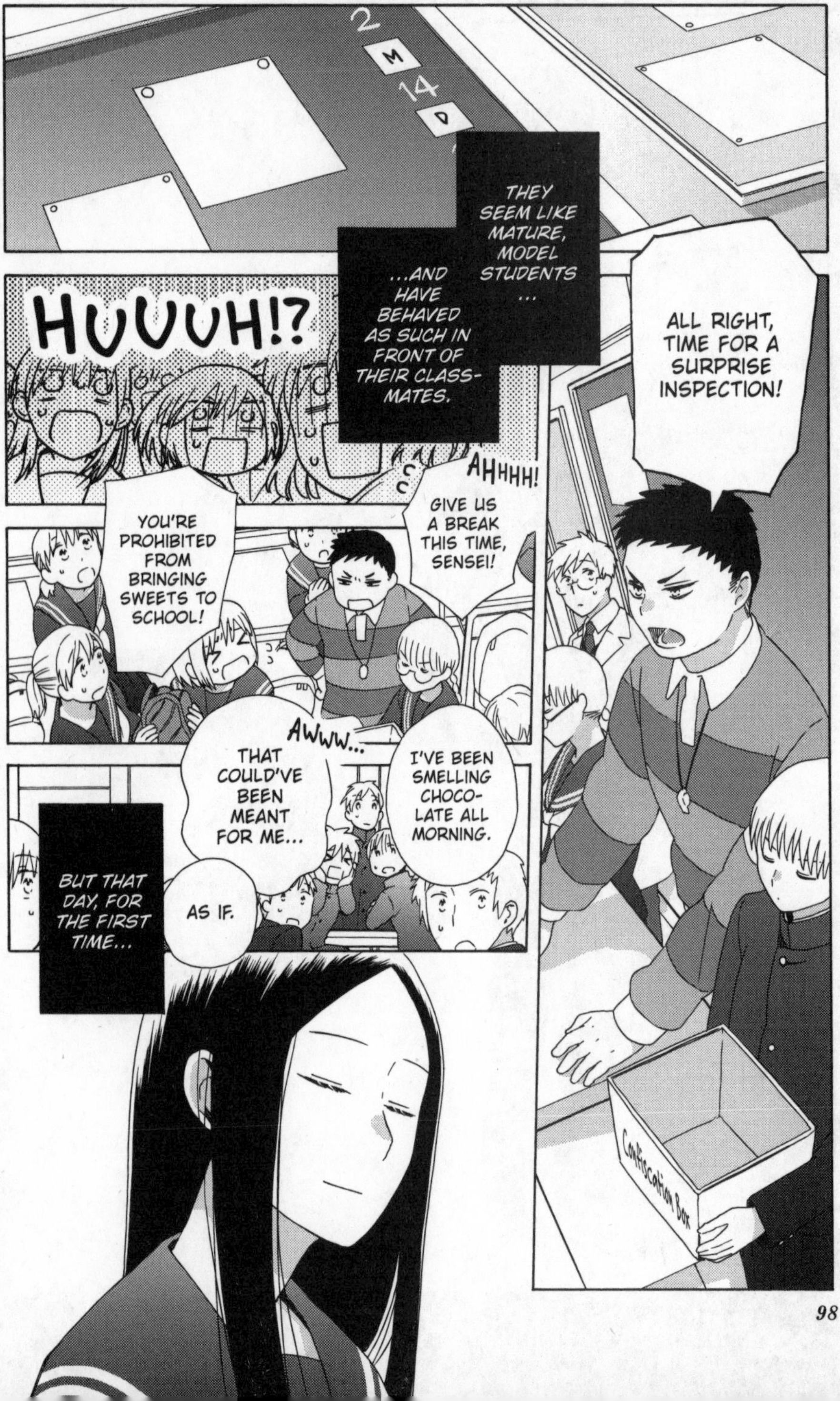
2
M
14
D
THEY SEEM LIKE MATURE, MODEL STUDENTS...
...AND HAVE BEHAVED AS SUCH IN FRONT OF THEIR CLASS-MATES.
ALL RIGHT, TIME FOR A SURPRISE INSPECTION!
Confiscation Box
HUUUH!?
AHHHH!
GIVE US A BREAK THIS TIME, SENSEI!
YOU'RE PROHIBITED FROM BRINGING SWEETS TO SCHOOL!
I'VE BEEN SMELLING CHOCO-LATE ALL MORNING.
AWWW...
THAT COULD'VE BEEN MEANT FOR ME...
AS IF.
BUT THAT DAY, FOR THE FIRST TIME...

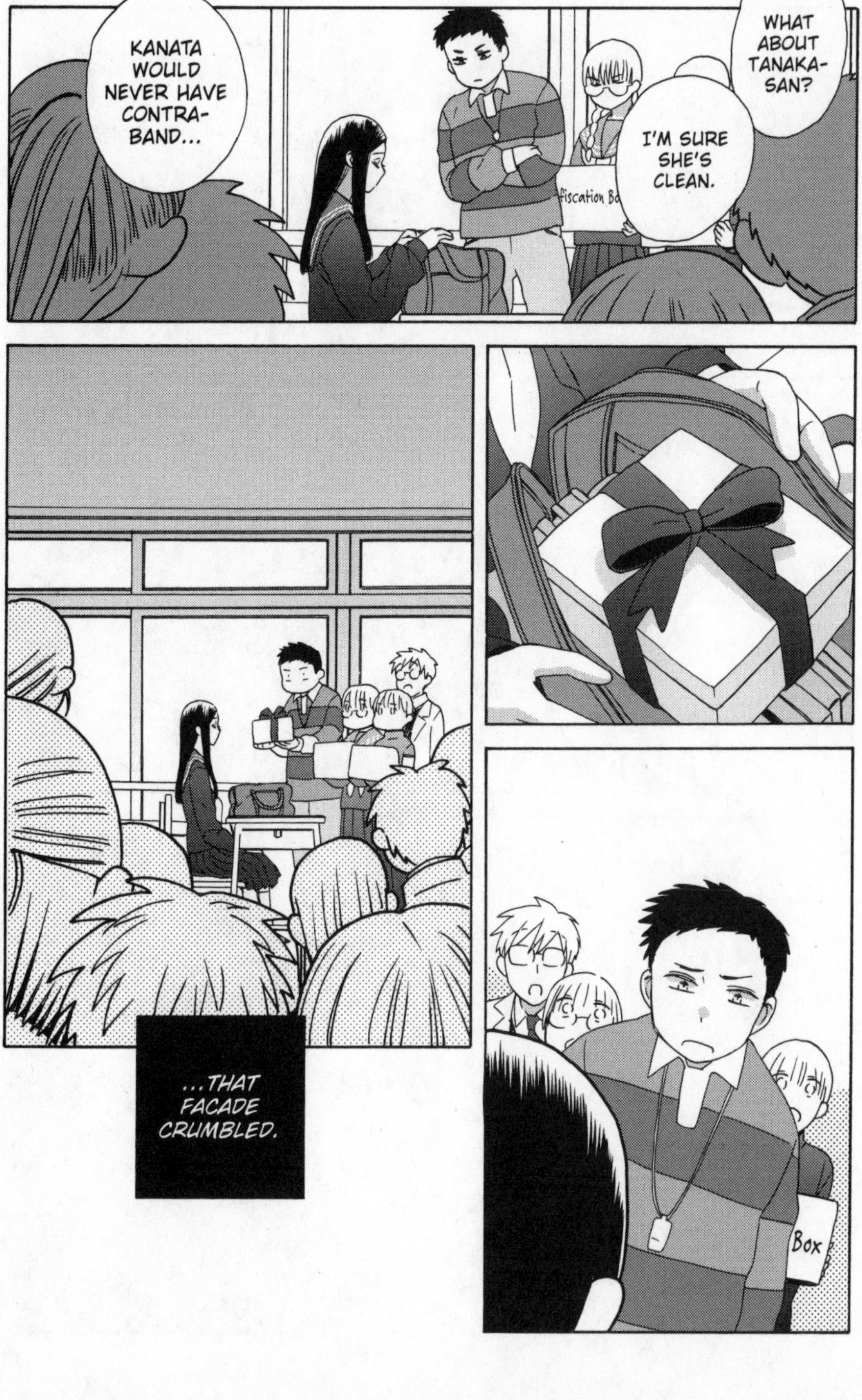
WHAT ABOUT TANAKA-SAN?
I'M SURE SHE'S CLEAN.
fiscation Bo
KANATA WOULD NEVER HAVE CONTRA-BAND...
Box
...THAT FACADE CRUMBLED.

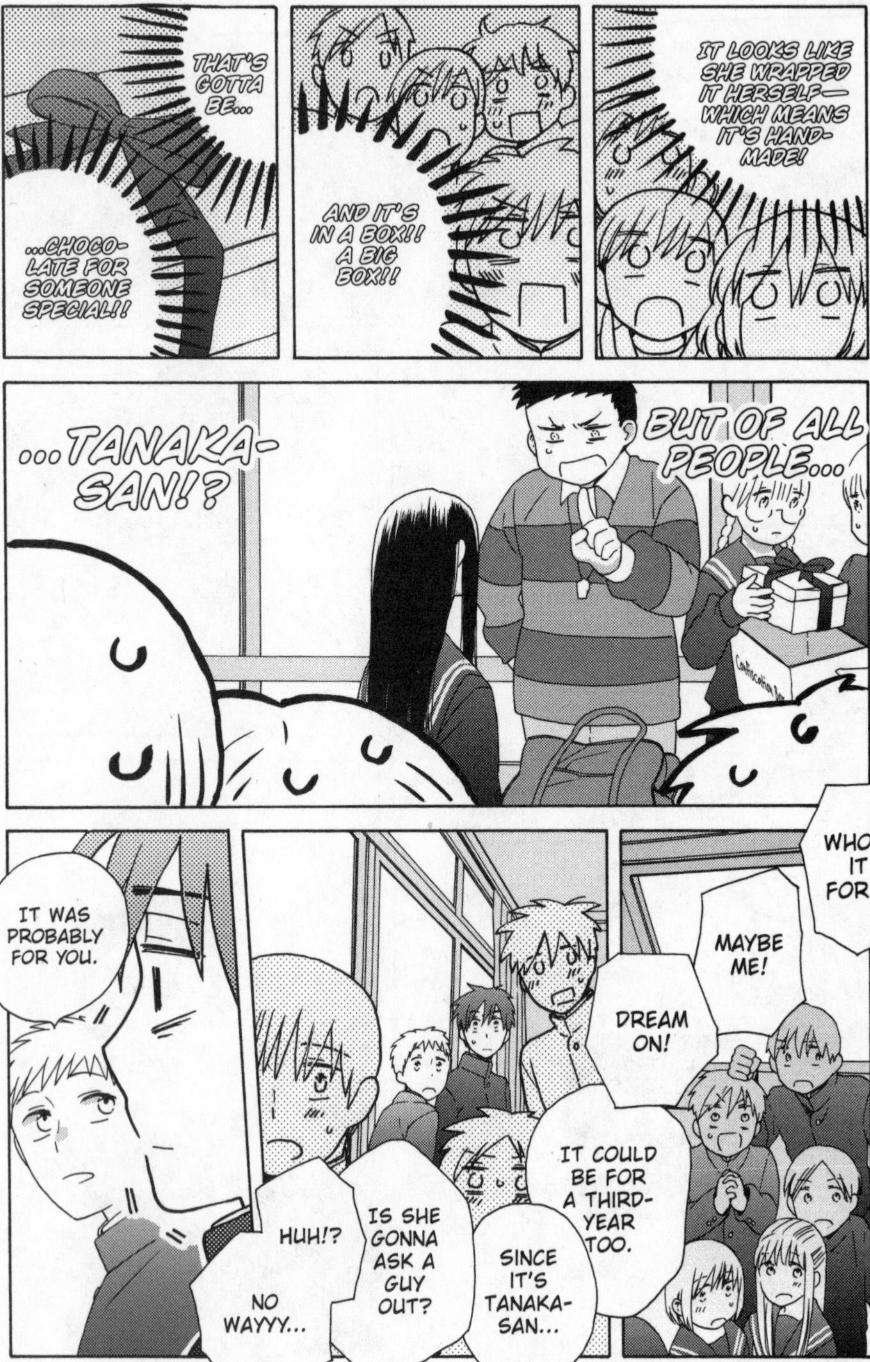
IT LOOKS LIKE SHE WRAPPED IT HERSELF—WHICH MEANS IT'S HAND-MADE!
AND IT'S IN A BOX!! A BIG BOX!!
THAT'S GOTTA BE...
...CHOCO-LATE FOR SOMEONE SPECIAL!!
BUT OF ALL PEOPLE...
...TANAKA-SAN!?
WHO'S IT FOR!?
MAYBE ME!
DREAM ON!
IT COULD BE FOR A THIRD-YEAR TOO.
SINCE IT'S TANAKA-SAN...
IS SHE GONNA ASK A GUY OUT?
HUH!?
NO WAYYY...
IT WAS PROBABLY FOR YOU.

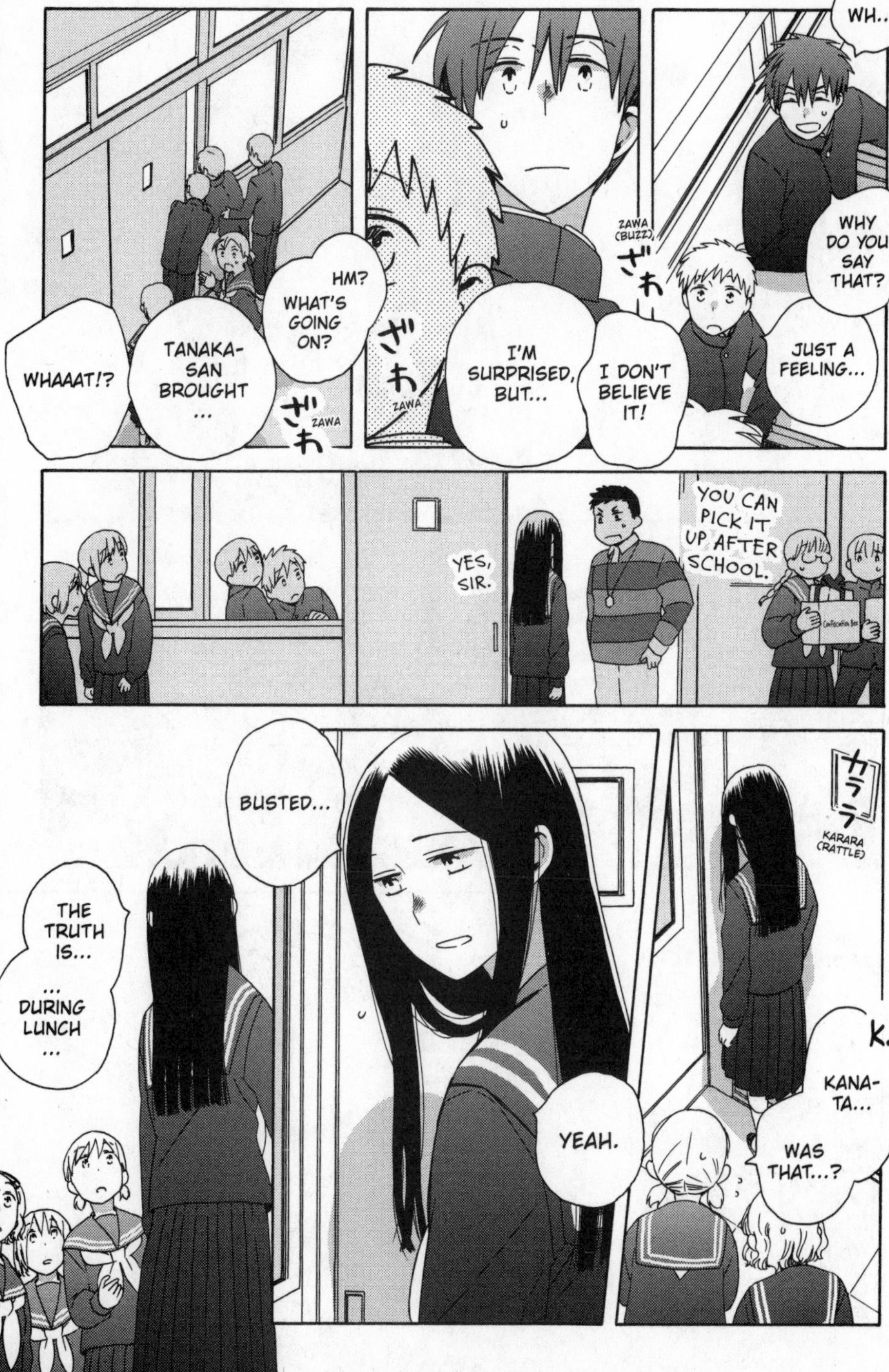
WH...
WHY DO YOU SAY THAT?
ZAWA (BUZZ) ざわ
JUST A FEELING...
I DON'T BELIEVE IT!
HM? WHAT'S GOING ON?
I'M SURPRISED, BUT...
ざわ ZAWA
TANAKA-SAN BROUGHT ...
ざわ ZAWA
WHAAAT!?
YOU CAN PICK IT UP AFTER SCHOOL.
YES, SIR.
カララ KARARA (RATTLE)
K...
KANA-TA...
WAS THAT...?
BUSTED...
YEAH.
THE TRUTH IS...
... DURING LUNCH ...

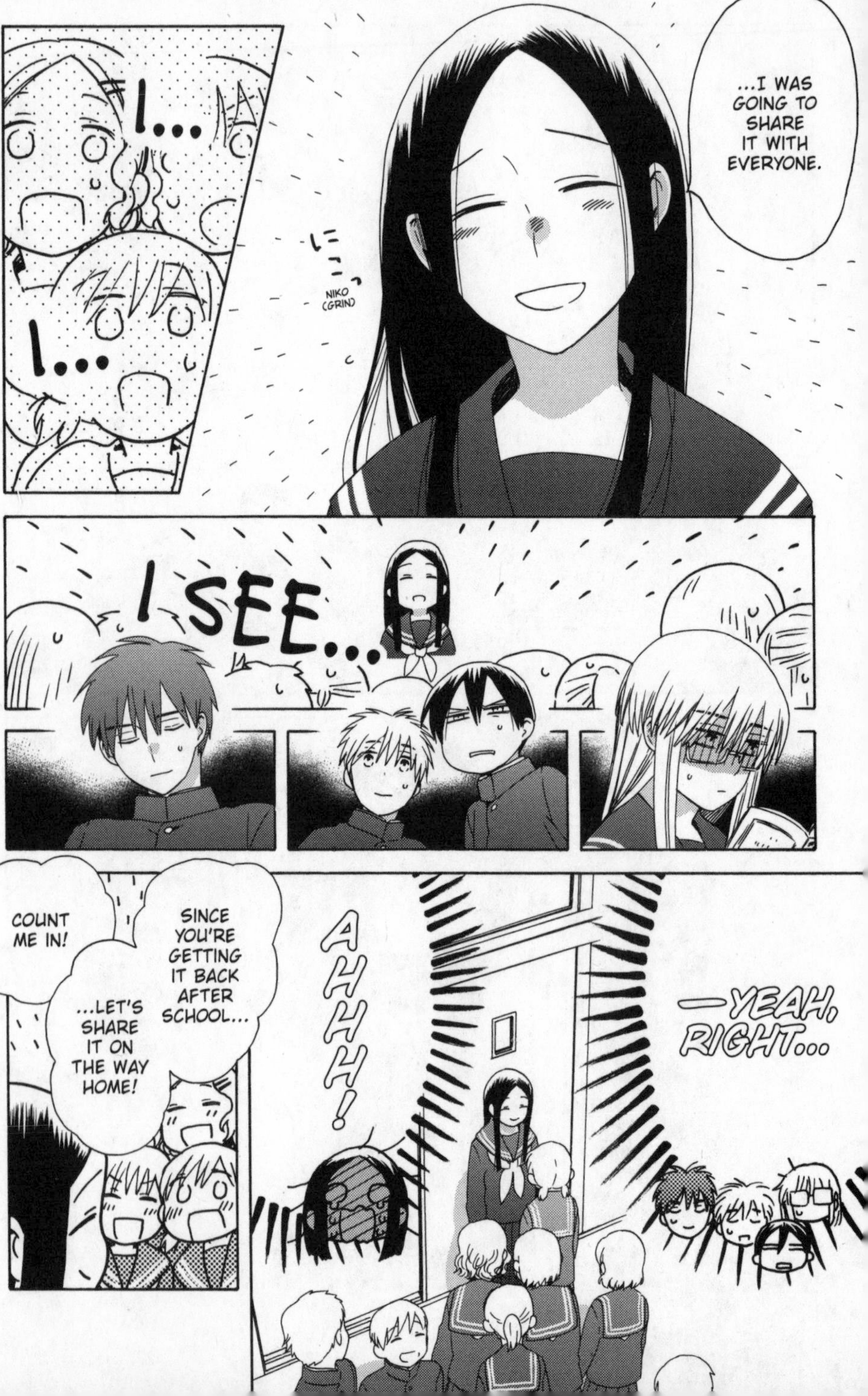
...I WAS GOING TO SHARE IT WITH EVERYONE.
NIKO (GRIN)
I... I...
I SEE...
—YEAH, RIGHT...
AHHHH!
SINCE YOU'RE GETTING IT BACK AFTER SCHOOL...
COUNT ME IN!
...LET'S SHARE IT ON THE WAY HOME!

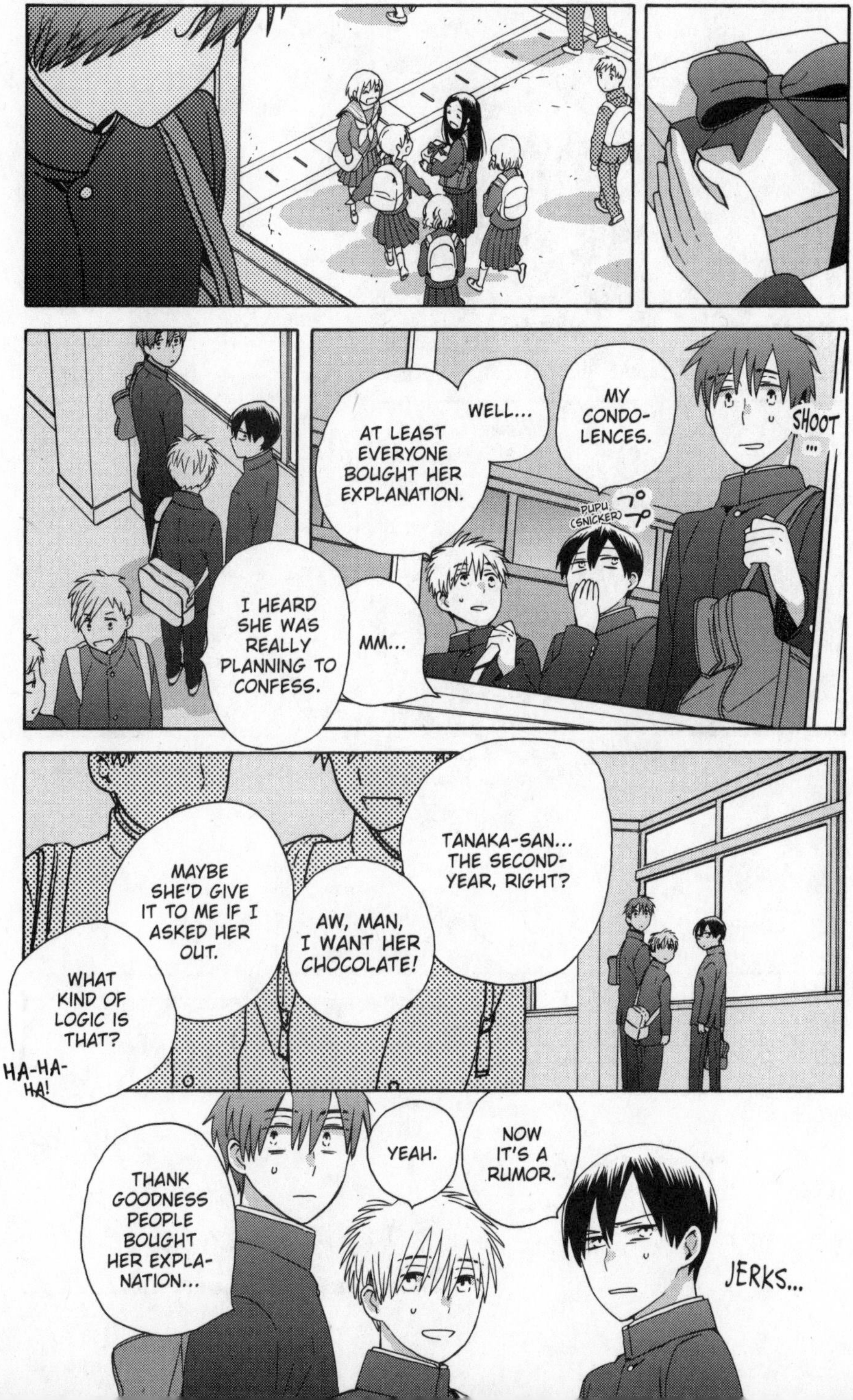
SHOOT...
MY CONDOLENCES.
WELL... AT LEAST EVERYONE BOUGHT HER EXPLANATION.
PUPU (SNICKER)
MM...
I HEARD SHE WAS REALLY PLANNING TO CONFESS.
TANAKA-SAN... THE SECOND-YEAR, RIGHT?
AW, MAN, I WANT HER CHOCOLATE!
MAYBE SHE'D GIVE IT TO ME IF I ASKED HER OUT.
WHAT KIND OF LOGIC IS THAT?
HA-HA-HA!
JERKS...
NOW IT'S A RUMOR.
YEAH.
THANK GOODNESS PEOPLE BOUGHT HER EXPLANATION...

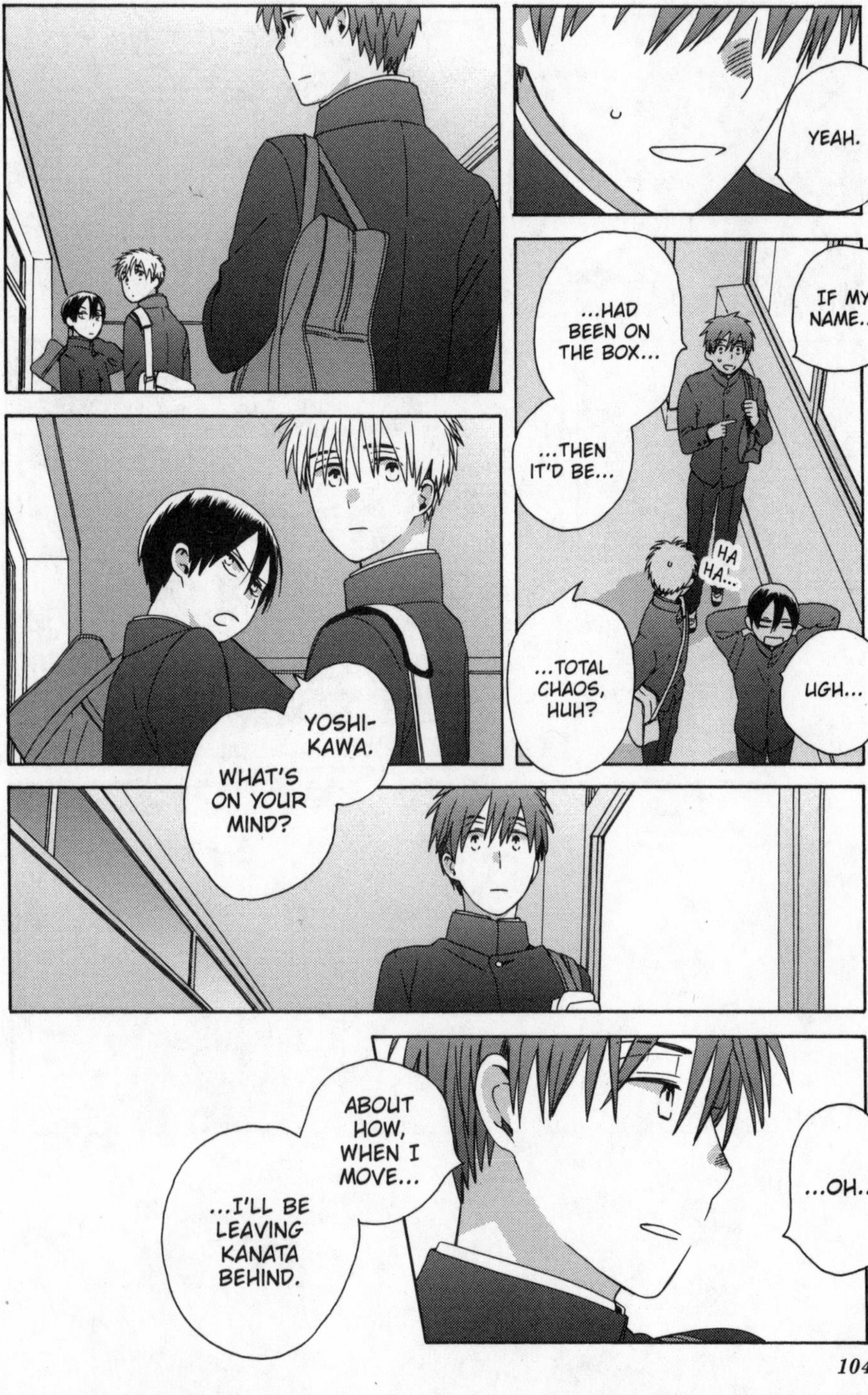
YEAH.
IF MY NAME...
...HAD BEEN ON THE BOX...
...THEN IT'D BE...
HA HA...
...TOTAL CHAOS, HUH?
UGH...
YOSHIKAWA.
WHAT'S ON YOUR MIND?
...OH...
ABOUT HOW, WHEN I MOVE...
...I'LL BE LEAVING KANATA BEHIND.

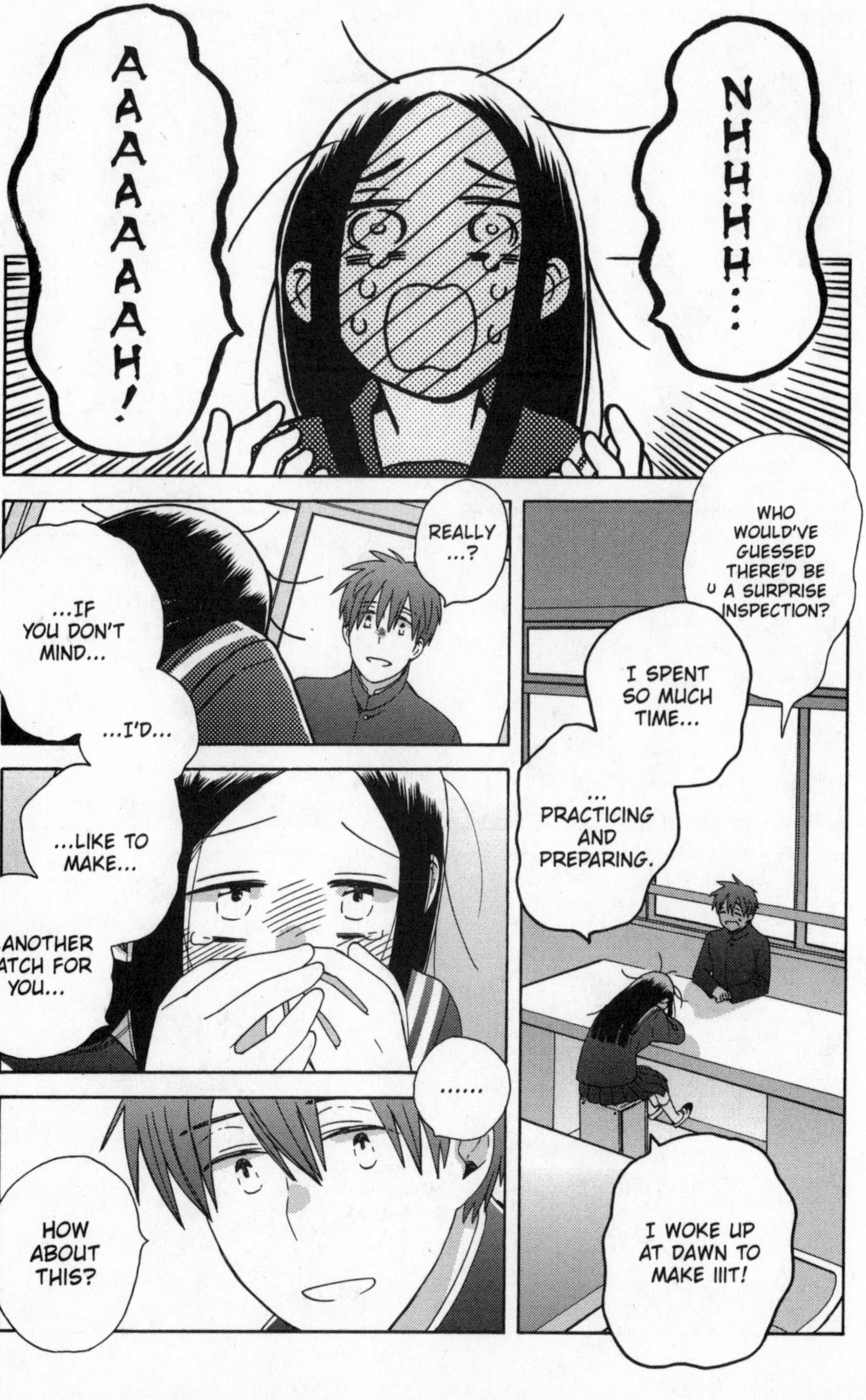
NHHHH...
AAAAAAAH!
WHO WOULD'VE GUESSED THERE'D BE A SURPRISE INSPECTION?
I SPENT SO MUCH TIME...
...PRACTICING AND PREPARING.
I WOKE UP AT DAWN TO MAKE IIIT!
REALLY...?
...IF YOU DON'T MIND...
...I'D...
...LIKE TO MAKE...
...ANOTHER BATCH FOR YOU...
......
HOW ABOUT THIS?

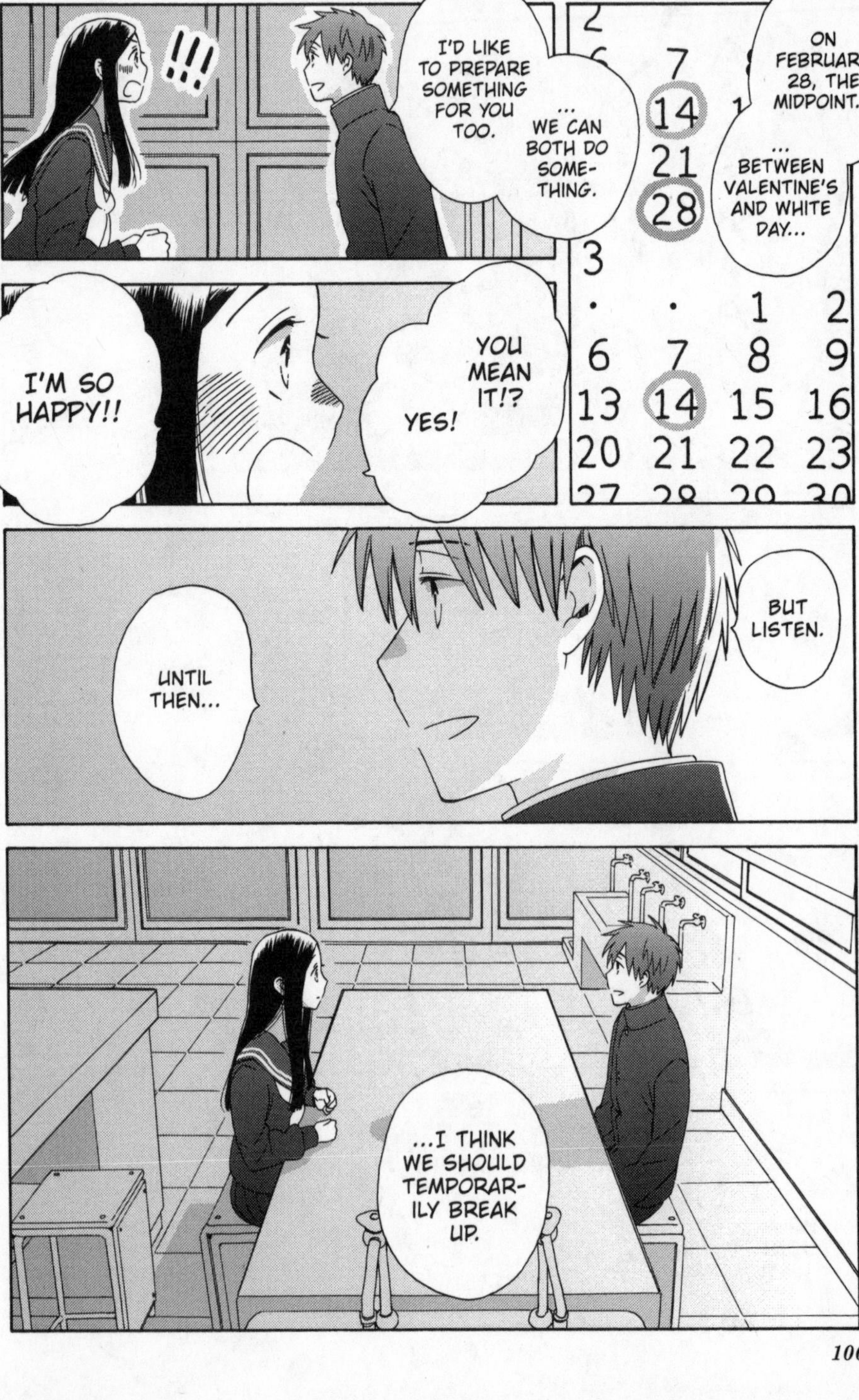
ON FEBRUARY 28, THE MIDPOINT...
...BETWEEN VALENTINE'S AND WHITE DAY...
I'D LIKE TO PREPARE SOMETHING FOR YOU TOO.
...WE CAN BOTH DO SOME-THING.
!!!
YOU MEAN IT!?
YES!
I'M SO HAPPY!!
BUT LISTEN.
UNTIL THEN...
...I THINK WE SHOULD TEMPORAR-ILY BREAK UP.

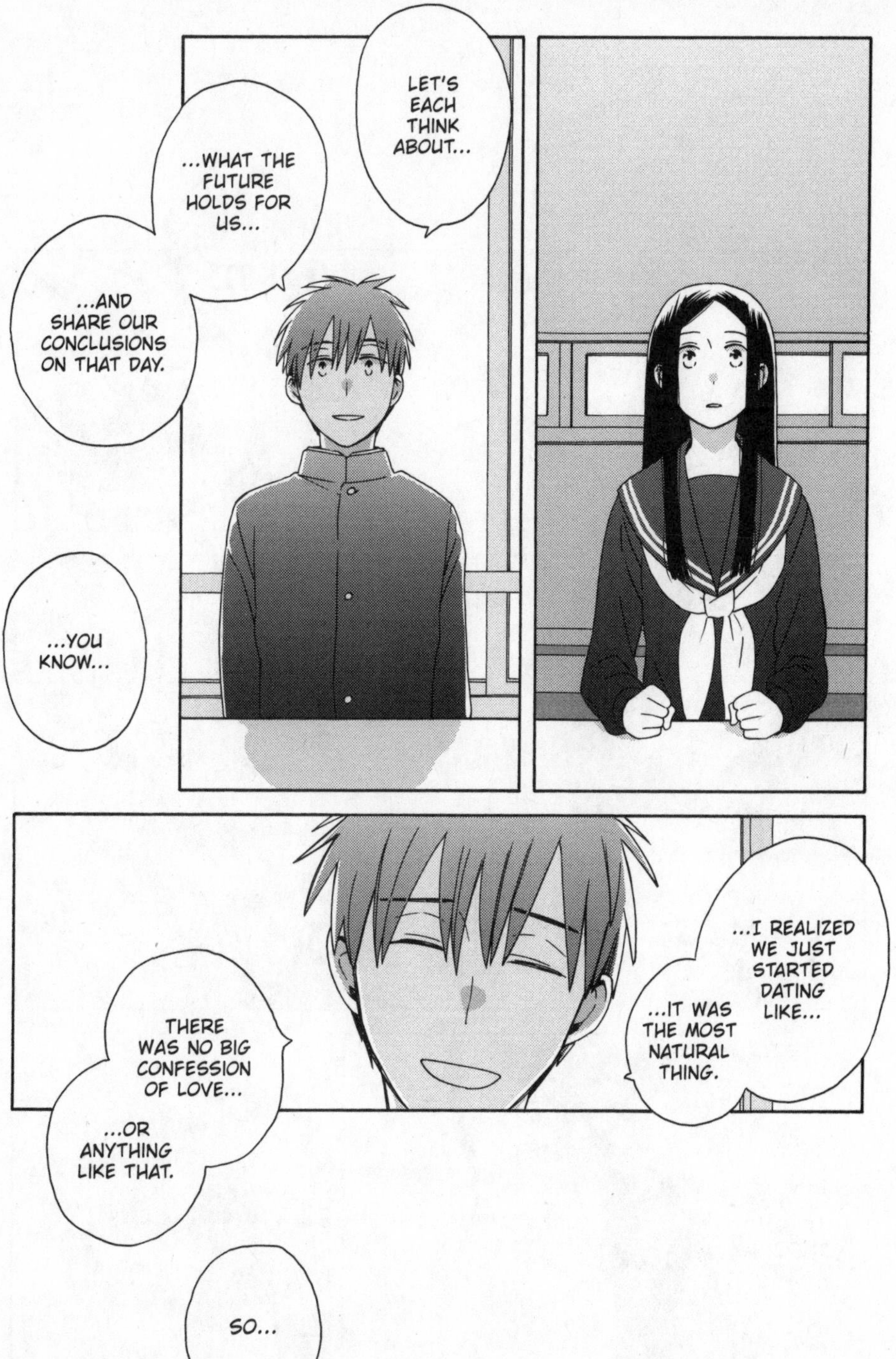
LET'S EACH THINK ABOUT...
...WHAT THE FUTURE HOLDS FOR US...
...AND SHARE OUR CONCLUSIONS ON THAT DAY.
...YOU KNOW...
...I REALIZED WE JUST STARTED DATING LIKE...
...IT WAS THE MOST NATURAL THING.
THERE WAS NO BIG CONFESSION OF LOVE...
...OR ANYTHING LIKE THAT.
SO...

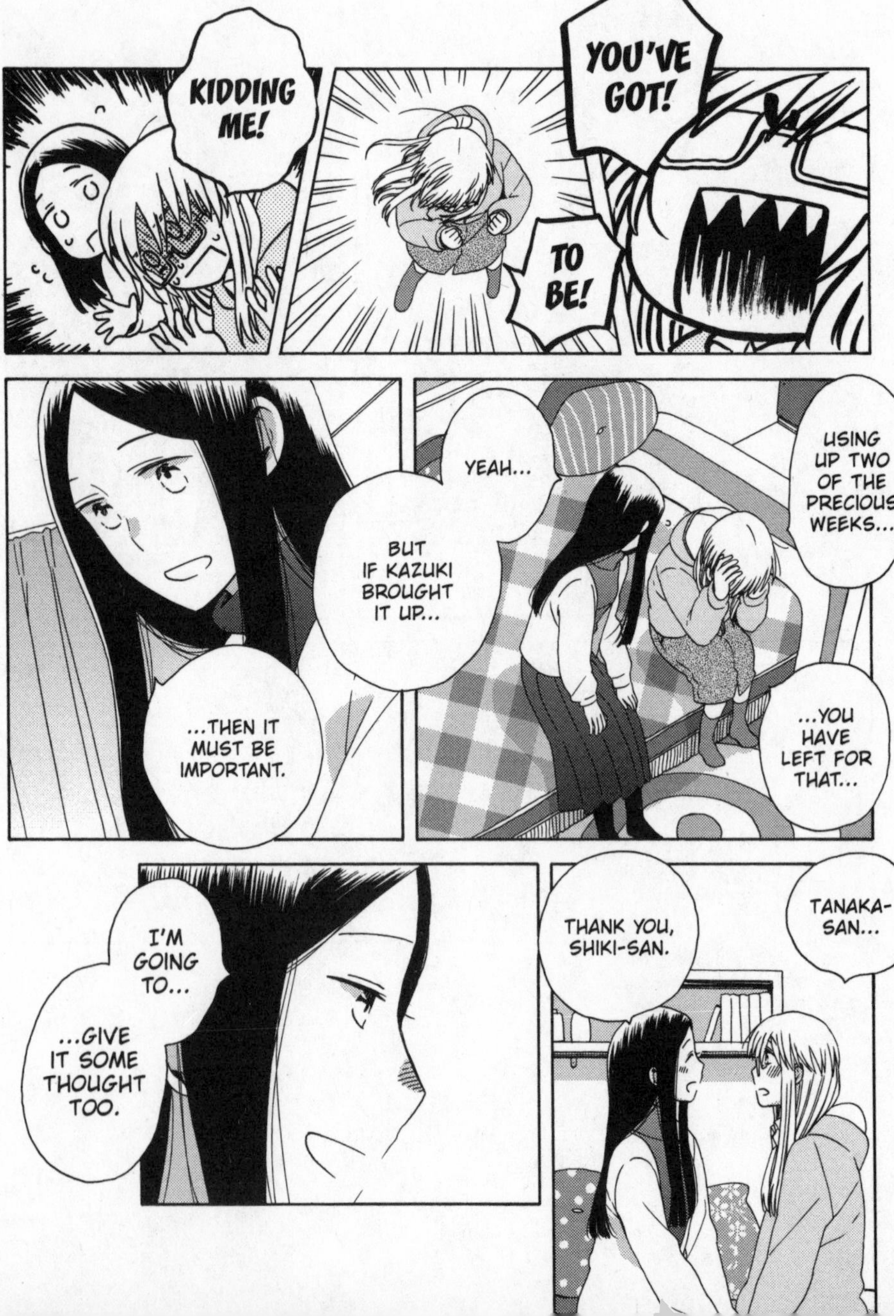
YOU'VE GOT!
TO BE!
KIDDING ME!
USING UP TWO OF THE PRECIOUS WEEKS...
...YOU HAVE LEFT FOR THAT...
YEAH...
BUT IF KAZUKI BROUGHT IT UP...
...THEN IT MUST BE IMPORTANT.
TANAKA-SAN...
THANK YOU, SHIKI-SAN.
I'M GOING TO...
...GIVE IT SOME THOUGHT TOO.

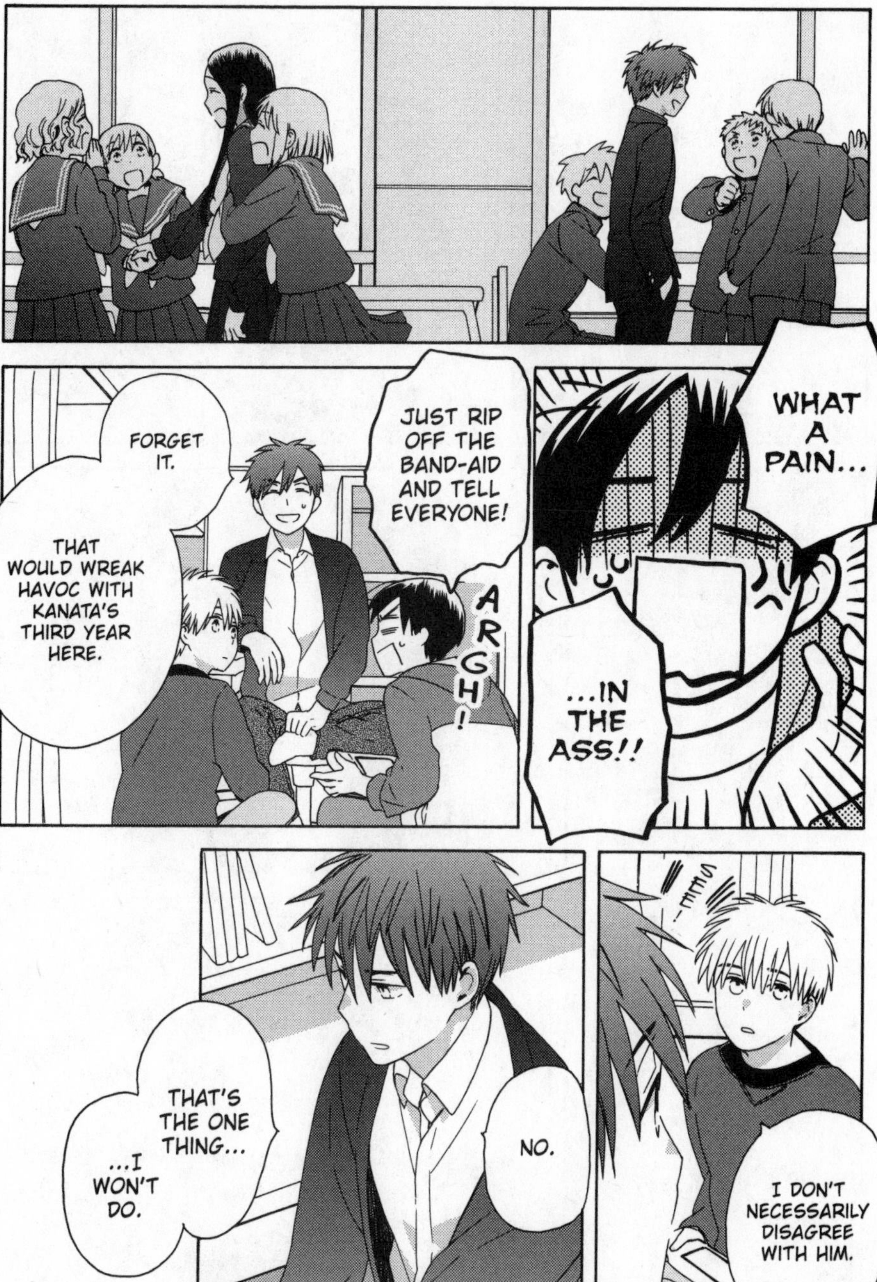
WHAT A PAIN...
...IN THE ASS!!
JUST RIP OFF THE BAND-AID AND TELL EVERYONE!
ARGH!
FORGET IT.
THAT WOULD WREAK HAVOC WITH KANATA'S THIRD YEAR HERE.
SEE!
I DON'T NECESSARILY DISAGREE WITH HIM.
NO.
THAT'S THE ONE THING...
...I WON'T DO.

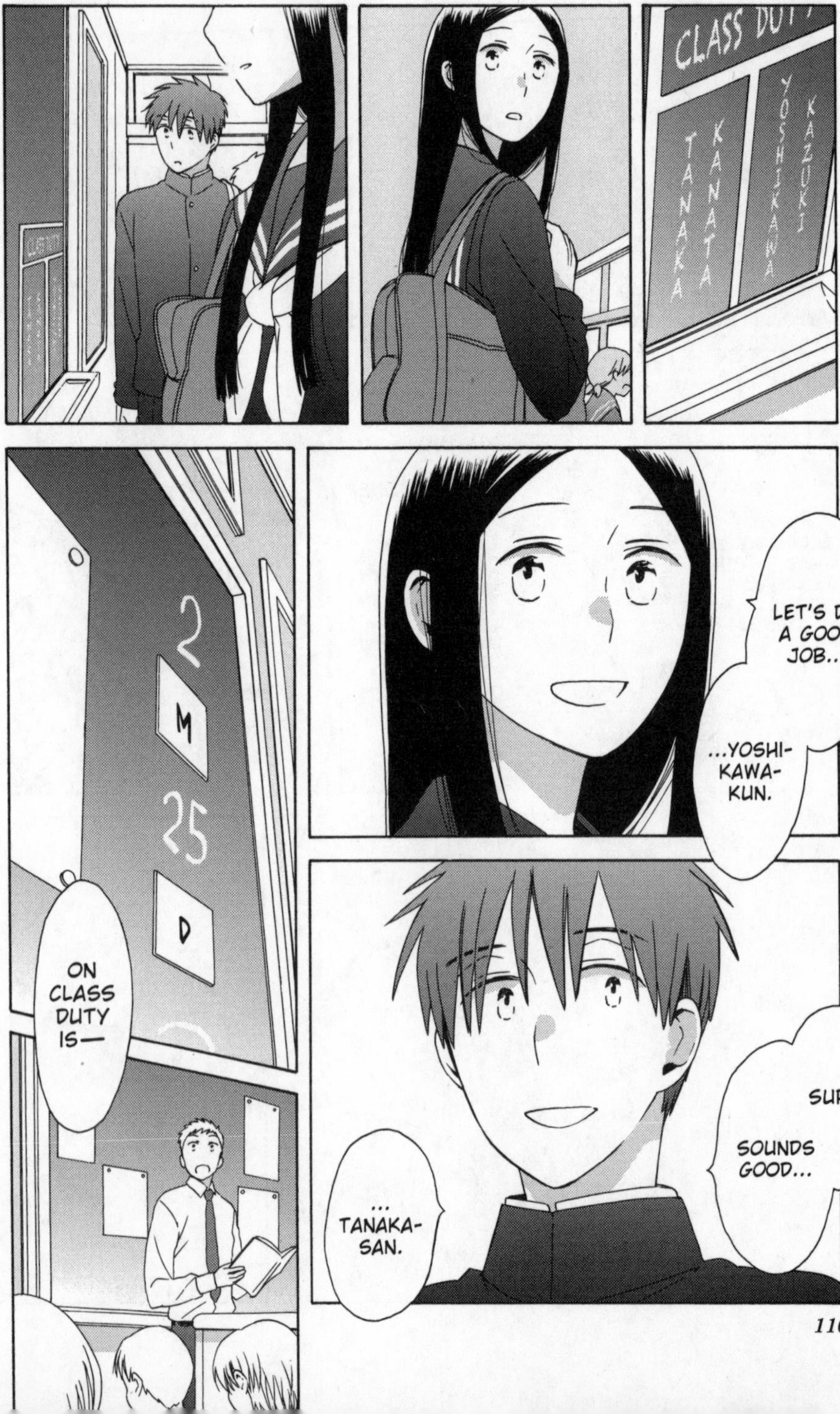
CLASS DUT
TANAKA KANATA
YOSHIKAWA KAZUKI
LET'S DO A GOOD JOB...
...YOSHI-KAWA-KUN.
SURE.
SOUNDS GOOD...
... TANAKA-SAN.
2 M 25 D
ON CLASS DUTY IS—

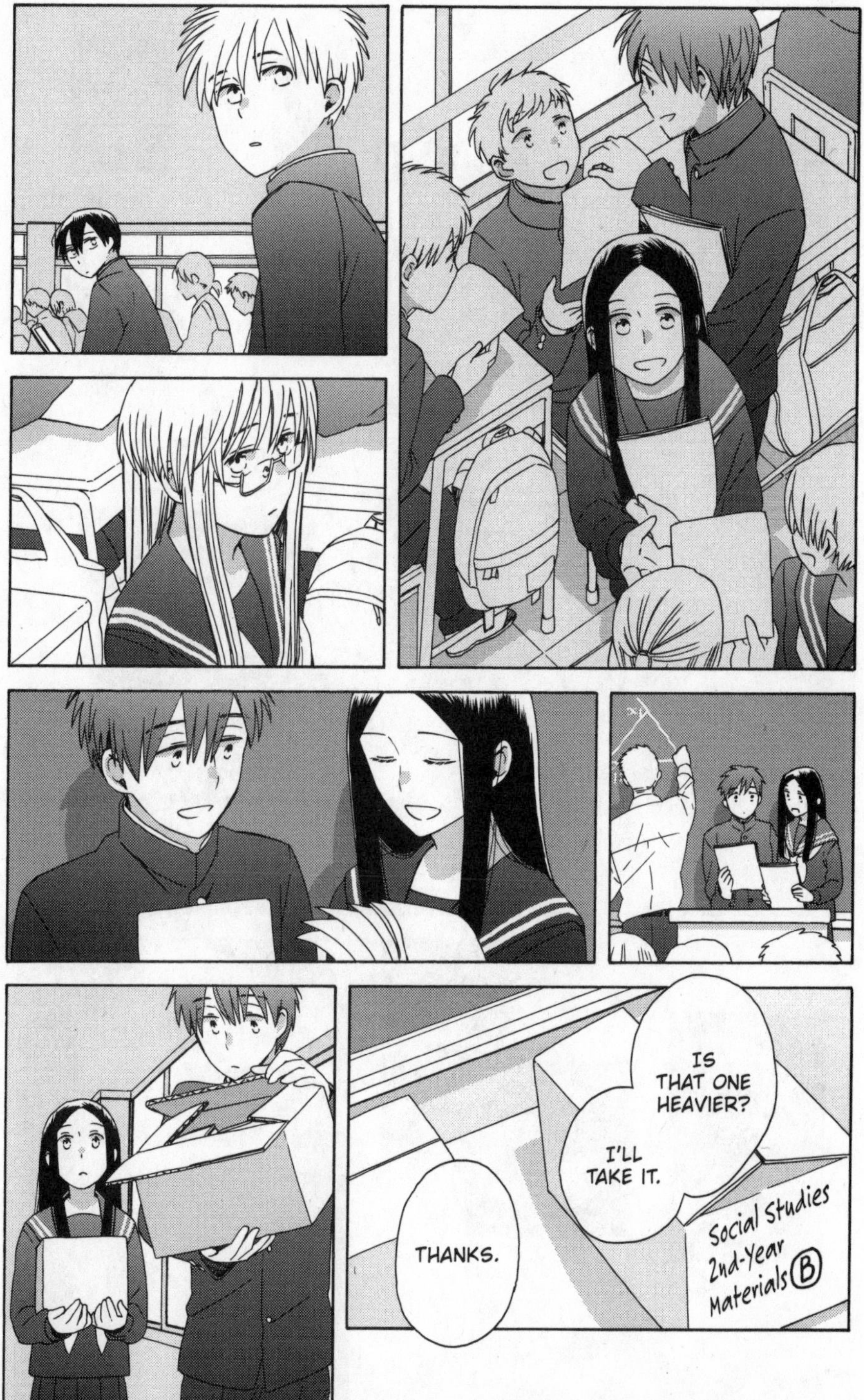
IS THAT ONE HEAVIER?
I'LL TAKE IT.
Social Studies 2nd-Year Materials (B)
THANKS.

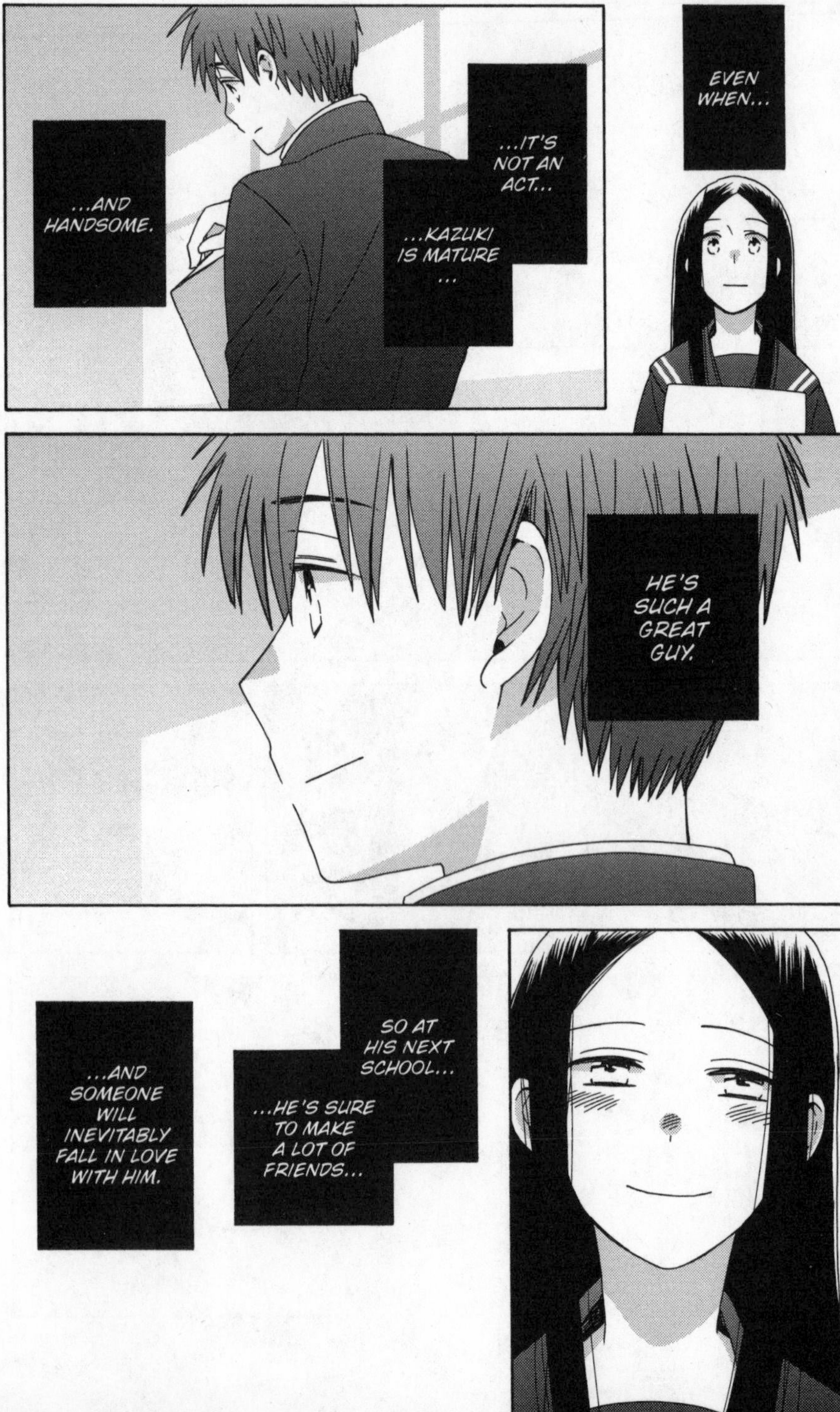
EVEN WHEN...
...IT'S NOT AN ACT...
...KAZUKI IS MATURE ...
...AND HANDSOME.
HE'S SUCH A GREAT GUY.
SO AT HIS NEXT SCHOOL...
...HE'S SURE TO MAKE A LOT OF FRIENDS...
...AND SOMEONE WILL INEVITABLY FALL IN LOVE WITH HIM.

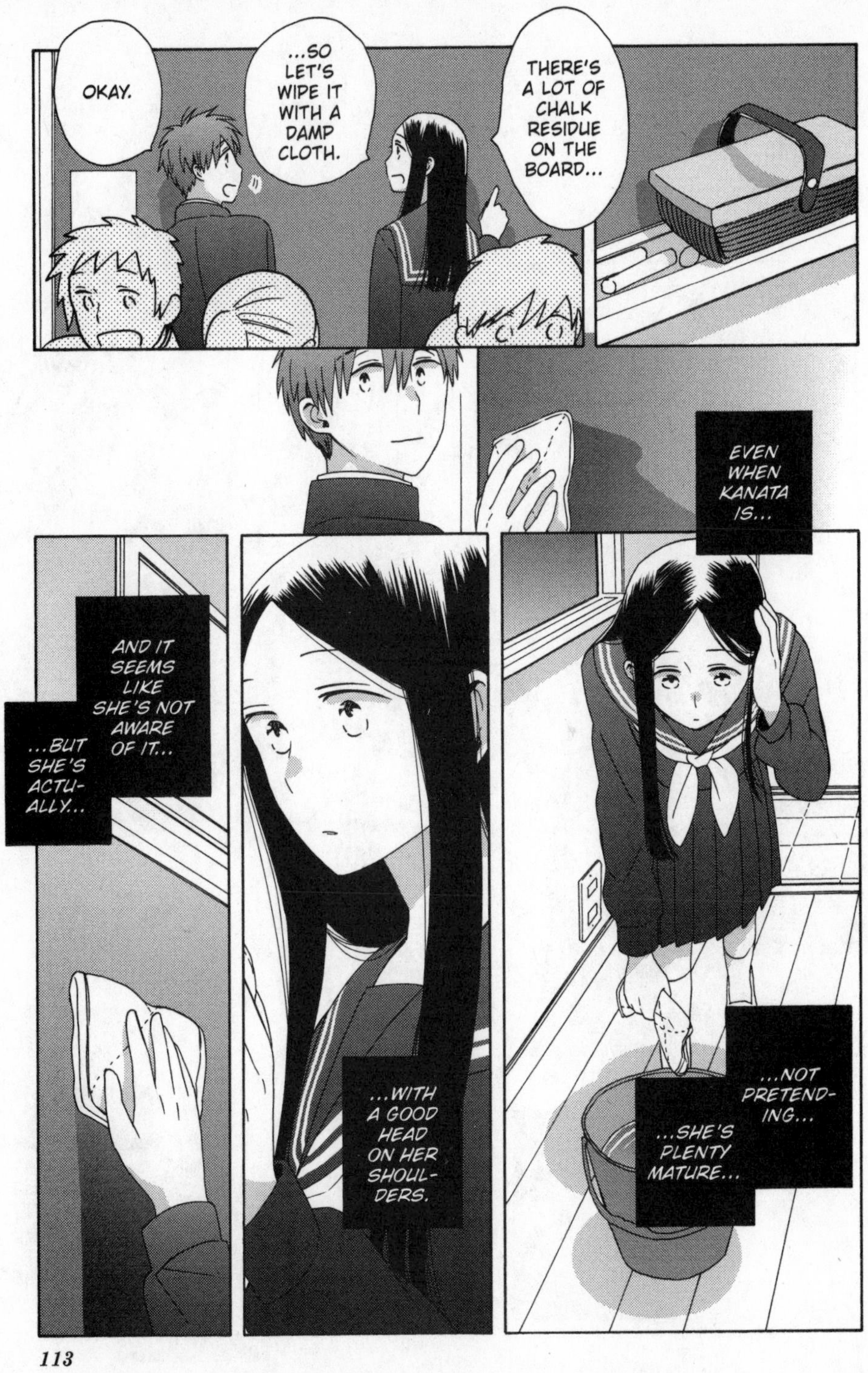
THERE'S A LOT OF CHALK RESIDUE ON THE BOARD...
...SO LET'S WIPE IT WITH A DAMP CLOTH.
OKAY.
EVEN WHEN KANATA IS...
...NOT PRETEND-ING...
...SHE'S PLENTY MATURE...
...WITH A GOOD HEAD ON HER SHOUL-DERS.
AND IT SEEMS LIKE SHE'S NOT AWARE OF IT...
...BUT SHE'S ACTU-ALLY...

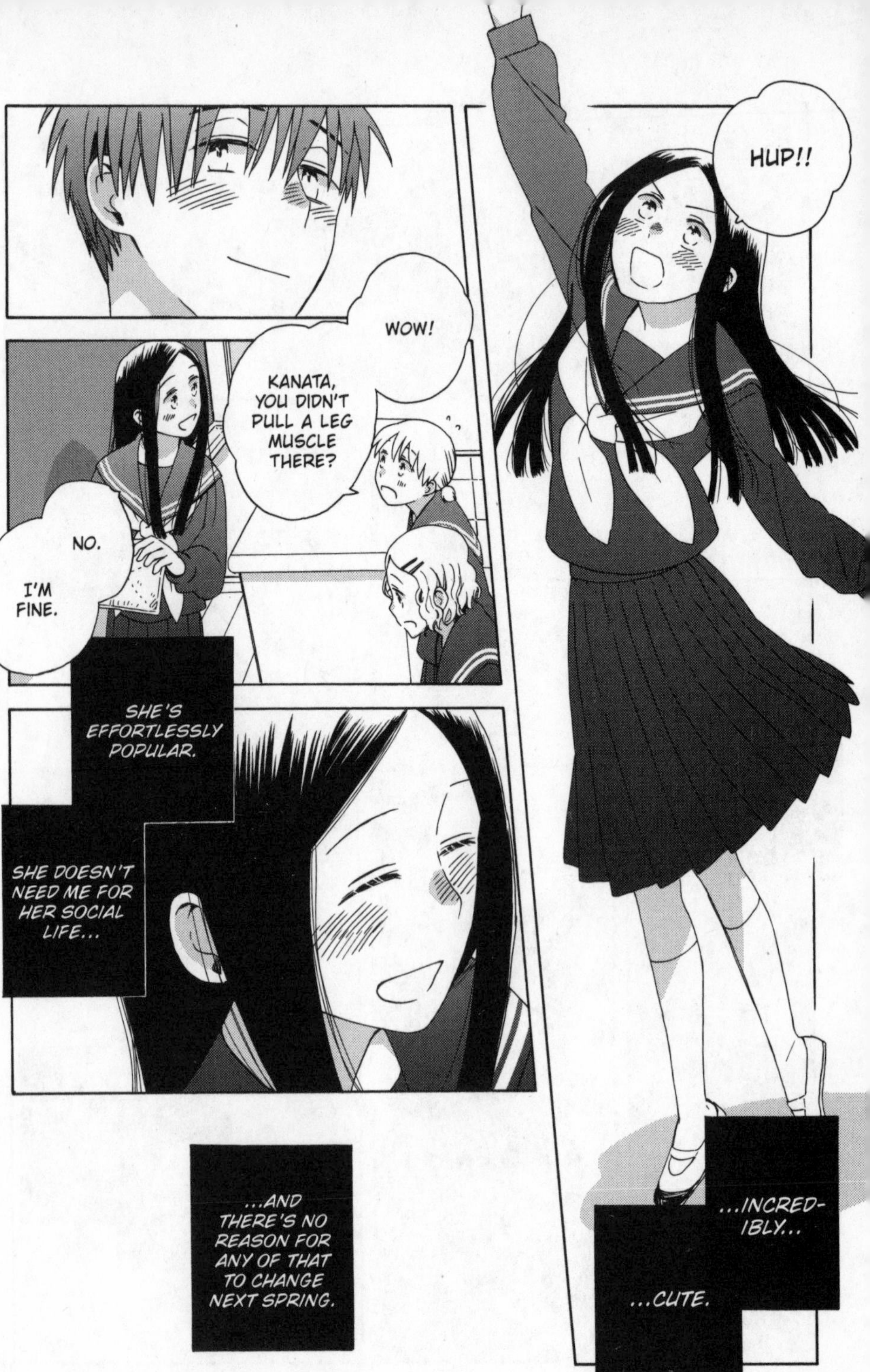
HUP!!
...INCRED-IBLY...
...CUTE.
WOW!
KANATA, YOU DIDN'T PULL A LEG MUSCLE THERE?
NO.
I'M FINE.
SHE'S EFFORTLESSLY POPULAR.
SHE DOESN'T NEED ME FOR HER SOCIAL LIFE...
...AND THERE'S NO REASON FOR ANY OF THAT TO CHANGE NEXT SPRING.

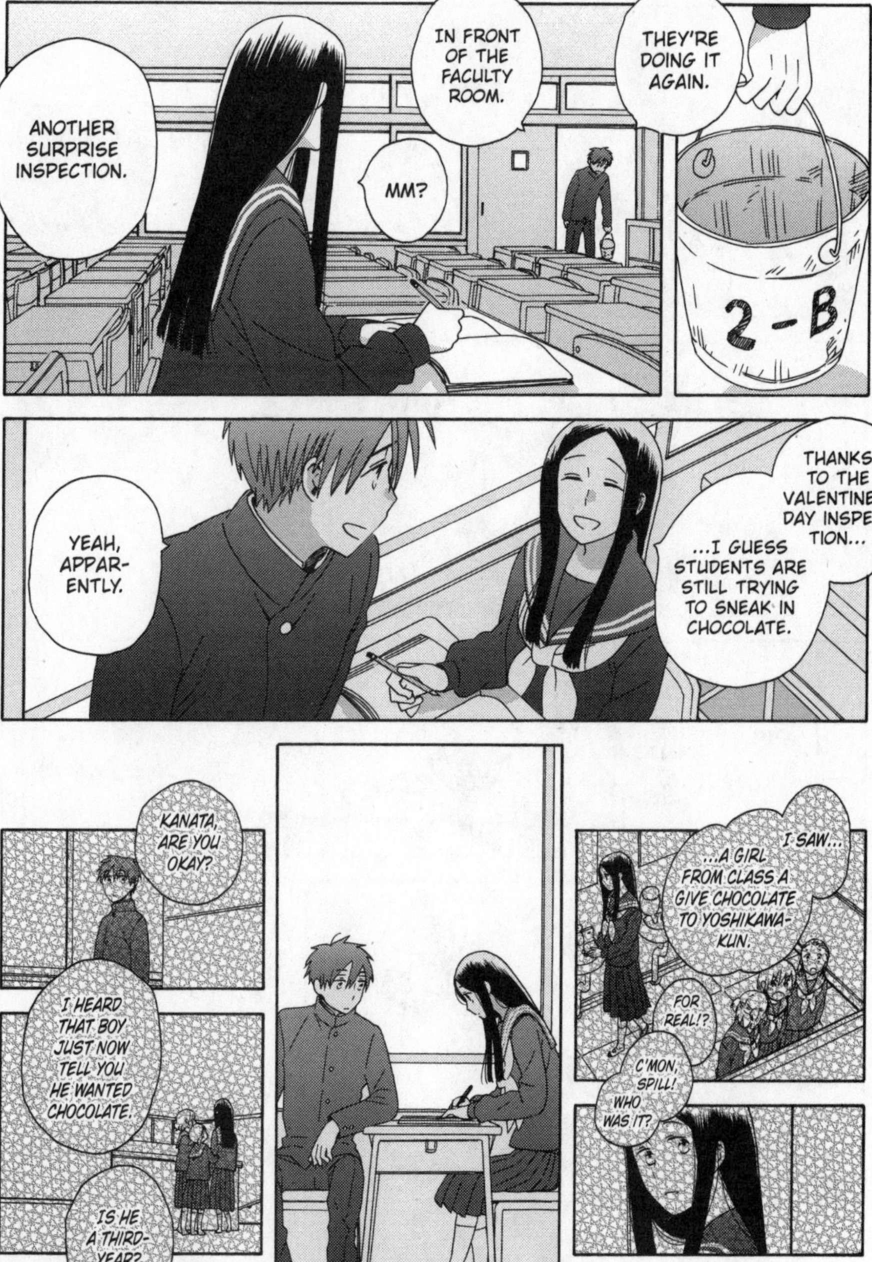
THEY'RE DOING IT AGAIN.
IN FRONT OF THE FACULTY ROOM.
MM?
ANOTHER SURPRISE INSPECTION.
2-B
THANKS TO THE VALENTINE'S DAY INSPECTION...
...I GUESS STUDENTS ARE STILL TRYING TO SNEAK IN CHOCOLATE.
YEAH, APPARENTLY.
I SAW...
...A GIRL FROM CLASS A GIVE CHOCOLATE TO YOSHIKAWA-KUN.
FOR REAL!?
C'MON, SPILL! WHO WAS IT?
KANATA, ARE YOU OKAY?
I HEARD THAT BOY JUST NOW TELL YOU HE WANTED CHOCOLATE.
IS HE A THIRD-YEAR?

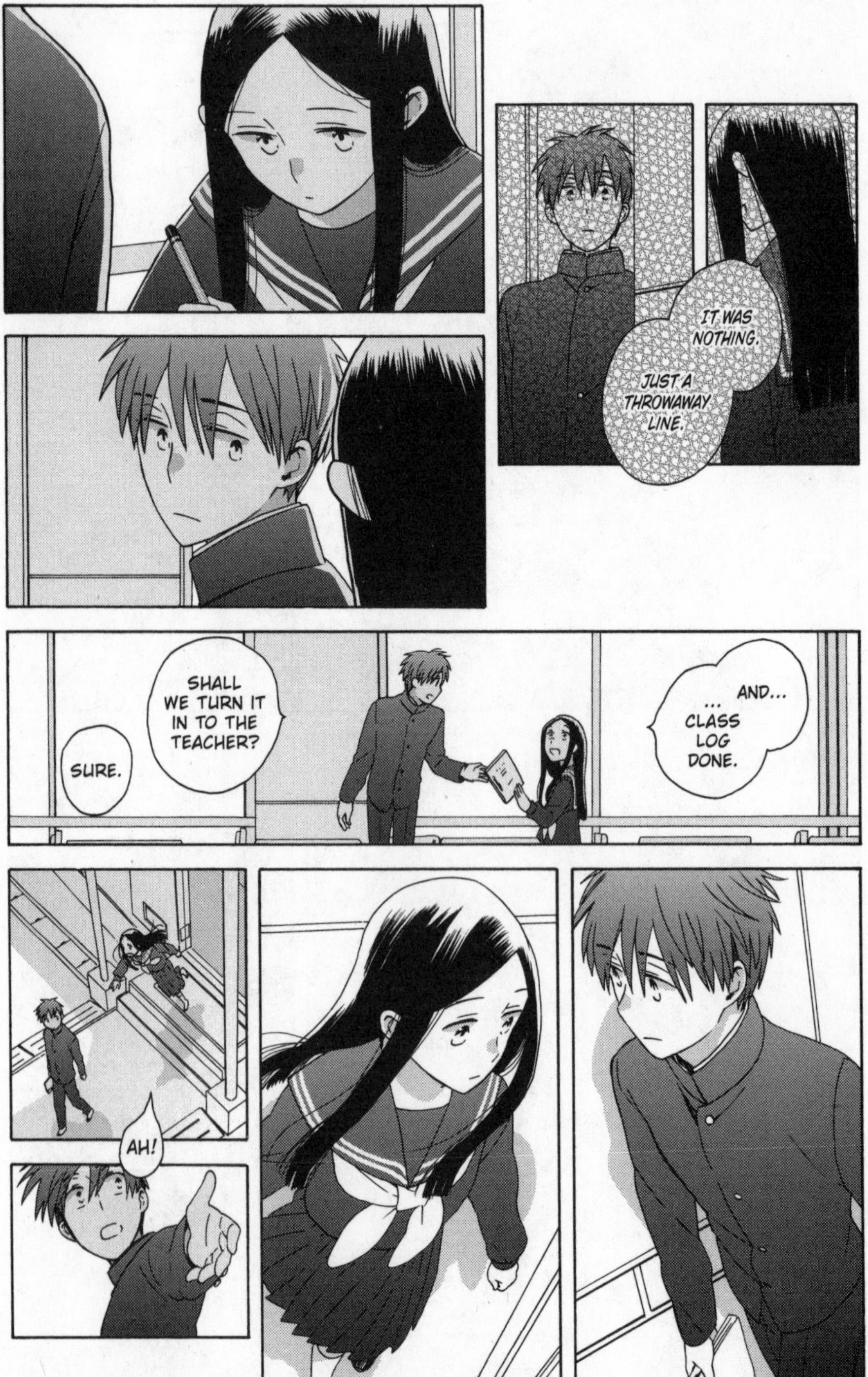
IT WAS NOTHING.
JUST A THROWAWAY LINE.
AND...
... CLASS LOG DONE.
SHALL WE TURN IT IN TO THE TEACHER?
SURE.
AH!

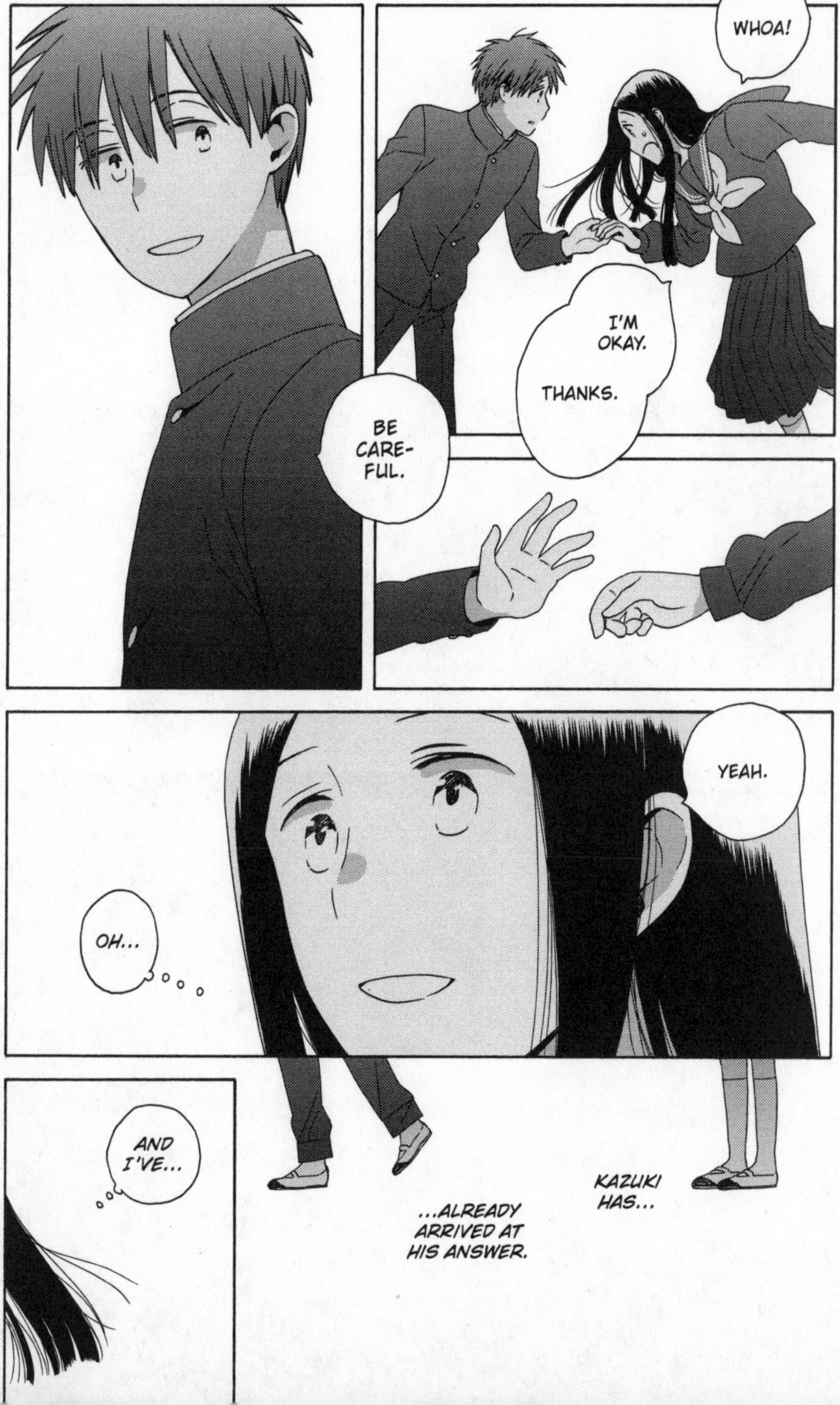
WHOA!
BE CARE-FUL.
I'M OKAY.
THANKS.
YEAH.
OH...
KAZUKI HAS...
...ALREADY ARRIVED AT HIS ANSWER.
AND I'VE...

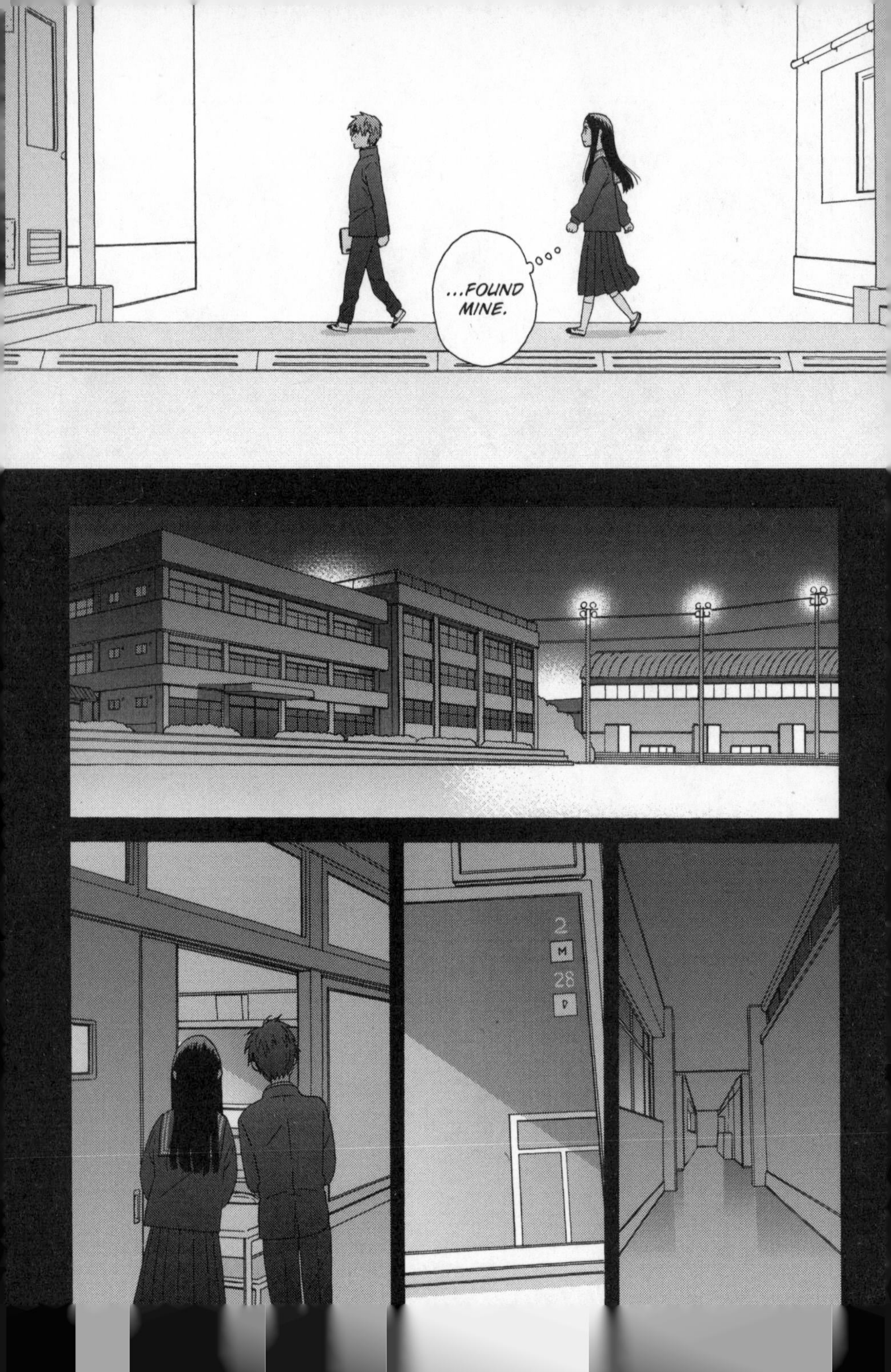
...FOUND MINE.
2 M 28 D

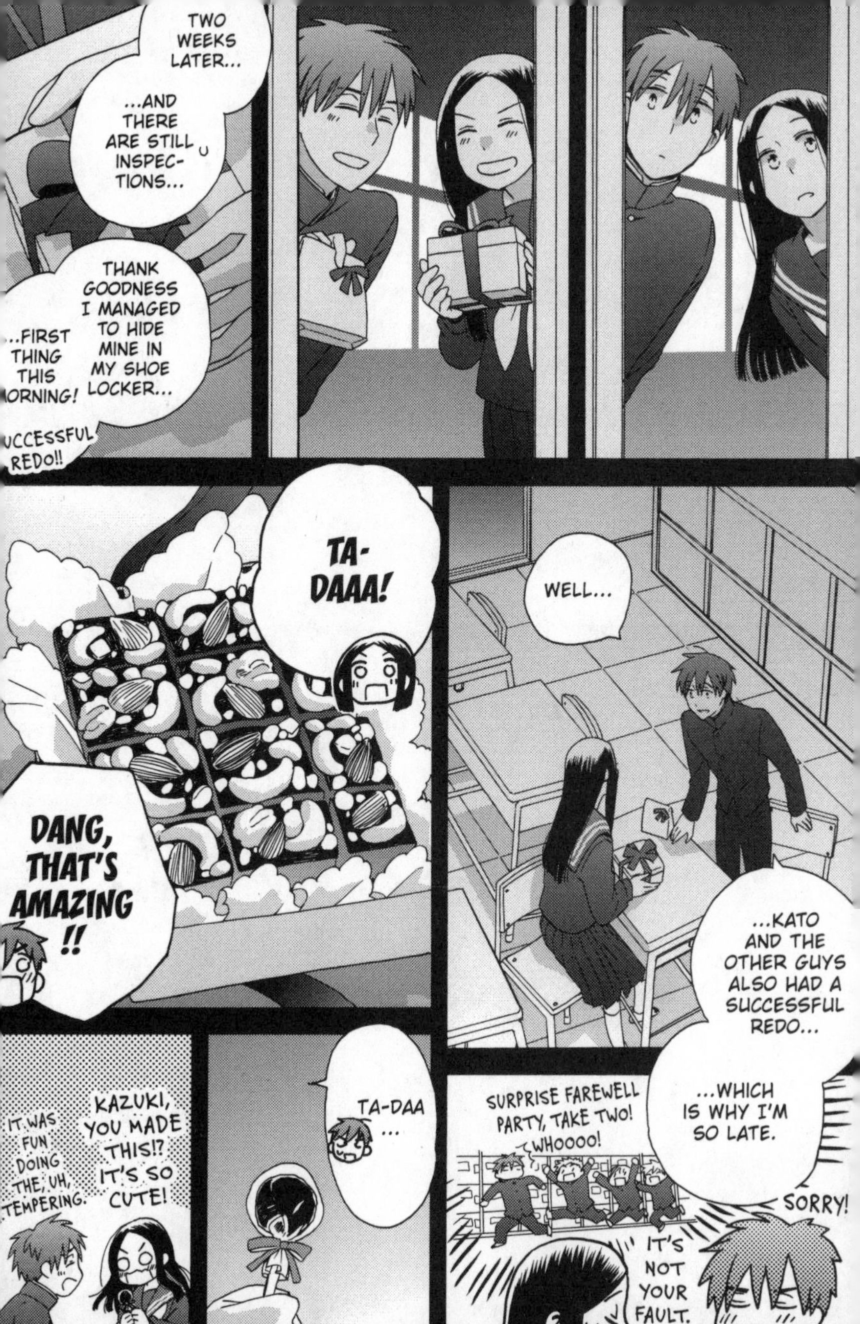
TWO WEEKS LATER...
...AND THERE ARE STILL INSPECTIONS...
THANK GOODNESS I MANAGED TO HIDE MINE IN MY SHOE LOCKER...
...FIRST THING THIS ORNING!
UCCESSFUL REDO!!
WELL...
...KATO AND THE OTHER GUYS ALSO HAD A SUCCESSFUL REDO...
TA-DAAA!
DANG, THAT'S AMAZING!!
...WHICH IS WHY I'M SO LATE.
SURPRISE FAREWELL PARTY, TAKE TWO!
WHOOOO!
SORRY!
IT'S NOT YOUR FAULT.
TA-DAA ...
KAZUKI, YOU MADE THIS!? IT'S SO CUTE!
IT WAS FUN DOING THE, UH, TEMPERING.

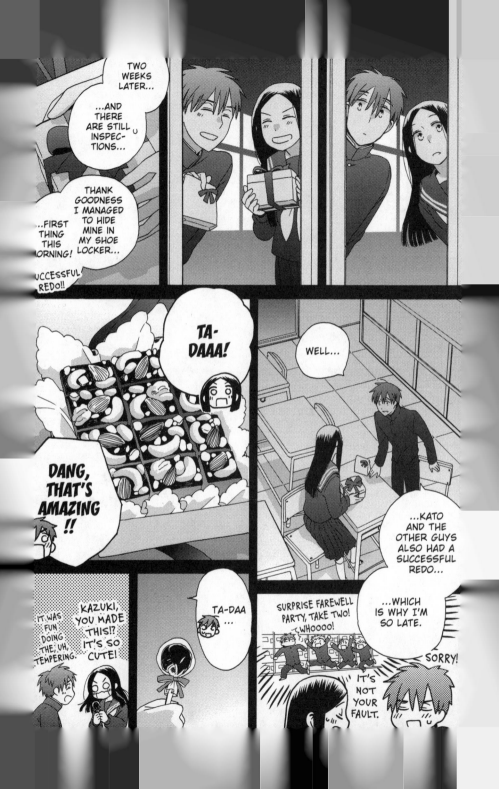

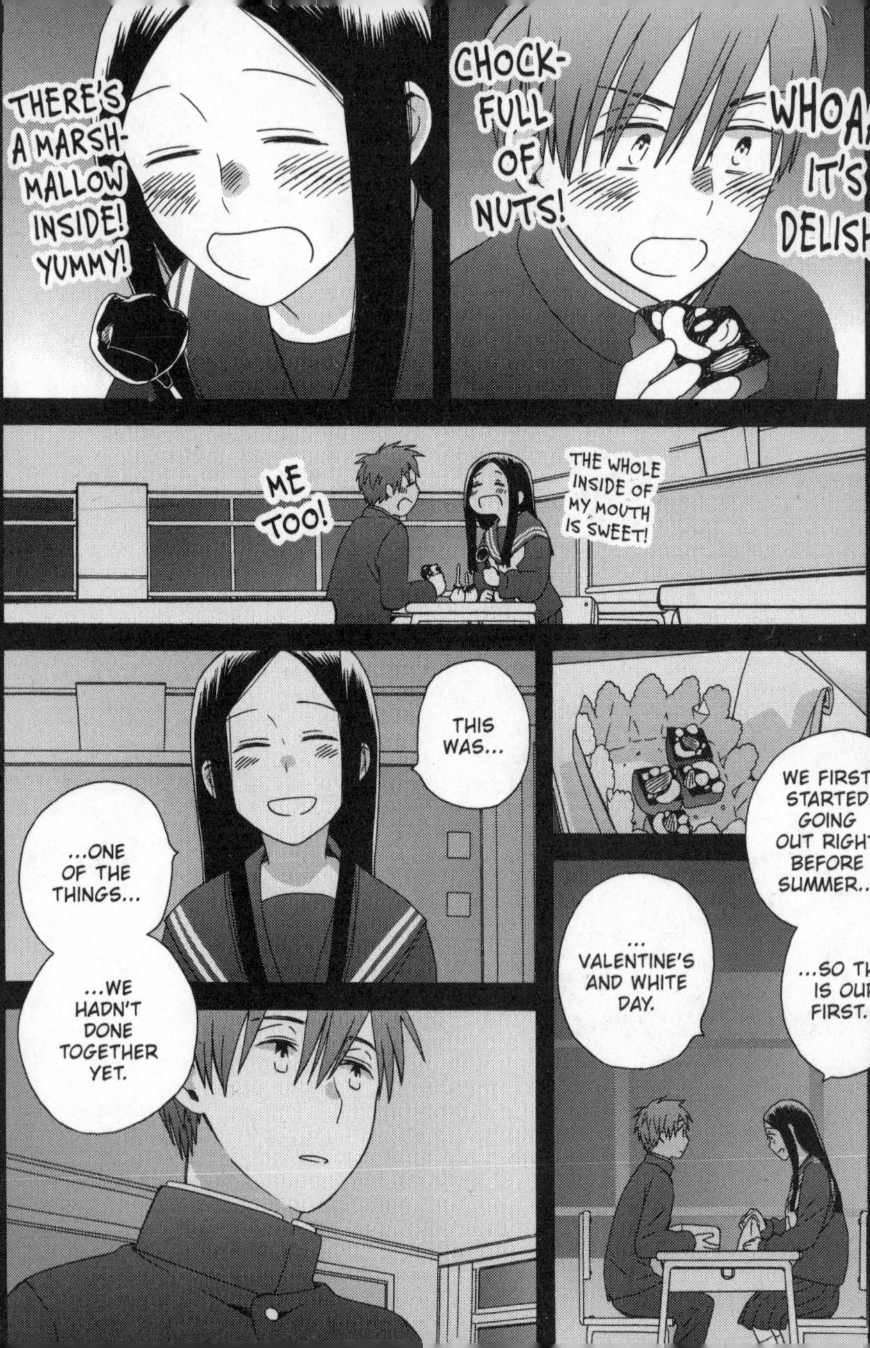
WHOAAA, IT'S DELISH!
CHOCK-FULL OF NUTS!
THERE'S A MARSHMALLOW INSIDE! YUMMY!
THE WHOLE INSIDE OF MY MOUTH IS SWEET!
ME TOO!
WE FIRST STARTED GOING OUT RIGHT BEFORE SUMMER...
...SO THIS IS OUR FIRST...
...VALENTINE'S AND WHITE DAY.
THIS WAS...
...ONE OF THE THINGS...
...WE HADN'T DONE TOGETHER YET.

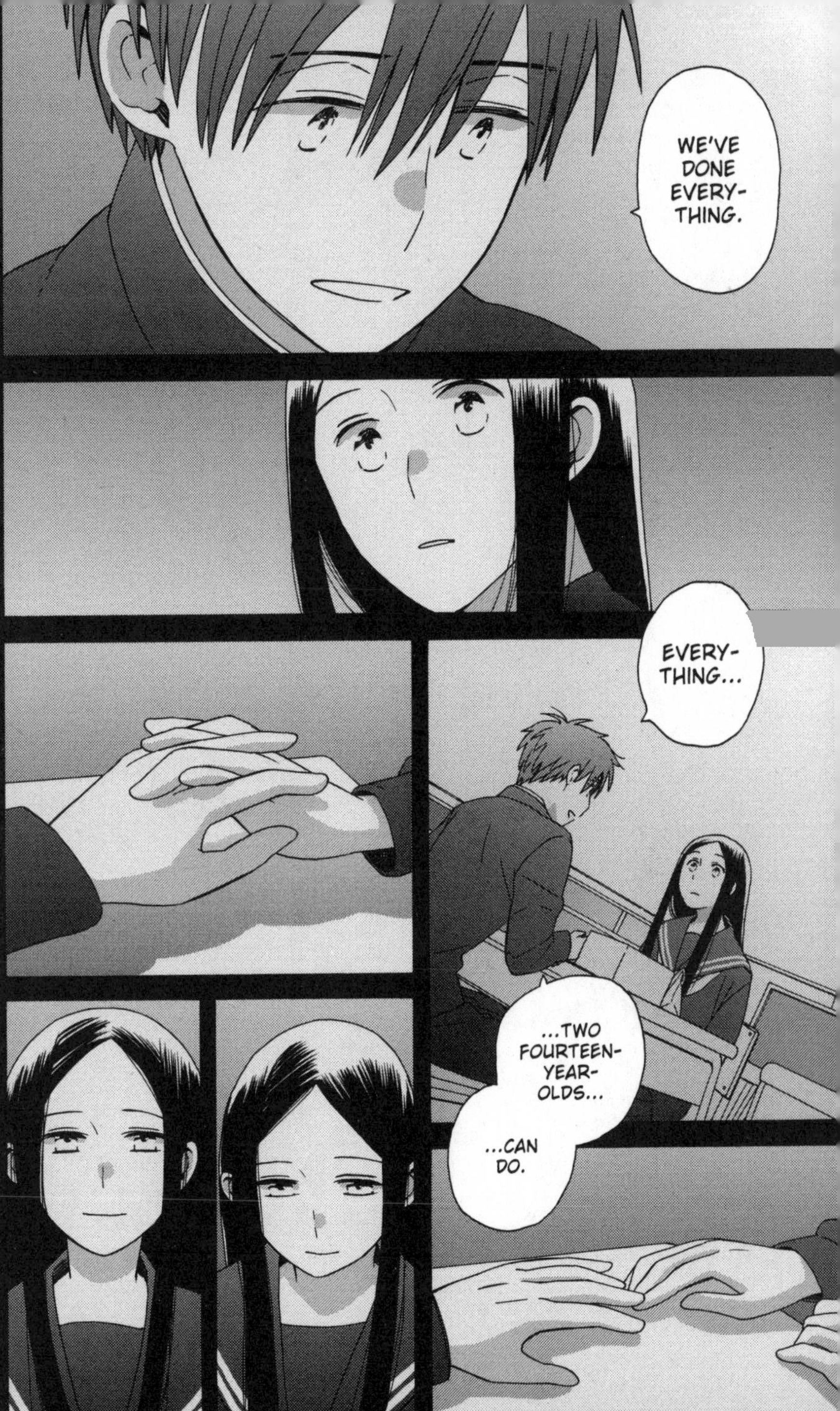
WE'VE DONE EVERY-THING.
EVERY-THING...
...TWO FOURTEEN-YEAR-OLDS...
...CAN DO.

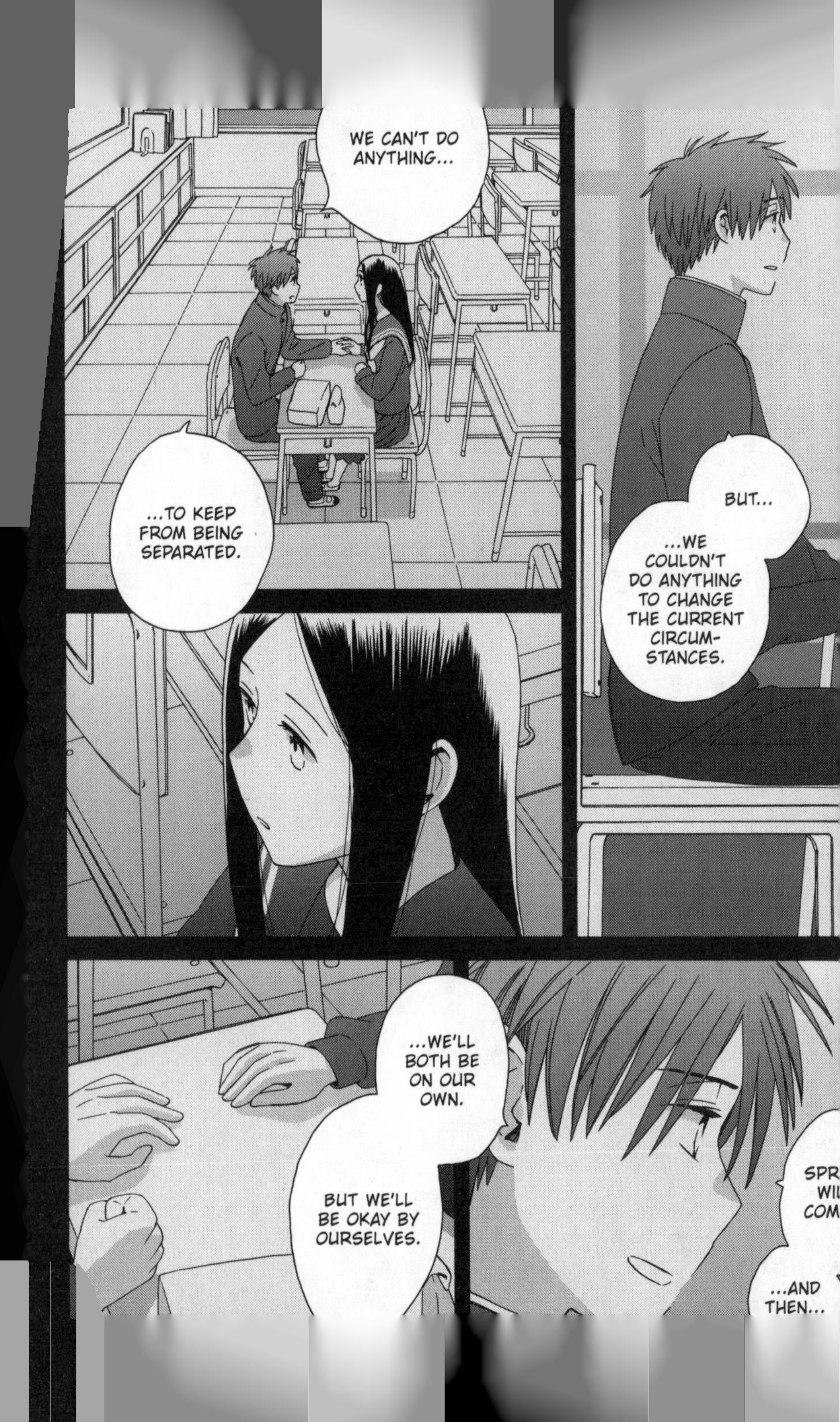
BUT...
...WE COULDN'T DO ANYTHING TO CHANGE THE CURRENT CIRCUM-STANCES.
WE CAN'T DO ANYTHING...
...TO KEEP FROM BEING SEPARATED.
...AND THEN...
...WE'LL BOTH BE ON OUR OWN.
BUT WE'LL BE OKAY BY OURSELVES.

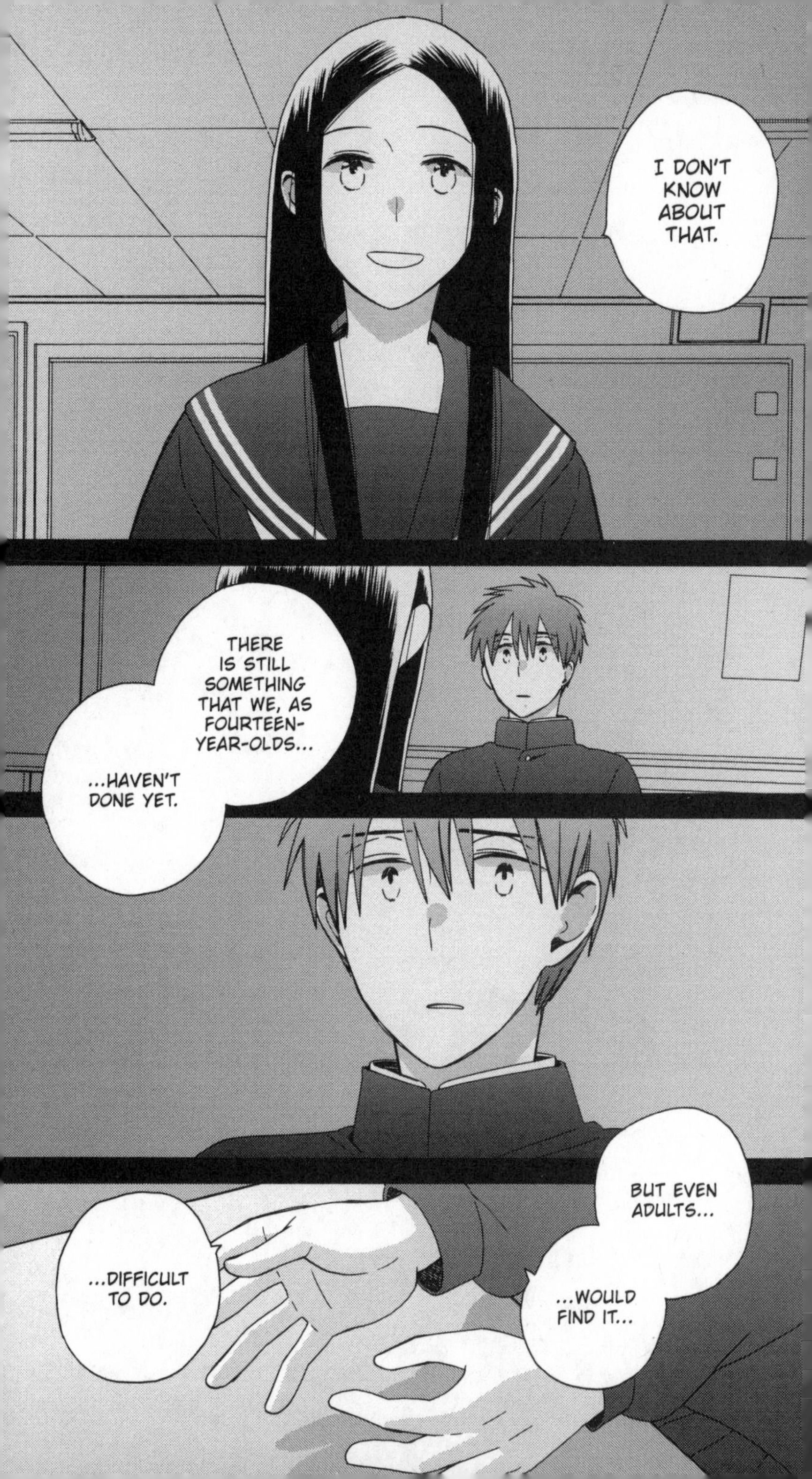
I DON'T KNOW ABOUT THAT.
THERE IS STILL SOMETHING THAT WE, AS FOURTEEN-YEAR-OLDS...
...HAVEN'T DONE YET.
BUT EVEN ADULTS...
...WOULD FIND IT...
...DIFFICULT TO DO.

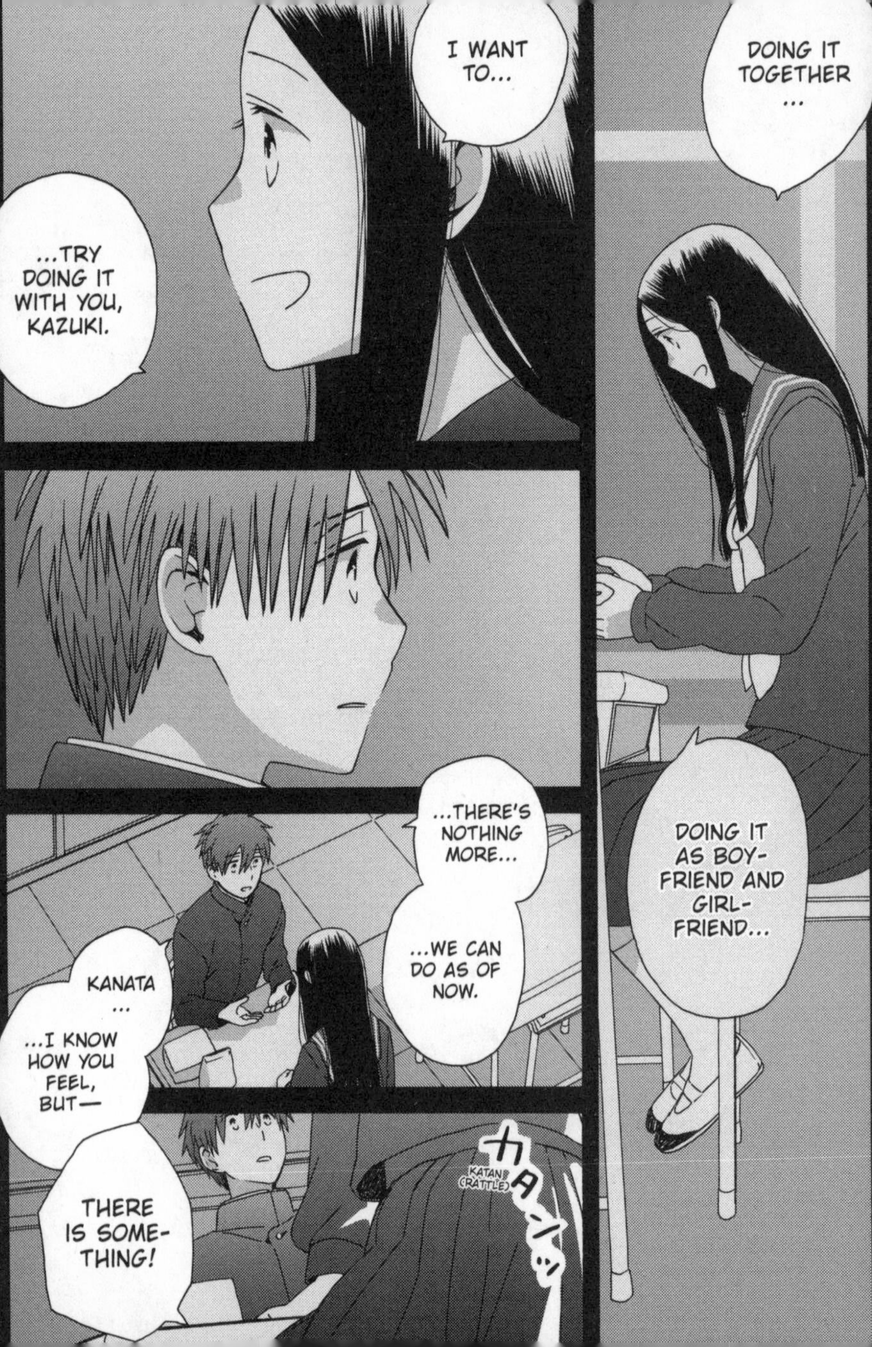
DOING IT TOGETHER ...
DOING IT AS BOYFRIEND AND GIRLFRIEND...
I WANT TO...
...TRY DOING IT WITH YOU, KAZUKI.
...THERE'S NOTHING MORE...
...WE CAN DO AS OF NOW.
KANATA ... ...I KNOW HOW YOU FEEL, BUT—
KATAN (RATTLE)
THERE IS SOMETHING!

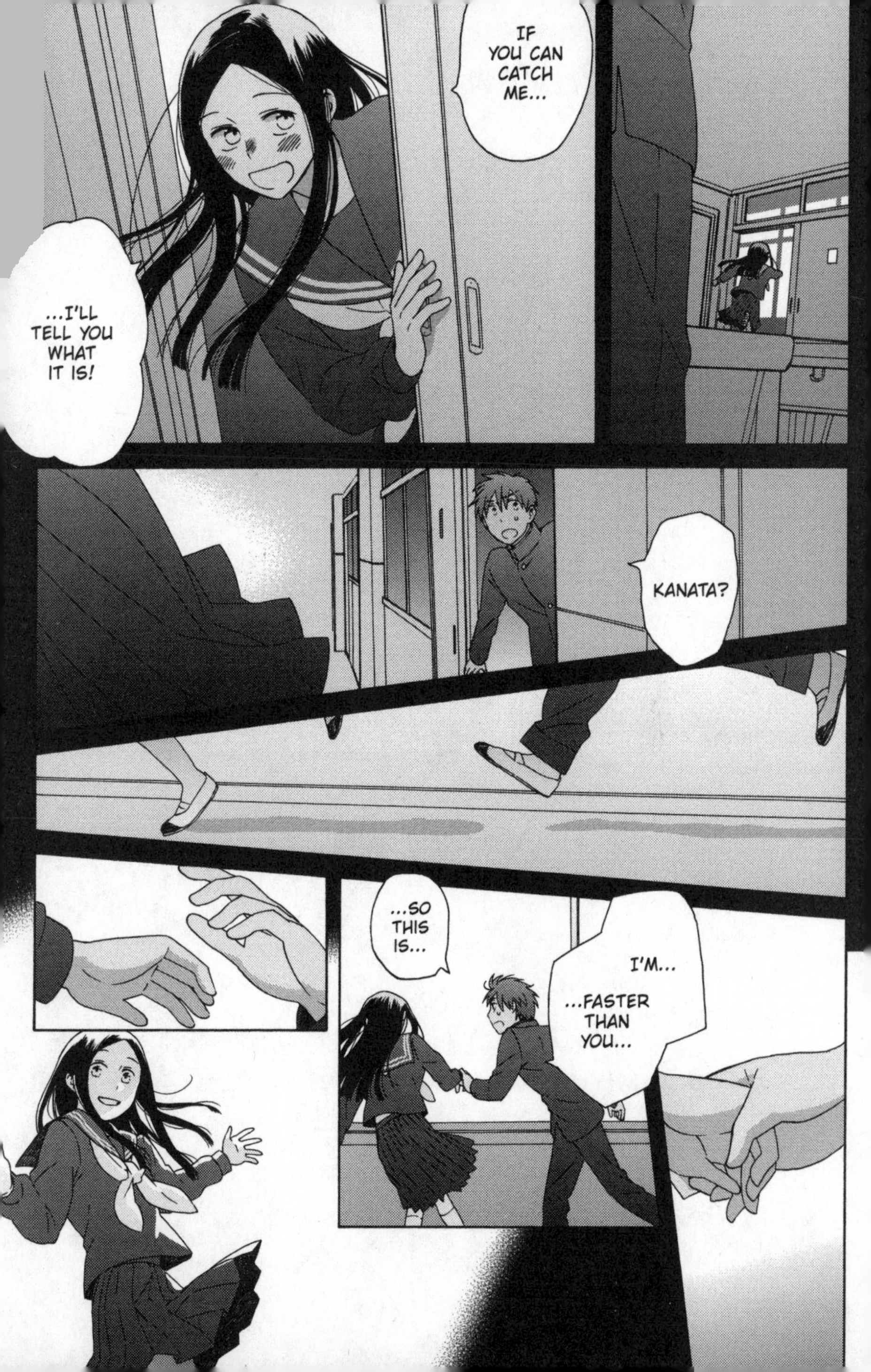
IF YOU CAN CATCH ME...
...I'LL TELL YOU WHAT IT IS!
KANATA?
I'M... ...FASTER THAN YOU...
...SO THIS IS...

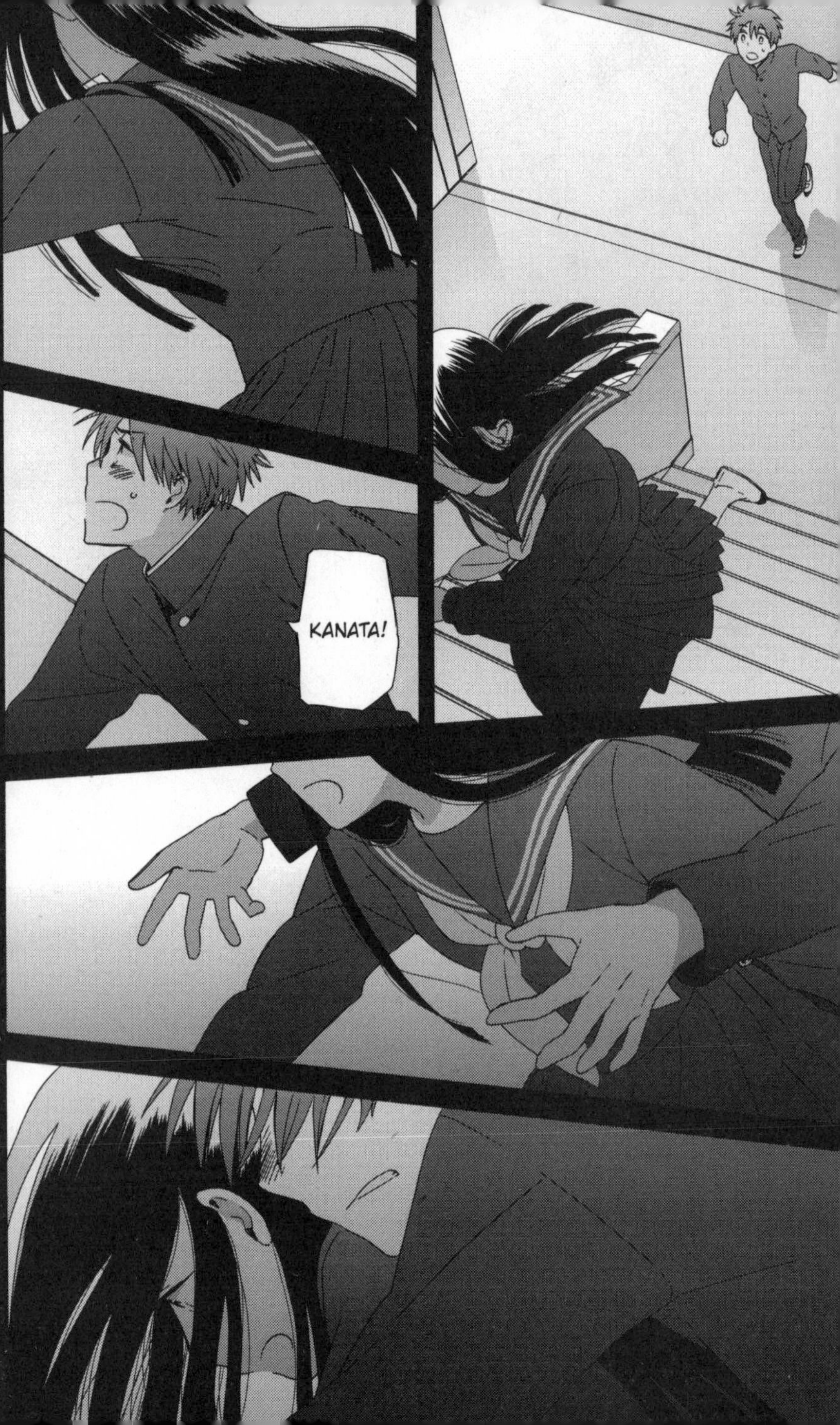
KANATA!

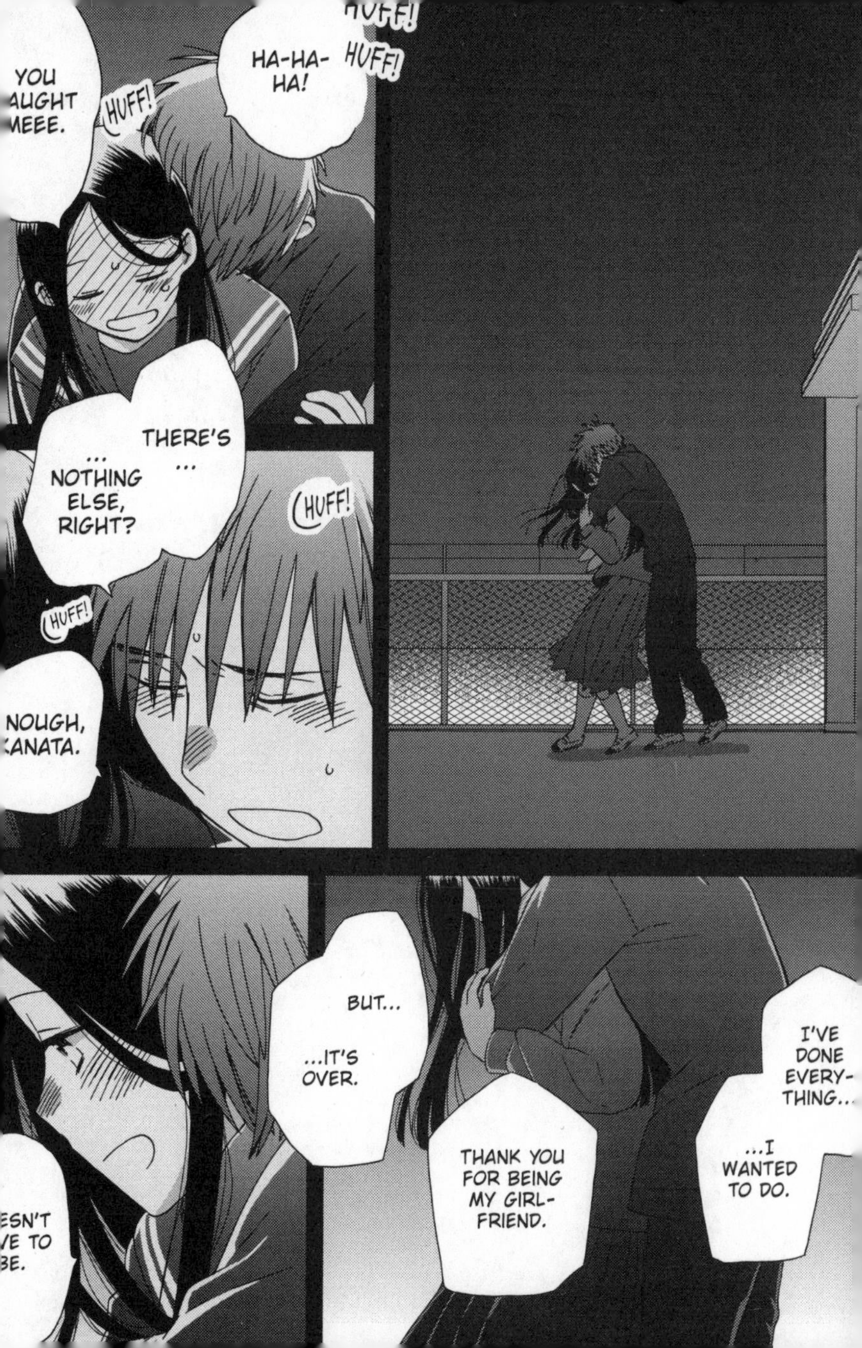
HUFF!
HUFF!
HA-HA-HA!
HUFF!
YOU
AUGHT
MEEE.
THERE'S ...
... NOTHING ELSE, RIGHT?
HUFF!
HUFF!
NOUGH,
ANATA.
I'VE DONE EVERY-THING...
...I WANTED TO DO.
BUT...
...IT'S OVER.
THANK YOU FOR BEING MY GIRL-FRIEND.
ESN'T
VE TO
BE.

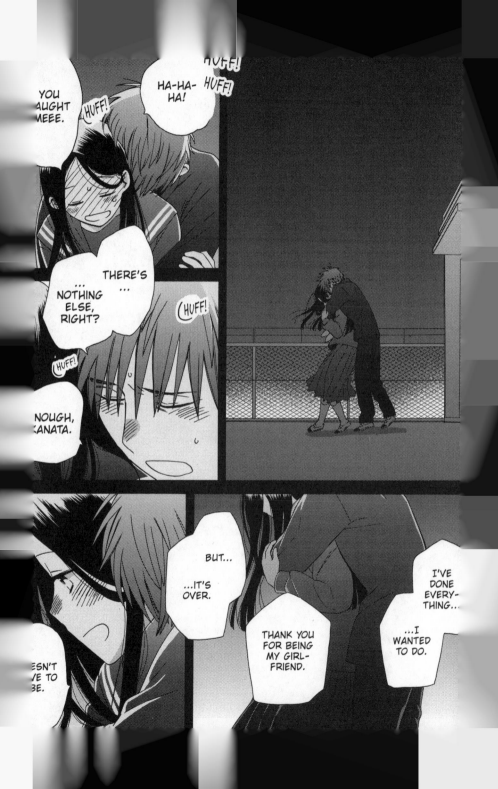

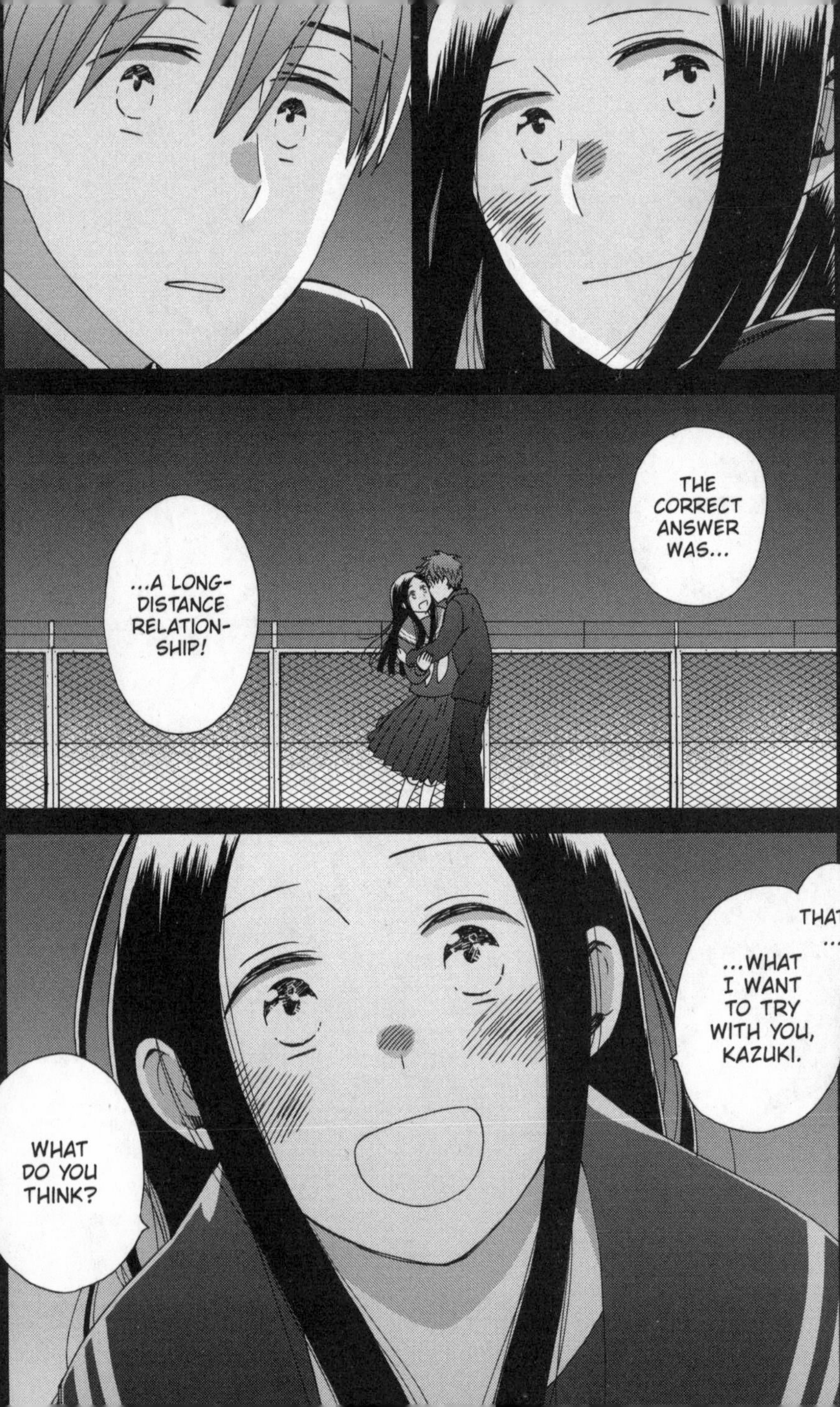
THE CORRECT ANSWER WAS...
...A LONG-DISTANCE RELATIONSHIP!
THAT'S...
...WHAT I WANT TO TRY WITH YOU, KAZUKI.
WHAT DO YOU THINK?

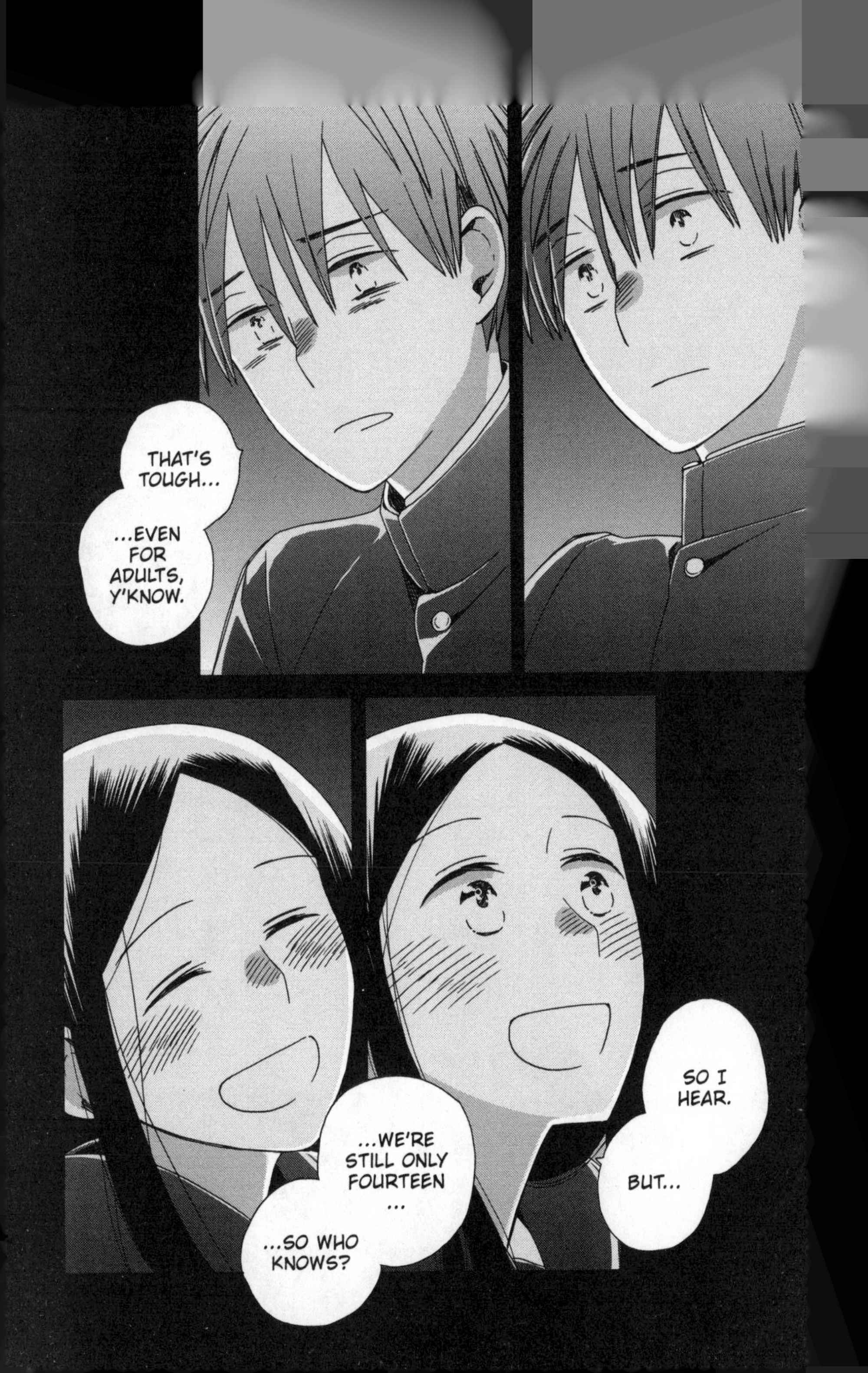
THAT'S TOUGH...
...EVEN FOR ADULTS, Y'KNOW.
SO I HEAR.
BUT...
...WE'RE STILL ONLY FOURTEEN...
...SO WHO KNOWS?

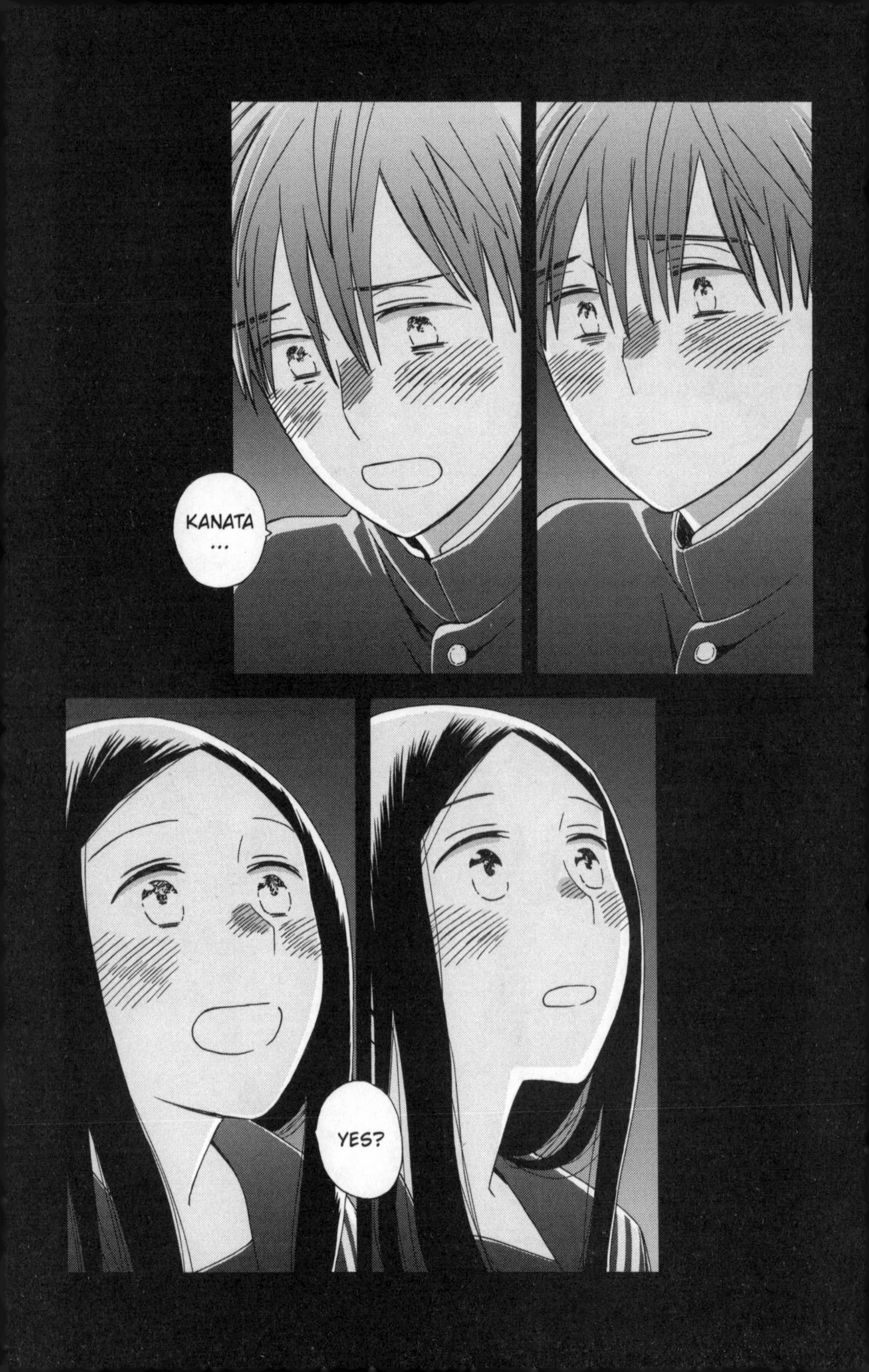
KANATA
...
YES?

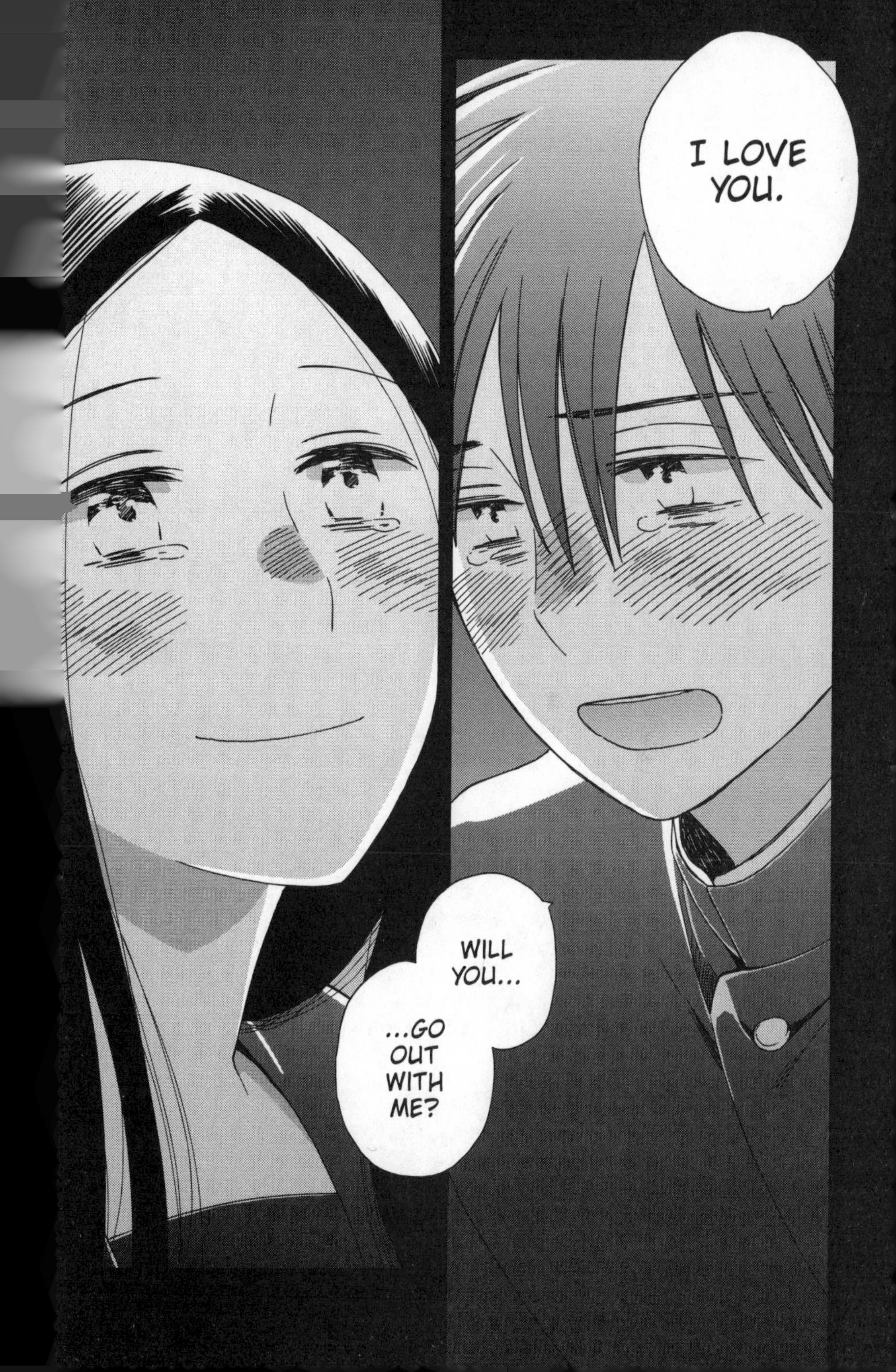
I LOVE YOU.
WILL YOU...
...GO OUT WITH ME?

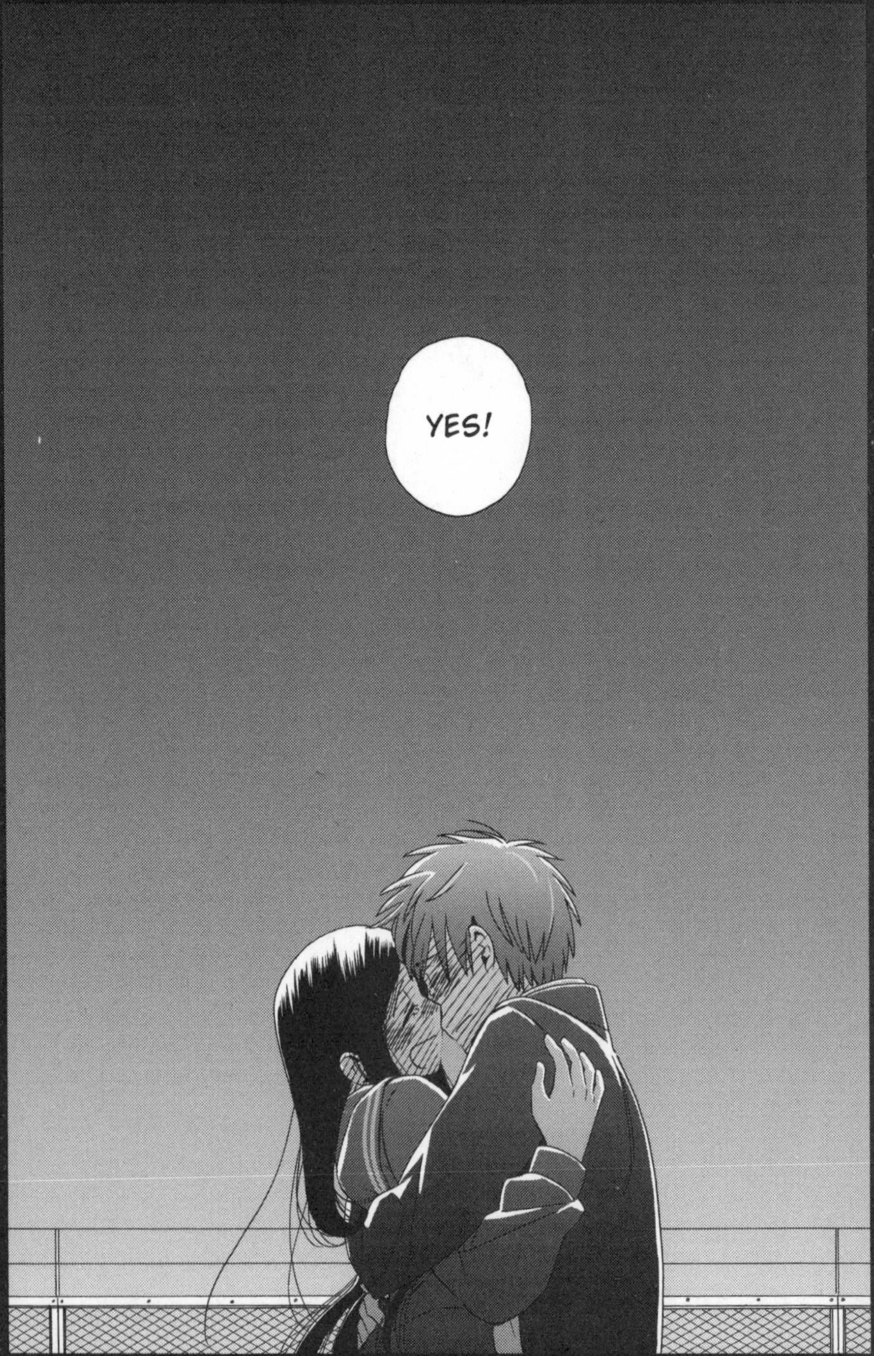
YES!

Fin

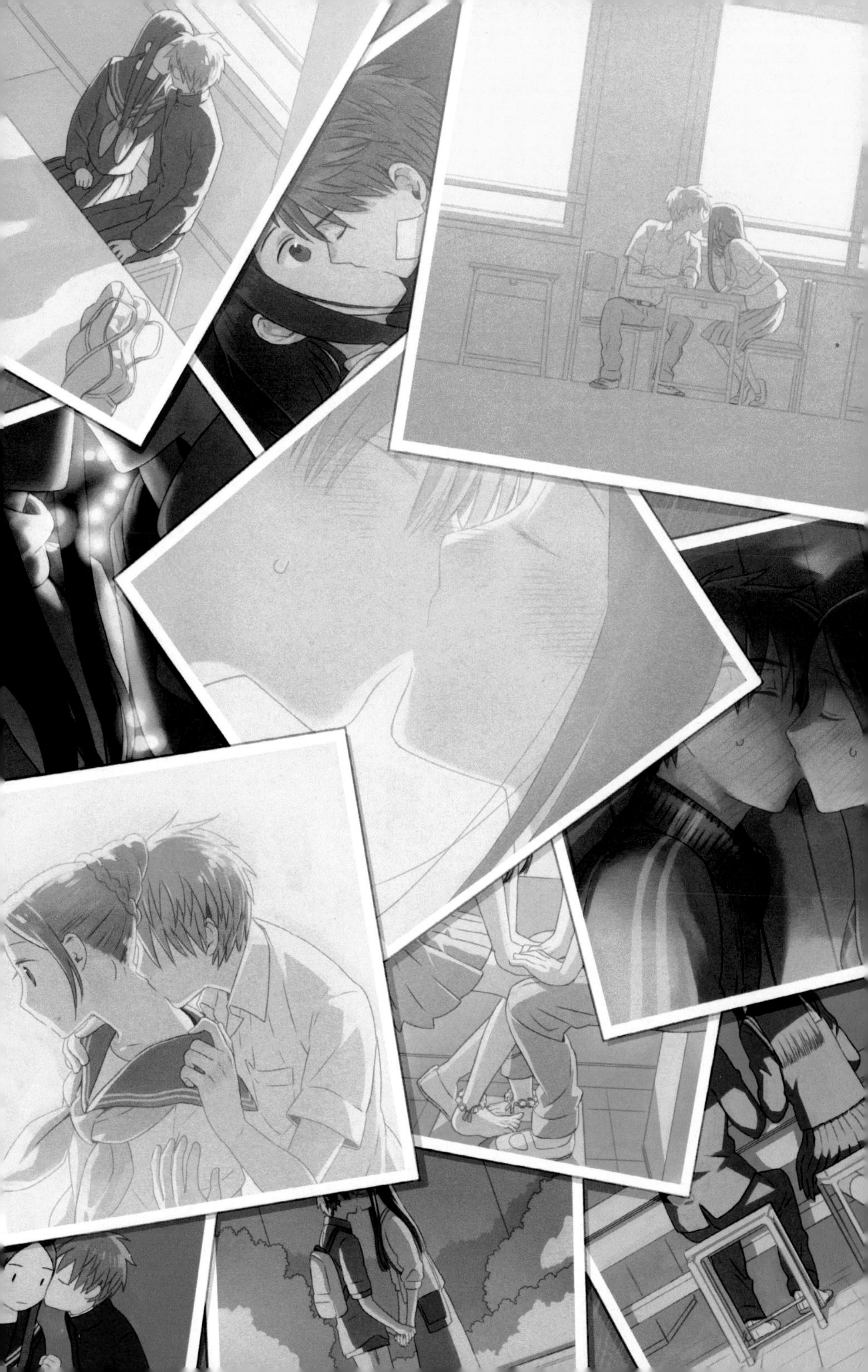

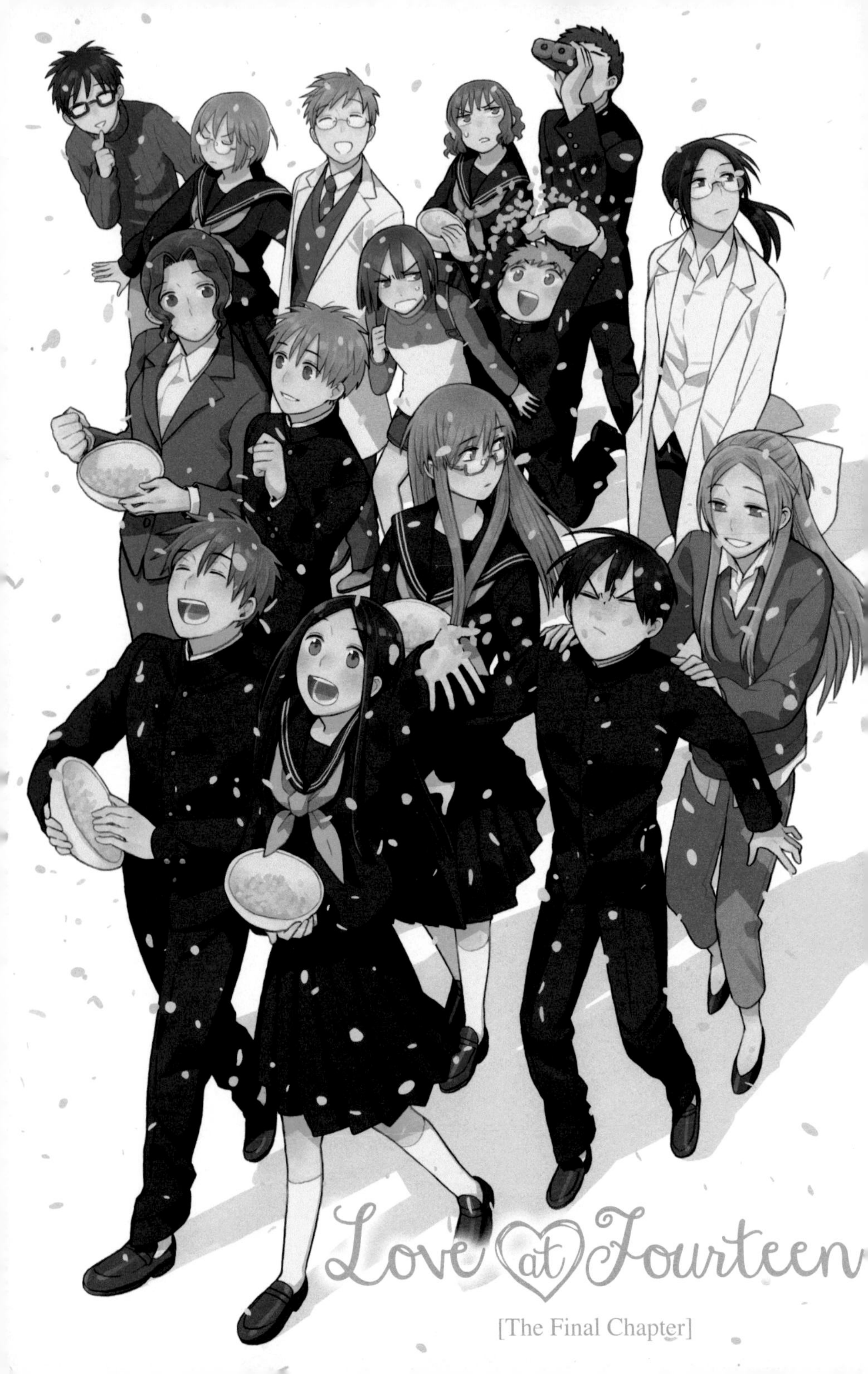
Love at Fourteen
[The Final Chapter]

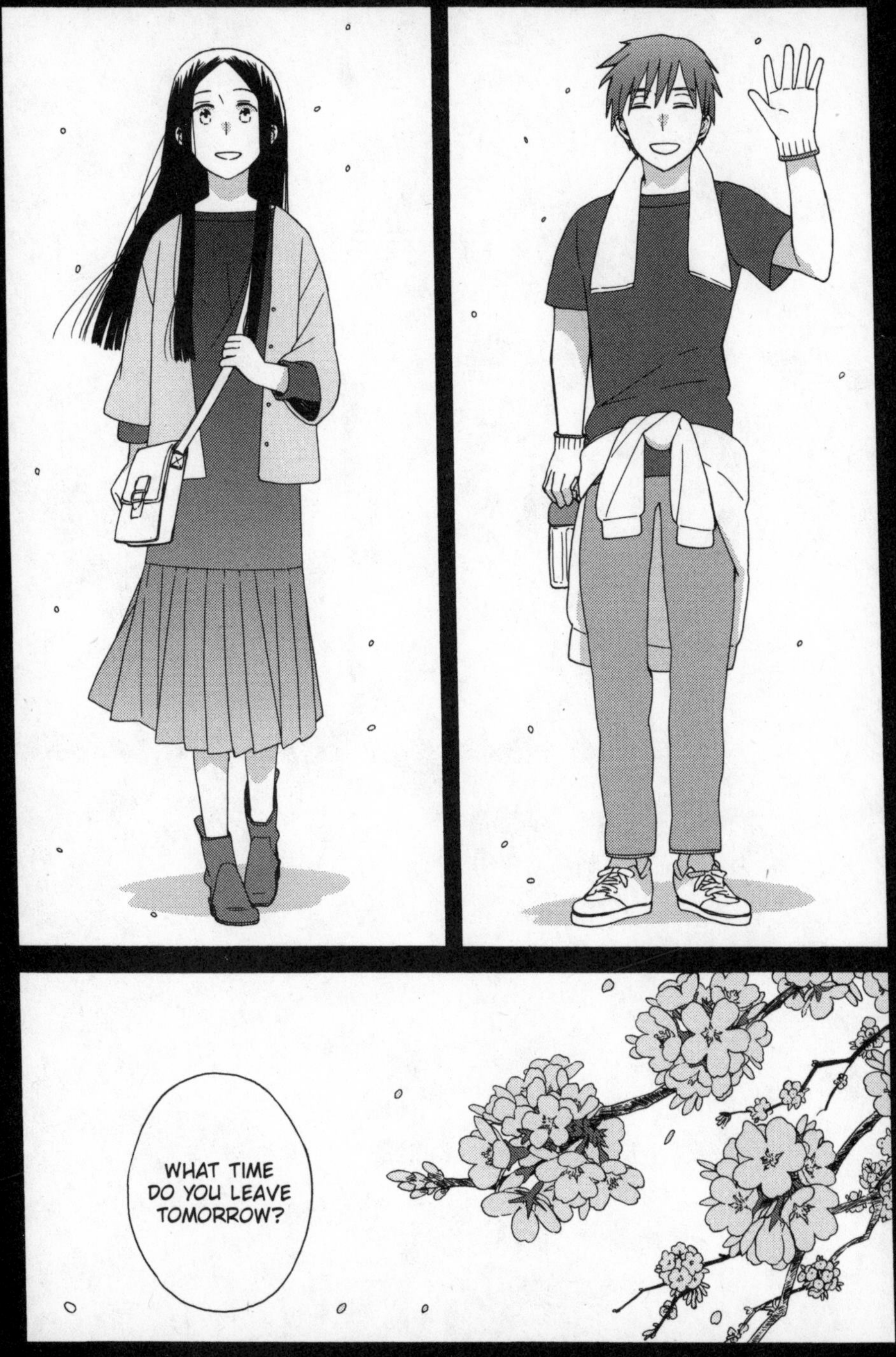
WHAT TIME DO YOU LEAVE TOMORROW?

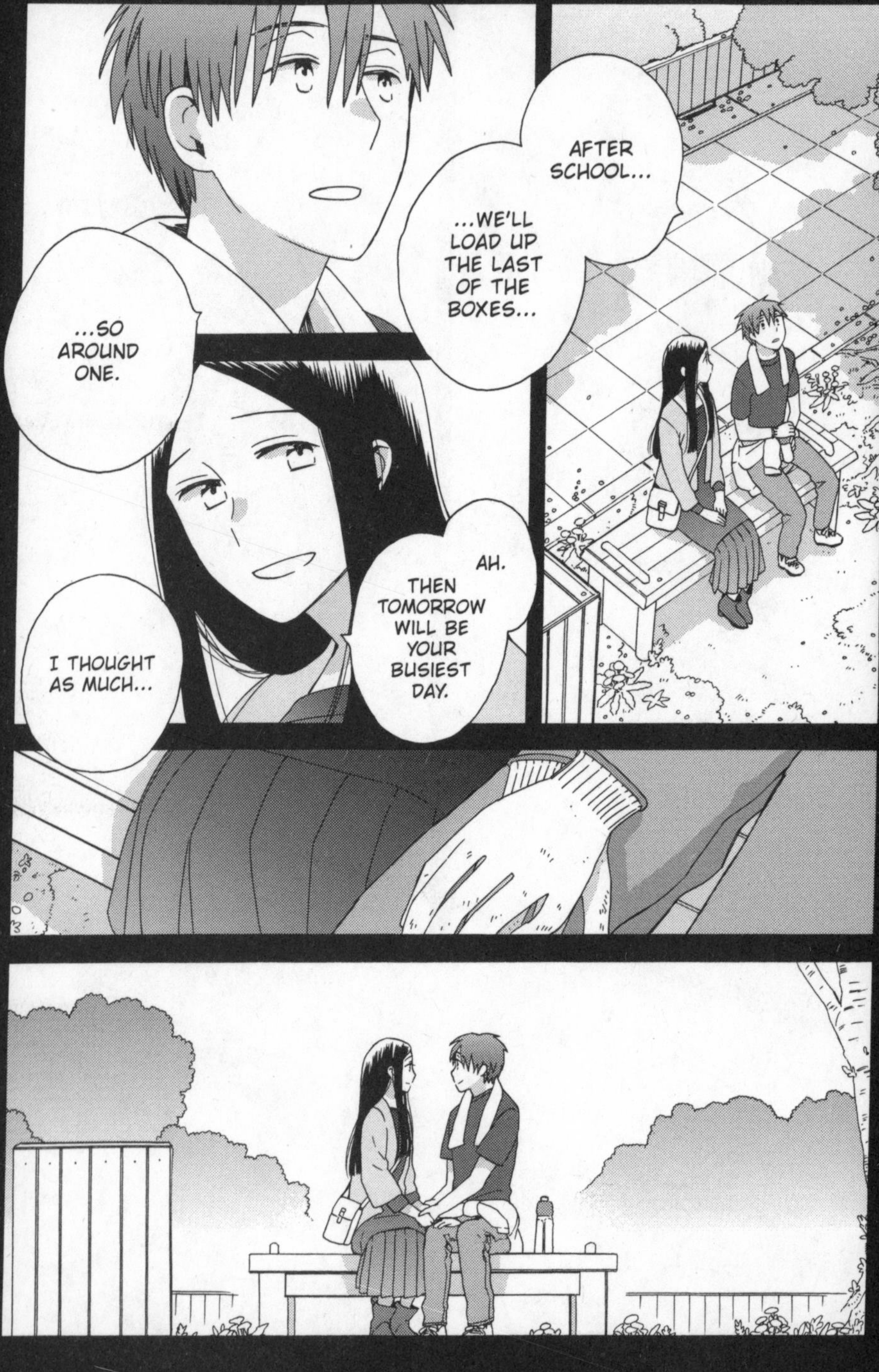
AFTER SCHOOL...
...WE'LL LOAD UP THE LAST OF THE BOXES...
...SO AROUND ONE.
AH. THEN TOMORROW WILL BE YOUR BUSIEST DAY.
I THOUGHT AS MUCH...

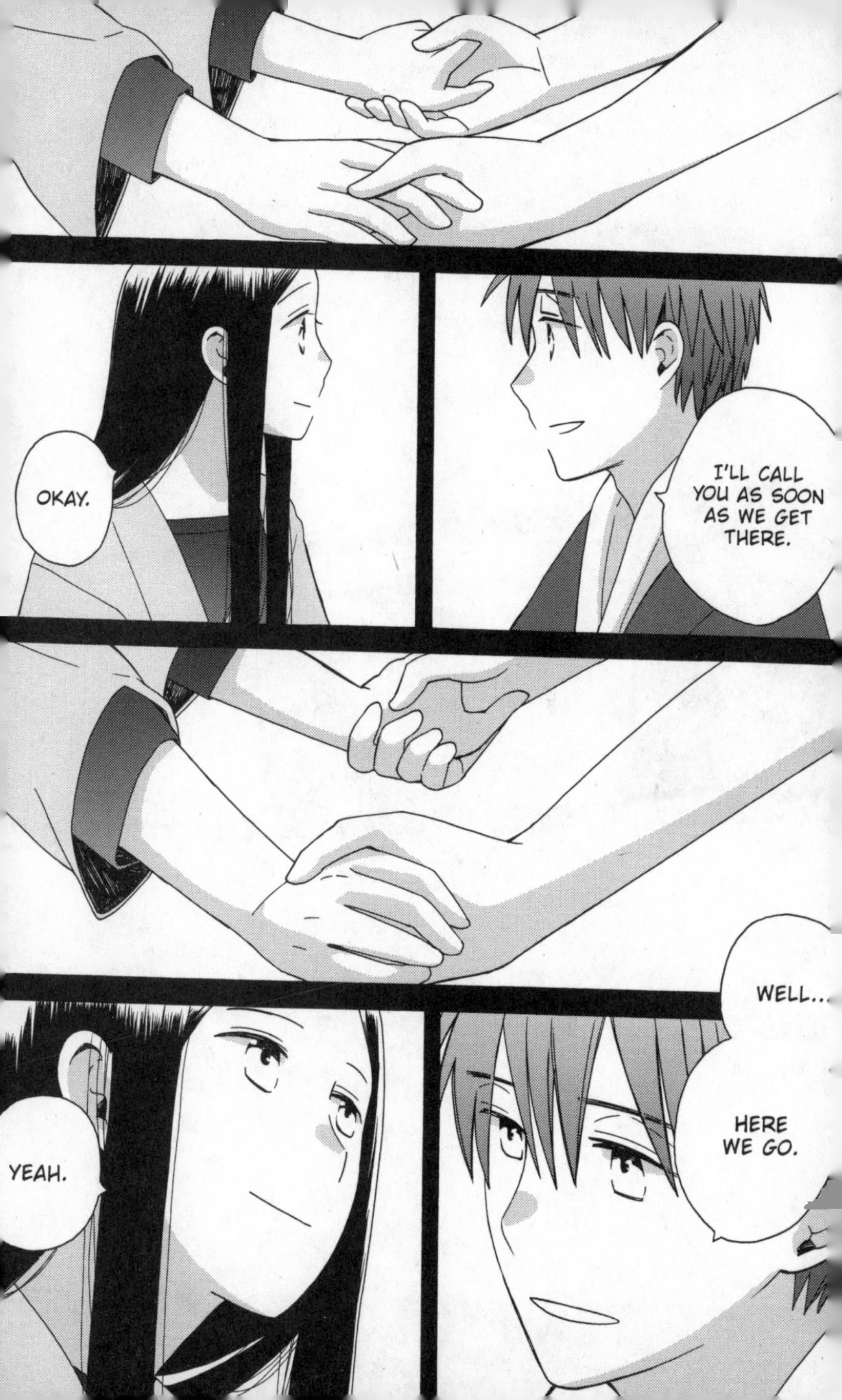
I'LL CALL YOU AS SOON AS WE GET THERE.
OKAY.
WELL...
HERE WE GO.
YEAH.

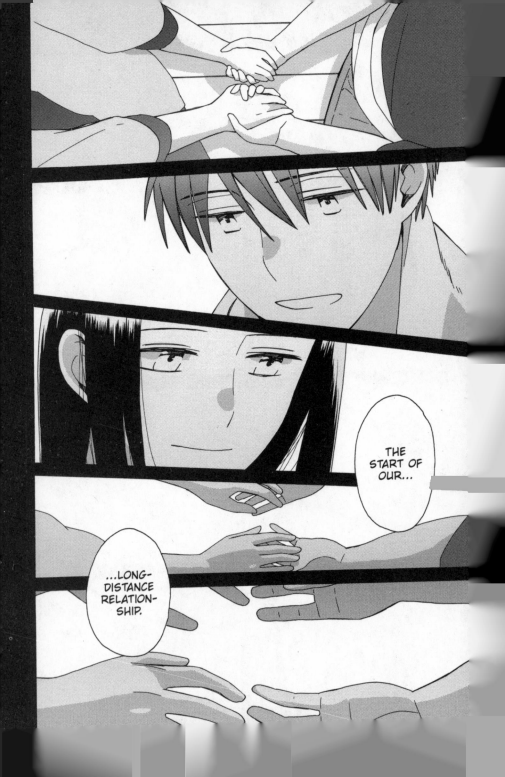

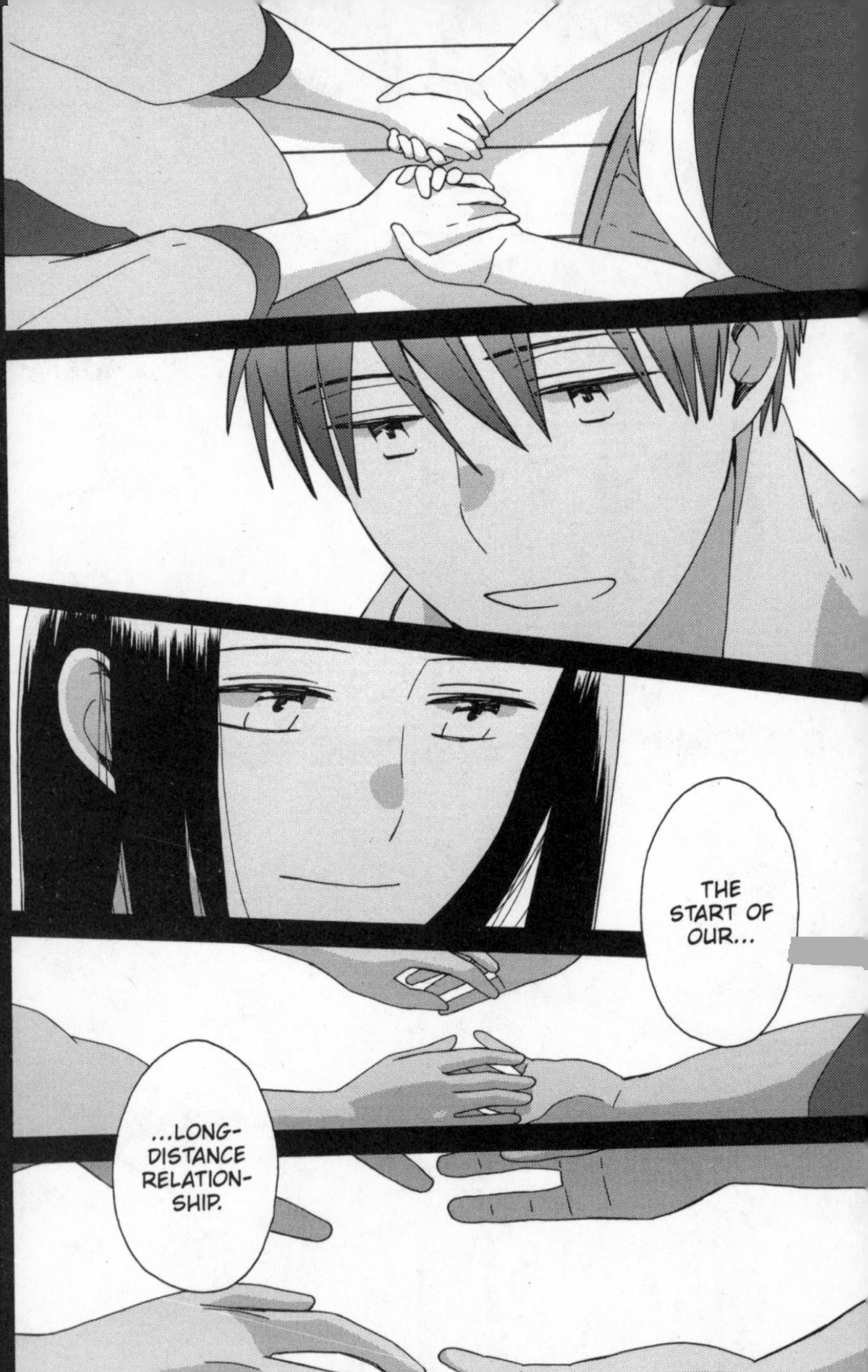
THE START OF OUR...
...LONG-DISTANCE RELATIONSHIP.

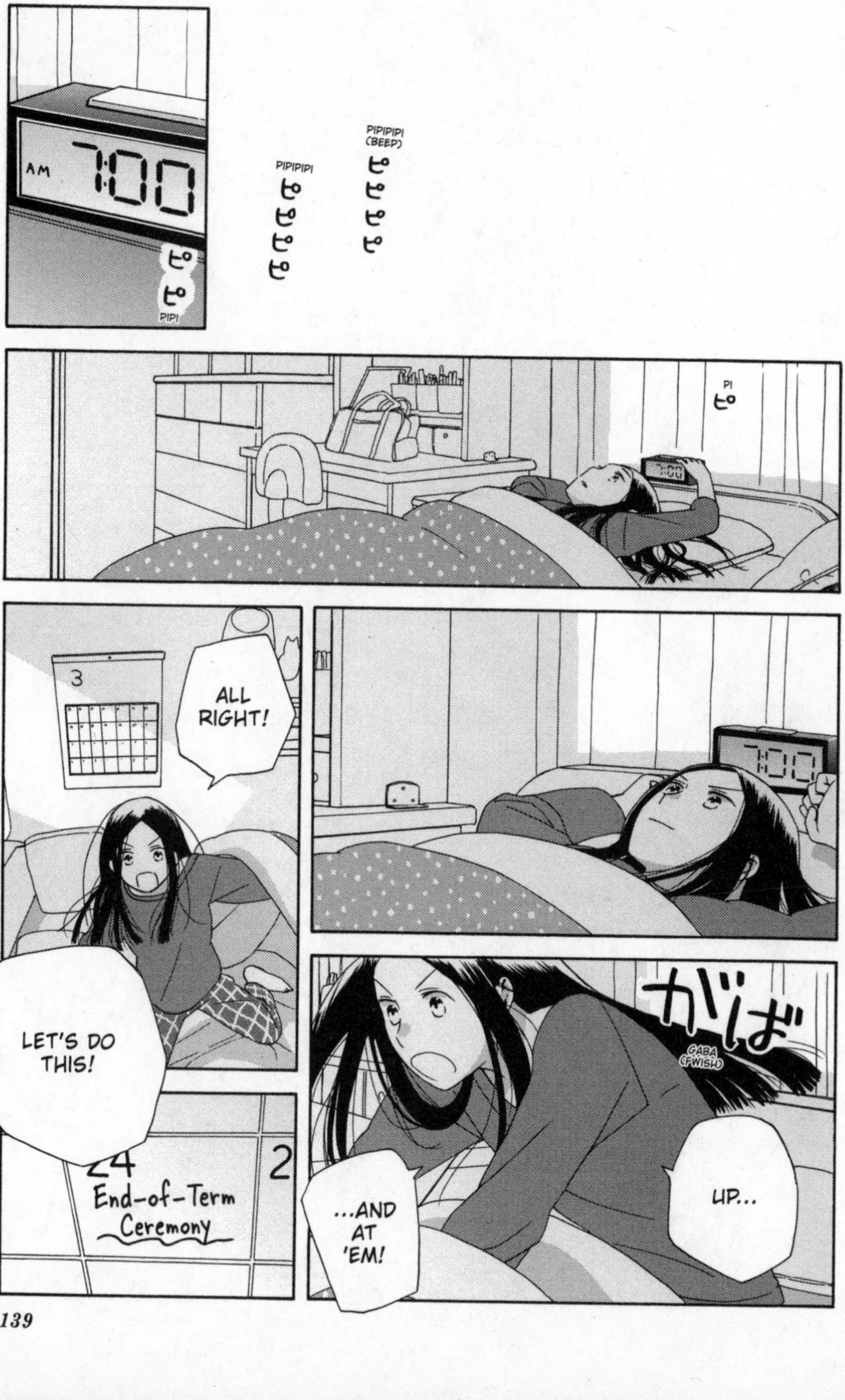

PIPIPIPI (BEEP)
PIPIPIPI
AM 7:00
PIPI
PI
GABA (FWISH)
UP...
...AND AT 'EM!
3
ALL RIGHT!
LET'S DO THIS!
24
End-of-Term Ceremony
2

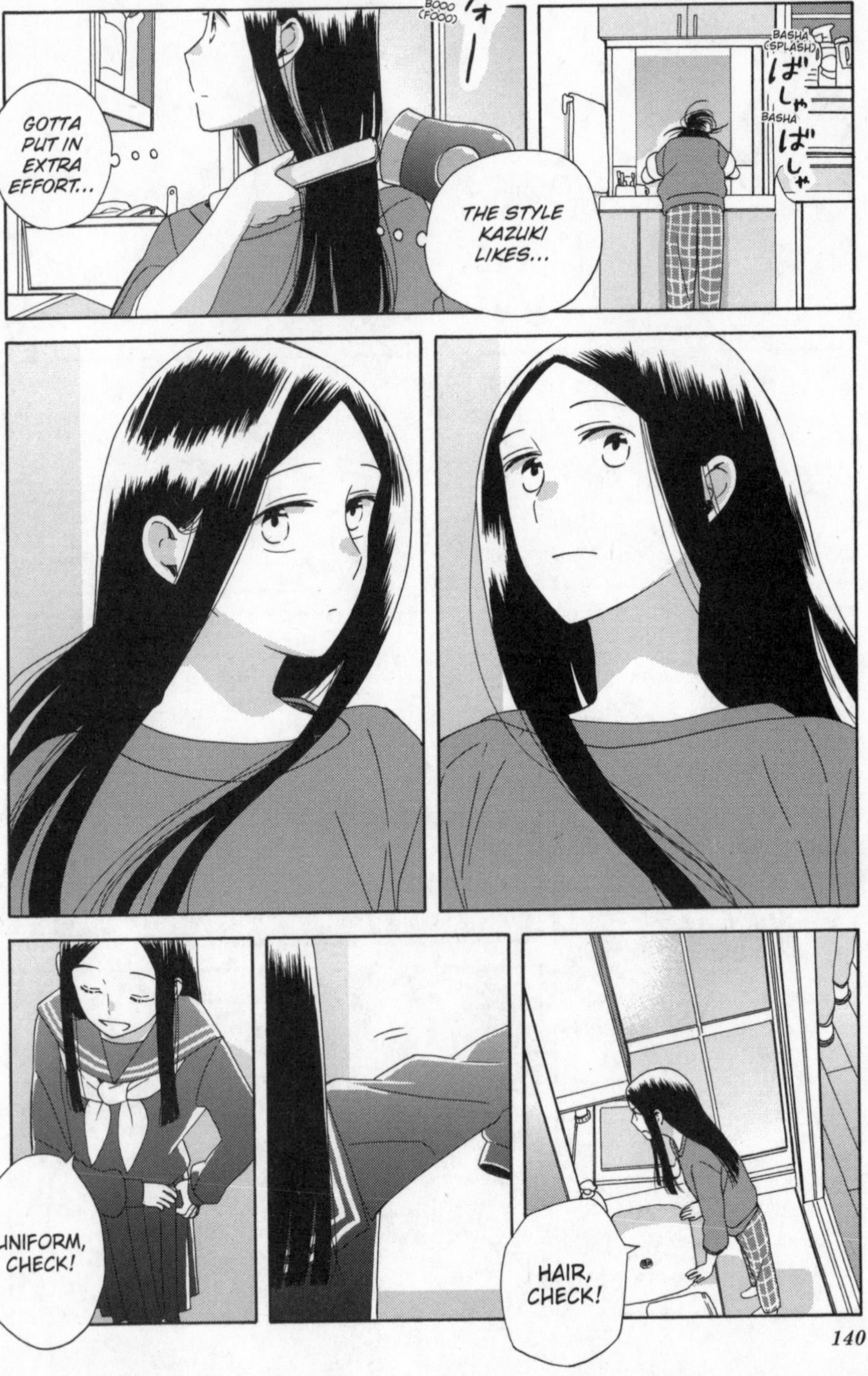
BASHA (SPLASH)
ばしゃ
BASHA
ばしゃ
BOOO (FOOO)
ブォー
THE STYLE KAZUKI LIKES...
GOTTA PUT IN EXTRA EFFORT...
HAIR, CHECK!
UNIFORM, CHECK!

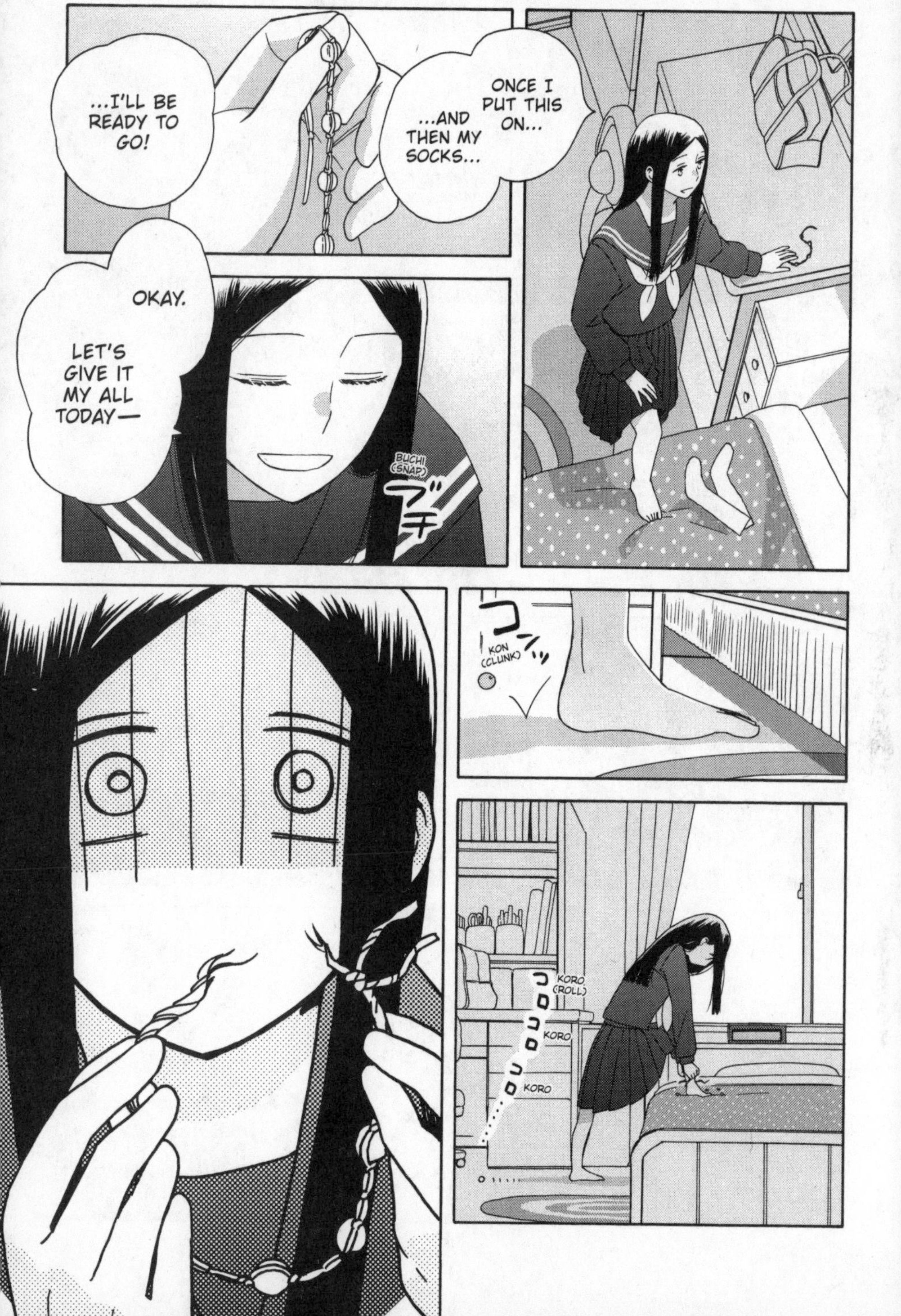
ONCE I PUT THIS ON...
...AND THEN MY SOCKS...
...I'LL BE READY TO GO!
OKAY.
LET'S GIVE IT MY ALL TODAY—
BUCHI (SNAP)
KON (CLUNK)
KORO (ROLL)
KORO
KORO

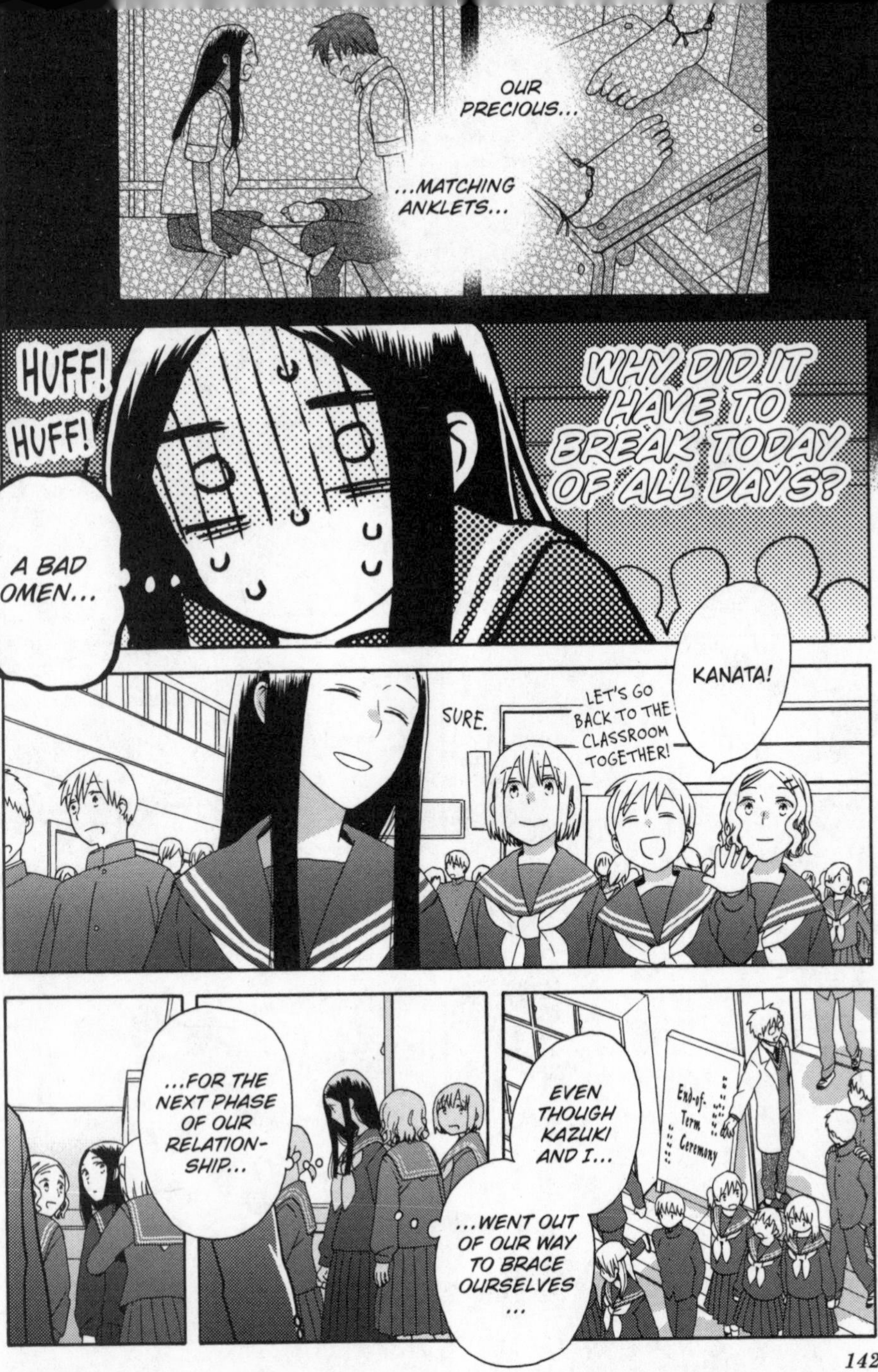
OUR PRECIOUS...
...MATCHING ANKLETS...
WHY DID IT HAVE TO BREAK TODAY OF ALL DAYS?
HUFF! HUFF!
A BAD OMEN...
KANATA!
LET'S GO BACK TO THE CLASSROOM TOGETHER!
SURE.
End-of-Term Ceremony
EVEN THOUGH KAZUKI AND I...
...WENT OUT OF OUR WAY TO BRACE OURSELVES...
...FOR THE NEXT PHASE OF OUR RELATIONSHIP...

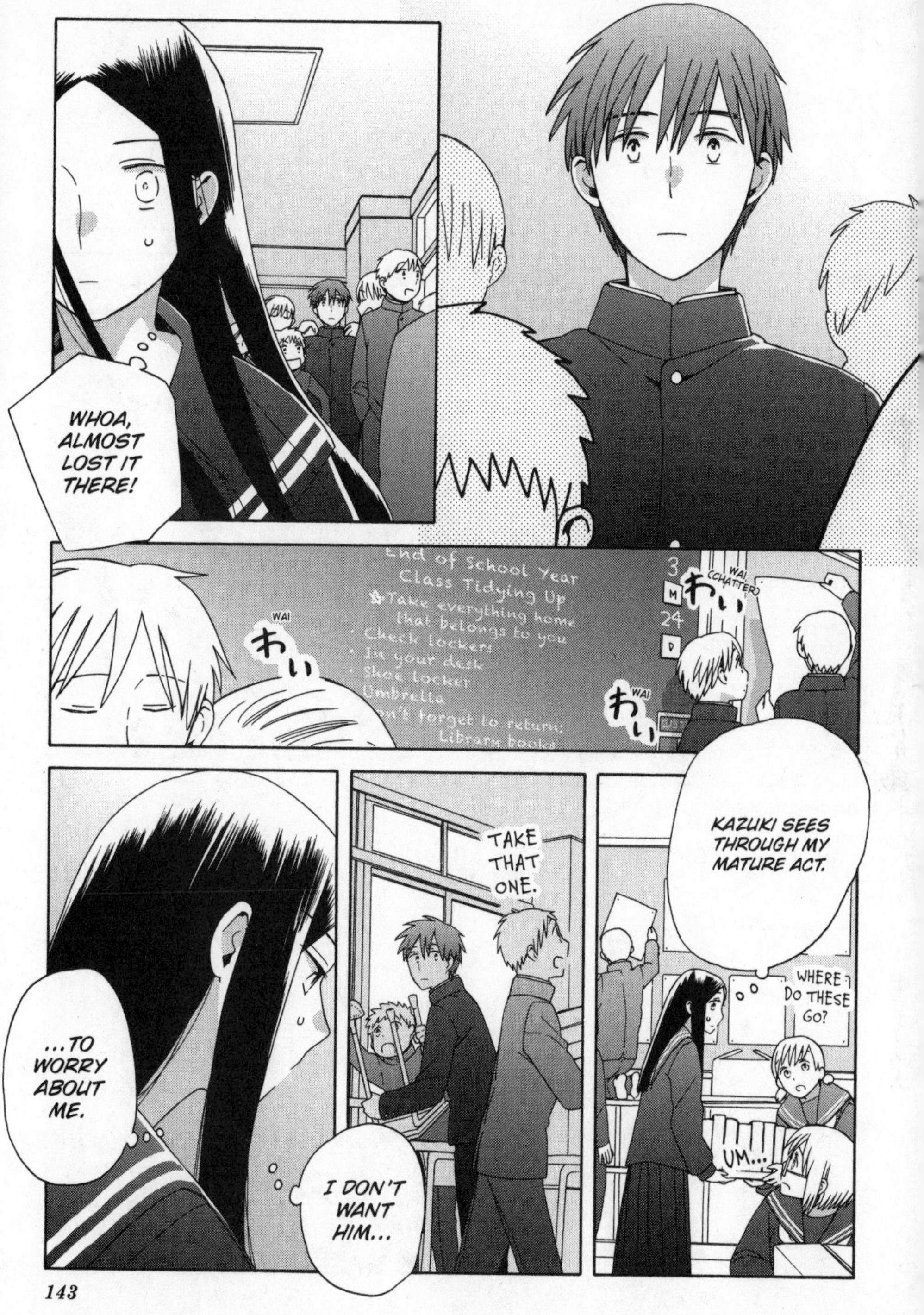
WHOA, ALMOST LOST IT THERE!
わい
WAI (CHATTER)
3 M 24 D
End of School Year
Class Tidying Up
Take everything home that belongs to you
・Check lockers
・In your desk
・Shoe locker
Umbrella
on't forget to return:
Library books
わい
WAI
わい
WAI
KAZUKI SEES THROUGH MY MATURE ACT.
WHERE DO THESE GO?
UM...
TAKE THAT ONE.
I DON'T WANT HIM...
...TO WORRY ABOUT ME.

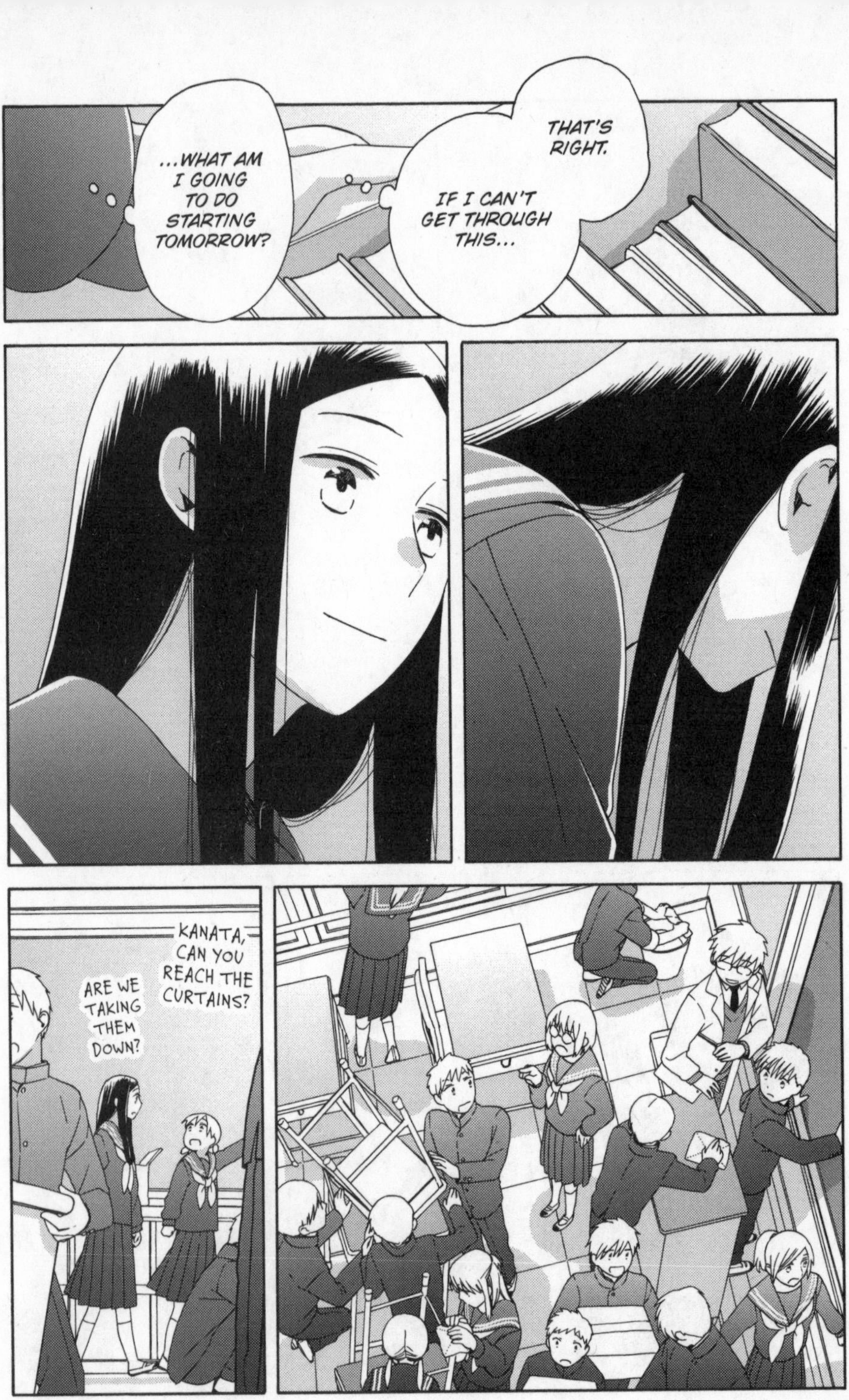
THAT'S RIGHT.
IF I CAN'T GET THROUGH THIS...
...WHAT AM I GOING TO DO STARTING TOMORROW?
KANATA, CAN YOU REACH THE CURTAINS?
ARE WE TAKING THEM DOWN?

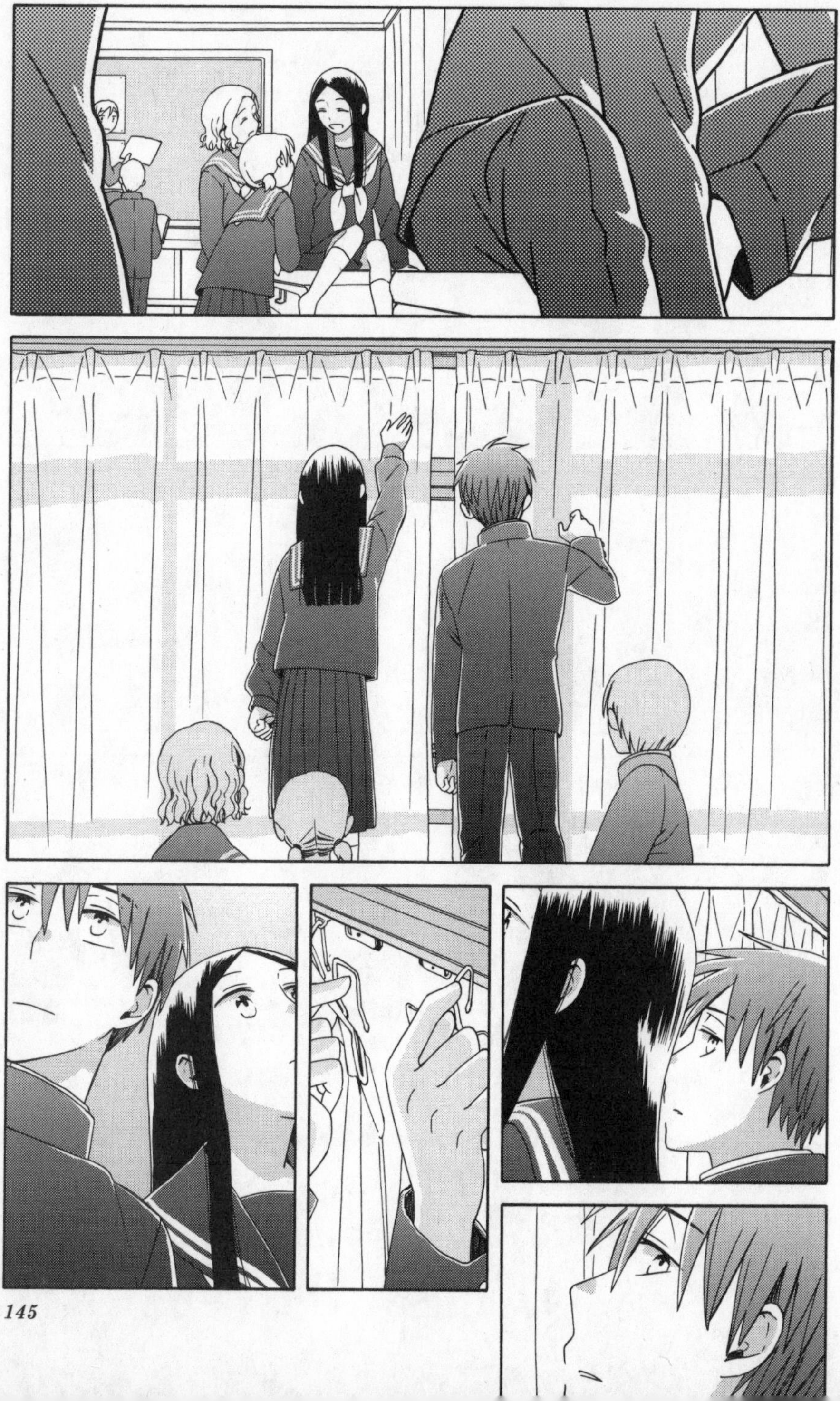

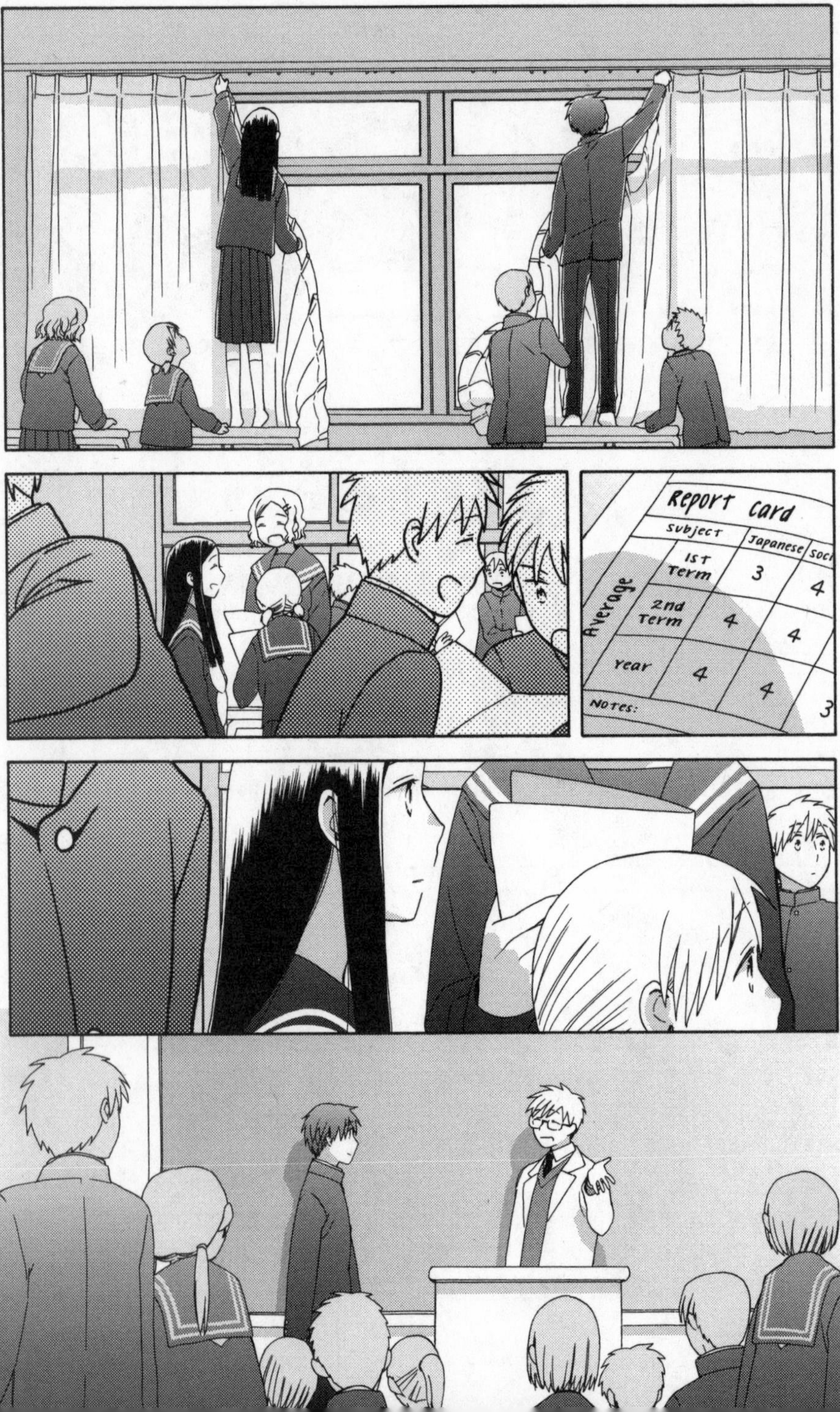

Report Card
Subject
Japanese
Average
1st Term
3
4
2nd Term
4
4
Year
4
4
Notes:
3

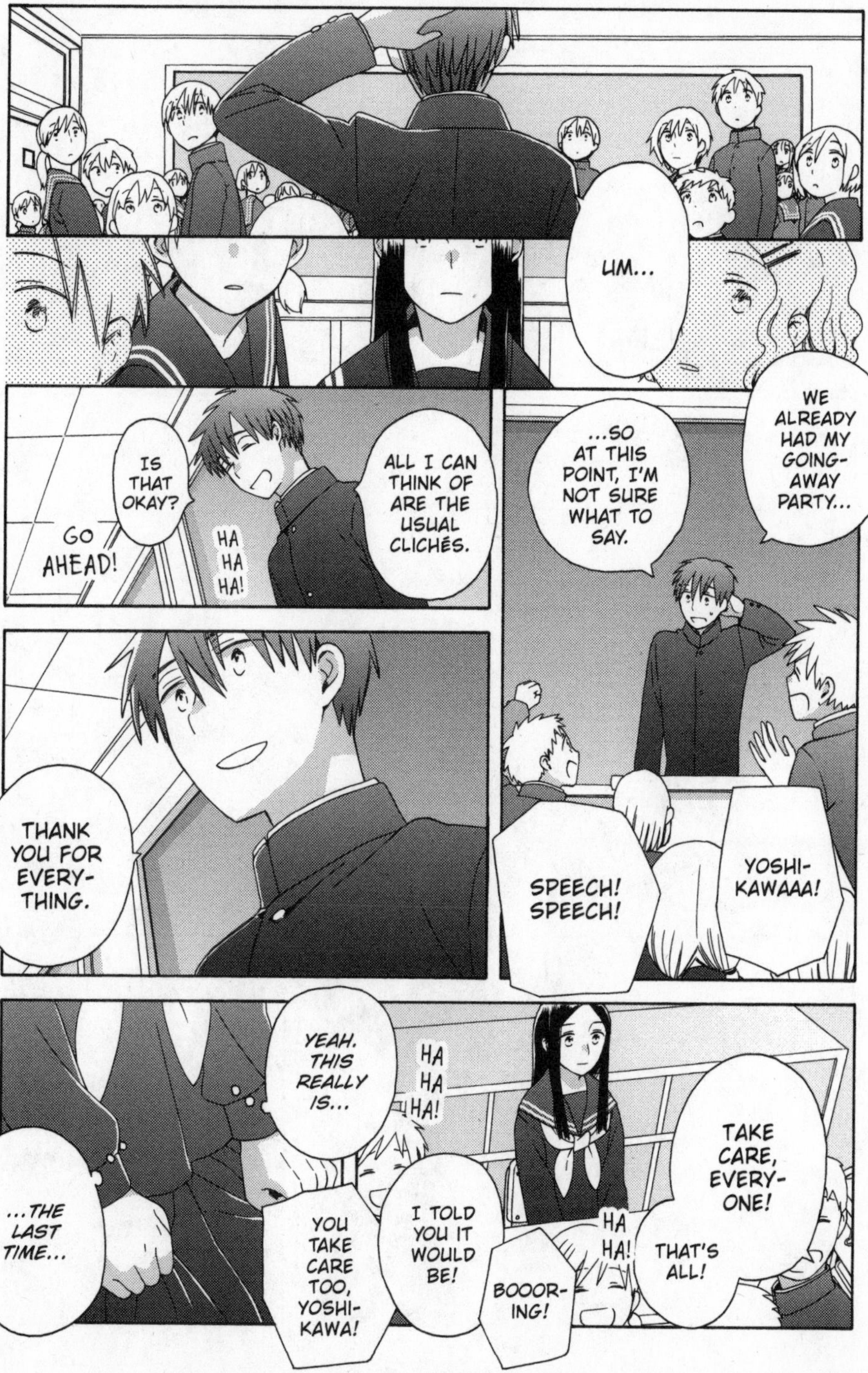
UM...
WE ALREADY HAD MY GOING-AWAY PARTY...
...SO AT THIS POINT, I'M NOT SURE WHAT TO SAY.
YOSHI-KAWAAA!
SPEECH! SPEECH!
ALL I CAN THINK OF ARE THE USUAL CLICHÉS.
HA HA HA!
IS THAT OKAY?
GO AHEAD!
THANK YOU FOR EVERY-THING.
TAKE CARE, EVERY-ONE!
THAT'S ALL!
HA HA!
BOOOR-ING!
HA HA HA!
YEAH. THIS REALLY IS...
I TOLD YOU IT WOULD BE!
YOU TAKE CARE TOO, YOSHI-KAWA!
...THE LAST TIME...

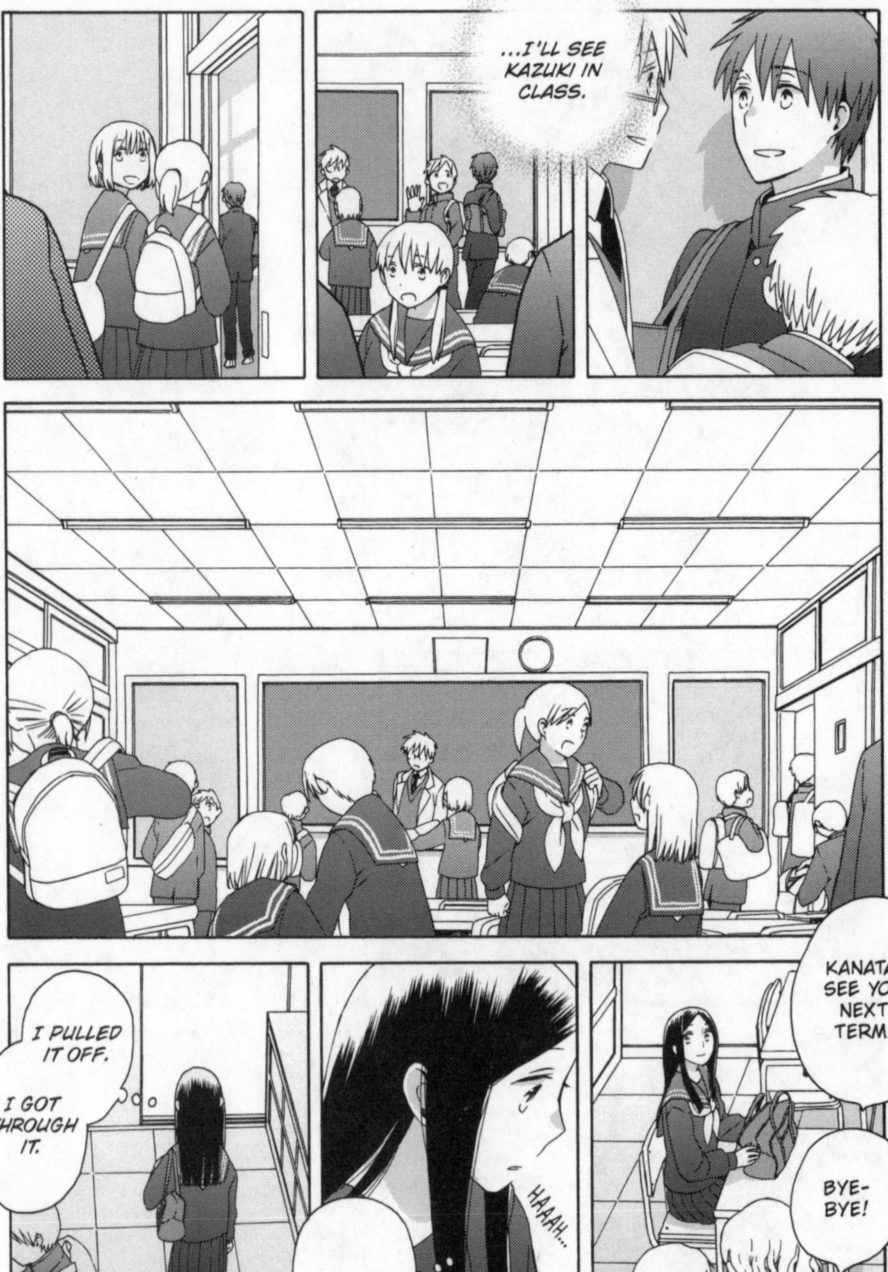
...I'LL SEE KAZUKI IN CLASS.
KANATA, SEE YOU NEXT TERM!
BYE-BYE!
HAAAH...
......I MADE IT.
I PULLED IT OFF.
I GOT THROUGH IT.

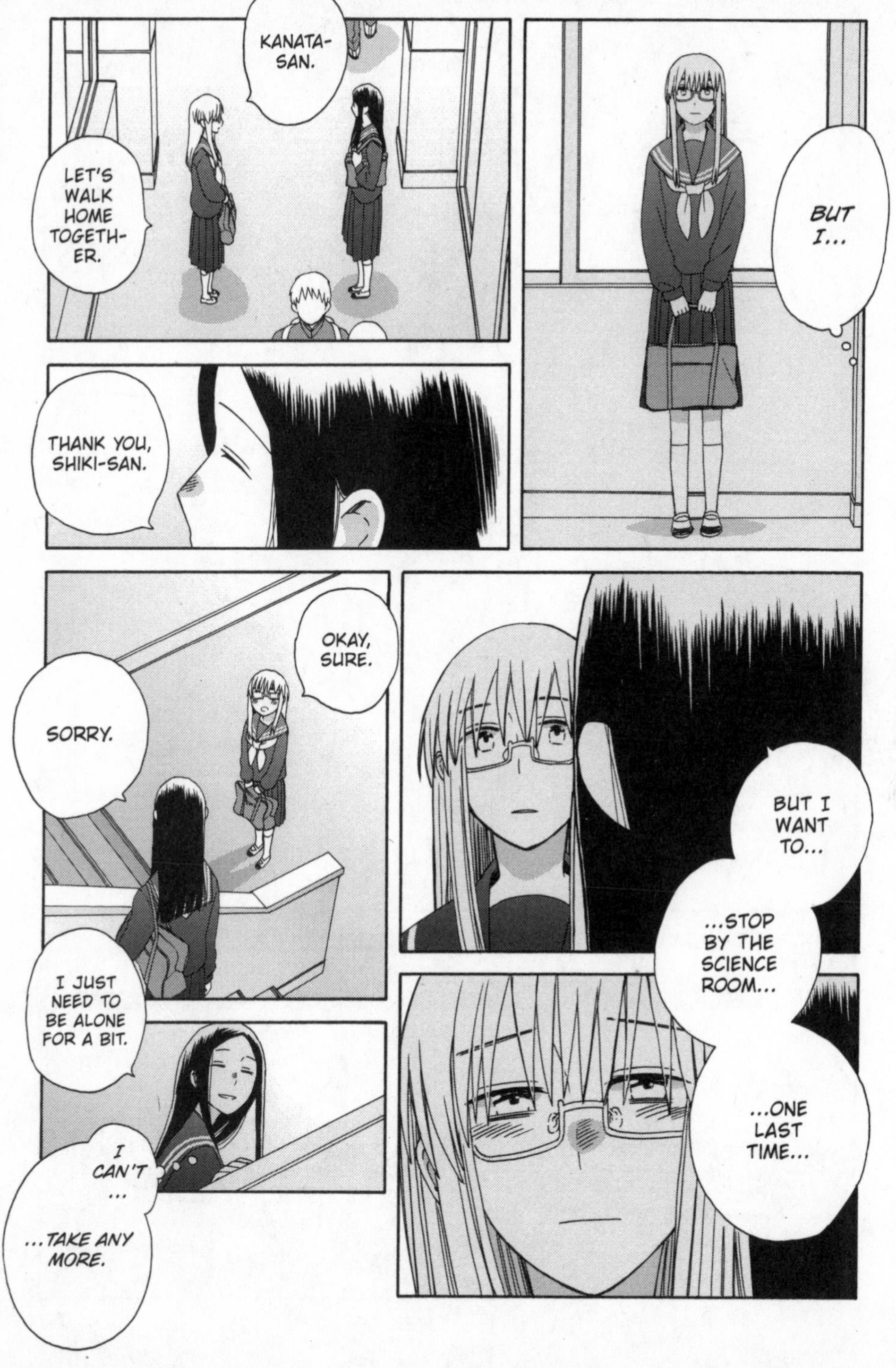
BUT I...
KANATA-SAN.
LET'S WALK HOME TOGETH-ER.
THANK YOU, SHIKI-SAN.
BUT I WANT TO...
...STOP BY THE SCIENCE ROOM...
...ONE LAST TIME...
OKAY, SURE.
SORRY.
I JUST NEED TO BE ALONE FOR A BIT.
I CAN'T ...
...TAKE ANY MORE.

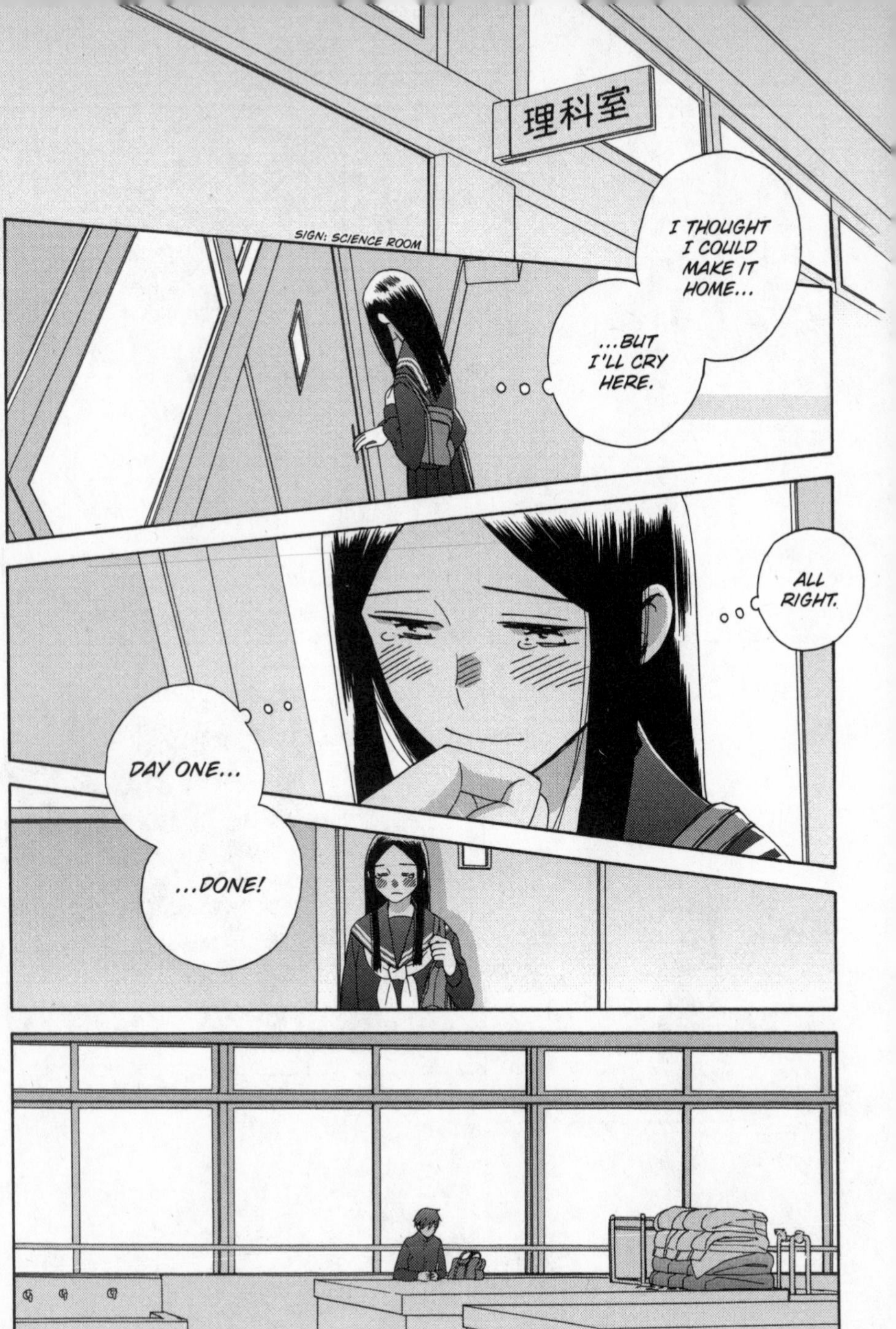
理科室
SIGN: SCIENCE ROOM
I THOUGHT I COULD MAKE IT HOME...
...BUT I'LL CRY HERE.
ALL RIGHT.
DAY ONE...
...DONE!

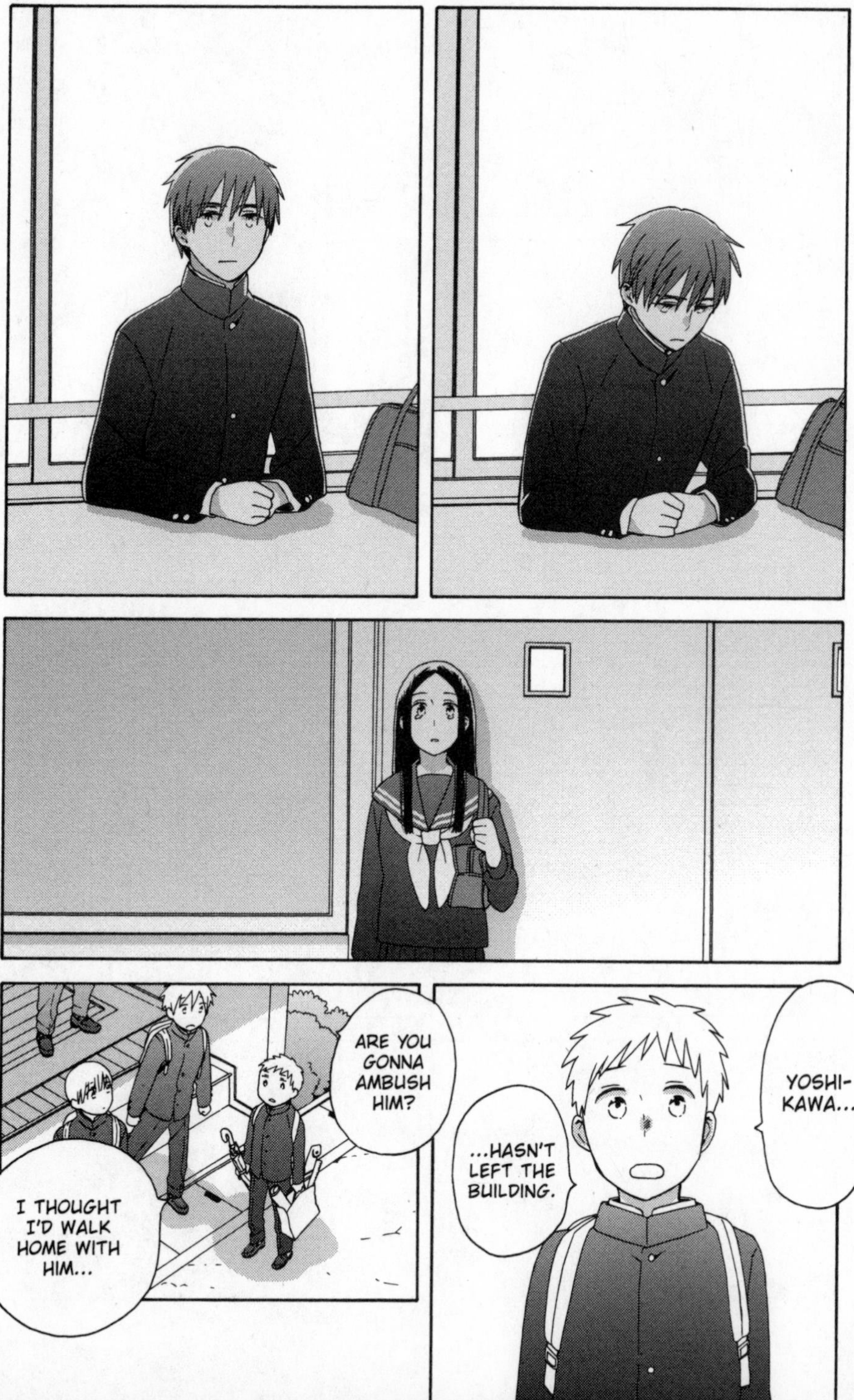
YOSHI-KAWA...
...HASN'T LEFT THE BUILDING.
ARE YOU GONNA AMBUSH HIM?
I THOUGHT I'D WALK HOME WITH HIM...

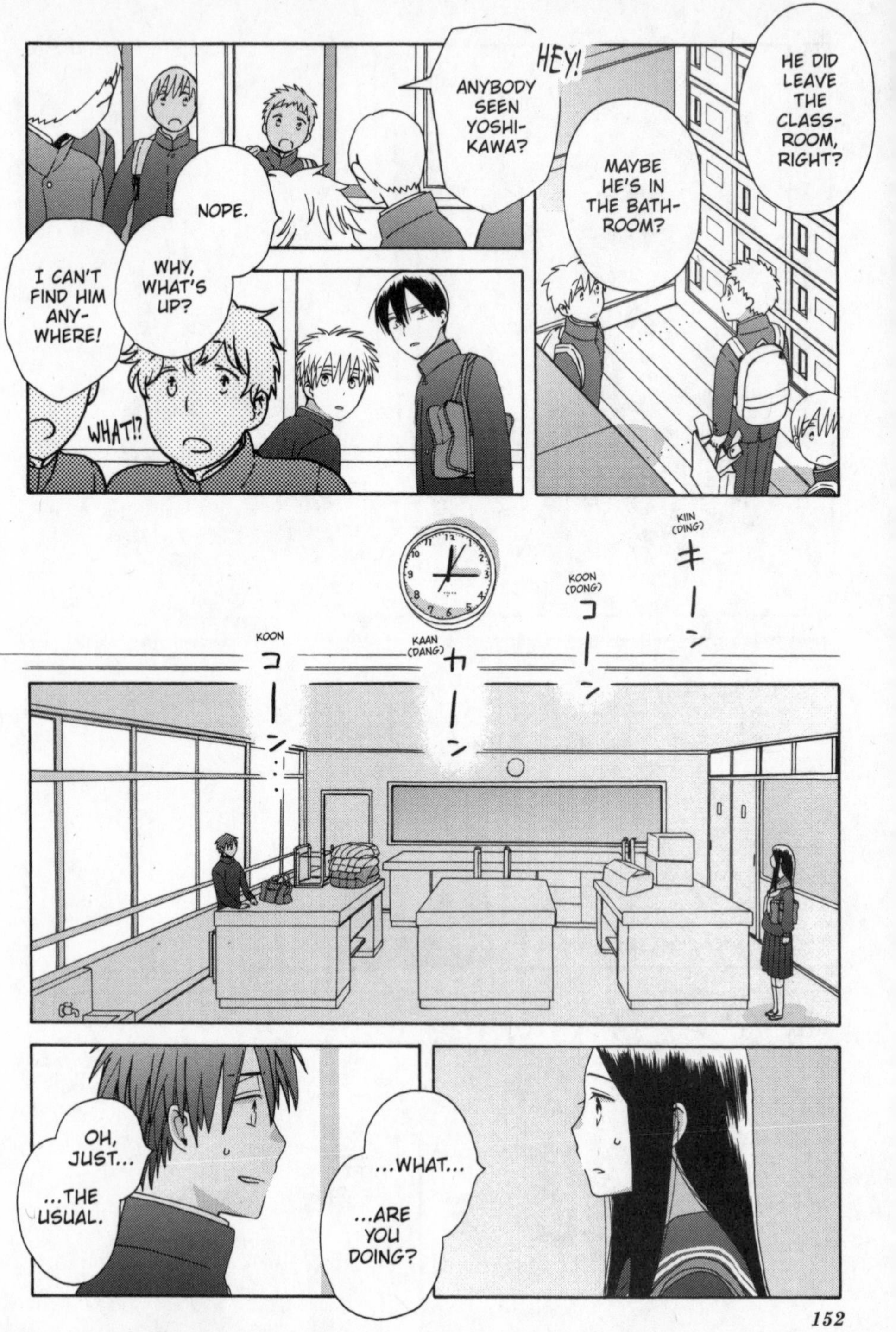
HE DID LEAVE THE CLASS-ROOM, RIGHT?
MAYBE HE'S IN THE BATH-ROOM?
HEY!
ANYBODY SEEN YOSHI-KAWA?
NOPE.
WHY, WHAT'S UP?
I CAN'T FIND HIM ANY-WHERE!
WHAT!?
KIIN (DING)
キーン
KOON (DONG)
コーン
KAAN (DANG)
カーン
KOON
コーン…
...WHAT...
...ARE YOU DOING?
OH, JUST...
...THE USUAL.

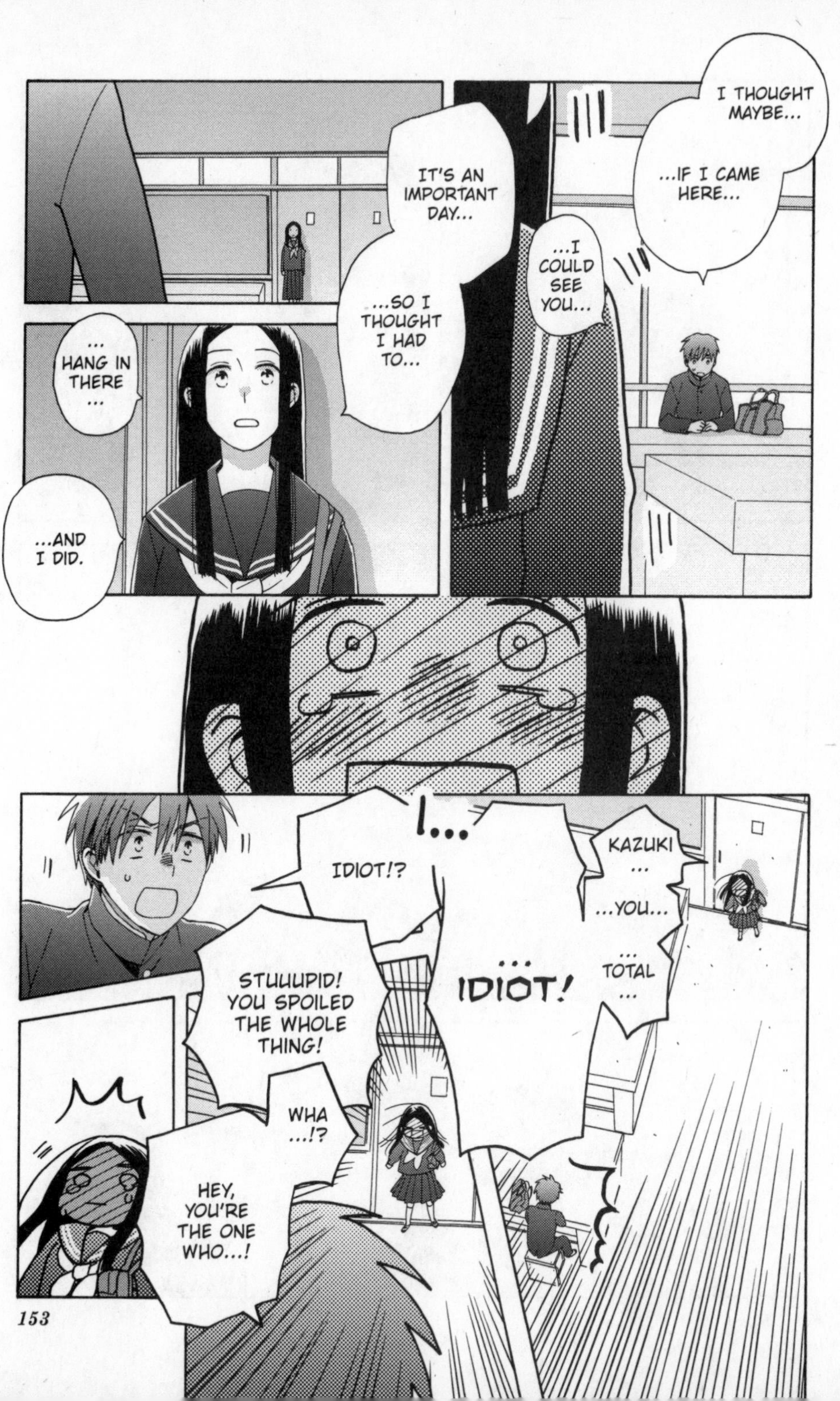

I THOUGHT MAYBE...
...IF I CAME HERE...
...I COULD SEE YOU...
IT'S AN IMPORTANT DAY...
...SO I THOUGHT I HAD TO...
...HANG IN THERE...
...AND I DID.
KAZUKI...
...YOU...
...TOTAL...
...IDIOT!
I...
IDIOT!?
STUUUPID! YOU SPOILED THE WHOLE THING!
WHA...!?
HEY, YOU'RE THE ONE WHO...!

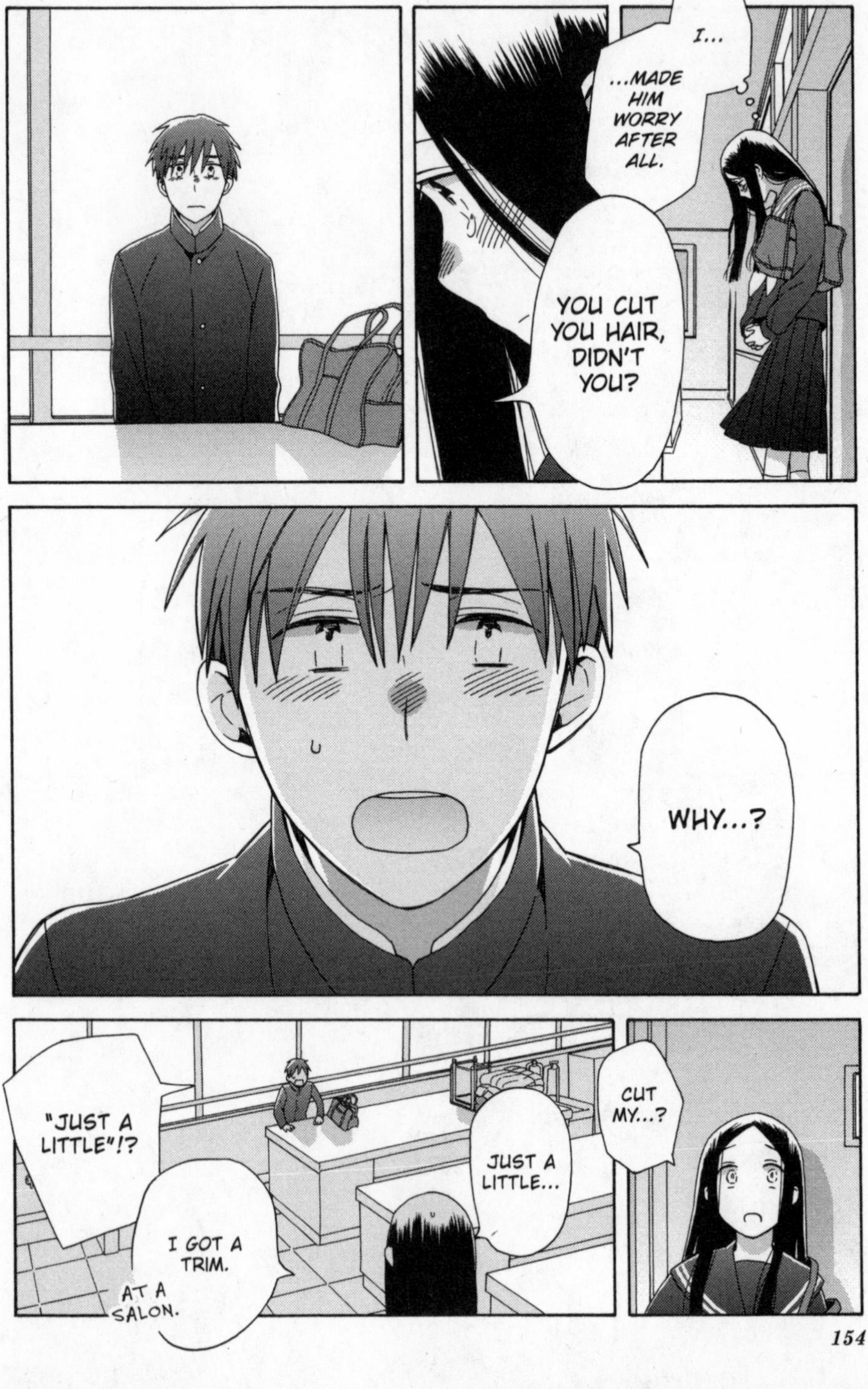
I...
...MADE HIM WORRY AFTER ALL.
YOU CUT YOU HAIR, DIDN'T YOU?
WHY...?
CUT MY...?
JUST A LITTLE...
"JUST A LITTLE"!?
I GOT A TRIM.
AT A SALON.

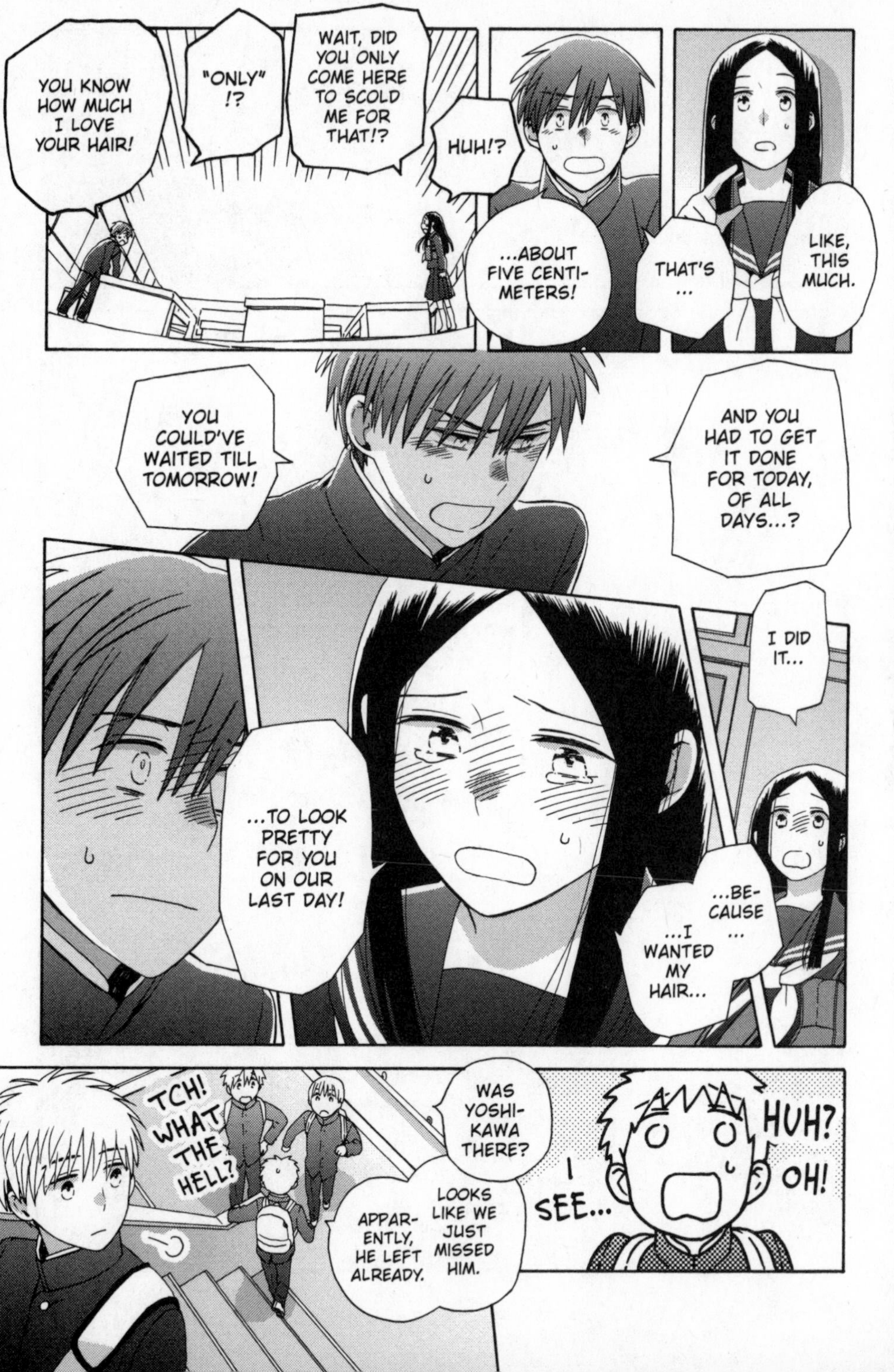
LIKE, THIS MUCH.
THAT'S ...
...ABOUT FIVE CENTIMETERS!
HUH!?
WAIT, DID YOU ONLY COME HERE TO SCOLD ME FOR THAT!?
"ONLY" !?
YOU KNOW HOW MUCH I LOVE YOUR HAIR!
AND YOU HAD TO GET IT DONE FOR TODAY, OF ALL DAYS...?
YOU COULD'VE WAITED TILL TOMORROW!
I DID IT...
...BECAUSE ...
...I WANTED MY HAIR...
...TO LOOK PRETTY FOR YOU ON OUR LAST DAY!
HUH? OH!
I SEE...
WAS YOSHIKAWA THERE?
LOOKS LIKE WE JUST MISSED HIM.
APPARENTLY, HE LEFT ALREADY.
TCH! WHAT THE HELL?

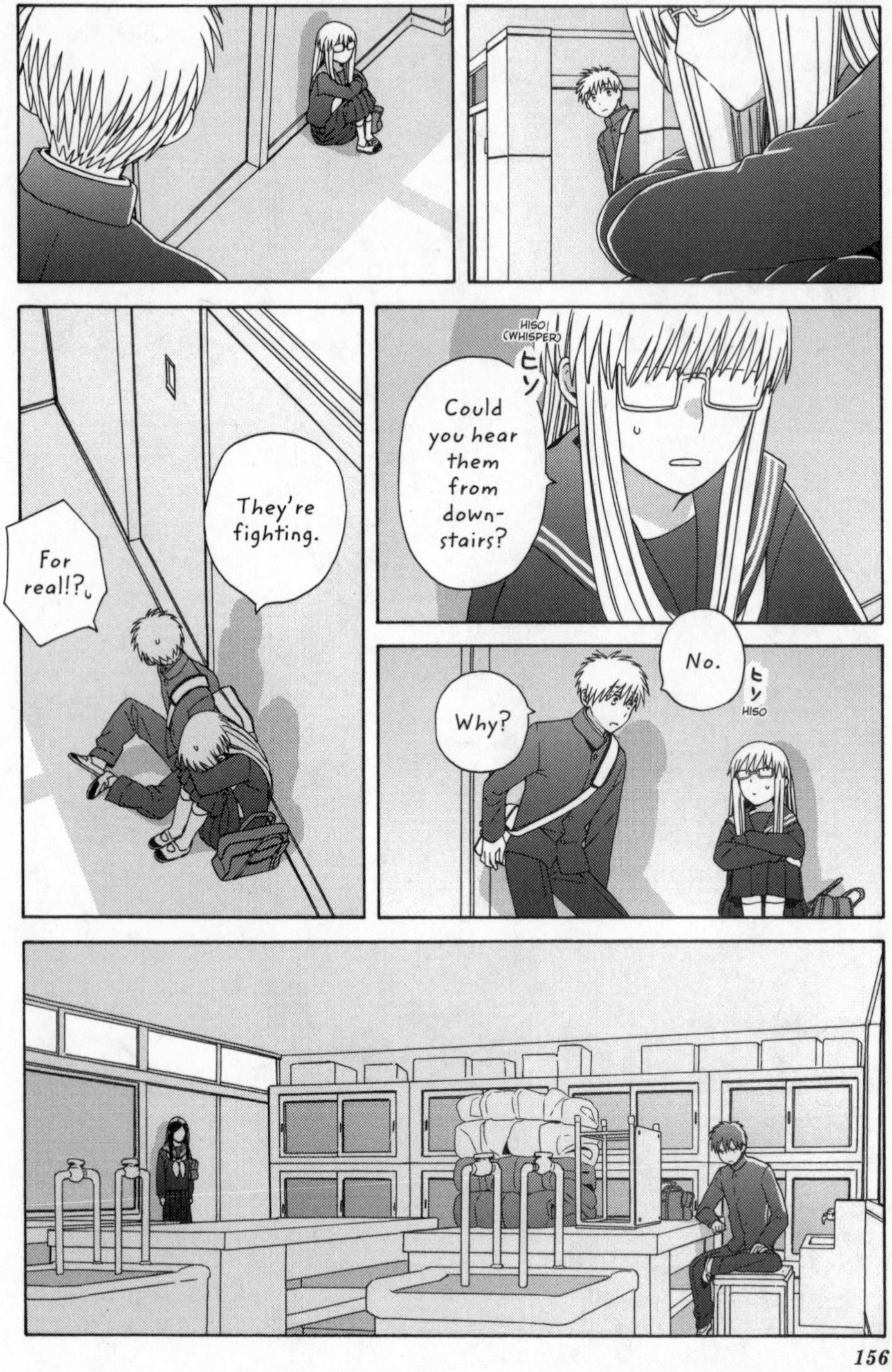
HISO! (WHISPER)
ヒソ
Could you hear them from downstairs?
No.
ヒソ
HISO
Why?
They're fighting.
For real!?

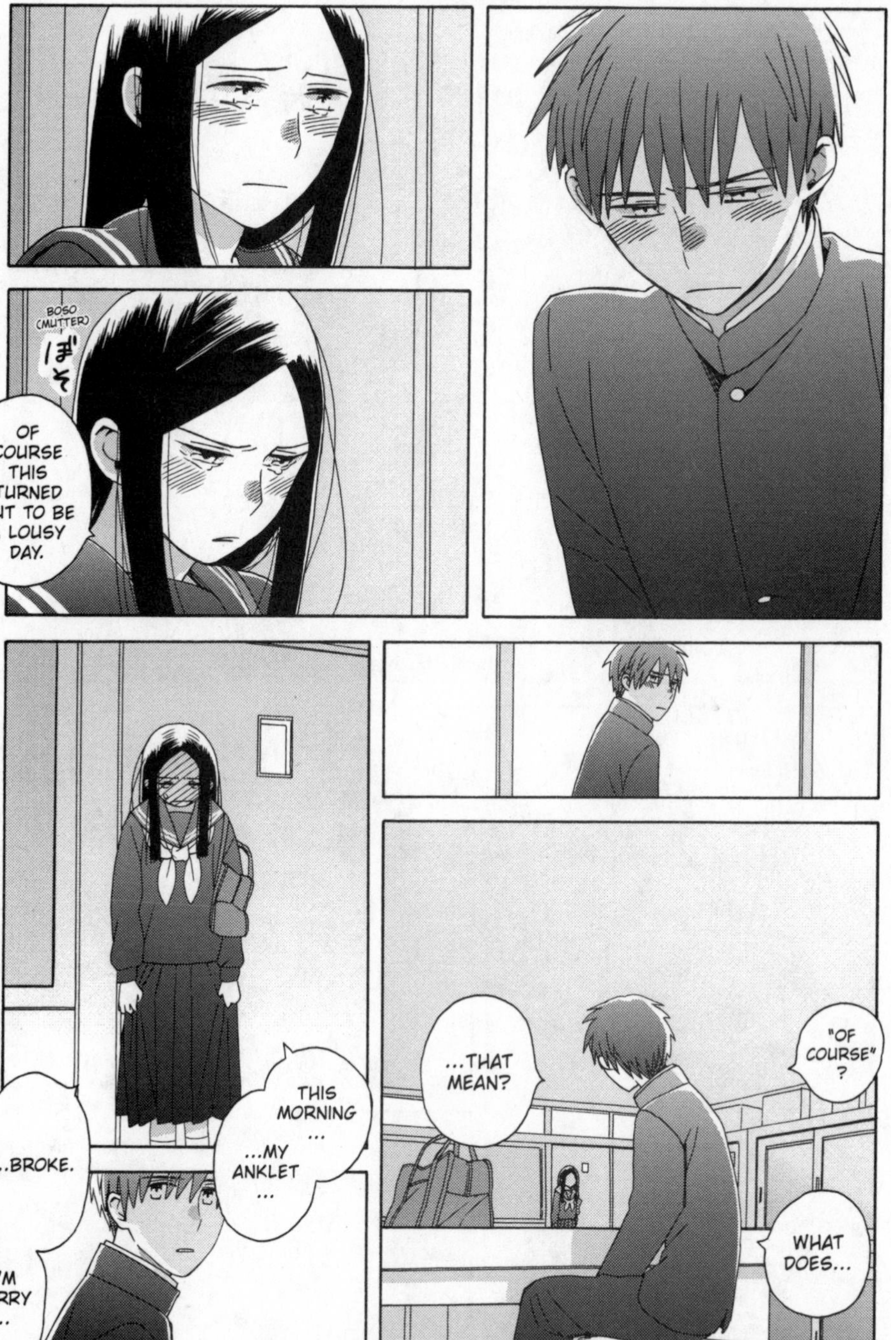
BOSO (MUTTER)
ぼそ
OF COURSE THIS TURNED OUT TO BE A LOUSY DAY.
"OF COURSE"?
WHAT DOES...
...THAT MEAN?
THIS MORNING ...
...MY ANKLET ...
...BROKE.
I'M SORRY ...

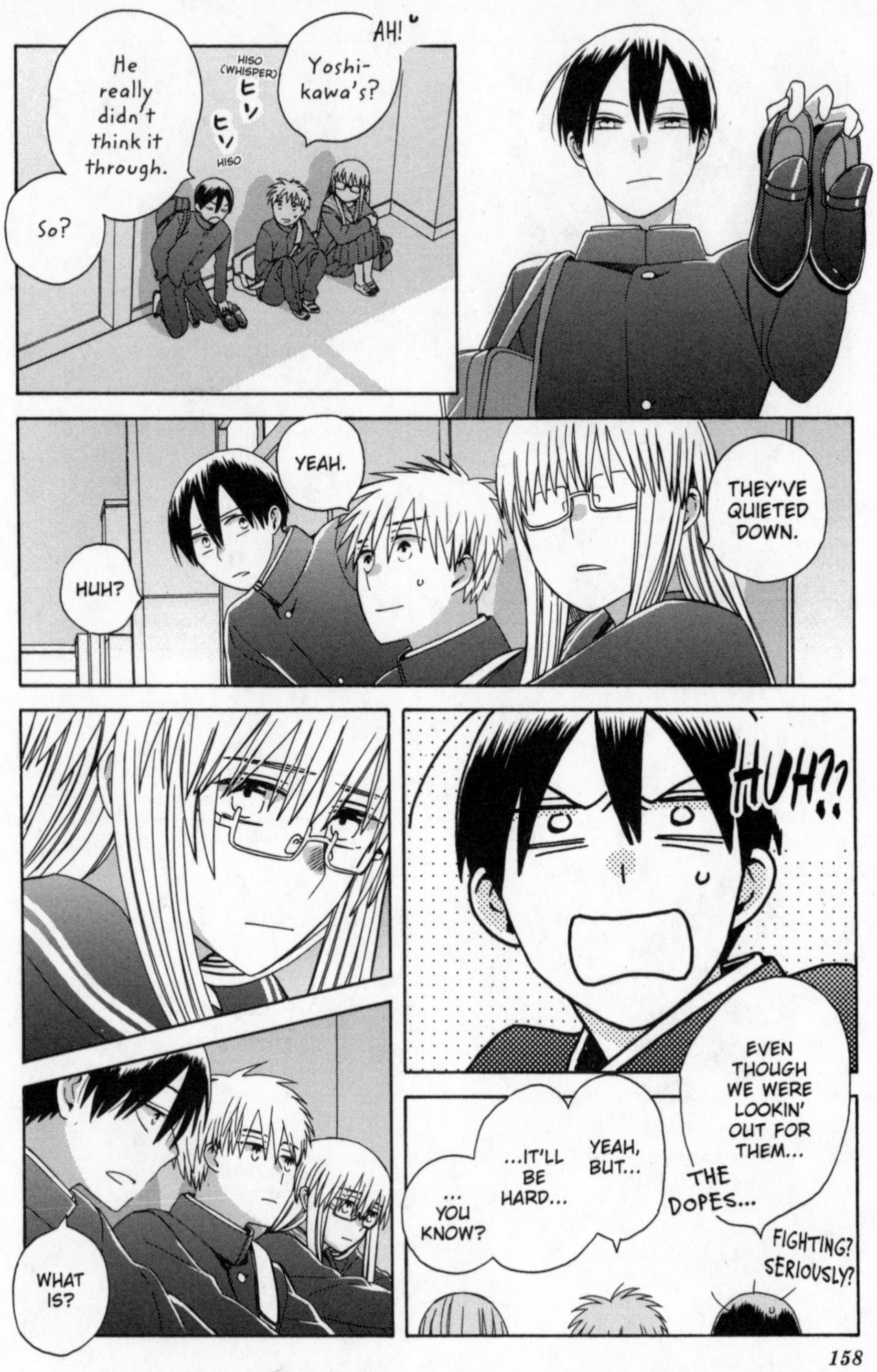
AH!
Yoshi-kawa's?
HISO (WHISPER) ヒソ
ヒソ HISO
He really didn't think it through.
So?
THEY'VE QUIETED DOWN.
YEAH.
HUH?
HUH??
EVEN THOUGH WE WERE LOOKIN' OUT FOR THEM...
THE DOPES...
FIGHTING? SERIOUSLY?
YEAH, BUT...
...IT'LL BE HARD...
...YOU KNOW?
WHAT IS?

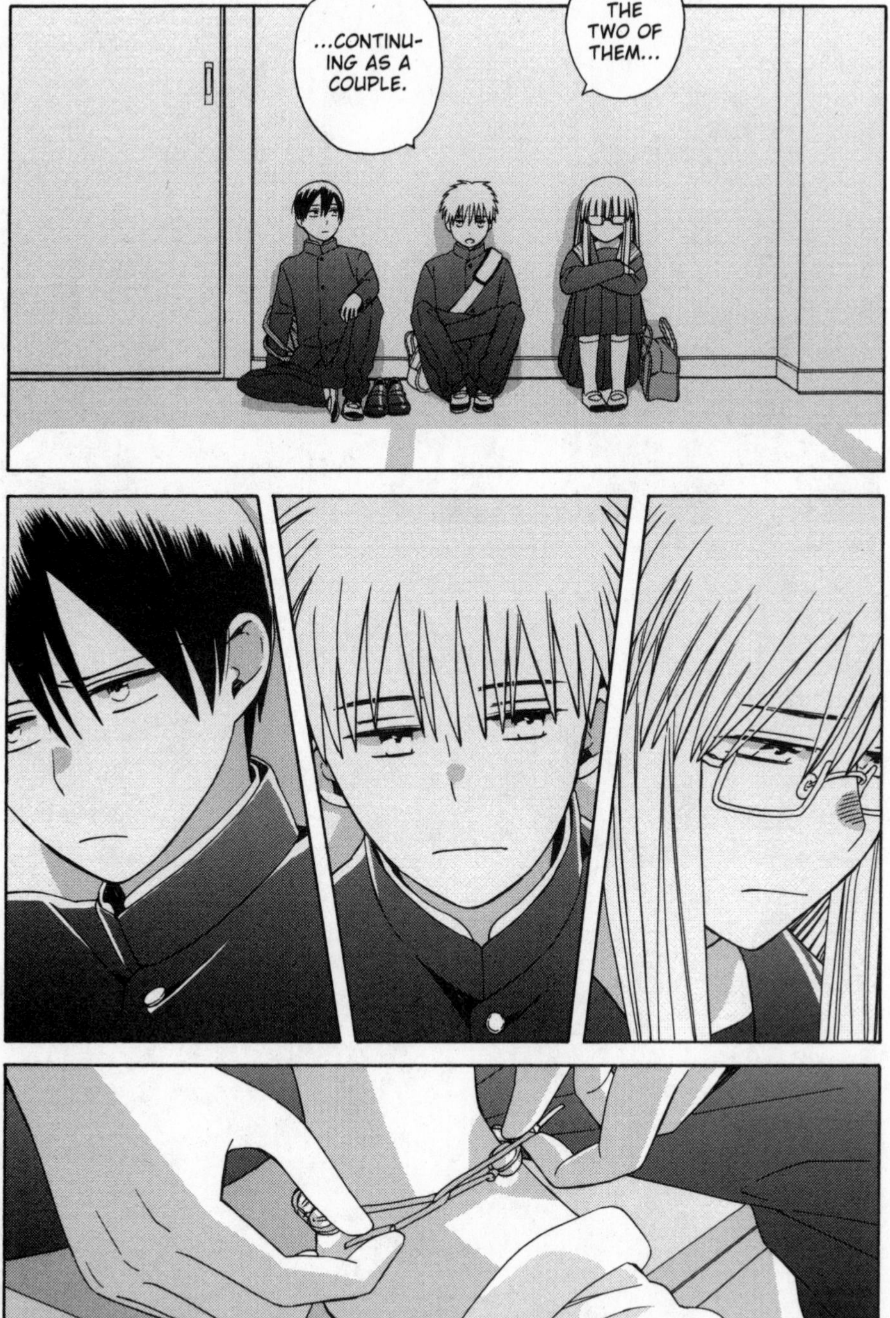
THE TWO OF THEM...
...CONTINUING AS A COUPLE.

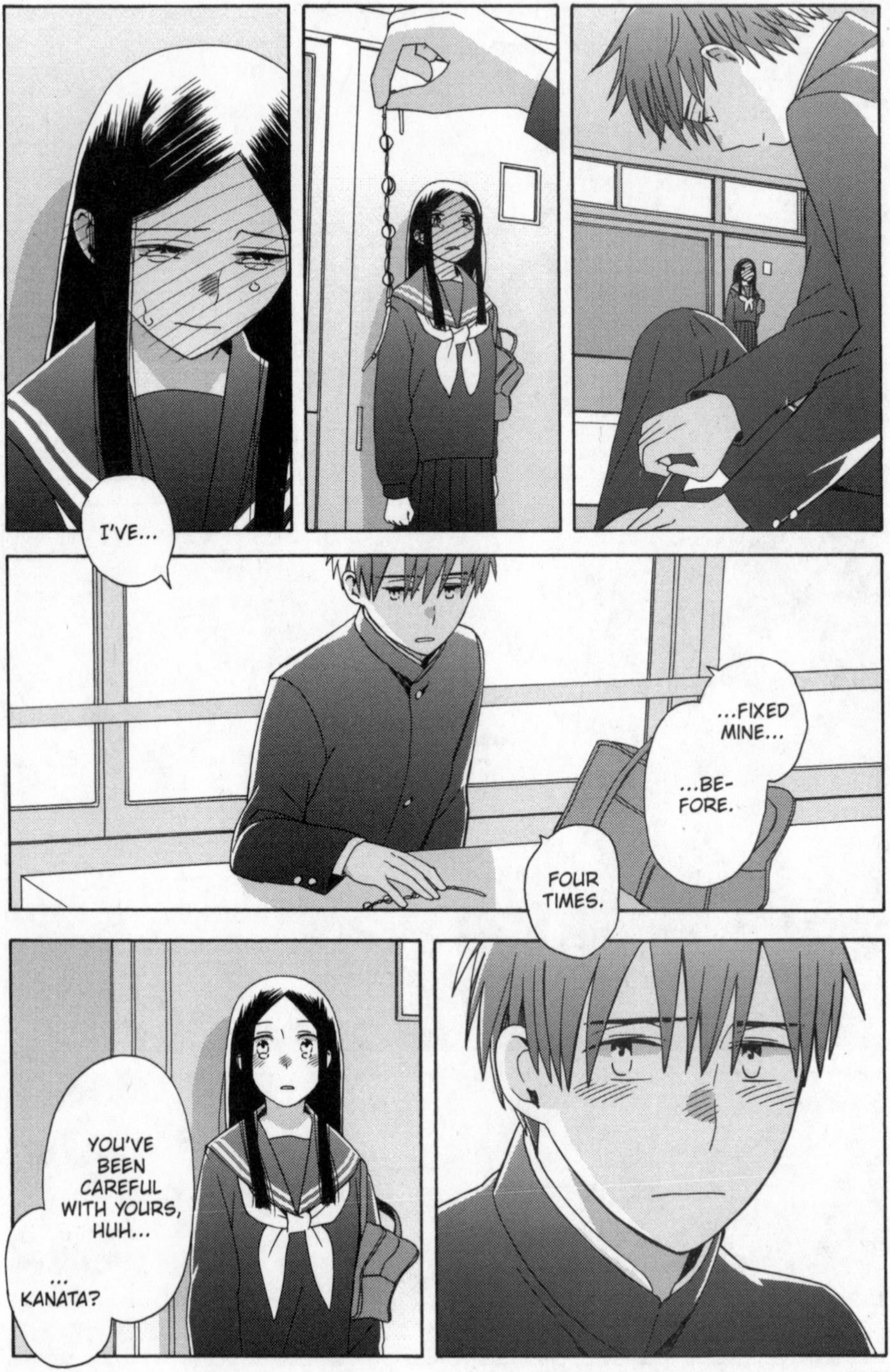
I'VE...
...FIXED MINE...
...BE-FORE.
FOUR TIMES.
YOU'VE BEEN CAREFUL WITH YOURS, HUH...
... KANATA?

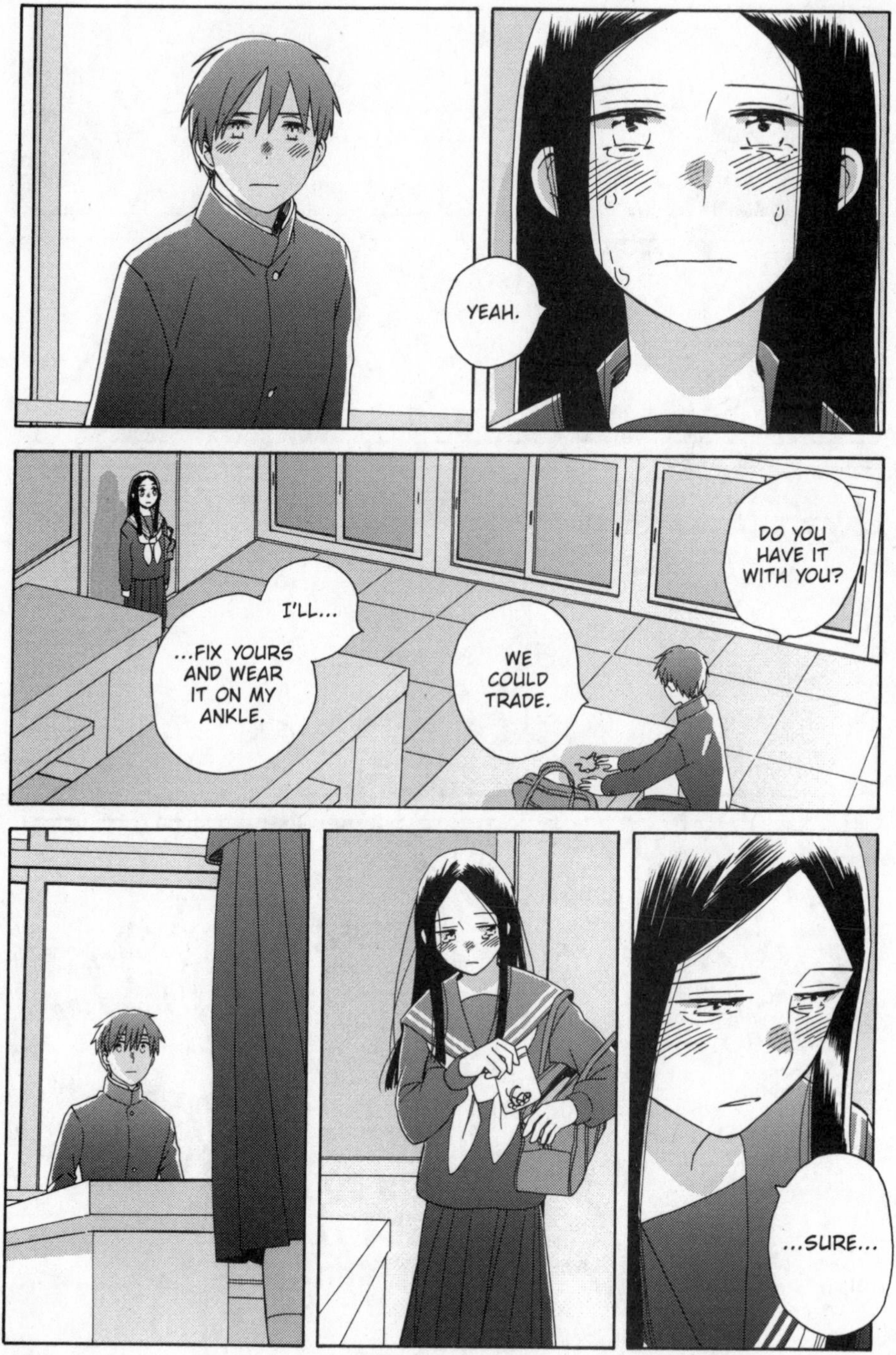
YEAH.
DO YOU HAVE IT WITH YOU?
WE COULD TRADE.
I'LL...
...FIX YOURS AND WEAR IT ON MY ANKLE.
...SURE...

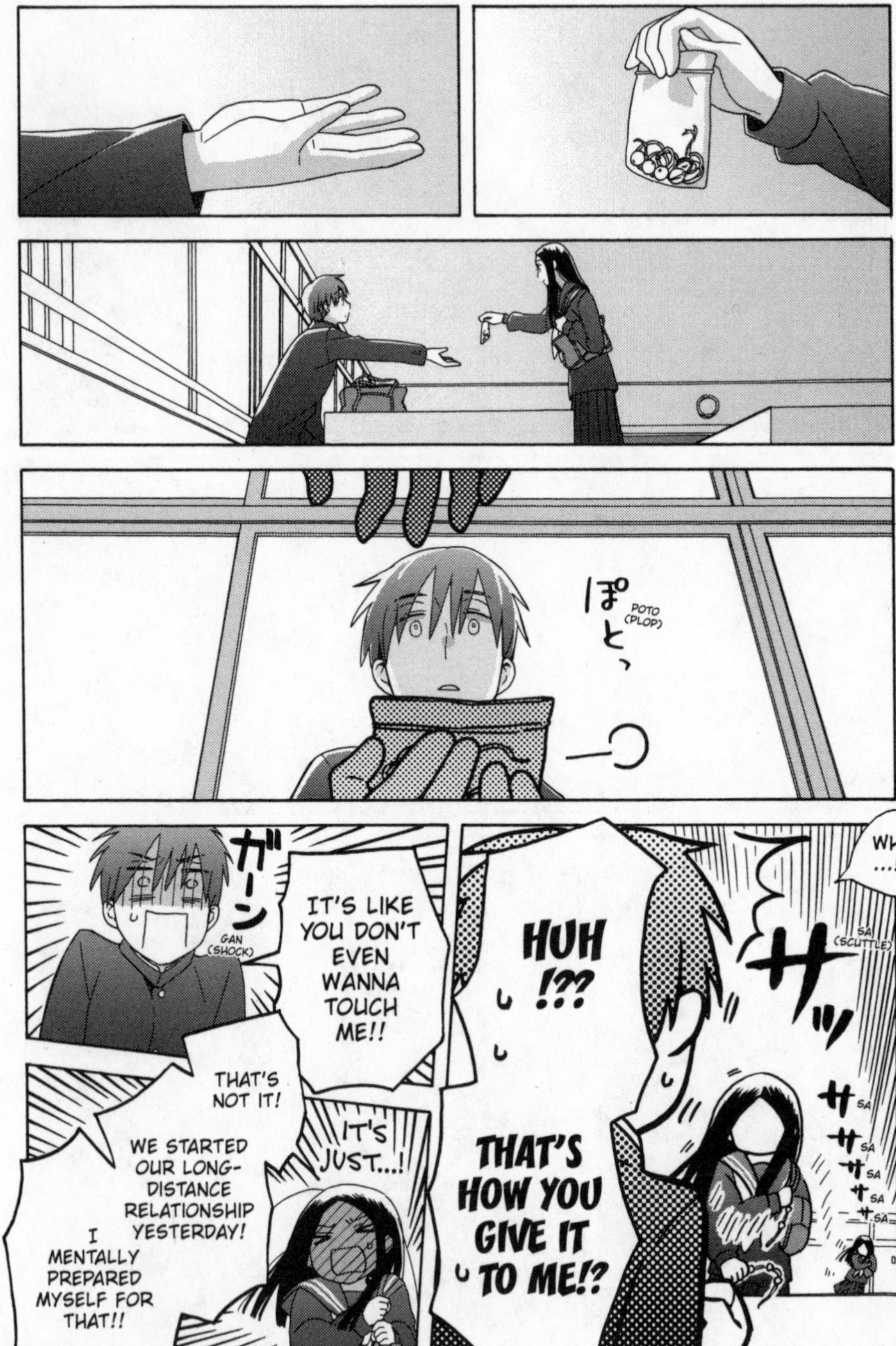
ぽと、
POTO (PLOP)
WHA ...!?
サッ
SA (SCUTTLE)
HUH !??
THAT'S HOW YOU GIVE IT TO ME!?
サ SA
サ SA
サ SA
サ SA
サ SA
ガーン
GAN (SHOCK)
IT'S LIKE YOU DON'T EVEN WANNA TOUCH ME!!
THAT'S NOT IT!
IT'S JUST...!
WE STARTED OUR LONG-DISTANCE RELATIONSHIP YESTERDAY!
I MENTALLY PREPARED MYSELF FOR THAT!!

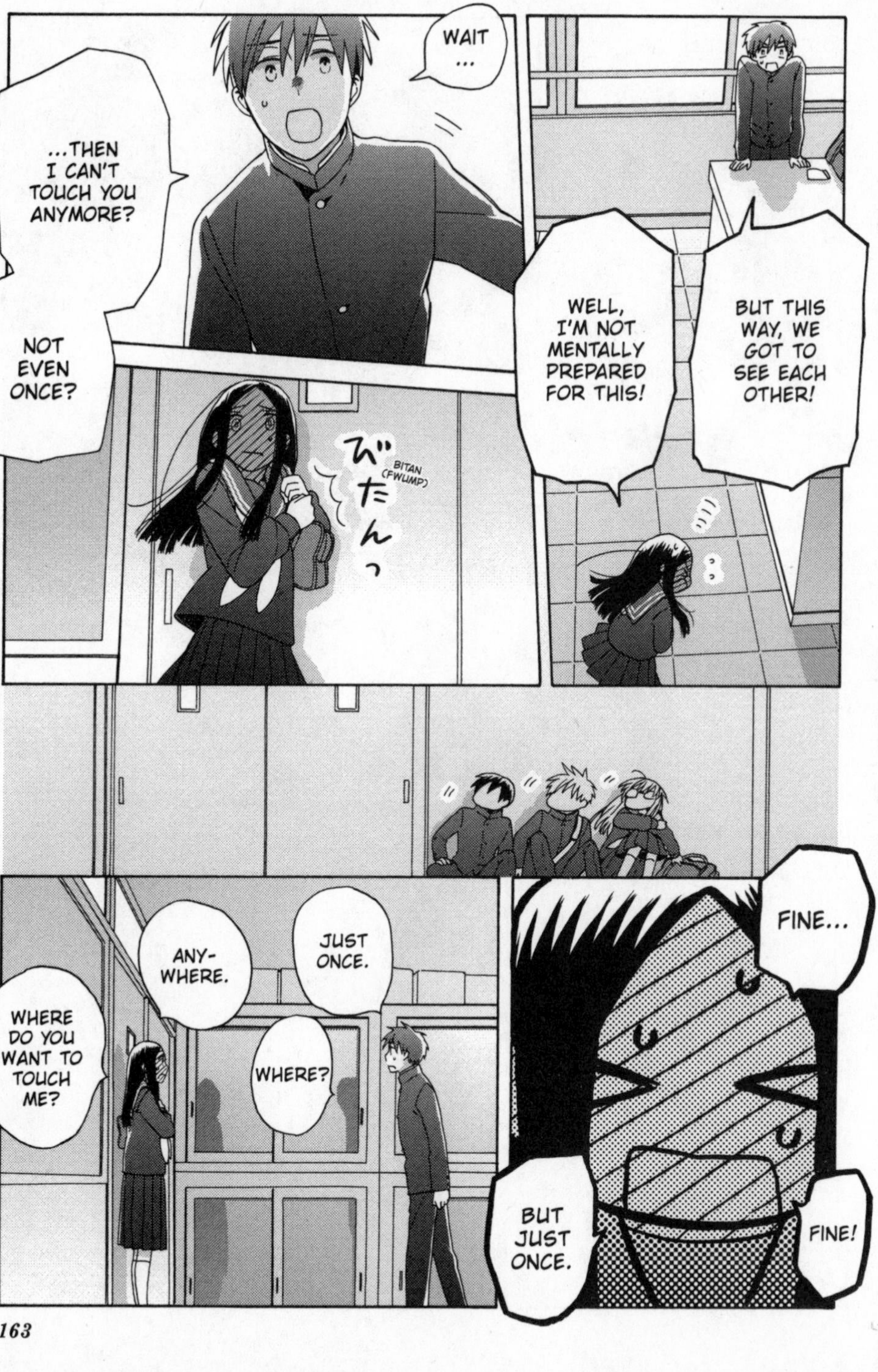
BUT THIS WAY, WE GOT TO SEE EACH OTHER!
WELL, I'M NOT MENTALLY PREPARED FOR THIS!
WAIT ...
...THEN I CAN'T TOUCH YOU ANYMORE?
NOT EVEN ONCE?
びたんっ
BITAN (FWUMP)
FINE...
FINE!
BUT JUST ONCE.
JUST ONCE.
ANY-WHERE.
WHERE?
WHERE DO YOU WANT TO TOUCH ME?

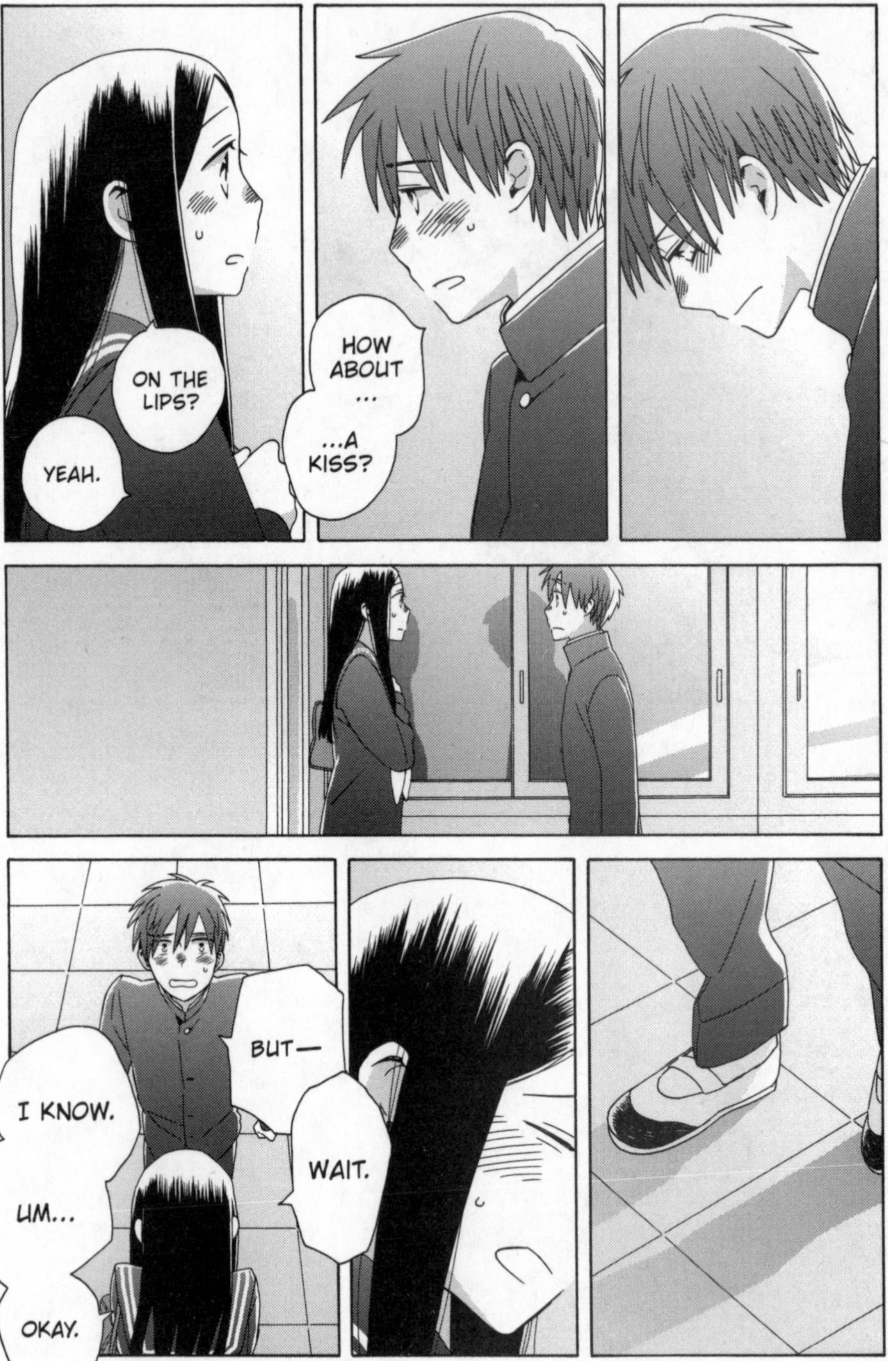
HOW ABOUT ...
...A KISS?
ON THE LIPS?
YEAH.
WAIT.
BUT—
I KNOW.
UM...
OKAY.

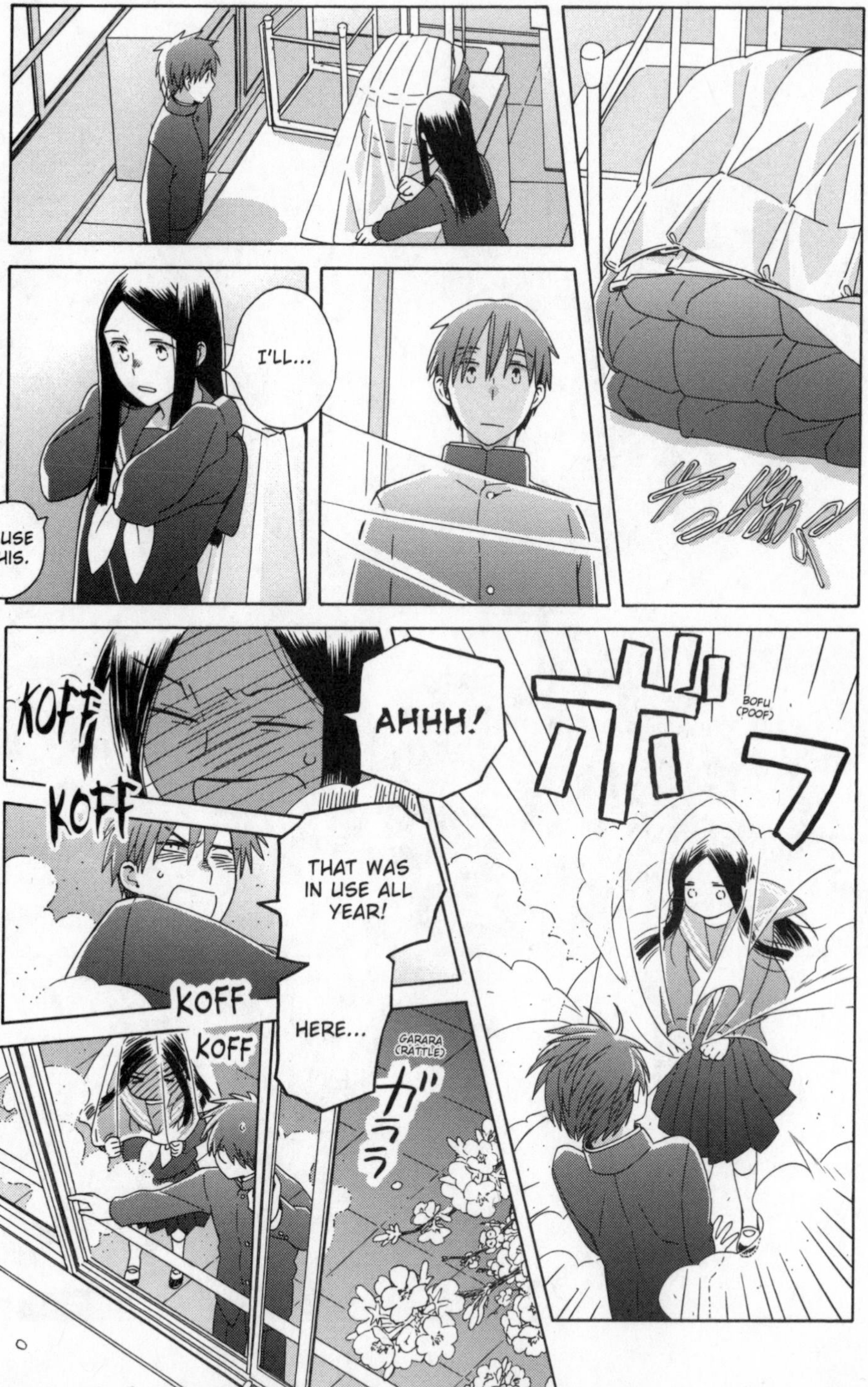

I'LL...
...USE THIS.
ボフ
BOFU (POOF)
KOFF
KOFF
AHHH!
THAT WAS IN USE ALL YEAR!
KOFF
KOFF
HERE...
ガララ
GARARA (RATTLE)

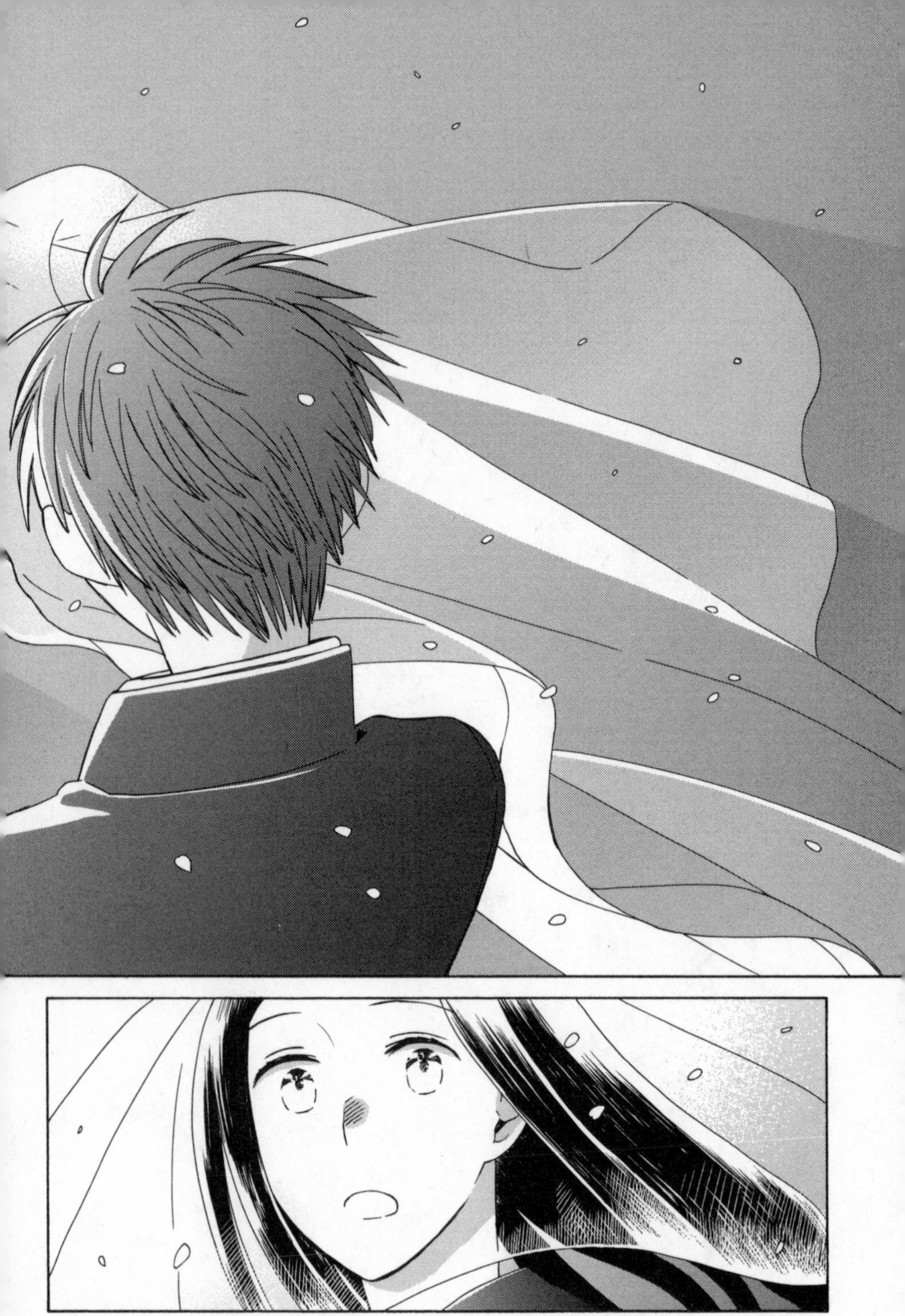

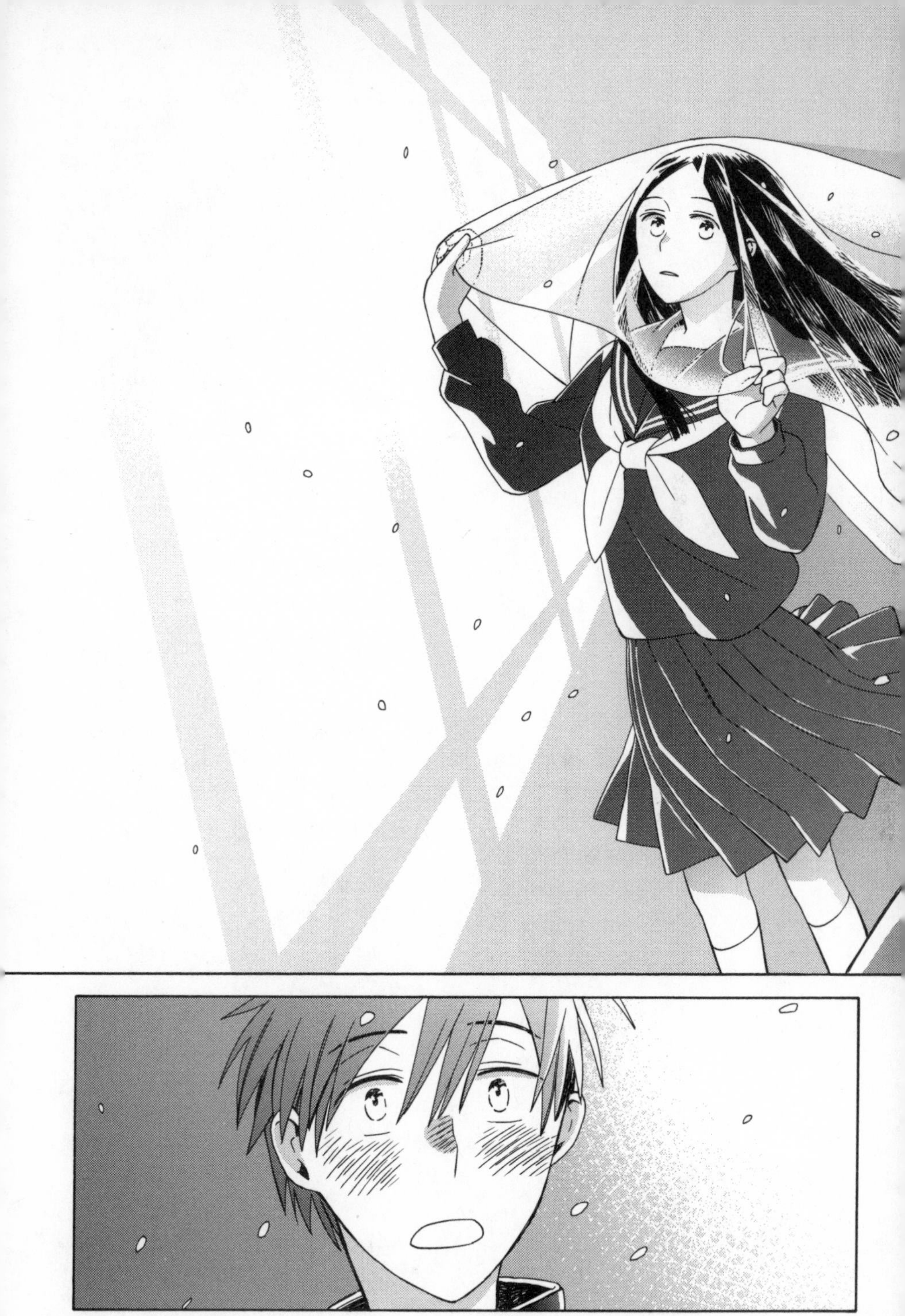

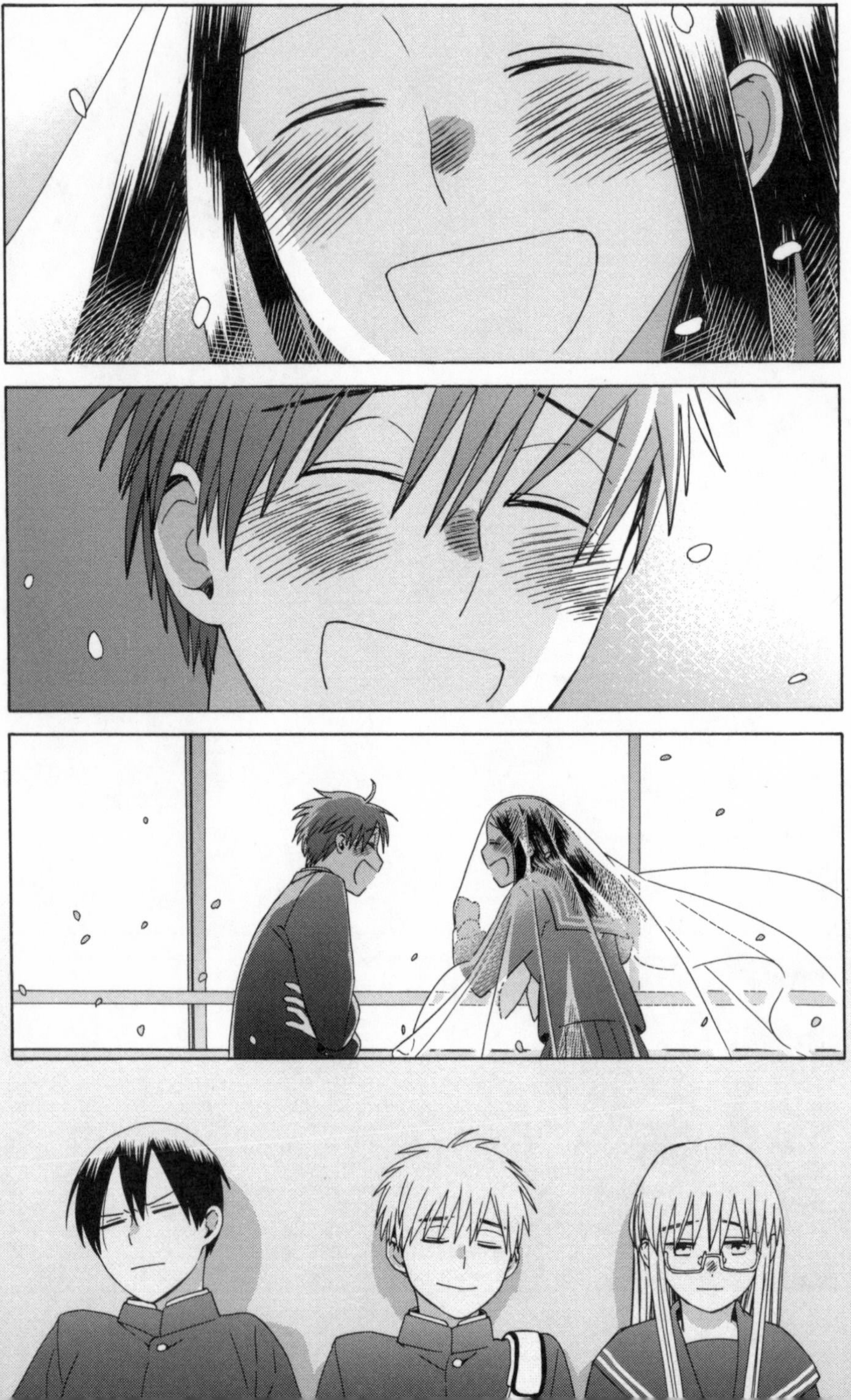

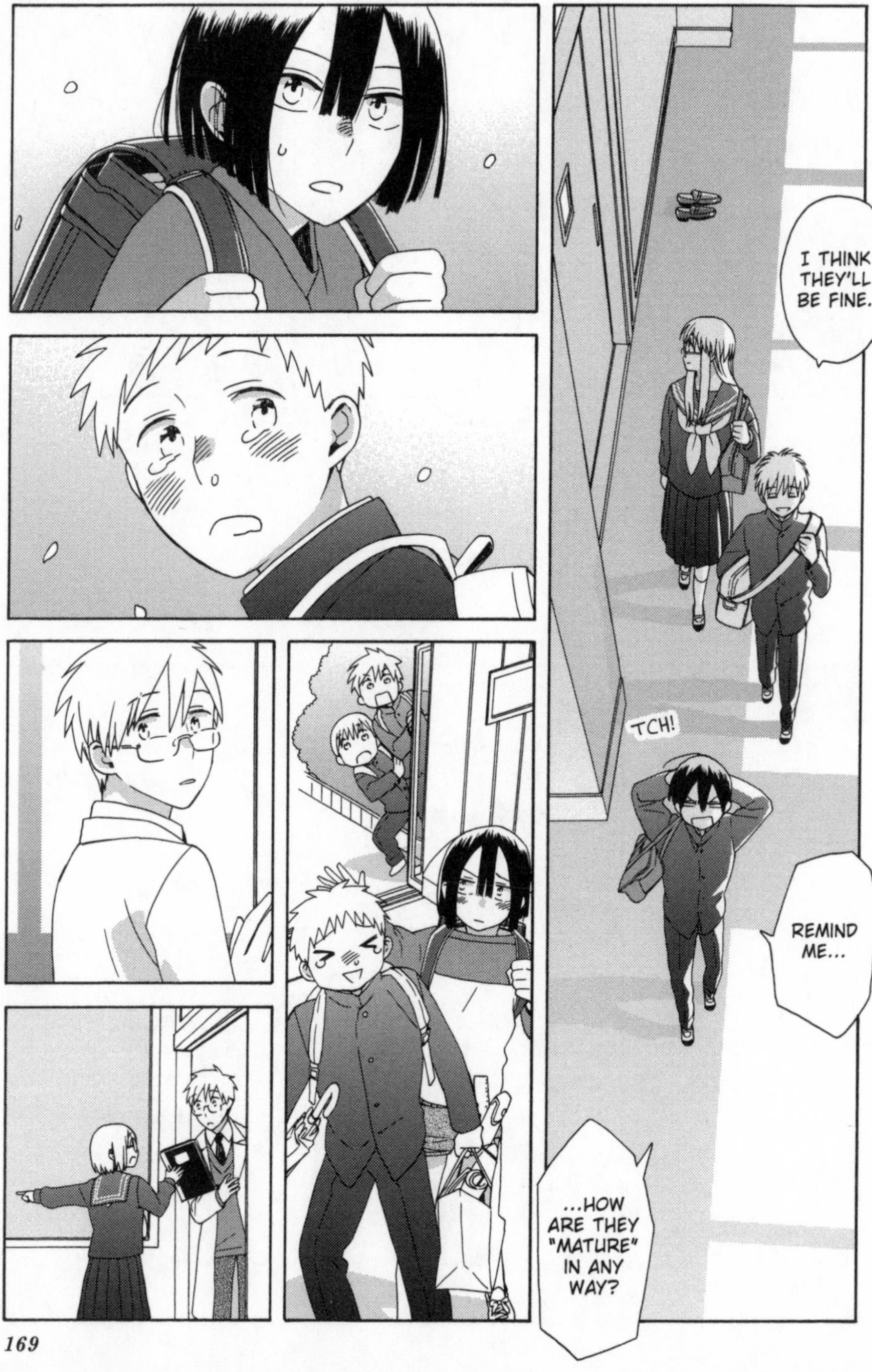
I THINK THEY'LL BE FINE.
TCH!
REMIND ME...
...HOW ARE THEY "MATURE" IN ANY WAY?

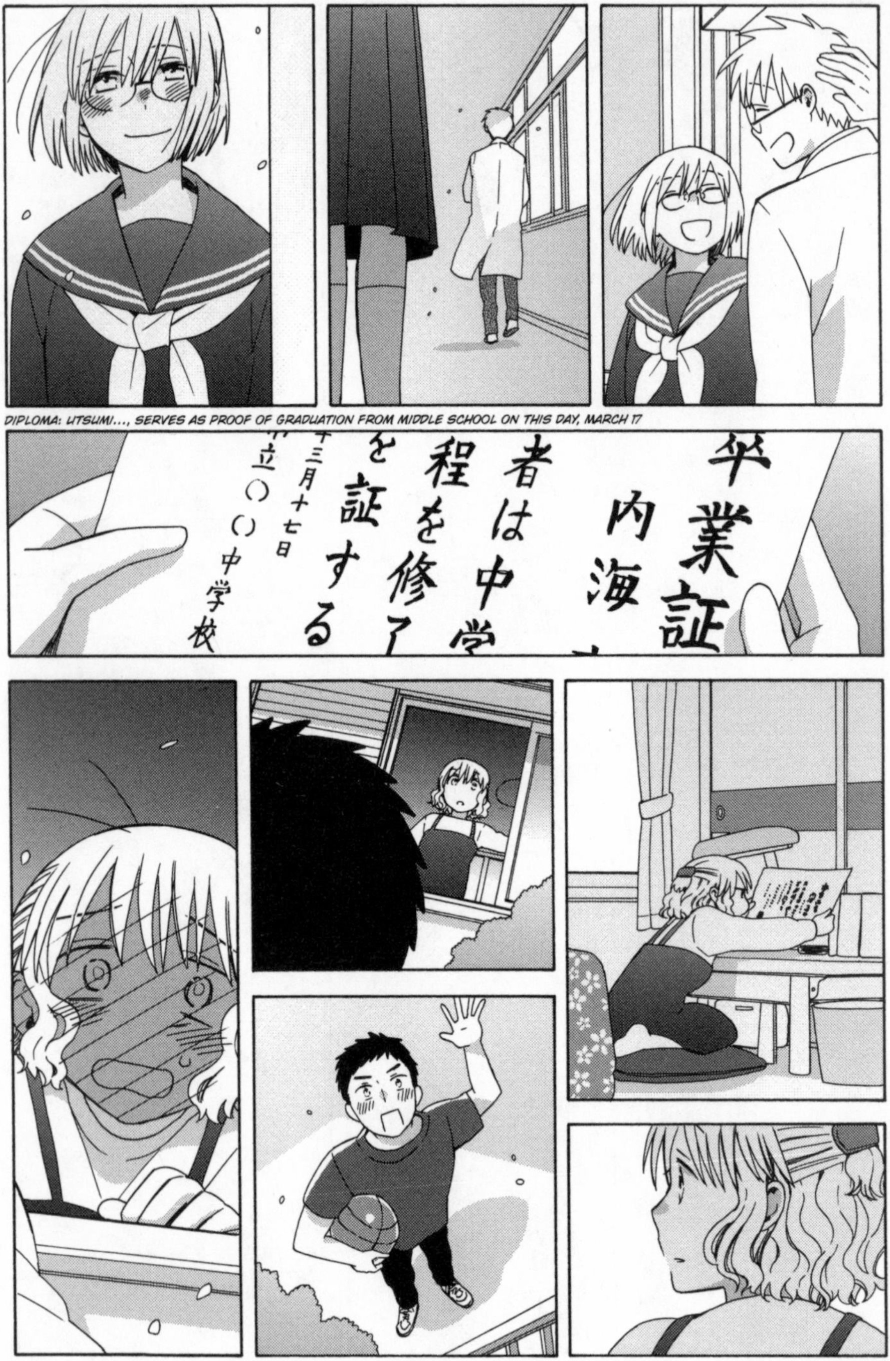
DIPLOMA: UTSUMI..., SERVES AS PROOF OF GRADUATION FROM MIDDLE SCHOOL ON THIS DAY, MARCH 17
業証
内海
者は中
程を修
を証する
三月十七日
立()()中学校

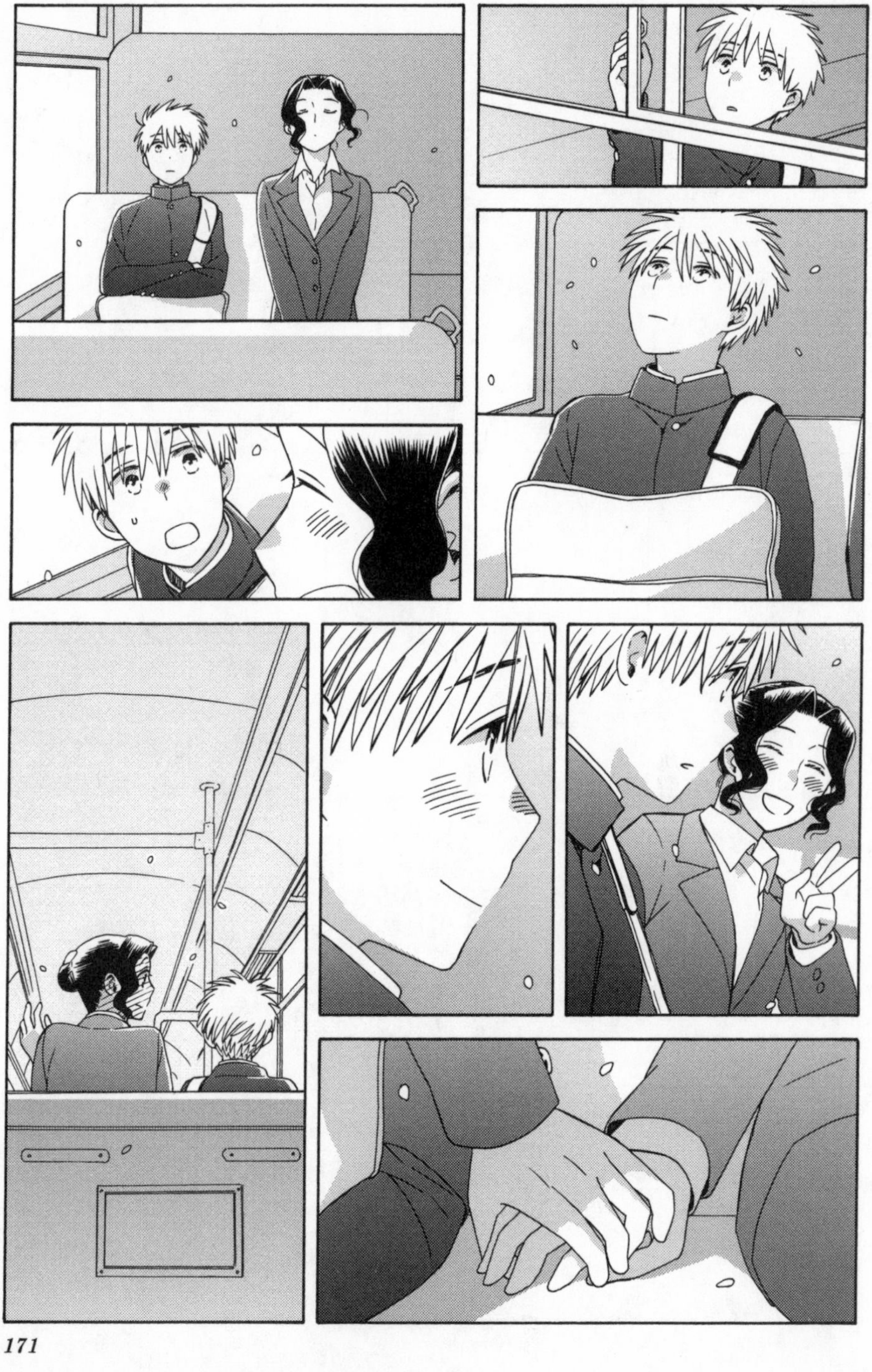

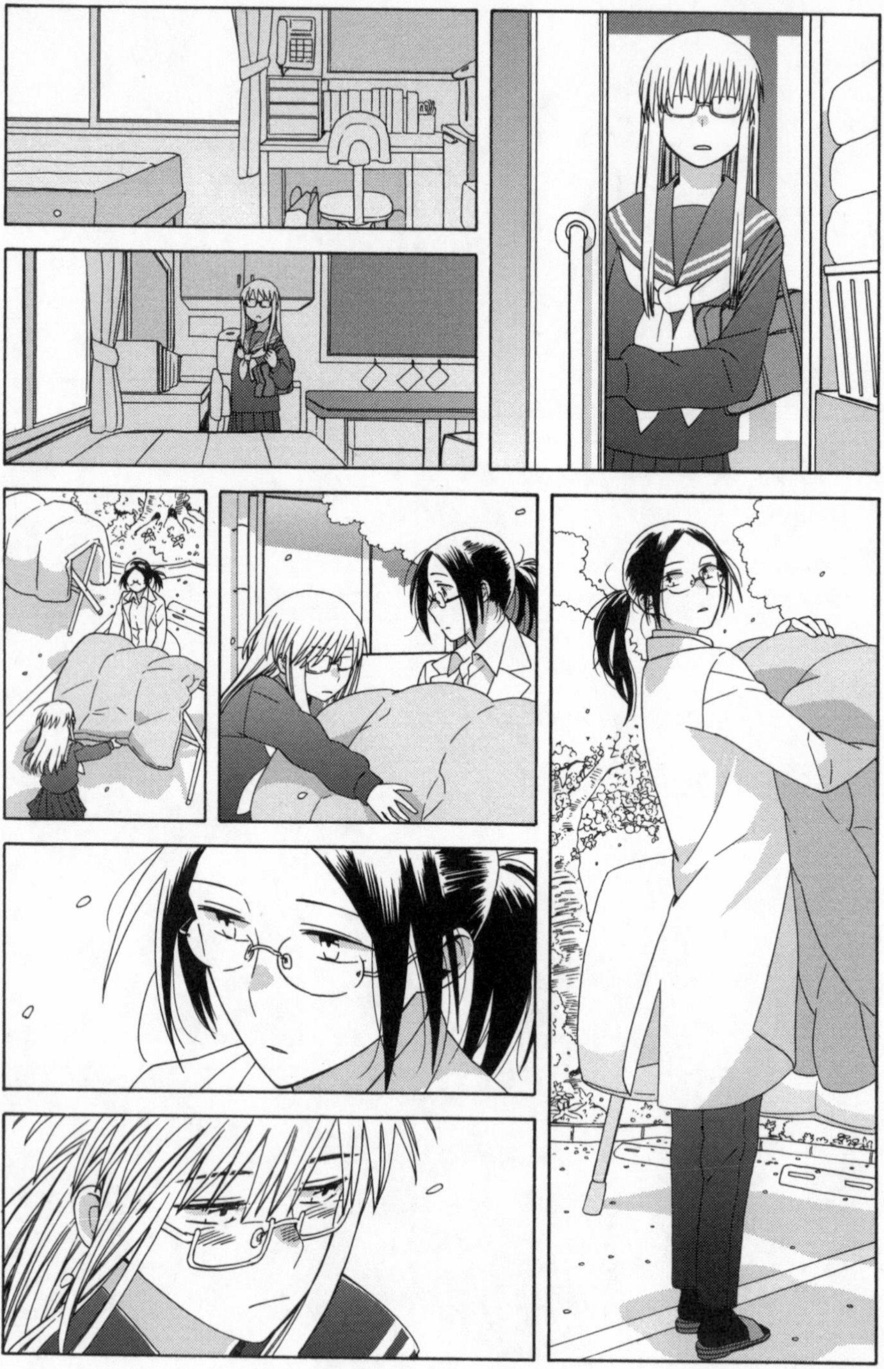

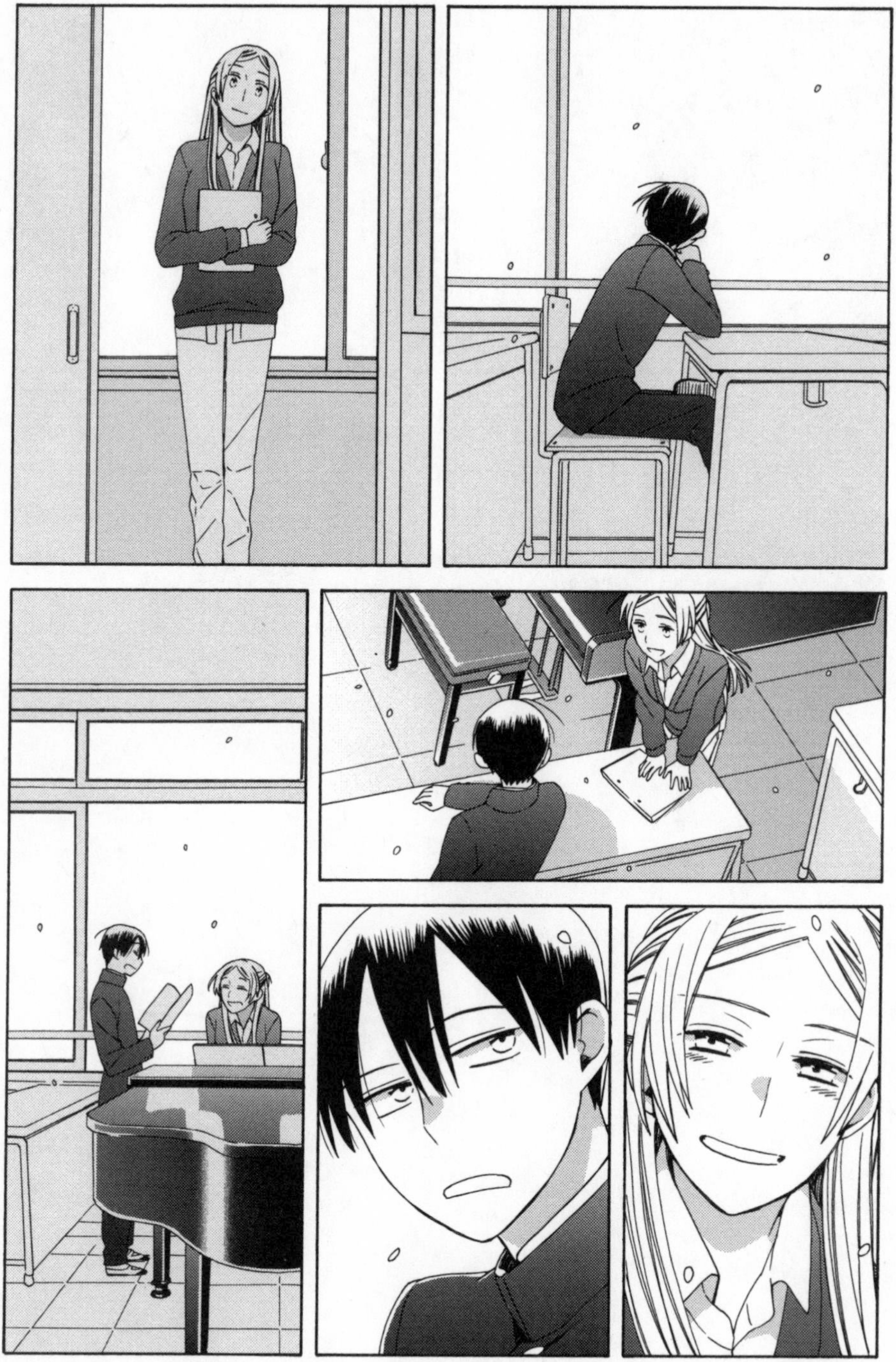

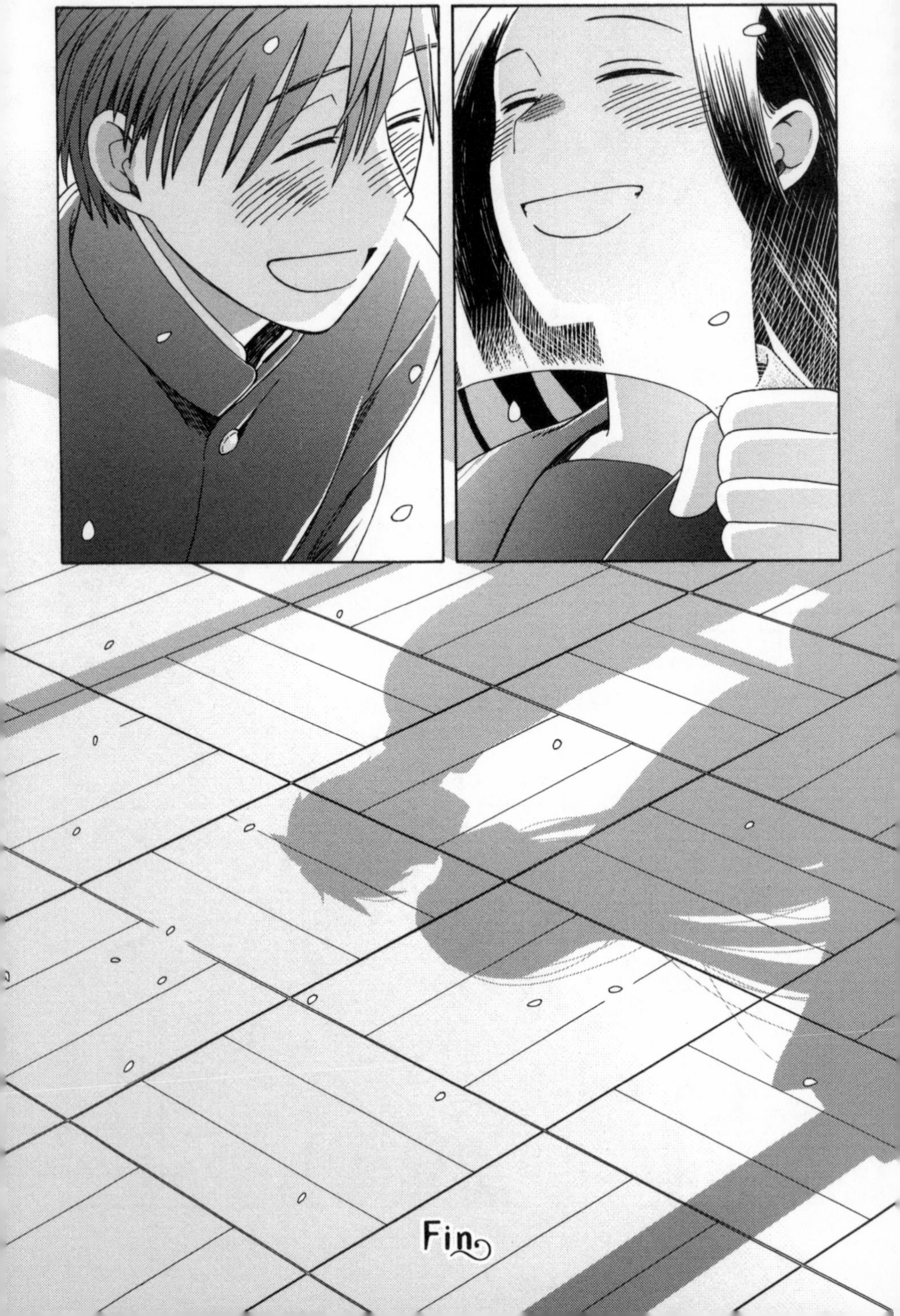

Fin

Love at Fourteen

[Encore]

IT WAS THE LAST TIME I SAW KAZUKI...

...AT THAT AGE.

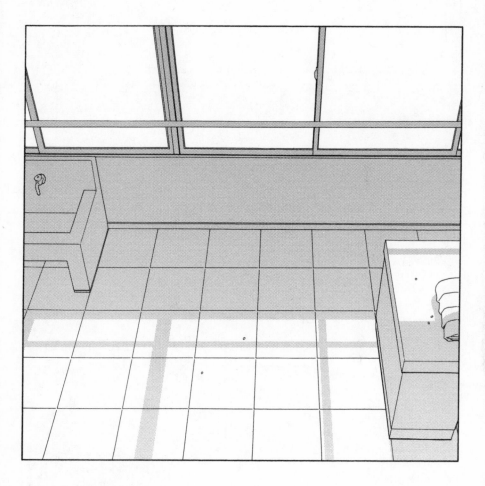

THAT DAY MARKED THE END OF OUR LOVE AT FOURTEEN.

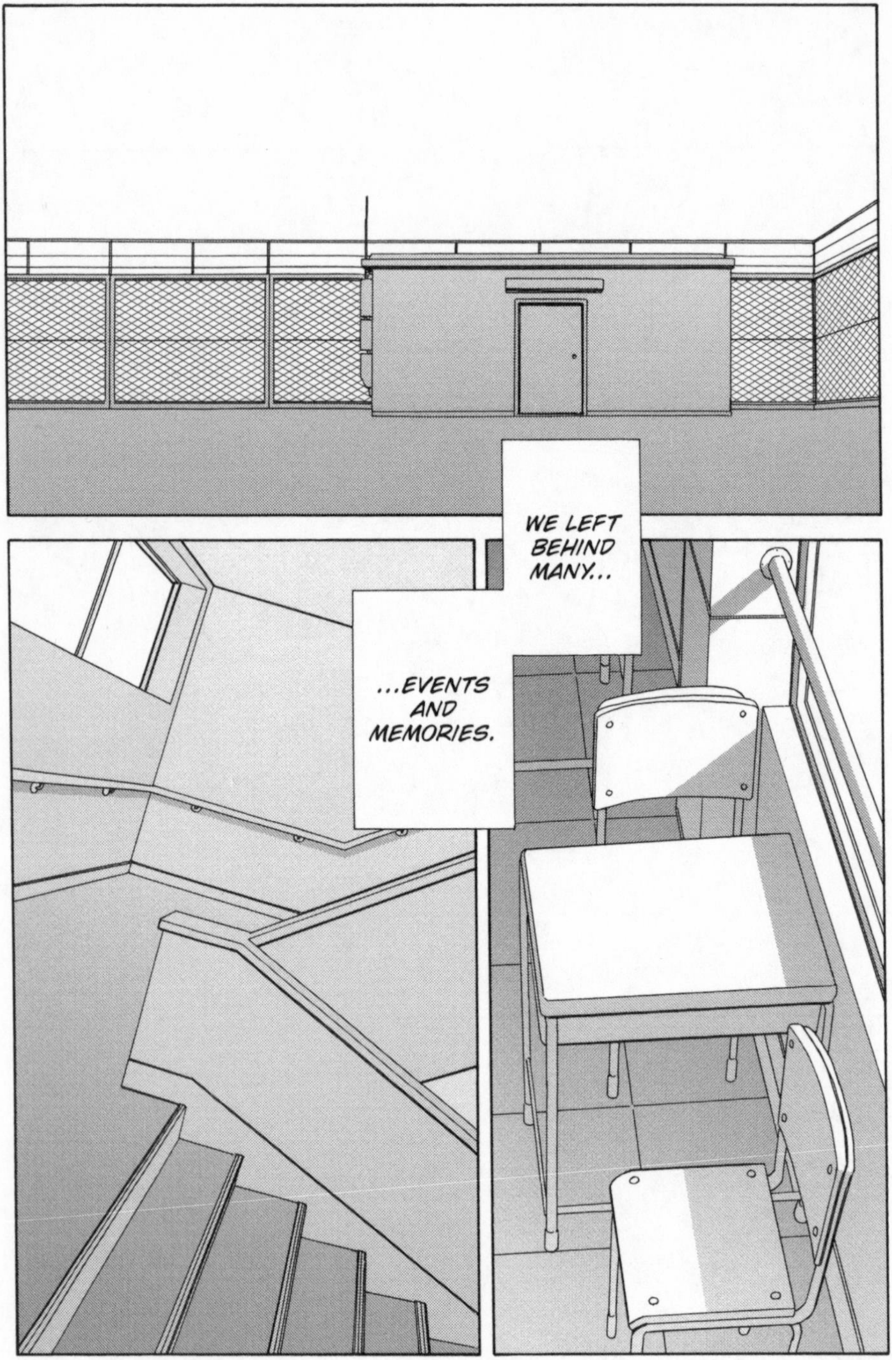
WE LEFT BEHIND MANY...
...EVENTS AND MEMORIES.

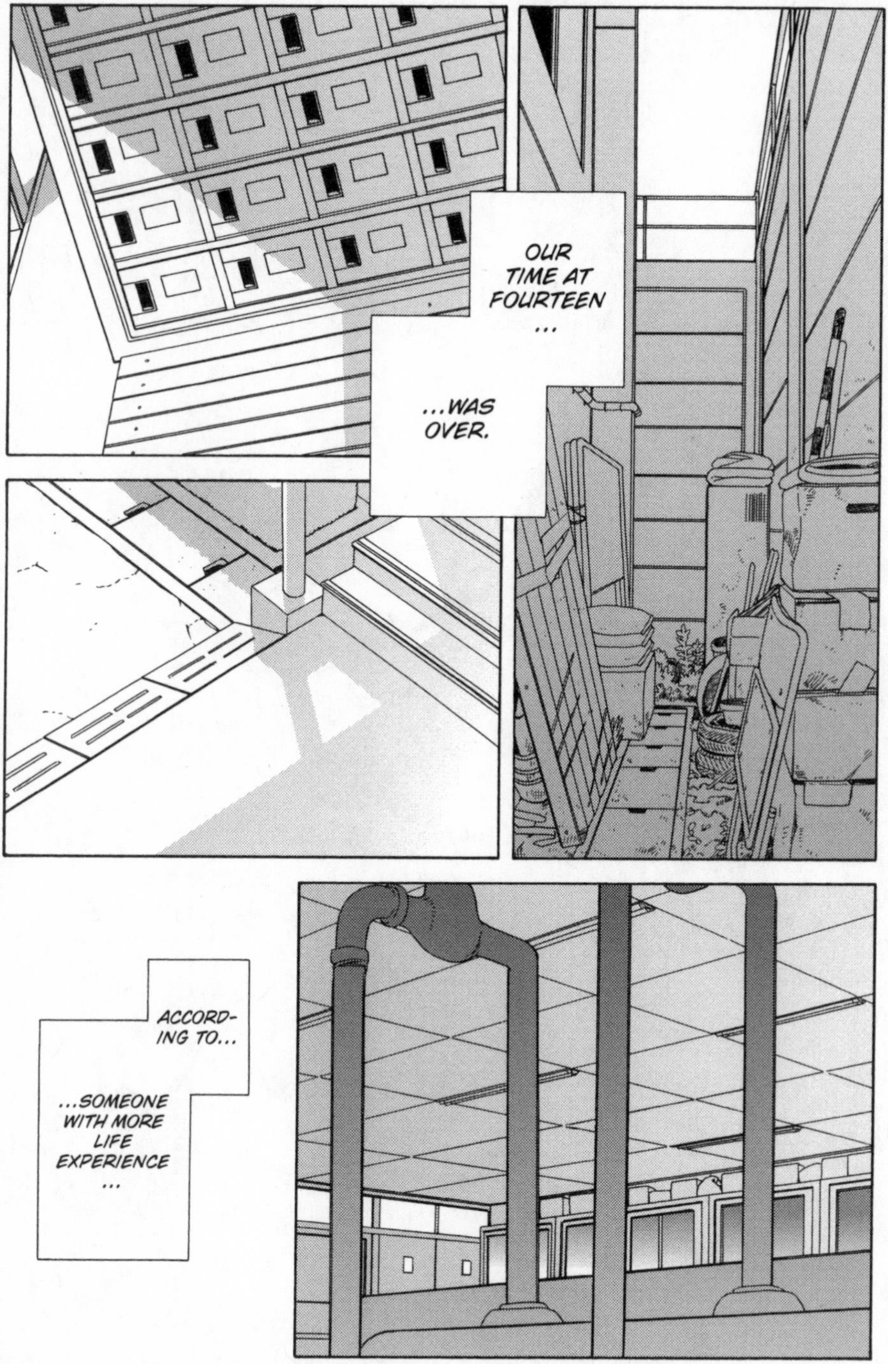
OUR TIME AT FOURTEEN ...
...WAS OVER.
ACCORD-ING TO...
...SOMEONE WITH MORE LIFE EXPERIENCE ...

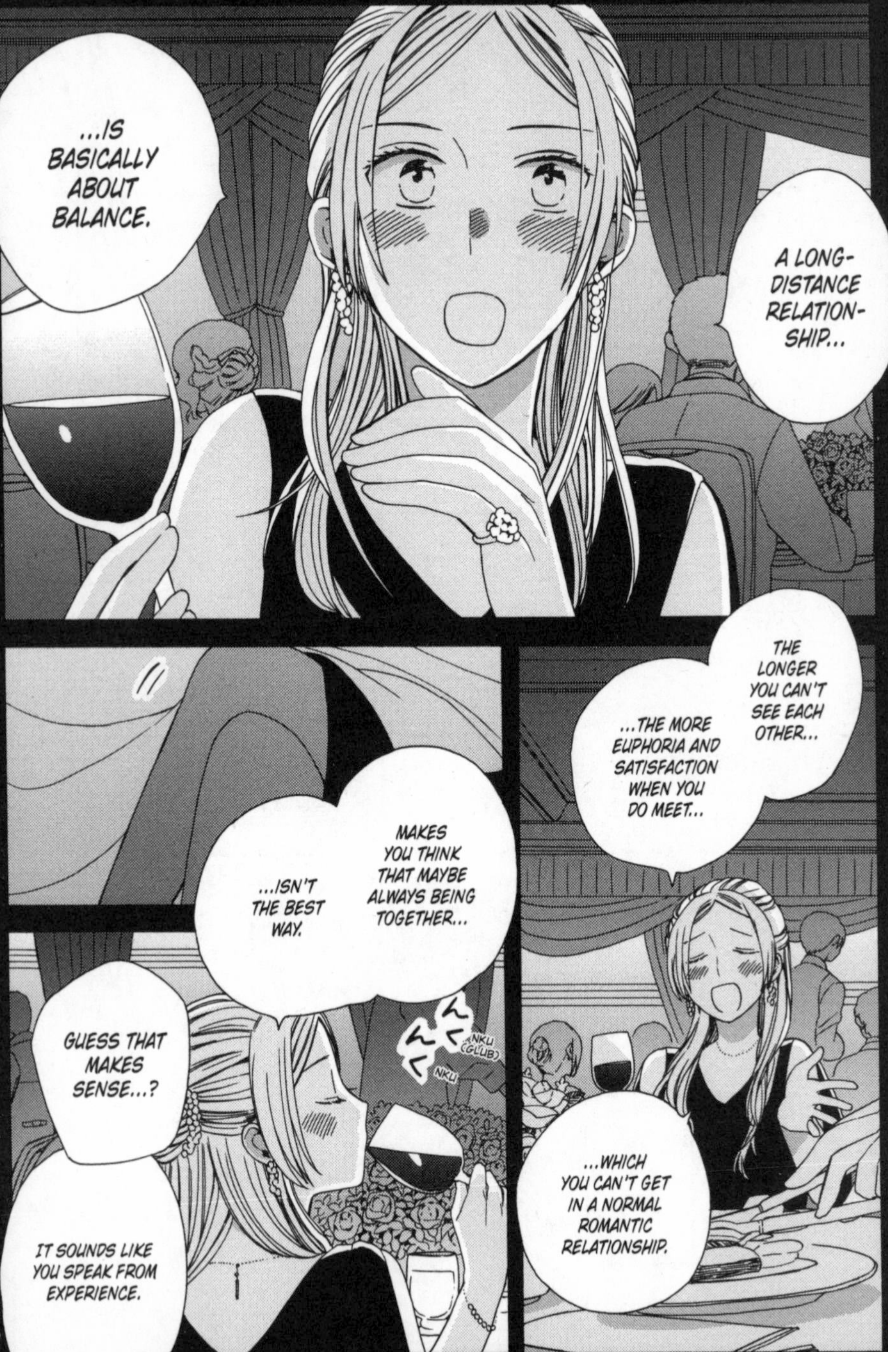
A LONG-DISTANCE RELATIONSHIP...
...IS BASICALLY ABOUT BALANCE.
THE LONGER YOU CAN'T SEE EACH OTHER...
...THE MORE EUPHORIA AND SATISFACTION WHEN YOU DO MEET...
...WHICH YOU CAN'T GET IN A NORMAL ROMANTIC RELATIONSHIP.
MAKES YOU THINK THAT MAYBE ALWAYS BEING TOGETHER...
...ISN'T THE BEST WAY.
NKU (GLUB)
NKU
GUESS THAT MAKES SENSE...?
IT SOUNDS LIKE YOU SPEAK FROM EXPERIENCE.

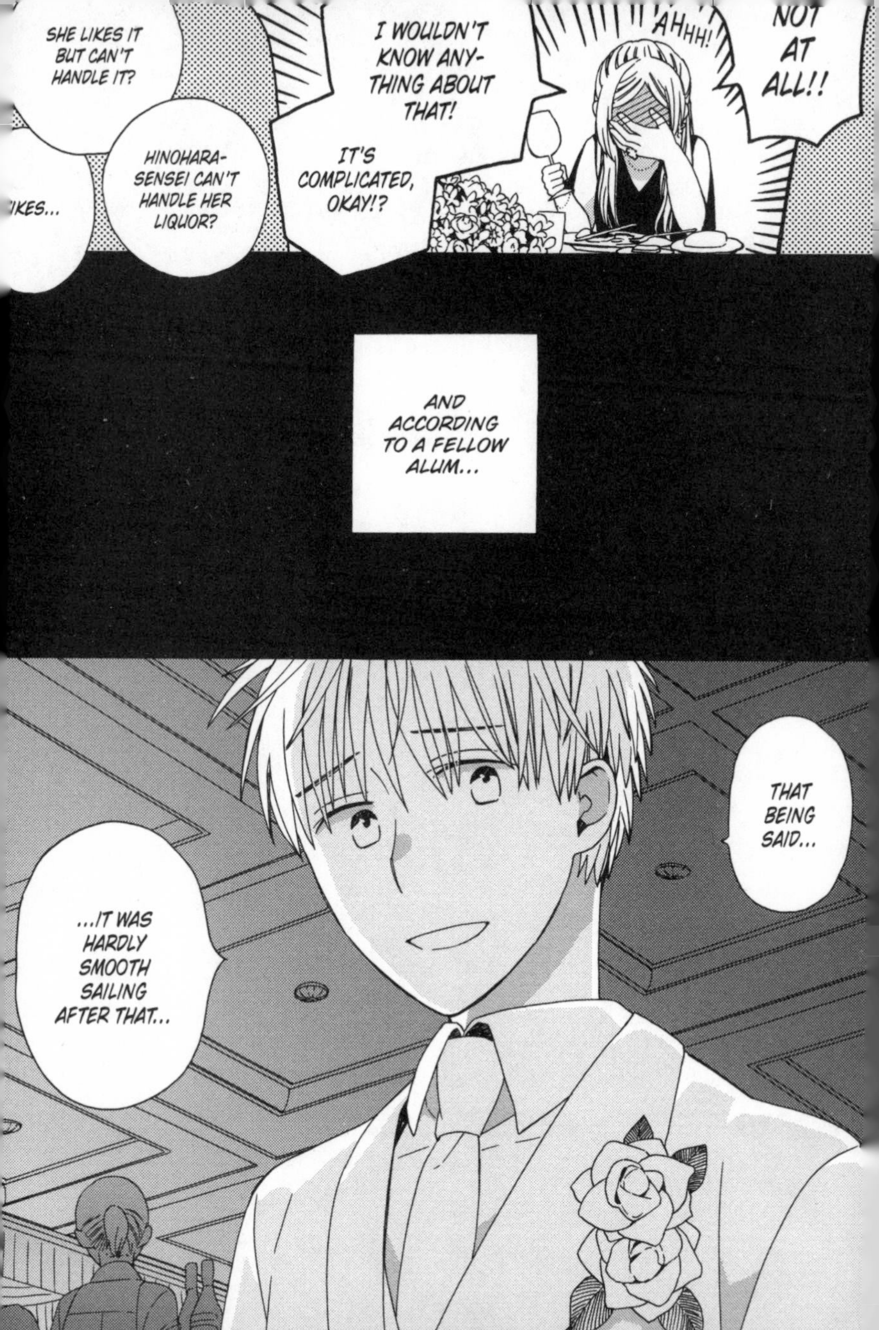
AHHH!
NOT AT ALL!!
I WOULDN'T KNOW ANYTHING ABOUT THAT!
IT'S COMPLICATED, OKAY!?
SHE LIKES IT BUT CAN'T HANDLE IT?
HINOHARA-SENSEI CAN'T HANDLE HER LIQUOR?
IKES...
AND ACCORDING TO A FELLOW ALUM...
THAT BEING SAID...
...IT WAS HARDLY SMOOTH SAILING AFTER THAT...

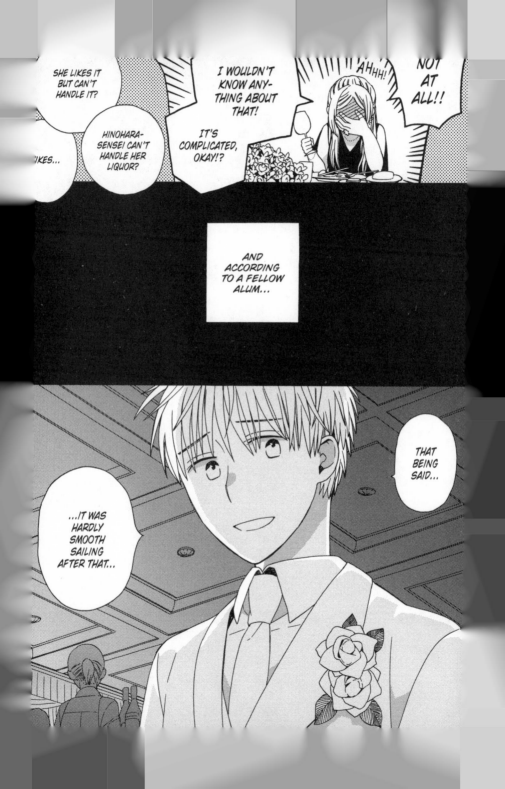

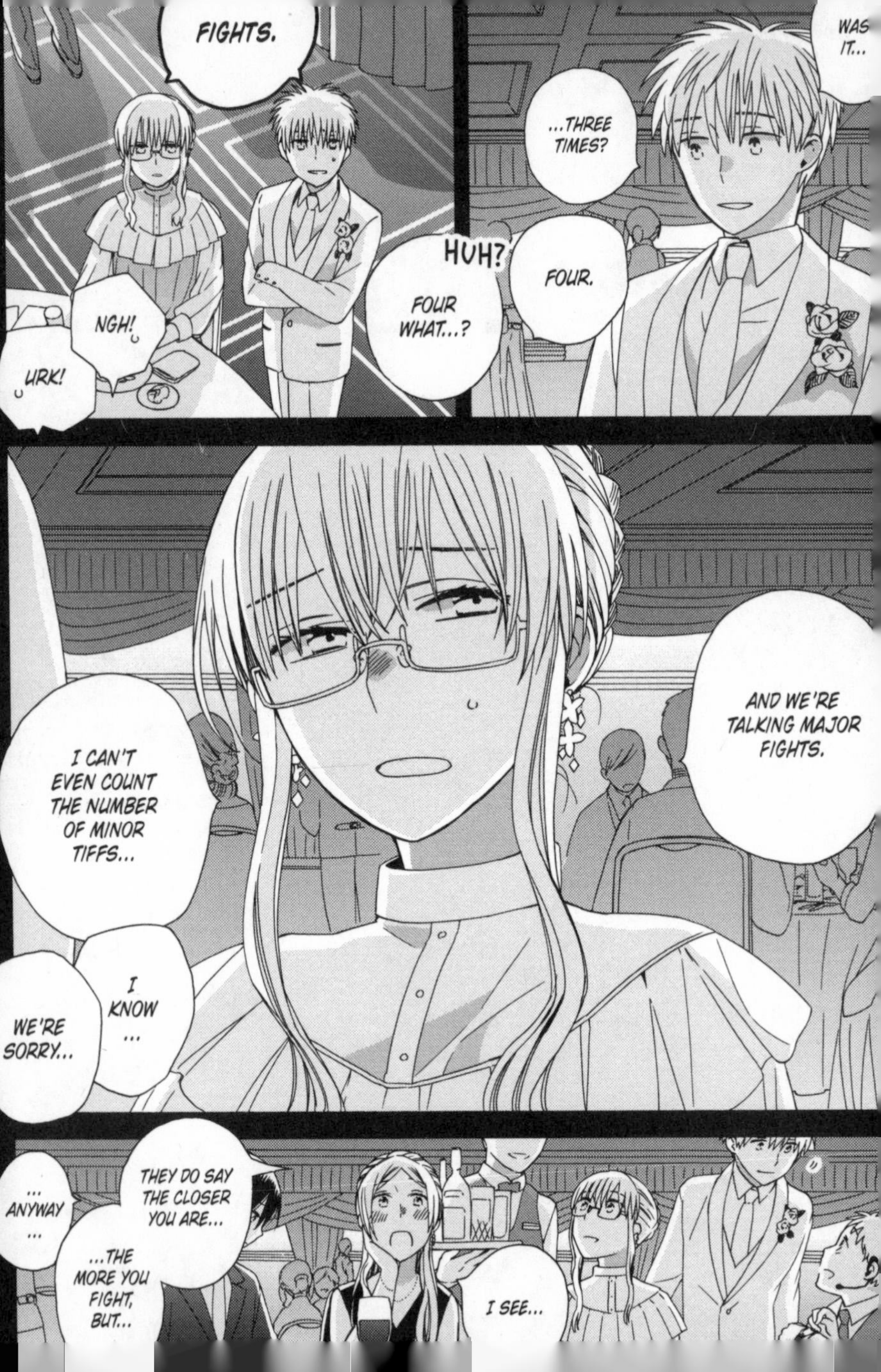
WAS IT...
...THREE TIMES?
FOUR.
HUH?
FOUR WHAT...?
FIGHTS.
NGH!
URK!
AND WE'RE TALKING MAJOR FIGHTS.
I CAN'T EVEN COUNT THE NUMBER OF MINOR TIFFS...
I KNOW...
WE'RE SORRY...
I SEE...
THEY DO SAY THE CLOSER YOU ARE...
...THE MORE YOU FIGHT, BUT...
...ANYWAY...

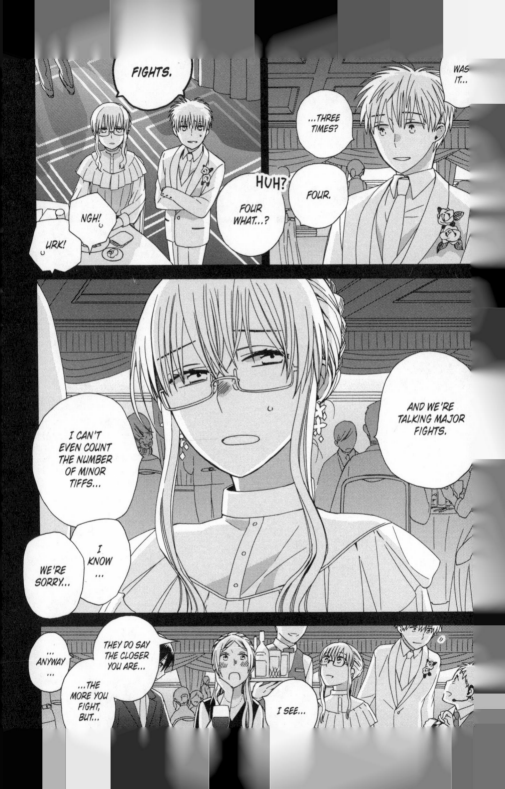

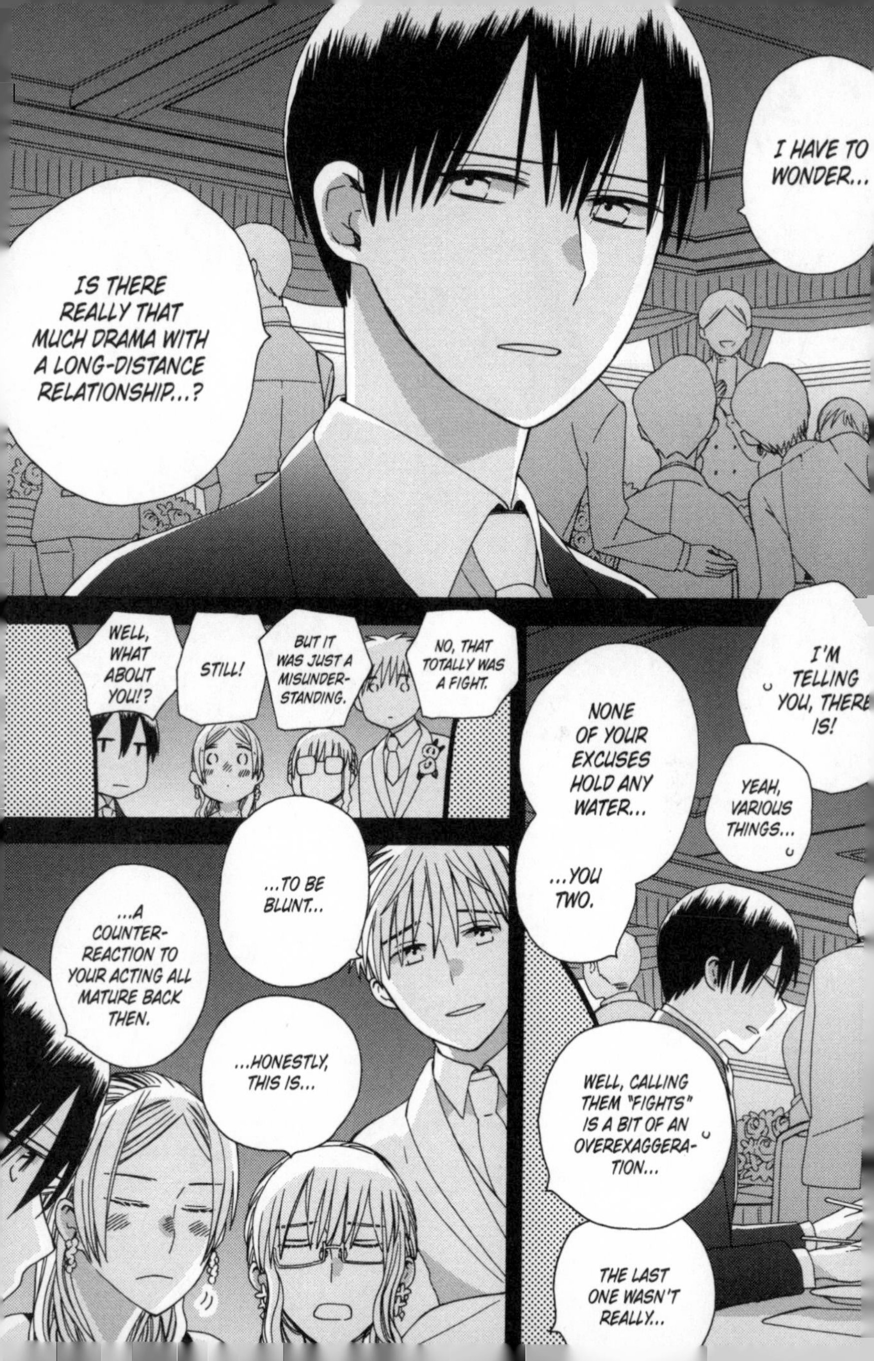
I HAVE TO WONDER...
IS THERE REALLY THAT MUCH DRAMA WITH A LONG-DISTANCE RELATIONSHIP...?
I'M TELLING YOU, THERE IS!
NONE OF YOUR EXCUSES HOLD ANY WATER...
YEAH, VARIOUS THINGS...
...YOU TWO.
WELL, CALLING THEM "FIGHTS" IS A BIT OF AN OVEREXAGGERATION...
THE LAST ONE WASN'T REALLY...
NO, THAT TOTALLY WAS A FIGHT.
BUT IT WAS JUST A MISUNDERSTANDING.
STILL!
WELL, WHAT ABOUT YOU!?
...TO BE BLUNT...
...A COUNTER-REACTION TO YOUR ACTING ALL MATURE BACK THEN.
...HONESTLY, THIS IS...

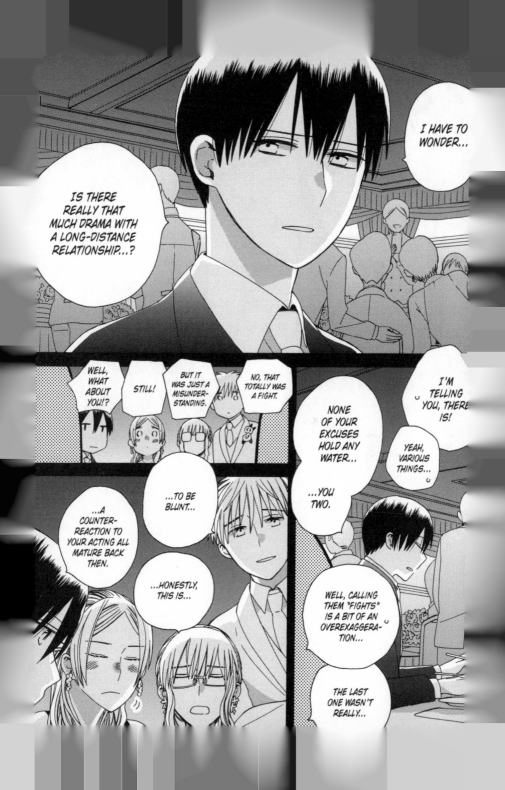

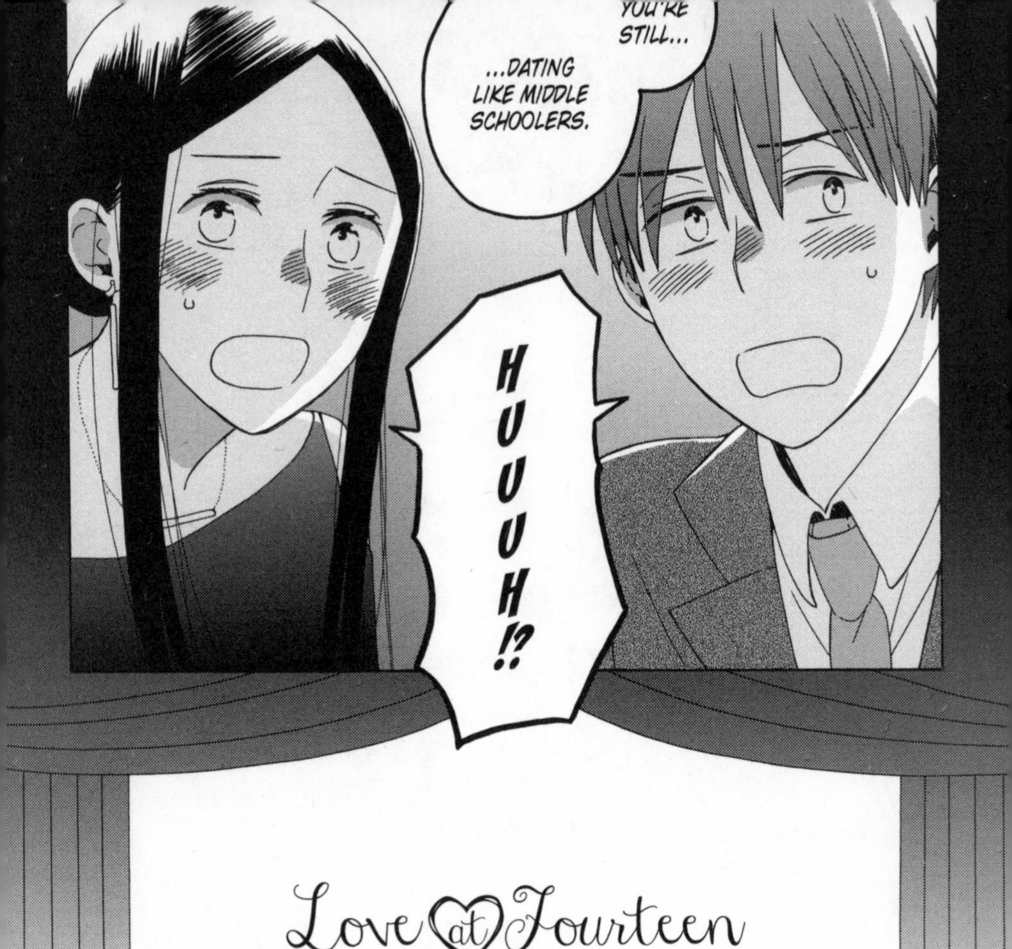
YOU'RE STILL...
...DATING LIKE MIDDLE SCHOOLERS.
HUUUUH!?

Love at Fourteen

[Encore]

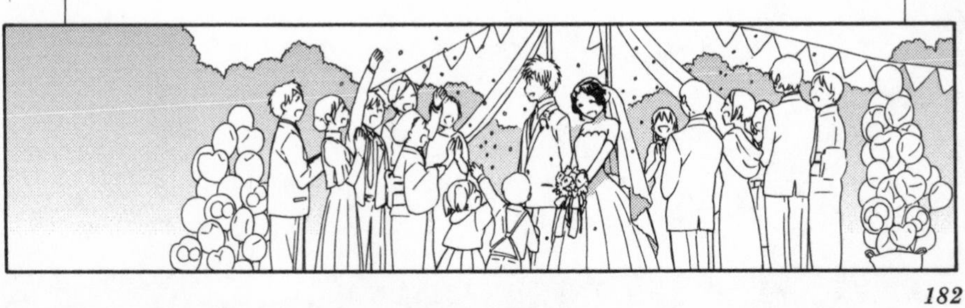

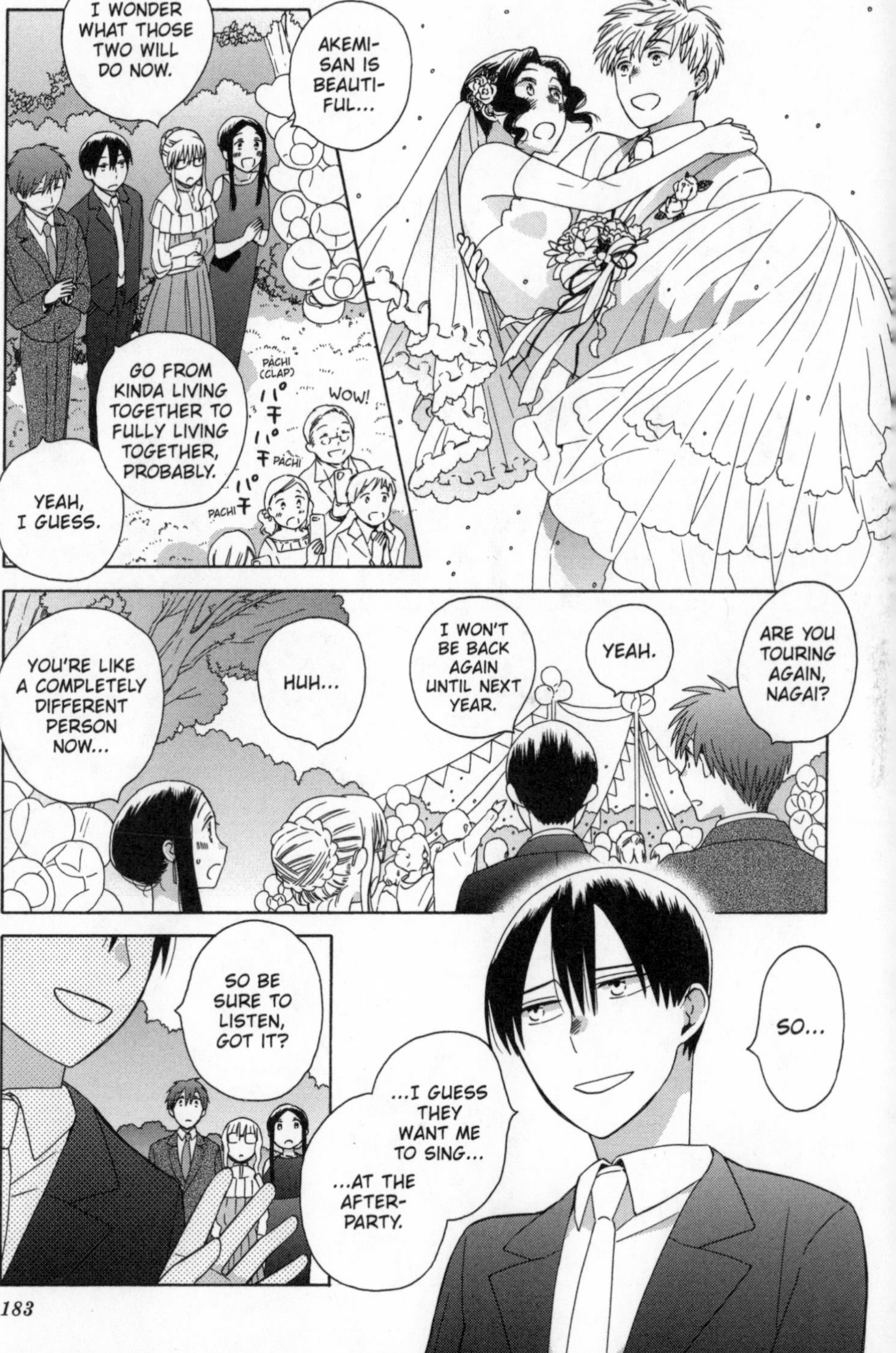
AKEMI-SAN IS BEAUTIFUL...
I WONDER WHAT THOSE TWO WILL DO NOW.
GO FROM KINDA LIVING TOGETHER TO FULLY LIVING TOGETHER, PROBABLY.
PACHI (CLAP)
パチ
WOW!
パチ PACHI
パチ PACHI
YEAH, I GUESS.
ARE YOU TOURING AGAIN, NAGAI?
YEAH.
I WON'T BE BACK AGAIN UNTIL NEXT YEAR.
HUH...
YOU'RE LIKE A COMPLETELY DIFFERENT PERSON NOW...
SO...
...I GUESS THEY WANT ME TO SING...
...AT THE AFTER-PARTY.
SO BE SURE TO LISTEN, GOT IT?

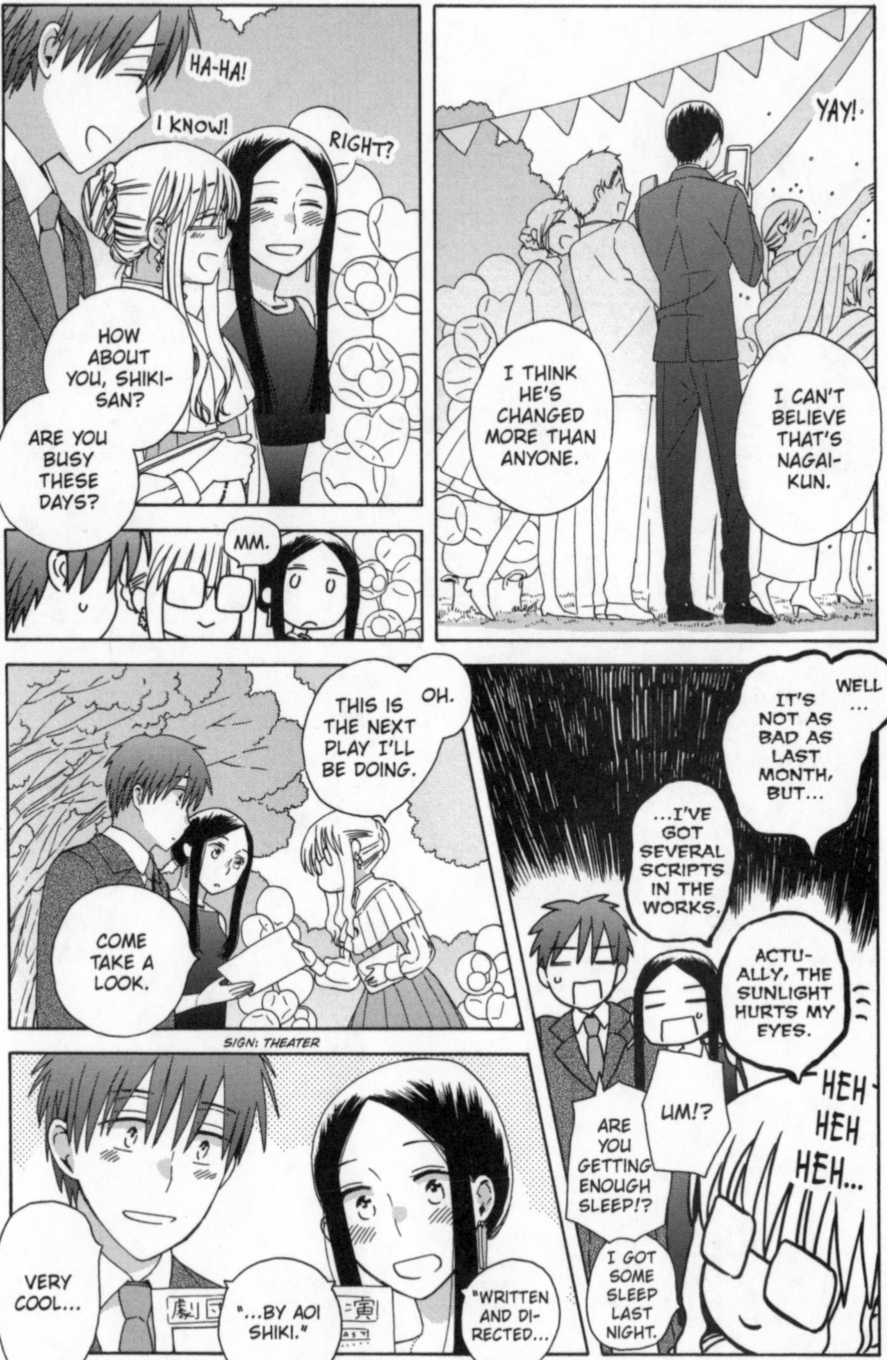
YAY!
I CAN'T BELIEVE THAT'S NAGAI-KUN.
I THINK HE'S CHANGED MORE THAN ANYONE.
HA-HA!
RIGHT?
I KNOW!
HOW ABOUT YOU, SHIKI-SAN?
ARE YOU BUSY THESE DAYS?
MM.
WELL ...
IT'S NOT AS BAD AS LAST MONTH, BUT...
...I'VE GOT SEVERAL SCRIPTS IN THE WORKS.
ACTU-ALLY, THE SUNLIGHT HURTS MY EYES.
HEH HEH HEH...
UM!?
ARE YOU GETTING ENOUGH SLEEP!?
I GOT SOME SLEEP LAST NIGHT.
OH.
THIS IS THE NEXT PLAY I'LL BE DOING.
COME TAKE A LOOK.
SIGN: THEATER
"WRITTEN AND DI-RECTED...
"...BY AOI SHIKI."
VERY COOL...

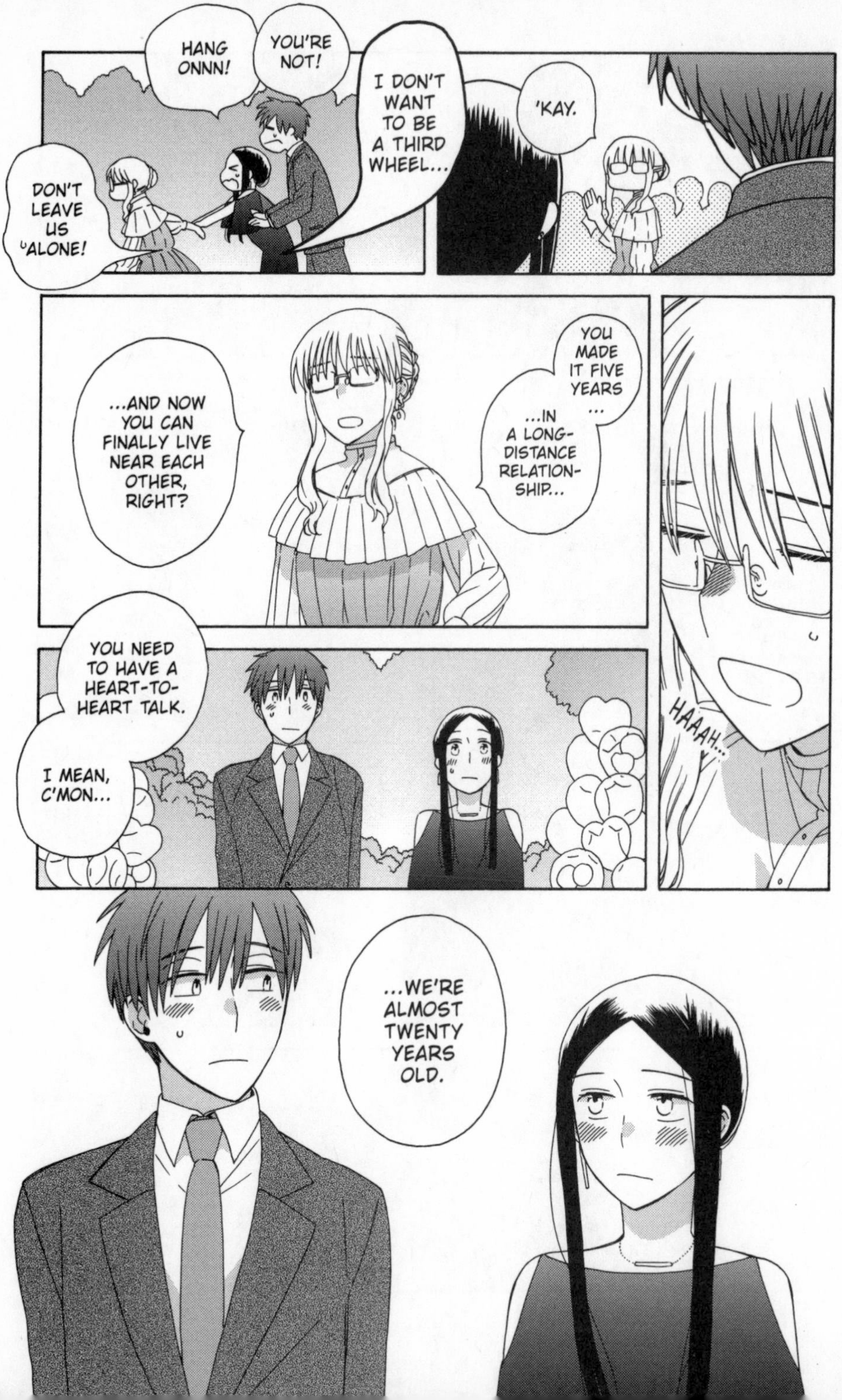

'KAY.
I DON'T WANT TO BE A THIRD WHEEL...
YOU'RE NOT!
HANG ONNN!
DON'T LEAVE US ALONE!
HAAAH...
YOU MADE IT FIVE YEARS...
...IN A LONG-DISTANCE RELATIONSHIP...
...AND NOW YOU CAN FINALLY LIVE NEAR EACH OTHER, RIGHT?
YOU NEED TO HAVE A HEART-TO-HEART TALK.
I MEAN, C'MON...
...WE'RE ALMOST TWENTY YEARS OLD.

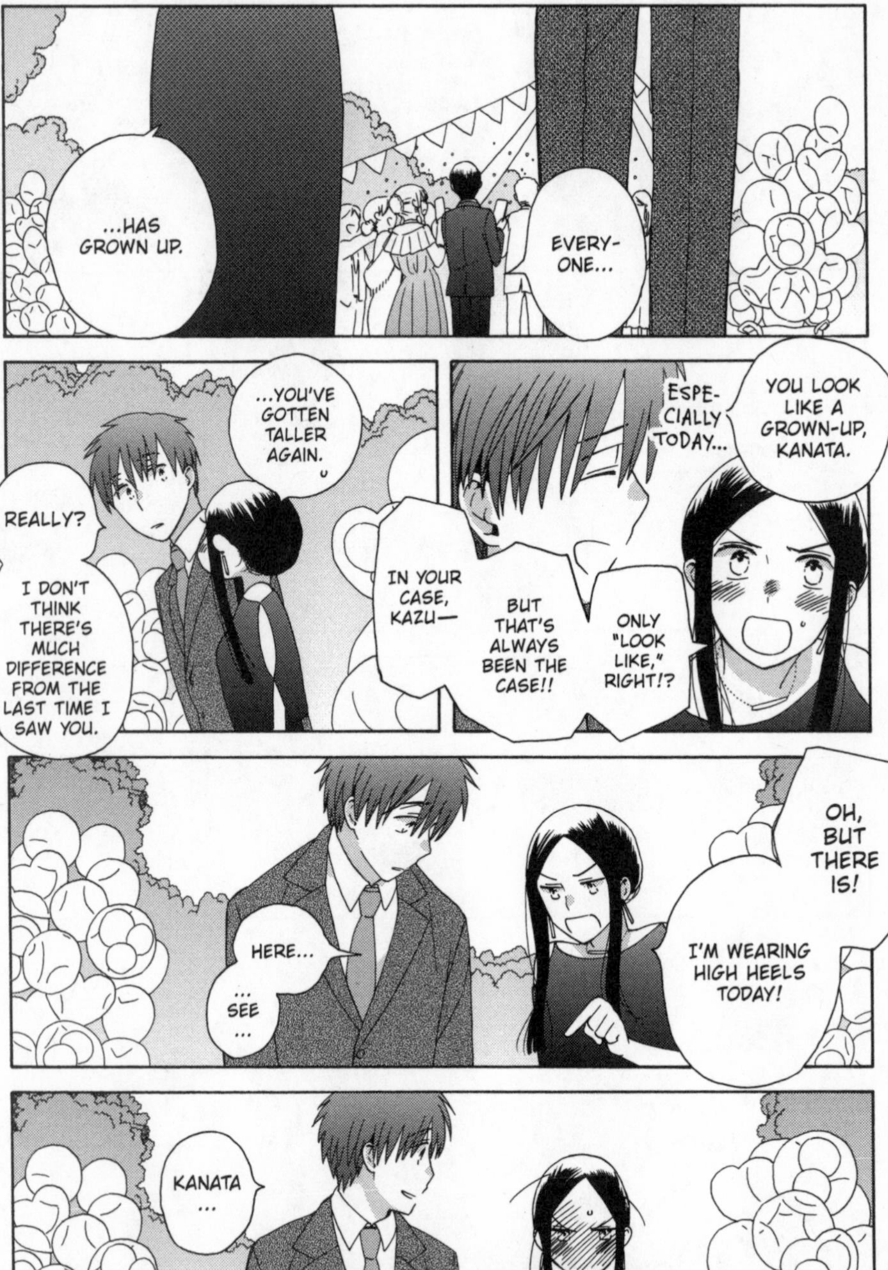
EVERY-ONE...
...HAS GROWN UP.
YOU LOOK LIKE A GROWN-UP, KANATA.
ESPE-CIALLY TODAY...
ONLY "LOOK LIKE," RIGHT!?
BUT THAT'S ALWAYS BEEN THE CASE!!
IN YOUR CASE, KAZU—
...YOU'VE GOTTEN TALLER AGAIN.
REALLY?
I DON'T THINK THERE'S MUCH DIFFERENCE FROM THE LAST TIME I SAW YOU.
OH, BUT THERE IS!
I'M WEARING HIGH HEELS TODAY!
HERE...
...SEE...
KANATA...

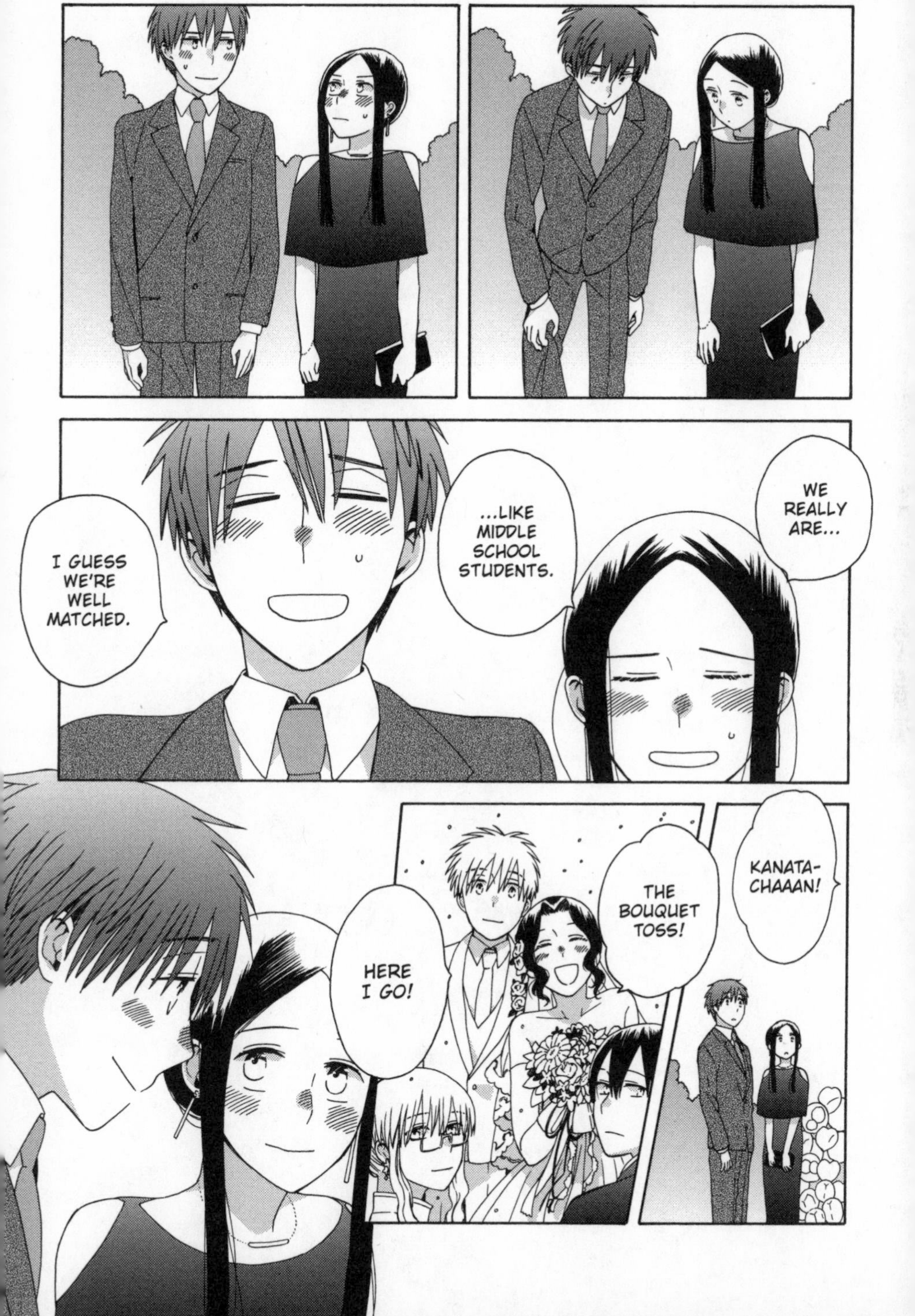
WE REALLY ARE...
...LIKE MIDDLE SCHOOL STUDENTS.
I GUESS WE'RE WELL MATCHED.
KANATA-CHAAAN!
THE BOUQUET TOSS!
HERE I GO!

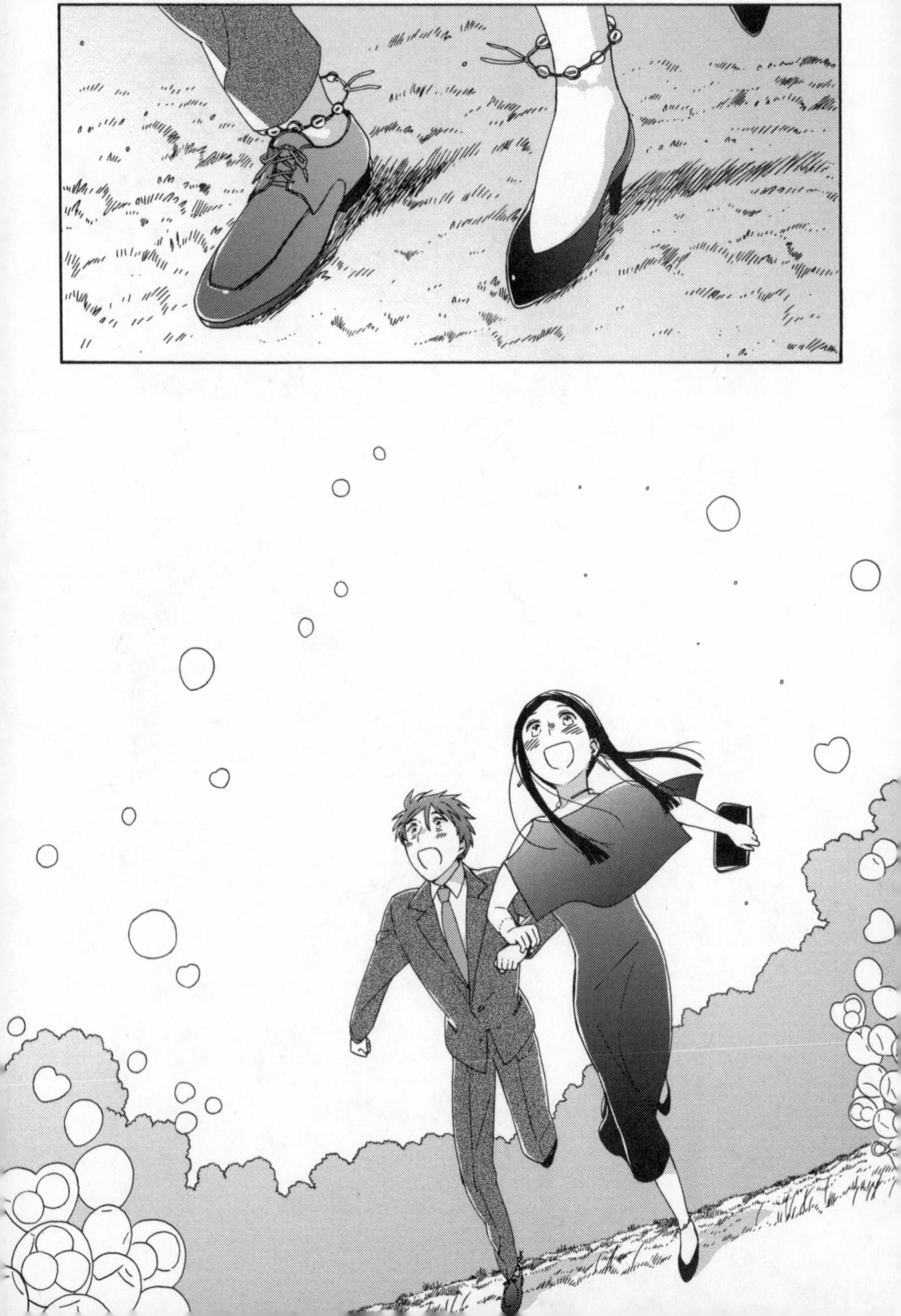

Fin

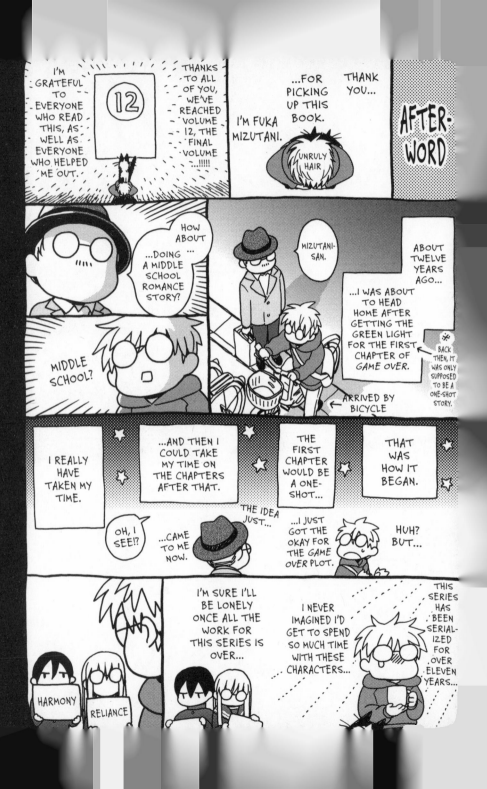

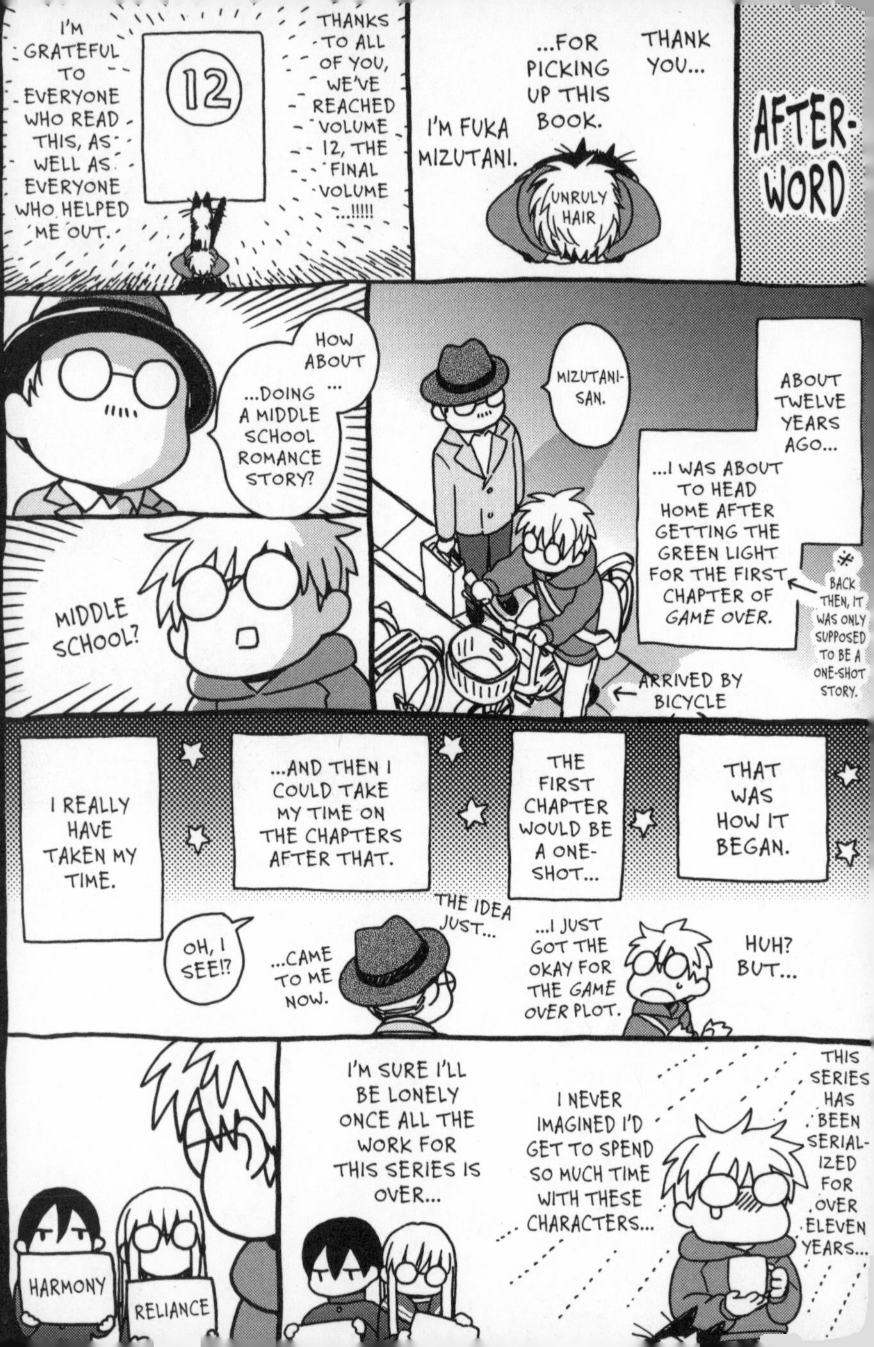
AFTER-WORD
THANK YOU...
...FOR PICKING UP THIS BOOK.
I'M FUKA MIZUTANI.
UNRULY HAIR
THANKS TO ALL OF YOU, WE'VE REACHED VOLUME 12, THE FINAL VOLUME...!!!!!
12
I'M GRATEFUL TO EVERYONE WHO READ THIS, AS WELL AS EVERYONE WHO HELPED ME OUT.
ABOUT TWELVE YEARS AGO...
...I WAS ABOUT TO HEAD HOME AFTER GETTING THE GREEN LIGHT FOR THE FIRST CHAPTER OF GAME OVER.
※ BACK THEN, IT WAS ONLY SUPPOSED TO BE A ONE-SHOT STORY.
MIZUTANI-SAN.
ARRIVED BY BICYCLE
HOW ABOUT ...
...DOING A MIDDLE SCHOOL ROMANCE STORY?
MIDDLE SCHOOL?
THAT WAS HOW IT BEGAN.
THE FIRST CHAPTER WOULD BE A ONE-SHOT...
...AND THEN I COULD TAKE MY TIME ON THE CHAPTERS AFTER THAT.
I REALLY HAVE TAKEN MY TIME.
HUH? BUT...
...I JUST GOT THE OKAY FOR THE GAME OVER PLOT.
THE IDEA JUST...
...CAME TO ME NOW.
OH, I SEE!?
THIS SERIES HAS BEEN SERIALIZED FOR OVER ELEVEN YEARS...
I NEVER IMAGINED I'D GET TO SPEND SO MUCH TIME WITH THESE CHARACTERS...
I'M SURE I'LL BE LONELY ONCE ALL THE WORK FOR THIS SERIES IS OVER...
RELIANCE
HARMONY

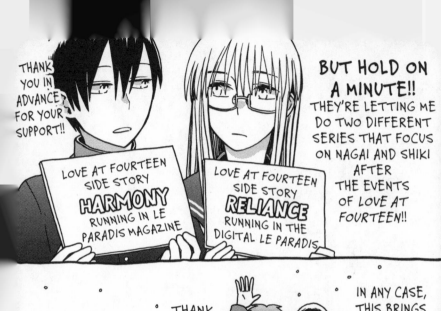

BUT HOLD ON A MINUTE!! THEY'RE LETTING ME DO TWO DIFFERENT SERIES THAT FOCUS ON NAGAI AND SHIKI AFTER THE EVENTS OF LOVE AT FOURTEEN!!
LOVE AT FOURTEEN SIDE STORY RELIANCE RUNNING IN THE DIGITAL LE PARADIS
LOVE AT FOURTEEN SIDE STORY HARMONY RUNNING IN LE PARADIS MAGAZINE
THANK YOU IN ADVANCE FOR YOUR SUPPORT!!

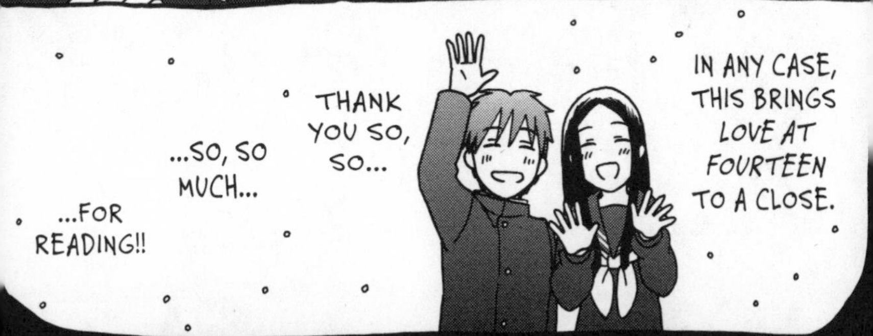

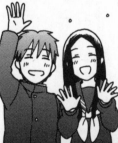

IN ANY CASE, THIS BRINGS LOVE AT FOURTEEN TO A CLOSE.
THANK YOU SO, SO...
...SO, SO MUCH...
...FOR READING!!

Special Thanks.

Iida-sama

Kohei Nawata DeSign

My family

My great friends

Digital Resources Sangatsu-sama

Sayo Murata-chan

And all of you who are reading this now.

Winter 2021

水谷フーカ.
Fuka Mizutani

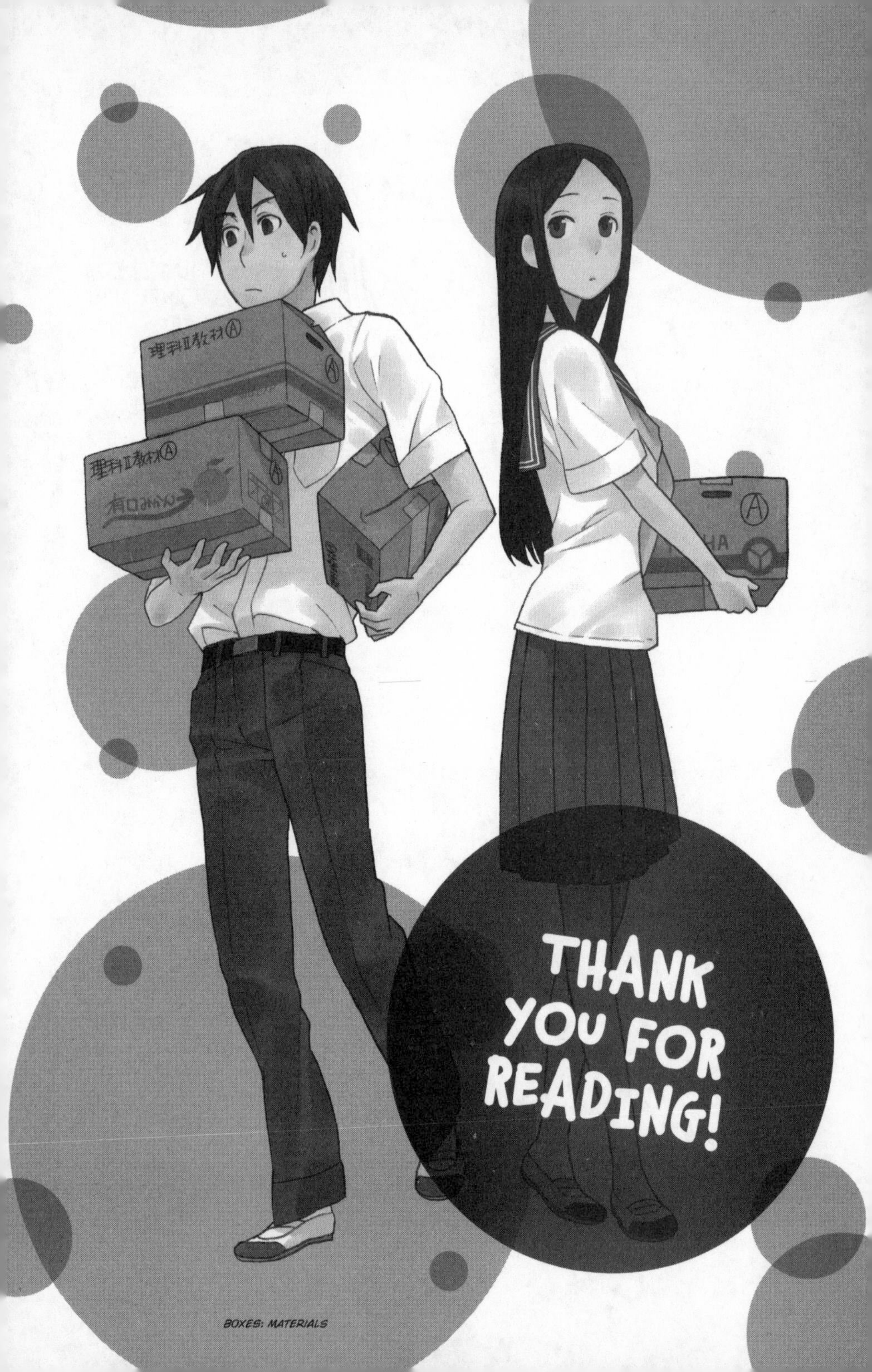
理科Ⅱ教材
理科Ⅱ教材
THANK YOU FOR READING!
BOXES: MATERIALS

TRANSLATION NOTES

COMMON HONORIFICS:

no honorific: Indicates familiarity or closeness; if used without permission or reason, addressing someone in this manner would constitute an insult.

-san: The Japanese equivalent of Mr./Mrs./Miss. If a situation calls for politeness, this is the fail-safe honorific.

-sama: Conveys great respect; may also indicate that the social status of the speaker is lower than that of the addressee.

-kun: Used most often when referring to boys, this indicates affection or familiarity. Occasionally used by older men among their peers, but it may also be used by anyone referring to a person of lower standing.

-chan: An affectionate honorific indicating familiarity used mostly in reference to girls; also used in reference to cute persons or animals of either gender.

-senpai: A suffix used to address upperclassmen or more experienced coworkers.

-sensei: A respectful term for teachers, artists, or high-level professionals.

PAGE 77

Second button: There's a Japanese tradition on graduation day for male students to give the second button on their uniform to the female student they like—the second button being the one closest to the heart on older uniforms. These days, girls will also proactively ask their crushes for the buttons, in which case the boys would save the button for the one they like the most.

PAGE 93

Sakuramochi: A Japanese confection that consists of a rice cake dyed pink like cherry blossoms—known as *sakura* in Japanese—with red bean paste in the center and a pickled cherry blossom leaf wrapped around it. It's usually enjoyed in the spring when the cherry blossom trees are in bloom.

PAGE 106

Valentine's and White Day: In Japan and many other Asian countries, women traditionally give men chocolate, whether it be to their acquaintances (known as *giri choco*, or "obligatory chocolate") or as a means of confessing their feelings (known as *honmei choco*, or "heartfelt chocolate"). Men will then give return gifts a month later on White Day, March 14.

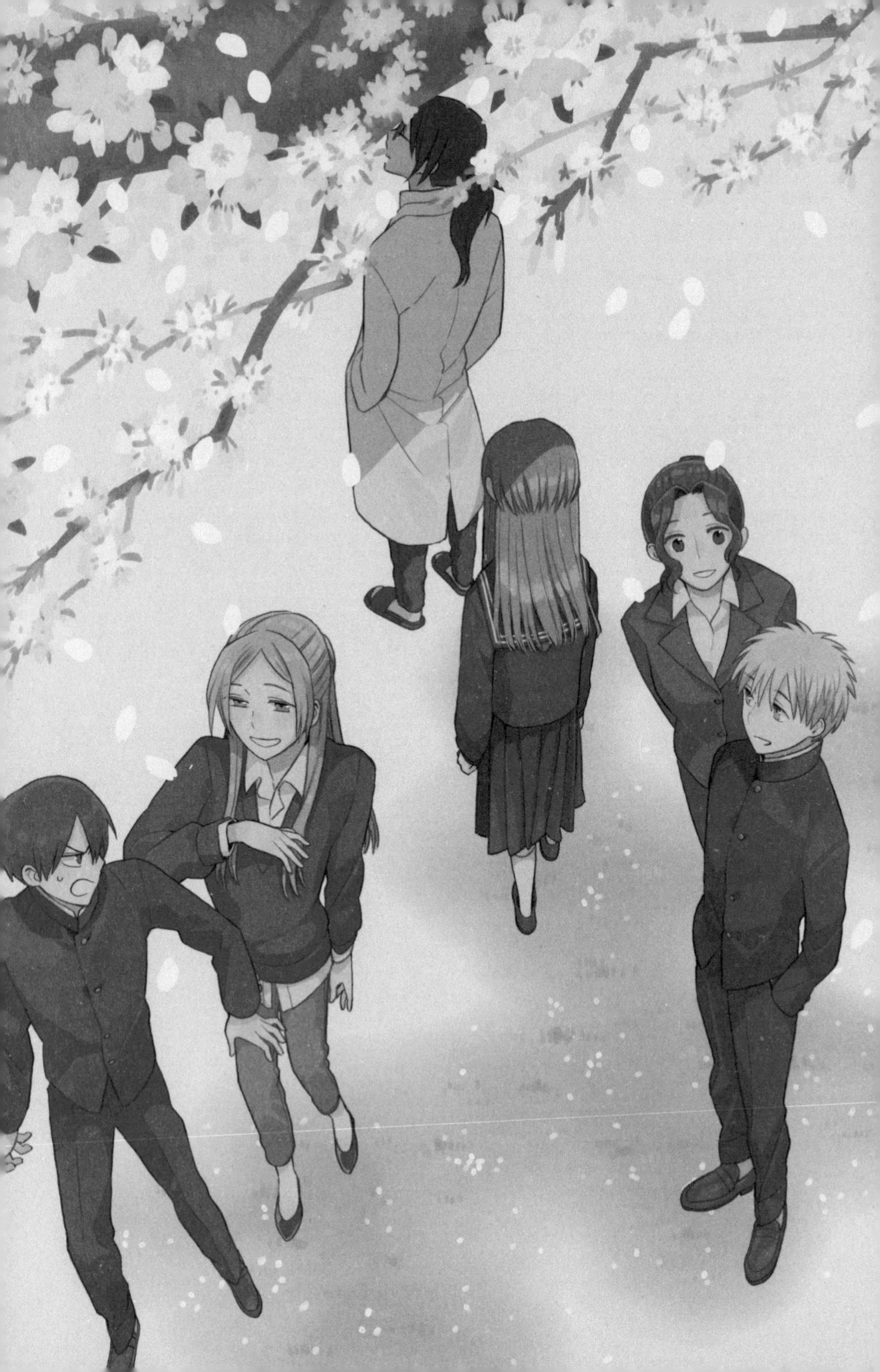

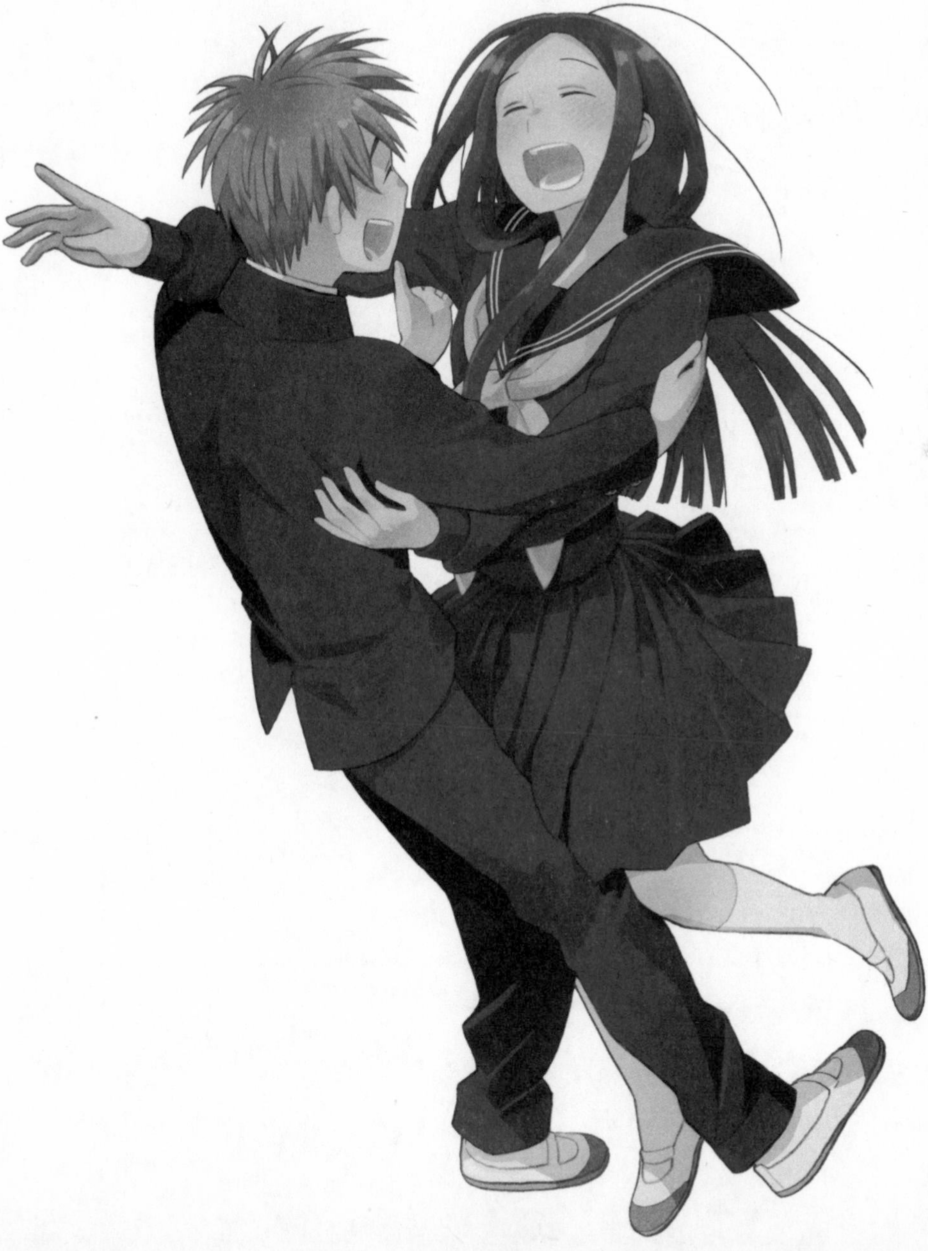

LOVE AT FOURTEEN ⑫

FUKA MIZUTANI

Translation: Sheldon Drzka

Lettering: Lys Blakeslee

JUYON-SAI NO KOI by Fuka Mizutani
© Fuka Mizutani 2021
All rights reserved.
First published in Japan in 2021 by HAKUSENSHA, INC., Tokyo.
English language translation rights in U.S.A., Canada and U.K. arranged with
HAKUSENSHA, INC., Tokyo through Tuttle-Mori Agency, Inc., Tokyo.

English translation © 2022 by Yen Press, LLC

Yen Press
150 West 30th Street, 19th Floor
New York, NY 10001

Visit us at yenpress.com
facebook.com/yenpress
twitter.com/yenpress
yenpress.tumblr.com
instagram.com/yenpress

First Yen Press Edition: December 2022
Edited by Yen Press Editorial: Won Young Seo, JuYoun Lee
Designed by Yen Press Design: Liz Parlett

Yen Press is an imprint of Yen Press, LLC.
The Yen Press name and logo are trademarks of Yen Press, LLC.

Library of Congress Control Number: 2016297684

ISBNs: 978-1-9753-4942-4 (paperback)
       978-1-9753-4943-1 (ebook)

10 9 8 7 6 5 4 3 2 1

WOR

Printed in the United States of America